Fugue Macabre: Ghost Dance

by

C.J. Parker

Enjoy The Read
CJ Parker

Light Sword Publishing

Timeless Tradition; Word by Word

First Edition

Editing by:
Shawn Guideau

Cover design by:
Sean Dickey

Formatting by:
Laurie Christopherson

ISBN: 978-0-9792030-6-0

PUBLISHED BY LIGHT SWORD PUBLISHING

www.lightswordpublishing.com

Printed in the United States of America

Dedication

To Richard for letting me quit my day job so I could write full time.
To Sher and Pam for reading the same chapter over and over and . . .
To Judah Mahay for my web page.
To Judy Creekmore for all those author pictures.
To Anna Marie for just being my friend.
To June Baker, my personal cheerleader

Email: cjparker@fictionwriters.ws
www.cjparker.net
http://fuguemacabre.livejournal.com
myspace.com/fuguemacabre

Acknowledgements

Where does one start to give credit to so many people? I want to thank RWA and SOLA for their support. My online critique groups, Word Critters and Critique World, deserves a mention for all those chapters they had to slog through and were kind enough to not say "Give up already!" Thanks to the girls at the Covington Library who helped me more than they'll ever know. Big thanks go to Sher Hames Torres and Pamela Reese for coming to my rescue when I started banging my head on the keyboard.

Last but not least, thank you, Linda Daly, for believing in me and, Shawn Guideau, editor extraordinaire for finding the silly mistakes I missed (and those damned commas).

www.cjparker.net

One

New Orleans

Reporters were already clogging the cemetery entrance when Detective Derek Bainbridge pulled alongside the police units sitting end to end like a funeral procession down Basin Street. He leaned his head against the steering wheel. Bile burned his throat, and his stomach cramped from fighting nausea. He knew what awaited him--another dead child and not a trace of evidence-- nothing to help him find the lunatic doing this.

A sharp knock at the window drew Derek's head up with a snap. Detective Karney smiled through the glass like the brainless idiot he was. "What?" Derek shouted.

"Oh, nothing. Just wondered if you were going to get out of the car during this century. The kid is gonna start getting ripe."

Gritting his teeth, Derek opened the door and exited his SUV. "You got business here, Karney, or just sightseeing?"

"I heard the call and was nearby. I'm leaving now." Karney jerked his head toward the scene. "Don't envy you this one. The governor's giving the chief a lot of shit." His smile widened baring crooked, stained teeth. "And it's gonna run downhill all over you, Bainbridge."

Derek swung the car door shut, forcing Karney to move or be knocked down. Derek made his way to the yellow crime scene tape stretched around an area containing eight elaborate crypts and what he knew would be the body of ten-year-old Selma Fortier. Thunder rumbled overhead, echoing through St. Louis Cemetery Number One as though the occupants of this necropolis were angry at the intrusion of the living.

He surveyed the scene and pulled in a deep breath, instantly regretting it. Musty scents of centuries-old tombs and ever-damp soil intermingled with sticky-sweet aromas of gardenias and jasmine in bloom. Summer's noontime heat settled over him in a humid, suffocating cloak, making the air seem that much denser.

"Detective." A uniformed officer stepped up beside him, breathing hard.

Derek nodded once. "Who found her?"

Turning red-rimmed eyes to his left, the young officer indicated an old black man losing his lunch behind a grave. Sounds of his retching bounced from one tomb to another. The officer drew another deep breath. "Name's Earl Levy. Came to visit his wife and found the girl's body."

"This your first murder?"

"No, sir. First kid, though. I got a son 'bout that age."

The officer swallowed so hard Derek heard his throat clench and then release. "You okay?"

"Yeah. I nearly got sick when I saw her, though. They're not gonna let me live it down, either." He gestured with a tilt of his chin toward two detectives trying to keep the press at bay. More reporters and cameramen jammed the wrought iron entrance of the concrete wall surrounding the cemetery, shouting questions and snapping photographs.

"Don't let them fool you, kid. They've done their share of puking at crime scenes." Derek stooped under the tape and strode to the remains of the murdered child. The killer had taken the time to pose the girl's nude body against a mold-blackened tomb--legs crossed at the ankles, tiny hands folded in her lap and head tilted to one side. The pose would appear peaceful had her face not been streaked with dried blood from maroon hollows where innocent eyes once viewed her world. The girl's injuries exposed raw, bloody bone and ragged-edged flesh where her scalp belonged. As with the five children murdered before her, elaborate symbols had been carved into her torso.

Mrs. Fortier's tortured expression flashed across Derek's memory and tore at his gut. For the last three days, she'd come to the station begging for answers. Having to tell the woman her baby was dead made his insides twist painfully.

A cocksure photographer from some supermarket rag made it over the wall and dashed close enough to snap a shot of the naked victim before two officers tackled him to the ground and confiscated his camera.

Frustration and anger fueled Derek's temper. "Why don't we have a blind up? Hasn't the ME been here yet?"

The young cop's back stiffened. "No, sir. Not yet. I roped off the area and kept everybody away. Crime scene's not been messed with."

Derek's eyes were drawn to the front of the crypt where words written in blood taunted him. Always the same enigmatic message: *Ogou La Flambo, Lieutenant of burning battlefields, gorge with this blood and grant me my revenge.*

He turned when Detective Frank Panner approached. Running fingers through his sandy-blond hair, Panner shouted orders to nearby men to blind the scene with tarpaulins. He glanced at Derek. "Found out what that Ogou La Flambo shit is." He flipped his cigarette beyond the cordoned area. "Voodoo head honcho. Some war god or something."

"You think this could be a cult gone bad?"

Frank reached into his shirt pocket and pulled out another Marlboro. "Best motive I've heard so far. Isn't this the cemetery where Marie Laveau's supposed to be planted? Maybe. . . ." He wiggled his eyebrows and the corners of his mouth twitched with mirth.

"I'm in no mood for jokes, Frank. We have another dead kid. Or didn't you notice?"

"Yeah. Number six." Frank lit his cigarette and drew in a smoke-clogged breath. "The governor thinks you should be replaced, you know?"

Derek brought his face so close to Frank's he smelled a mixture of peppermint and smoke on his breath. "I don't give a damn what the governor thinks. Let him come out here and see these kids. Then see if he can tell me what I'm not doing to find the son-of-a-bitch doing this."

Frank held up his hands in stop-sign fashion. "Hey, man, I'm with you. Don't kill the messenger. I'm just telling you what he said."

Derek stepped away. "Sorry, man."

"No need. I understand. This case is eating at everybody."

"Have you talked to the guy who found her yet?"

With a shrug and a flick of his hand to dust a smear of dirt from his shirt, Frank said, "No. Figured I'd let you talk to him first. But, Derek, do him a favor. Soften up that scowl. You look like you have a mad-on for the whole damned world."

A shrill whistle drew their attention.

"Found something," an officer yelled.

Detectives and officers converged on a pale yellow sheet of notepaper with two bloody orbs placed on top. Four words mocked them: *She has to pay.*

"Is . . . is that. . . .?" The officer didn't finish his question. "Oh, God." He gagged and ran a few feet away before throwing up.

Frank whistled low. "You think those are the kid's eyes?"

Derek gritted his teeth. "Bastard's playing with us."

Memories of a twenty-year-old unsolved murder teemed inside his skull like the buzz of a low-hanging power line. As with this one, the killer's note baited him. The taunting message reverberated over and over like a mantra in his brain.

I couldn't let you have her.

Two

"Will someone . . . please . . . tell them I'm not dead?"

Drifting between sleep and wakefulness, Tabatha's defenses were at their lowest. She'd spent years training her mind to shut out the voices of the dead, but tonight she was too tired to keep them at bay. She slid one of her legs to the bed's edge until she had one foot on the floor. "Come on legs," she encouraged with a groan. "One down, one to go."

With great effort, she sat up and ran splayed fingers through her hair, twining it into a bun at the nape of her neck. Her pager vibrated against her hip. After glancing at the display, she reached for the phone and keyed in Emergency's number. "Dr. Gray."

"I have a patient for you." Tabatha recognized Dr. Boone's smooth, comforting voice instantly. "Slit wrists, thirteen years old. No hurry. We sedated her. Just need someone to sign her into psych."

"I'll be right down." She placed the receiver on its base and left the residents' sleep room.

Tabatha exited the elevator and headed into a glassed-off area restricted to all but medical personnel. "You look like death whipped to a peak, Dr. Boone."

He slumped into the nearest chair. "All hell broke loose in the city tonight. So many gunshot wounds have come in I've lost count. One man with a knife sticking out of his chest kept insisting the Japanese were invading. Another strolled in with a broken wine bottle sticking out of his skull. Just walked in like he had nothing more serious than a splinter." He slumped deeper into the chair and rubbed his face. "Yours is in room one. Think I'll try to sneak in five minutes of rest before the next wave."

~

Tabatha moved to the girl's side and patted her shoulder. Despite the heavy sedation, the girl trembled uncontrollably. "It's going to be okay, Miss O'Connor."

"Mary. My name is Mary."

"Fine, Mary it is. Now, tell me why you did this to yourself. Nothing could be that bad, could it?"

"My daddy." She swallowed a sob and shook her head. "No. Forget it."

"Forget what, Mary?"

"Nothing."

Tabatha dragged a stool over to the side of the examination table. "Not nothing. It has to be something pretty awful to make you do something like this."

"I just wanted it to be over." The girl's eyes rolled in their sockets, and Tabatha watched her struggle to focus. She must have tremendous strength not to succumb to the meds Boone gave her.

"What happened, Mary?"

"He . . . Mom doesn't believe me. Why should you? Go away and let me go home." A sob nearly choked her as she uttered the last word.

"I can't go away, and you can't go home. You tried to kill yourself."

The girl shot her a shocked look. "No, I didn't. I just. . . ." She raised her bandaged arms and stared at them. "I just wanted him to stop." She burst into tears and rolled into the fetal position, her back to Tabatha. Sobs shook her body violently. "She called me a troublemaker, said I just wanted attention."

Tabatha's heart sank to the pit of her stomach. "What did your father do, Mary?"

Silence spoke the unspeakable truth.

"I know this is hard to talk about." Tabatha focused all her emotions on the girl, and ran a feather-light touch over Mary's forehead, willing her to calm down. "Mary, I need you to tell me everything."

"He . . . did the dirty," she wailed. "He told me it was okay. He loved me. But it's not okay, is it?"

"No." Tabatha paused, taking several deep breaths. "Was this the first time?"

"No."

Tabatha pressed her lips together and gritted her teeth.

Mary wiped her nose with the heel of her hand. "Don't be mad at that other doctor." Her face flamed scarlet. "He asked me the same things, but I just couldn't tell him. I was ashamed."

"It's not your fault, Mary. You did nothing wrong." Tabatha flung the door of room one open and yelled for the charge nurse. "Martha, bring me a rape kit." She paused to calm her anger before she spoke again. "And call the police."

An hour later the police had their questions answered. Social Services had been notified and Mary was wheeled away to a private room with orders that her parents were not allowed to visit. Tabatha leaned against the wall and tried to convince herself she'd done everything she could for Mary. A warrant for her father's arrest was being processed. Her family doctor had been notified. It was out of Tabatha's hands now. She glanced around for anything to take her mind off of Mary and saw the nurses' attendant, Bobbie Luckman, trying to maneuver two sheet-draped gurneys toward the service elevator.

"You can't do that by yourself, woman." Tabatha grimaced. "You'll pull a muscle and end up a patient here yourself."

Bobbie glanced at Tabatha, pulled the tie out of her long ebony ponytail and gathered the wisps of stray hair back into the tie's bindings. "They're swamped down here. I was just going to get these out of the way. Patients get spooked when they see bodies lying about. I'll take this one and come back for the other."

"I know Dr. Boone said it's been crazy tonight, but can't the orderlies do this?"

The charge nurse slapped a pile of paperwork on her counter. "No! I can't spare them right how. It's not going to kill her to take them down."

"I'll help you," Tabatha said.

"That's not your job, Dr. Gray," the charge nurse shouted, as if ordering her to step down.

"It's not Bobbie's job either." She turned her back to the nurse and grasped the edge of the gurney. The sheet flew back as if it had been ripped away by an invisible hand. The cadaver's arm fell limply over the side, swinging as if the dead man's hand were searching for something to grip.

A cleaning lady gasped and stumbled against the wall, fear sculpting her face as she clawed at a chain around her neck. She drew a crucifix from under her scrubs, holding it out like a shield. "Stay away from me. You got the touch of the Devil."

"Oh for Pete's sake, Edda," Bobbie said. "It was just the air conditioner switching on, and I must have jostled the body trying to maneuver the gurney, causing the arm to slide over the edge."

Tabatha reached out to touch the cross. "I'm afraid you have your mystical creatures mixed up, Edda. I'm not a vampire. A piece of jewelry has no effect on me."

The old woman's eyes widened when Bobbie lifted the corpse's arm into place and drew the sheet over the body. Her gaze darted from the body to Tabatha. "I've heard about the things you do. People talk."

"That's enough, Edda," the charge nurse said. "Watch your mouth and get back to work."

"No, that's all right." Tabatha strove for a kind, reassuring smile, hoping it hid the nervousness that was threatening to make her sweat. "Where are you from, Edda?"

The woman cleared her throat and looked down her nose at Tabatha. "Jamaica."

Tabatha wasn't sure if she felt pity or disdain for the woman. "I know what you mean about people talking." She pulled Mary's paperwork out of the slot next to the door and signed the transfer form. "They say everyone in Jamaica practices voodoo."

The woman clutched her cross, sputtered, and then looked away.

"Don't worry, Edda, I'm way too smart to believe everything I hear." Tabatha held back the smile that threatened when Edda's face reddened. "Lead the way, Bobbie?"

Bobbie pointed down the hall. "Elevator's that way."

The nurse reached out to touch a stack of papers. "Bobbie, take these discharge prescriptions to the outpatient pharmacy. You'll be in the basement anyway."

Bobbie pulled off one latex glove to take the prescriptions off the spindle and stuffed them into her pocket. "Do I need to wait for the medications?"

"No. The pharmacy tech will run them up during his rounds."

Bobbie and Tabatha arranged the gurneys in the large service elevator. Bobbie pressed the down button with her elbow and watched the numbers on the display count down.

An uncomfortable silence settled over them. Tabatha cleared her throat. "Edda really freaked."

Bobbie cut her eyes speculatively at Tabatha. "Edda hates working around the dead."

Tabatha straightened the sheet over the body and changed the subject. "Have their families been called?"

"Yours is a John Doe. No ID, no wallet. Nothing."

Tabatha warred with herself whether to lower her psychic shields and ask his name, but with Bobbie in the elevator, she didn't dare. "Sad. Someone could be worried about him."

When the elevator stopped, the women pushed the gurneys to the morgue. Bobbie punched the access code into the keypad, and the heavy door opened to the anteroom.

Tabatha said, "Looks like the staff is busy. I'll stay with the bodies until someone can come out and sign for them. You run those prescriptions, and then I'll help you return the gurneys to the ER."

Bobbie nodded. "Great. Thanks."

The quiet of the morgue held an odd sense of peace for Tabatha. The cold stainless steel room smelled of paraldehyde, its odor acrid, sour. She peeked inside the first autopsy room and found it as silent as Central Park after midnight. Each table had its own hanging scale for weighing excised organs, and hoses for rinsing waste and body fluids away. Trays of instruments--retractors, saws, scalpels--all the necessary accoutrements lay nearby. Tabatha walked to the door of the isolation room, peeked in the small window, and saw three people wearing protective paper suits and headgear. She pressed the intercom. "I have two customers for you."

A voice blurted through the speaker. "You'll have to wait. We're finishing up here. Ten, maybe fifteen minutes."

Approaching the John Doe, Tabatha looked around to make sure no one lurked in the shadows. She lowered the sheet, then drew in a deep breath, held it for a moment and opened her mind to his soul.

"Who are you?"

David Pike.

"What happened to you, David?"

I'd just got home and was jumped while I unlocked my door.

"Who did this, and what did they look like?"

Three men--two white, one with short dark hair, the other with blond; one Hispanic-- black hair, tall, walked with a limp.

"Did you know any of them?"

No. Where am I?

"Hospital morgue. You're dead, David," she said gently.

Panic surrounded him in a coppery-scented mist. She ran her gloved fingers through his blood-stiffened hair and spoke softly. "Be at peace, David. It's the beginning of a new life."

Tabatha turned away and was met with a solid wall of cold, dry flesh. She panicked for a moment, looking around to see if anyone had seen.

"Oh, hell. Where did you come from?"

His head tilted to one side as if trying to understand her question. His arm lifted, and he pointed toward an open cooler drawer. The long, crudely sewn autopsy incisions glared against white skin. He was young, probably not more than twenty-three or twenty-four. In life he had been strong and healthy, good looking.

Damn, she hated when they showed up like this. She always felt sorry for them. Their lives were cut short too early, too violently. They were confused by what had happened. Most didn't even know they were dead. Years of dealing with this type of situation had not lessened her concern for them. She still wanted to put them at ease; to help them accept what had happened to them and make their transitions go quickly.

"What's your name?"

"Francis Wade." His voice escaped in a shaky rasp.

"Well, Francis, you have to go back. You're dead."

He glanced down at his nakedness and then at her. "Dead?"

Tabatha looked into his eyes and saw nothing but death's black void. His soul gone, only an empty shell remained. She took him by the hand and led him to the cooler. The cold of his skin ran a chill up her spine. "Lie down, Francis."

He did as she said.

"Go to sleep and wake only when God calls you."

Before turning to leave, she watched his face immobilize into a lifeless mask. Closing the drawer, she turned. Her heart fell to her feet when she saw Bobbie standing next to the other body-draped gurney.

Though she tried to appear nonchalant, standing with arms crossed, leaning against the morgue entry, her expression was almost comical, wide-eyed and slack-jawed. "I knew it. Damn, Tabatha, the rumors are true, aren't they?"

"I'll be gone in a couple of days. It won't be your problem. I've never hurt anyone and I'd never hurt you. I only wanted to help our John Doe. We needed to know how to contact his family. But that one," Tabatha pointed toward Francis' temporary resting place, "I didn't mean for that to happen. Sometimes the power breaks free when I have my guard down."

Bobbie took several steps back until she stood in the hallway, looked one way, and then the other. "Power? You mean you can raise anyone? Talk to anyone that's dead?"

Fatigue and disappointment weighted Tabatha's heart. Bobbie was the only friend she'd made since she'd come to New York, and now she'd managed to screw that up. "Only the first three days after death."

"How could you talk to the cool pop? Wade's been dead for over a week."

Tabatha rubbed her forefinger over her eyebrow. "A soul remains with the body for three days. I can hear their voices calling, asking for my help. Once a soul is gone, they're silenced. But sometimes when I'm really tired, a corpse will rise without my trying. Mr. Wade's body rose, but his soul is gone. I can talk to him but only his memories are available to me. With no soul, there is no emotion, no passion."

"I see, but how. . . .?"

"I was born with this . . . ability to raise the dead. I've spent years learning to control it."

Bobbie seemed to think about that for a moment then nodded, averting her eyes. "Do they know what's going on when we do their autopsy?"

"I know they don't feel pain, but do they know what's going on? I don't know." Tabatha sighed. "Want me to raise another and ask?"

Bobbie's hands flew out in front of her. "No! I'd rather not see any more dead bodies walking around, if you don't mind."

So she wouldn't have to look Bobbie in the eye, Tabatha filled out an identification tag and slipped it onto David's big toe.

Bobbie glanced back down the hall again. "I never see you at the hangouts. Do you ever go out?"

"No."

Stepping into the room, Bobbie stopped next to the body bag holding David Pike's remains. "Look. We all have our secrets. I can live with this secret as long as you don't pull that stunt again; at least not with me around. Creepy." She shuddered.

Bobbie's eyes were filled with so much sincerity that Tabatha nearly wept with relief. "Thank you." Bobbie started for the door, but Tabatha couldn't resist the urge to ask, "What's *your* secret?"

Bobbie did a quick turnabout. "What?"

"You said we all have secrets. What's yours?"

A smile lit Bobbie's face. "That's a story for another day. Not here." She laid her hand atop the second body and a rush of sadness filled her eyes. "This is my brother. He was murdered this morning. I have to take him home to New Orleans for his ceremony."

"New Orleans? That's where I'm going. Do you have family and friends there?"

"A few." Bobbie drew a deep breath and released it. "Maybe we'll. . . ."

Two men exited the isolation room. "What do you have for us?"

~

Tabatha guided her black Grand Am into the drive and slowed to a stop. Fifteen years had passed since she'd last been to New Orleans. Cold, like winter-chilled fingers, crept up her spine and into the dark recesses of her mind. Death drew near. She closed her eyes and forced her shields up to prevent what she knew would come next. The voices. Voices of a soul not yet passed over to the next realm. After a moment, with her psychic shields in place, a consoling quiet flowed through her like the warmth of morning sunshine, chasing away the darkness trying to envelope her.

She took a deep breath and opened her eyes, raking her gaze over her childhood home. The six Doric columns supporting the overhanging roof were in dire need of repair. Four narrow picture windows flanked the front door, their green hurricane shutters off-kilter, and great spans of paint were missing from the brick façade.

"Paw-Paw must be pacing in his crypt," she mumbled in disgust.

Located in the Garden District, the old mansion sat in the center of two acres of perfectly manicured landscape. Centuries-old oaks spread their limbs, offering a green canopy of shaded relief from New Orleans' summers.

Movement to her left caught Tabatha's attention, and goose bumps of excitement covered her skin despite the ninety-plus degree temperature. Nyssa Bouchard ran toward her as fast as her old legs would carry her, waving her arms wildly and calling Tabatha's name. She had been the groundskeeper at Gray Manor practically forever and was Tabatha's lifelong friend. Tabatha jumped from the car, started toward her, and threw herself into Nyssa's embrace.

"A doctor." A myriad of emotions laced the old woman's voice. "I'm so proud of you. But why have you stayed gone so long? I've missed you."

Tabatha struggled to understand Nyssa's sobbed words. "I've missed you, too." She jutted her chin toward the house. "Why has she let it get so run down?"

Nyssa shrugged her thin shoulders and stepped from Tabatha's embrace. "Carla still can't accept that your grandfather left Gray Manor to you. She was angry when she lost the last appeal. Thinks it should be hers."

"It is Mom's home, Nyssa."

"It's not enough to live here." She glanced at the second floor, lowering her voice to a whisper. "You must be careful while you're home. I think she wishes you bad gris-gris."

Tabatha smiled and ran her fingers through her friend's long black hair. "No voodoo spells can harm me. You should know that."

"Yes, I suppose you're right. Your powers are still strong. Even now, I can feel them surging from you."

Tabatha saw as well as sensed disapproval in her friend's gaze. "Something wrong?"

"Who taught you to dress, girl?" Nyssa asked, tugging on one sleeve of Tabatha's black silk bomber jacket while glaring at the torn knees of her jeans.

"You're one to talk. When did you become such a clotheshorse? There's no denying the style and cut of an Armani." Black and tailored to fit like a glove, the suit gave Nyssa the aura of a wealthy professional instead of a groundskeeper. With a smile and wink, Tabatha said, "I must be paying you too much."

"My salary is set firm in your grandfather's will. You have no power to change it." Her frown vanished as quickly as it appeared. "Now, stop changing the subject. Why are you dressed like a beggar?"

With a shrug, Tabatha said, "I should have changed into something else when I stopped for the night but didn't have the energy to pull any luggage out of the trunk. And I'll have you know I paid a pretty penny for these jeans." Tabatha glanced up in time to see the bedroom drapes being pulled aside and caught a glimpse of her mother before she turned and vanished into darkness beyond the curtains. "Why don't we go in?"

Anger tugged at the corners of Nyssa's mouth. "Let's go to my place. We can talk there without her listening."

Tabatha ran an alert eye over Nyssa. "What's wrong? Why don't you want me in there?"

Nyssa glossed her tongue over her lips, slumped her shoulders, drew a deep breath through her nose and slowly released it. "You're right. Might as well get it over with."

The sight that greeted Tabatha upon entering the great room of the mansion shocked, then enraged her. The once-beautiful ivory ceiling medallions looked as if someone had tried to pry them off, leaving the old plaster decorations beyond repair. The hardwood floors were marred with scuffmarks and deep gouges, and the raised paneled walls were in no better shape. "Where is Grandfather's furniture? Where is the clock, the artwork, the damn rug?"

A knock at the door drew Tabatha's attention away. "What now?" she mumbled and crossed the room in long exaggerated strides, impatience building with each step. She fully intended on sending away whoever was there, but the shock of seeing the girl in the doorway replaced her anger with curiosity.

She'd not seen that face since grade school. Memories of the girl's angry, taunting words rose afresh in Tabatha's mind and brought a rush of old pain. She hadn't changed much since Tabatha had seen her last. Her red hair hung unkempt past her shoulders, a sprinkling of freckles dotted the bridge of her nose, and her overlarge clothing hung in unflattering sags and folds.

"Meads? Rhonda Meads, right?"

Rhonda dropped her gaze to her feet. "I need your help."

"You want help from me?" She gritted her teeth and tried to remain calm. "What could 'Witch Tabatha' possibly help you with?"

"Tabatha!" Nyssa said, but Tabatha's pointed finger quieted her.

Rhonda cleared her throat. "Just hear me out, please."

"Could this wait for a couple of days? I just got home and I'm tired."

"No. I need to talk to you now. It'll only take a few minutes. I promise."

With an irritated sigh, she moved aside and waved Rhonda in. "What is it you want?"

"Are the stories about you true?" Rhonda kept her gaze downcast, as if afraid to look at Tabatha. "Please, let them be true."

Tabatha crossed her arms. "Which story do you need to be true?"

"Can you raise the dead?"

Stumbling backward, Tabatha's throat closed off the air she desperately needed. An unwelcome memory of terror-stricken mourners and her grandfather's casket trembling on its stand returned in an unwanted rush. "What? Why would you ask me such a thing?"

"Miss Bouchard said--"

Tabatha's legs gave out, and she landed hard on one of two chairs left in the room. "Get out."

"Please. . . ."

"Get out!"

Draping her arm over Tabatha's shoulders, Nyssa said, "Child, hear this out. Let her tell you the reason. The magic can be used to good."

Tabatha glared at her best friend. "Nyssa, you don't know what you're asking of me. I don't do--"

"Just listen to her. It's a birthright, not a curse." Nyssa's voice had taken on a gruff, irritated tone.

Tabatha forced herself to face Rhonda. She would listen, but would do and say anything to make Rhonda leave and never return. "Talk. Make it short."

"I'm adopted." She held out her arms in a pleading gesture. "I found my birth mother, but she died before I could find out . . . something. Something I need to know."

"It's your birth mother you want raised?"

Rhonda nodded.

"Why?"

"I need to know why she abandoned me. Do you know what it's like to think your own mother didn't want you?"

Tabatha struggled to swallow the lump of hostility forming in her throat. "You tormented me all through our childhood. My only escape was being sent away to live with strangers. Do I know what it's like not to be wanted? Yes. I do. Go away, Rhonda. Only God can raise the dead."

"Don't lie to me. I saw it on that TV show, *Hidden Truths Revealed.*" Rhonda turned pleading eyes toward Nyssa. "Help me make her understand."

Tabatha swallowed a sigh of disgust. That damned show had somehow gotten hold of an old film of a necromancer raising a body and splattered it all over the airwaves. The man's powers were not as strong as hers, and the body rose in a half decayed state, sending everyone into frenzy of shock and revulsion. "Nyssa does not control me, Rhonda. I, only I, can make this decision, and I've made it. Even if I could, I wouldn't do this for you. Ever."

"I'm not asking," Rhonda said, her voice angry and sullen. "You *are* going to help me. I'm not taking no for an answer."

At the sound of footsteps, Tabatha spun around. Her mother moved toward them. She was dressed in an elegant royal-blue kimono embroidered with a fire-breathing dragon which seemed to snake up her thin body. Her long black hair hung to her waist, swaying with each step.

"My daughter told you to remove yourself from my home. Do so." Carla waved her hands in a shooing motion. "You are not welcome here."

Rhonda backed away. "This isn't over. I'll be back. I need your help."

Tabatha rose, grabbed Rhonda roughly by the arm and led her to the door, slamming it behind her. She rested her forehead against the cool wood. Her heart jumped into her throat when Carla pulled her into her arms.

"You understand why I sent you away, now. Don't you? You've shaken the curse."

Tabatha tried to speak, but a wash of emotions filled her throat. If she told her mother the truth, how long would this embrace last?

Carla ran her hand over Tabatha's hair; a slight frown creased her brow as she gazed at the silver tresses. "There was so much evil here. I needed you to see that and learn the realities of life. I love you, Tabatha. I didn't want you to be like them." She loosened her hold on Tabatha and turned her head with a jerk toward Nyssa. "What are you doing here? I may have to put up with you on the grounds, but not in my home."

"Mother, it's my home as well and Nyssa is my friend."

A moment of hatred hardened her mother's features before disappearing so quickly that Tabatha wasn't sure she'd seen it at all.

Carla smiled and returned her attention to Tabatha. "My beautician could do so much with that hair. A little color, a perm." She stared at Tabatha's ice-blue eyes. "Colored contacts maybe?"

"No color. No perm. No contacts. You have to accept me the way I am, Mother."

She felt herself being drawn into Carla's embrace again. The scent of Chanel No. 5 engulfed her. She'd wanted this for so long, but fear and a deep sense of warning chilled her. She had to question, was this her real mother or the monster she remembered from her childhood?

Three

Why did Tabatha have to come back? Did she think I wouldn't recognize her? I'd know her instantly. Oh, the face has matured, but it's her. Those naive blue eyes she used to charm my man haven't changed. How many times do I have to kill her? Why doesn't she stay dead? Could she know? Will she tell?

I have to calm down. This is her home.

No, it's mine. She stole it from me. Perfect Tabatha. Always so coy, so innocent. She doesn't fool me. She's crazy, hears voices in her head.

I should have taken care of that other one. Tabatha only came to see her.

Look at the ungrateful bitch. Floating around half naked on the back porch as if no one can see her. Tae Kwon Do she calls it. Showing off for anyone who will look.

How I long to draw my rotting circle of death on her smooth white belly. I love how she screams when I touch her. She's learned what it's like to hurt.

A car . . . who is this, now?

Yes. Yes. Here comes that girl. She can help me. Everyone will understand why I did it. They'll thank me. They'll see how evil Tabatha is.

~

Dropping out of her trained stance, Tabatha grabbed a towel from a nearby lawn chair. Taking several deep breaths, she glanced toward the sound of approaching footsteps. She raised her hand to shade her eyes from the sun's glare. "Who's there?" she shouted when she saw nothing but her empty backyard.

Rhonda rounded the corner of the house, stopping a good distance away. A blast of hot air lifted her red hair like strands of coiled flames above her head. "I want to talk to you."

Tabatha released her breath with a hiss. "What do you want now? I'm not going to raise--"

"I've heard of neco . . . necman. . . ."

"You can't even say the word." Tabatha wrapped her arms around her waist. "Necromancer; or animator if you prefer."

Rhonda nodded and looked around the yard as if checking to make sure they were alone.

"Even if I could do this, do you realize what it would involve? You'd need a sacrifice to raise a body."

Rhonda's head snapped around, and her eyes filled with terror. "Not a human!"

Lowering her face into the towel, Tabatha groaned with frustration. "No. An animal. A goat or chicken, depending on how long the corpse has been dead." She watched for a reaction. Rhonda's body went limp with what Tabatha assumed was relief. Hope bounded to the surface. For a few brief moments she thought she'd talked Rhonda out of her foolishness. She needed only to push the right buttons. "You know it's considered evil. Ungodly. If the church found out, you could be excommunicated."

Rhonda nodded.

"And you still want to go ahead with it?" Tabatha asked.

"Yes." Jutting out her chin, Rhonda stared Tabatha in the eyes for the first time. "I'm scared, but not enough to walk away. I have to know why she didn't want me."

Tabatha saw Nyssa crossing the yard and turned to her. "Are you in on this?"

"She came looking for you two days ago. I told her when you'd be home." Nyssa glanced at Rhonda. "I did think she'd wait a while to let you get settled." She looked down her nose at Rhonda and sniffed the air. "If you'll excuse me, I have work to do." She turned and made her way to the garage and shut the door behind her.

Rhonda cleared her throat. "I didn't mean it. It's just . . ."

"Didn't mean what?"

"The things I did back then. I'm sorry."

"Sorry?" Tabatha swallowed the anger nearly choking her. *Sorry for calling me Death Monger? Or maybe you're sorry for stealing those dead dogs from the animal hospital and putting them on my porch after my grandfather's funeral?* She shook the unspoken questions from her mind. "I can't do it." She tried to pass, but Rhonda blocked her way.

"I'm sorry for the way we treated you, Tabatha. Really sorry." Rhonda's fingers toyed with the frayed waistband of her sweatshirt. Her expression filled with regret; real or not, Tabatha wasn't sure. "We were wrong. I'll do anything to make it up to you."

"I don't believe your apology is sincere. You want something from me and you think I'll be so grateful for your attention I'll fall to my knees and do anything you ask. I'm not a kid anymore, Rhonda." Tabatha looked at the girl standing before her--really looked at her. "Did you think coming here dressed in Goodwill Chic would make me feel sorry for you? Poor little Rhonda, her mommy left her all alone and now she can't even afford Wal-Mart." She cringed at the cruel words that spouted from her mouth.

Rhonda's face flushed crimson and twisted in anger. "How dare you! Not everyone has a rich family to pay their way through life."

Tabatha's momentary guilt faded. She narrowed her eyes with anger. "No one paid my way."

"Please. I'll do anything. You have to help me." Tears ran down her cheeks and her lower lip quivered.

"Can you give me one acceptable reason why I should help you? Go home and think on this. Answer one question and I'll do what you ask."

Rhonda inhaled deeply then released her breath in a whoosh. "What?"

"Why?" Tabatha had no doubt there was more to this than what Rhonda was saying. She was scared--desperate. "Why should I help you?" Tabatha shoved past Rhonda and went into the house.

Pulling a chair from the small dinette, she sat down and tried to calm herself. But there was little calm here. She glanced around the kitchen. Institutional white from ceiling to floor; the room felt sterile and cold. She remembered her grandfather's cook, Bertha, rushing around, singing old spirituals as she prepared their meals. The memory of her soulful smile, ebony skin and blue uniform brought life to Tabatha's otherwise empty surroundings. She closed her eyes to ward off tears threatening to escape and wished Bertha was here now. She'd know what to do and say. She always did.

Tabatha gritted her teeth and turned at the sound of the door opening with a crash against the wall. "Damn."

Rhonda slammed her open wallet onto the table and pointed to a snapshot of a young boy. "That's my son, Shane."

Tabatha looked away.

"Look at him," Rhonda screeched. "His birthday was last week. He turned five."

"You're not telling me everything, Rhonda. I can smell the fear on you like a three-day-old cadaver. I'm going to add one more stipulation. The truth."

Rhonda's glare faltered, and she slid to her knees sobbing into her hands.

Tabatha wanted to feel resentment, but Rhonda's weeping, and the sight of her rail-thin body ripped away any barrier Tabatha had built against the world. She picked up Rhonda's wallet and looked into Shane's green eyes. The little redheaded boy smiling into the camera was the epitome of innocence. "What does Shane have to do with this?"

ℱour

Derek leaned back in his chair and surveyed his surroundings. At times he saw the stain-streaked walls and grimy, caged windows of the station house as a fitting stage for his growing discontent. The place smelled of smoke and stale coffee. The sounds of phones ringing, men talking, suspects yelling and keyboards clicking filled the air in a hodgepodge of static-like noise. In the holding cell, a street punk stood in a pool of his own urine, eyes wide with fear. Derek never understood how street-hardened punks could be scared of a few cops to the point of pissing themselves. Bleeding-heart liberals had outlawed 'friendly persuasion' techniques a long time ago. He glanced at the other detectives as they scuttled around the squad room, each with their own cases, their own problems to solve. This week alone there had been three fatal beatings, fifteen shootings, two stabbings; and it was only Wednesday.

He turned his gaze to photographs of six little girls lined up on a corkboard; their innocent, smiling faces stared back at him, beseeching him to find the monster responsible for their deaths.

Mandy Green, the youngest victim, disappeared one day before her fifth birthday. Sister to two older brothers. Father dead.

Adrianna Ronan turned six three months ago--an only child to Misty and John.

Torri Casale, also six, adopted but no less adored.

Deanna Ward, nine-years-old, a bit of a handful, according to her mother, Candy.

Ursola Babin, seven, a shy girl who never talked to strangers.

The victims attended different schools and lived in different sections of town. The killer had no preference for rich or poor. Their blue eyes and blond hair, and the fact that they were all girls were the only common denominators between the children. Their nude bodies always showed up in one of the local cemeteries three days after their disappearances.

He added a snapshot of ten-year-old Selma Fortier to the board. Brilliant but too trusting, she skipped second and fourth grades and played classical violin. In her daily visits to the precinct, Selma's mother reminded Derek of all Selma had going for her. "What are you doing to find my daughter, detective?" she would ask and hand him another picture of her daughter.

Those quiet, terror-filled words would haunt Derek until his dying day, reminding him he'd failed. Again.

He wanted to tell her the truth. Not enough. It's never enough when a kid turns up dead. Instead he tried to comfort and reassure her that they were doing everything in their power to find Selma.

Today she hadn't asked any questions.

Today Mrs. Fortier identified her daughter.

Today she cried.

Derek opened the voodoo primer sitting on his desk. He hadn't been able to find a link to the rituals performed on the bodies. The medical examiner's report concluded a skilled hand had removed the victims' eyes. Their scalps, however, appeared to have been jabbed and cut while the killer was in the throes of rage. Death had been by suffocation.

"Who killed you? What am I missing?"

"Talking to yourself, partner?" Frank asked before placing a styrofoam cup of coffee in front of Derek.

"Just thinking out loud. Trying to make something click into place." He moved his attention back to photographs of the crime scenes. Each child had been posed in the same seated position, grotesque empty sockets where their eyes had once been; their bodies, always bathed, smelling of deodorant soap. Signs of freezer burns were evident on the buttocks as though they'd sat in a deep-freezer waiting to be delivered.

"Have they talked to you yet?" Frank's question drew Derek from his thoughts.

"No, not yet. I'm listening though, just in case."

"Be nice if they could tell us who did this." Frank reached for the framed photograph on Derek's desk. "Don't you think it's time to put this away? It's been twenty years."

Derek yanked it out of Frank's hand and returned it to its proper place. Her picture was his reminder of why he became a cop. But hers was the one case he had never been able to solve--hers and the children's. "When I find her killer, I'll put her to rest."

Frank circled the desk and slumped in his chair. "Mary wants me to invite you to dinner Saturday night. She invited Melita Potts. Why don't you do her a favor and fuck her brains out? Make her a happy woman."

Derek groaned inwardly. "Hell no."

"Give me one good reason."

He cringed as an image of Melita's red frizzy hair and crooked, toothy grin flashed across his mind. "First, her voice could cut glass. Second, she licks her lips constantly. It drives me nuts." He pointed his finger and skimmed it over the others in the room. "Third, show me one man in this squad that hasn't had his turn in the sack with her. She's a squad follower. A cop's whore. No thanks. Make my excuses to Mary. Besides, I already have a date."

Frank straightened in his chair, eyebrows rose sharply. "With who? Do I know her?"

He glanced at the photograph again. "You did."

Frank let out a sigh. "Come on, man. Let Elizabeth go. It's time to move on. You're alive. She's dead."

Derek slammed his fist on the desk so hard every head in the office turned in their direction.

Frank held up his hands. "Okay. I give. Keep living with her ghost; but there are a lot of good women out there. Just remember this, buddy--you ain't getting any prettier and the girls ain't getting any younger."

Derek had turned forty a week earlier, but felt sixty. He knew time was running out, not so much for finding love, but for solving Lizzy's case. The hours, the stress and the frustration of the job settled on him like layers of fat around his heart.

He'd spent most of his waking hours watching his own back, living by his own rules. The department feared his ways but respected his results. Shoot first and ask questions later, was his motto. Derek's reputation on the streets kept the dark side always on the lookout for him. He didn't let women get close--for their own protection. Women were targets when the bad guys got even. He slept alone, ate alone, drank alone, and preferred it that way.

Standing, he jerked his jacket from his chair, drawing Frank's attention away from the case file he was reading. "Where you going?"

"I have an appointment." He paused at his friend's side. "Tell Mary I'll think about it, but not this Saturday and not with Snake Tongue Melita."

The room erupted with laughter. "Don't knock it until you try it, Bainbridge," a detective yelled from across the room.

Derek didn't look back or acknowledge the remark. His mind was on an anniversary and a dozen roses.

Five

Tabatha wrapped her arms around her waist, leaned against the kitchen table and waited. Her stomach clenched at what she saw. Cowering in the corner, her face hidden, Rhonda looked like a child concealing herself from the boogeyman. Tabatha wondered in what form Rhonda's fears took shape. Her bones pressed against the faded gray material of her sweatshirt, giving an impression of malnutrition. Copper-red hair hung limply around her shoulders, shrouding her face. Rhonda's sobs broke the quiet of the room, adding more depth to her lament.

"I'm waiting, Rhonda. Are you going to talk, or are you taking a time out over there?"

Rhonda turned, huddling against a cabinet. She half sobbed, half sighed. "My mother was . . . different."

"Different in what way?"

Tabatha dropped to her haunches to be at eye level with Rhonda and study her tear-streaked face. Worry creased her brow, and frown lines made themselves at home at the corners of her mouth. It occurred to her that Rhonda wasn't the child-bully who had made going to school torture for Tabatha, but a terrified full-grown woman.

"Like you," Rhonda whispered.

Tabatha's heart thumped wildly, each breath a struggle. Like me? No one is like me, she wanted to shout. "Stop talking in code. Like me how?"

"Psychic abilities." Rhonda slowly raised her eyes to meet Tabatha's. "She knew about you. They do, too."

Tabatha gritted her teeth. "They who?"

Rhonda lowered her face into her hands. "They told her they needed people with her gift. But they killed her. Now they want something she had, and I don't know what or where it is. They're going to kill Shane if I don't give it to them."

Tabatha sat hard on the floor. "They who?" She hated repeating herself and knew her voice held a hint of impatience.

"They call themselves Guardians Against Paranormal Sinners, but the few who know, call them the Guardians. My mother tried to tell me about them before she was killed, but I wouldn't listen. The police won't help me. They ruled her death a suicide." She wiped her nose on the sleeve of her sweatshirt. "I think they're afraid of the Guardians. When I mentioned their name, the look of fear that crossed the cop's face said it all. He made the sign of the cross and told me to never mention them again."

"These people have talked to you?"

"The Guardians?" She shook her head. "No. They broke into my house, ransacked every drawer, every closet."

"Do they have Shane?"

Rhonda ran her arm over her eyes, wiping away her tears. "No. He's with my mom."

"Wait. I'm confused again. I thought your mom was dead."

"Mom is the woman who adopted me. My birth mother is who I need you to raise."

"Okay. But what makes you think they'll hurt Shane or you?"

Reaching into her front pocket, Rhonda removed a folded piece of paper and handed it to Tabatha. "They left this for me."

Tabatha unfolded the gray, water marked stationary and read:

Your mother didn't play by the rules.

If you want to live, if you want your son to live,

you'll give it to us.

You have three days.

"That was two days ago. I have one day left. You gotta help me, Tabatha. Please."

Tabatha sat back against the table leg. "And you say they know about me?"

"Yeah."

"How do you know?"

Rhonda shrugged. "Mother said your name was on a list. That's all I know." Bordering on hysteria, she added, "I know you hate me, Tabatha. But I need to know what *it* is. Shane is all I have."

Tabatha had no doubt Rhonda believed what she'd said. She'd never seen such terror in anyone's eyes before.

"Please, I'm begging for my son's life. Please."

Tabatha ran her fingers through her hair and released a long-held breath. Numbness settled over her. Which was the greater evil here? Raise a dead mother to reap information that may save two lives? Or refuse and leave Rhonda to her own problems?

They know about you. The words sent a cold chill down her spine.

"God, forgive me." She knew what she had to do.

~

Derek sat on a concrete bench beside Elizabeth's grave. Pulling a small whiskbroom from his jacket pocket, he proceeded to clean dirt from the carved letters of her name. Had she not been killed just moments before their wedding, they would have been married twenty years today.

His throat was tight and dry. His head throbbed. "Elizabeth Ann Morrie," he whispered. Many times in the beginning, he'd crossed out her last name and written in Bainbridge. But the rains would come, washing it away and she would become a Morrie again.

"Happy anniversary, Lizzie. I brought your favorite--pink roses."

A smile lifted his lips in remembrance of Elizabeth's excitement over her wedding dress. When he allowed the memory of her to return, he still heard her laughter, saw the sparkle in her dark brown eyes, and smelled the scent of her perfume. His chance at happiness died with her. He'd accepted his lot to be alone.

"I still haven't found him, Lizzie. But I'm not giving up. I'll give you justice." He chuckled and shook his head. "Frank says I need to let you go, find someone else. What do you think?"

Voices a few tombs away caught his attention. His heart took on a thunderous pace when he saw a tall blond alongside a skinny little redhead. The blond's stride was confident, her face devoid of emotion; but it was her hair that intrigued him. The thick, long strands glowed mystically white in the dusk of sunset. Derek ran his gaze from her head to her booted toes. Slender, elegant in her movements, she was the model of perfection. He stepped behind a nearby tomb, wanting to keep her in sight without her noticing him.

They stopped at a crypt fifty feet away. She dropped to her knees and began to lay out an array of tools. His brows shot up at the sight of a chicken in a cage. "What are these girls up to, Lizzie?"

The blond muttered a chant as she formed a groove around the grave with a long bladed knife. She stopped where she began and pulled a vial from her bag and walked the circumference once again, this time filling in the groove with the vial's white contents. His curiosity turned to alarm when the woman assembled four symbols facing north, east, south and west. The symbols she drew weren't like the ones found on the children, but too similar for Derek's comfort.

"Are you sure you want to do this?" the blond asked.

"I have to know, Tabatha."

Derek whispered Tabatha's name, letting it roll over his tongue. It tasted sweet and alluring. He ducked behind the crypt when she turned toward him. After a few moments passed, he leaned around the crypt far enough to see the women again.

Tabatha paused, her eyes roaming over the cemetery before she removed the chicken from the crate. "Do not step out of this circle until I tell you it's safe, Rhonda. Do you hear me?" She released the latch on the chicken's cage.

Rhonda nodded, but said nothing.

The chicken squawked and flapped its wings in a futile fight for freedom. With a swift slice of a dagger, its head dropped away. Rhonda moved to the edge of the protective circle to escape the spray of blood splattering the crypt and Tabatha's clothing. Once again Tabatha traveled the circle letting the blood of the chicken form a second line inside the first. She strode to the crypt and placed her bloody hand on the entrance. "Live. I command you to live, Dorothy McShayne."

Derek nearly fell backward when the earth rumbled under his feet and a blast of thunder sounded from a cloudless sky. Tabatha retreated a few steps. The mortar binding the door to the crypt rained to the ground as though being chipped away from within. The grinding sound of stone against stone filled the silence and the door slid open. A hand reached out, touching the edge, then a second hand. A fall of long red hair appeared then her head lifted slowly to reveal the woman's face. She slid forward, her body levitating from the crypt's gaping mouth until she stood before them.

Cold surrounded Derek with whispers of unknown origin. A sensation of death-chilled breath brushed his cheek. The air became thick and heavy with the scent of decay. He landed hard on his backside. "Get away," he muttered batting at the sensation of another's nearness.

Tabatha swung around, arms spread outward from her sides. "Unclean spirits, I did not summon you. Go. Return to where you came. The living is not yours to taunt." Her eyes grew hard and angry. "Leave here!"

The day's heat returned and the air cleared. Silence once again ruled Derek's world. He sagged against the tomb and breathed deeply.

Silence hung like a thick curtain of indecision before Tabatha finally said, "Dorothy, my name is Tabatha Gray."

Dorothy tilted her head to one side then the other. "I know who you are. All of the dead know you."

Tabatha visibly shuddered. "Who killed you?"

The corpse held a steady lifeless gaze on Tabatha. "John Phelps."

"Why?"

"The Guardians discovered I was taping their conversations, copying their death list and keeping a record of those they murdered."

"Where are these things now?"

"Under Rhonda's bedroom floor; seventh board from the closet."

Tabatha nodded once then drew a deep breath. "How did the Guardians get my name?"

"Someone told them who you were, what your powers are, and when you were returning home."

"Do you know who that person was?"

"No."

Derek shifted to a more comfortable position as Tabatha turned to the other girl and asked, "Rhonda, is there anything else you need to know?"

"Why did you give me up, Mother? Didn't you want me?"

Dorothy didn't answer; instead her stare remained trained intently on Tabatha.

"Why did you give Rhody up for adoption, Dorothy?"

"Rhody?"

"Rhonda," she shouted. "I've not been called Rhody since grade school."

Tabatha massaged her temples with her fingertips. "Why did you give *Rhonda* up for adoption?"

"I wanted her to be safe and have a good life. A better life than I could give her."

Tabatha nodded. "Enough. Return to your resting place, Dorothy McShayne. Rise again only when God calls your name."

Derek fought for air. His throat grew tighter with each tortured breath. Dorothy lifted into the air and settled into her crypt. The concrete stone blocked the opening and its seal reformed. Silence that had encompassed the cemetery moments before was broken with sounds of crickets and distant voices. It was then Derek realized the sun had set, shrouding them in darkness. Tabatha collected her tools and replaced the dead chicken in its cage. Rhonda sobbed quietly.

Tabatha's undisturbed composure vexed Derek. She'd done something impossible but behaved as if it were an everyday occurrence. He wondered if, for her, it was.

"Wait," Rhonda wailed. "You have to bring her back. I want to ask her something else."

"Once I tell them to rise only when God calls them, I can't evoke them again. No one can."

"I just wanted to ask if she ever regretted leaving me."

Tabatha stopped but didn't turn. "Rhonda, your mother did what she thought was right for you. Was your life so bad?" Tabatha didn't wait for an answer but walked away, leaving Rhonda to either follow or stay. She followed, her sobs trailing them.

Derek stayed back the distance of six or seven crypts. His mind raced with possibilities. He could at last find out who took Elizabeth from him. His forward movement stopped abruptly as visions of the dead children appeared one by one, as if reminding him there were more pressing problems than finding Elizabeth's murderer. He needed to think. He had to talk to Tabatha. He took a step forward but froze. A short distance away a cobra coiled itself at his feet and stared at him as though daring him to move. Derek shouted a profanity and jumped back, landing hard against a crypt. When he looked again, the snake had vanished. He searched frantically to find where it had gone, but saw only a coiled vine reacting to a breeze. "Get a grip, Bainbridge." He drew a shaky breath and ran toward the cemetery gates.

When he reached the groundskeeper, the old man doffed his hat and smiled. "Didn't know you were here."

Derek gave a curt nod before racing past him. In the darkness he couldn't be sure of the Pontiac Grand Am's color, but he could partially see the New York vanity license plate. Mud blotted out the last two letters, but the visible letters read DOCTO.

He grunted in indignation. "Doctor indeed."

Six

Before driving away, Tabatha took one last look in her rearview mirror. She saw him standing outside the cemetery's gates, broad-shouldered, a stance of domination. His face, lit by the overhead streetlight, conveyed a strange combination of hope, panic and anger. Tabatha had no doubt he'd been the presence she'd sensed near the gravesite. Whoever he was, he'd seen her raise Dorothy McShayne. The heat of his fear turned to cool astonishment. That alone confused her. She'd never been able to experience another person's emotions; or feel a man's eyes warming her to her bones either. *Who are you?*

Derek Bainbridge, came his reply.

Her heart skipped a beat. Had she imagined that?

Rhonda hiccupped. "Will you go with me to find those things?"

"Of course." She forced herself to give Rhonda her full attention. "I want to see this list. Those behind this must be influential if the cops know about them and won't do anything." Tabatha's thoughts returned to Derek, but she shirked away from the vision of male perfection. He'd been writing something on a pad. Her license plate? She released a pent up breath. "What can he do? I didn't break any laws. I didn't kill anyone."

Rhonda's hands stopped halfway to her nose with a tattered tissue. "What?"

"Never mind. It's not important."

Rhonda stared at her for a moment, then leaned against the headrest. "Go to Esplanade and turn right. My house is only a few blocks." She blew her nose and dabbed at her eyes. "How did you make her look so perfect? When she was found, her face had been cut up real bad, and now her face is beautiful again."

Tabatha didn't know the answer but tried to give one. "When I tell them to live again, I think the body reforms itself into its living state. I guess that means before any damage has been done."

"I'm glad." Rhonda nodded, apparently satisfied. "You don't think my mom killed herself?"

Tabatha snorted. "The dead don't lie, Rhonda. She told me some guy named Phelps killed her, and I believe her."

"I've never heard of Phelps. You know him?"

Tabatha shook her head.

"Turn left at the next corner." Rhonda sighed heavily. "Why wouldn't she answer my questions? She seemed to hear and see only you."

"Whoever uses magic to raise the dead has control over them. I can make them do anything. I don't like that responsibility." Tabatha squirmed in her seat, uncomfortable with the direction of the conversation. She was relieved when Rhonda pointed at a one-story, shotgun-style house.

"It's that one."

Light from the windows spilled out across the driveway, casting a glow into the darkness. "Did you leave a lamp on?"

She nodded. "It makes me feel safer coming home at night."

Tabatha stepped out of the car and searched the tree-lined avenue, trying to see who or what lurked in the shadows. Not knowing the area, she wasn't sure what to look for--who belonged, what was normal, what wasn't. The sight of two men and an elderly woman watching them unnerved her. "Do you see anyone who doesn't fit, Rhonda? Someone you don't know?"

Rhonda ran a wide-eyed glance round the neighborhood before shaking her head. "No. That's just my neighbor. She lives in the big green house. The two men are her sons." She raised her hand and waved. They returned the gesture.

The steps creaked, and Tabatha knew if anyone were near, they'd just announced their arrival. The porch wasn't in much better condition and groaned from their combined weight.

"Before you unlock the door, make sure no one has tampered with it," Tabatha warned.

Rhonda pushed it with her fingers and jumped back at the sharp pop of a loose board. She giggled nervously and tried the knob. "Yeah, it's fine." She thrust a key into the lock and opened the door.

Tabatha placed a hand on Rhonda's shoulder. "Stay here until I check things out. Keep your eyes open."

The all-encompassing musty smells of mold, day-old cooking oil and onions, made the house oppressive and airless. Suffocating heat tried to swallow her whole. Perspiration beaded on her brow, trickled between her shoulder blades and dampened the waist of her jeans. She searched furtively, checking under and behind everything. She opened closets, looked out windows, not knowing what she'd do if she discovered someone hiding.

Satisfied, she signaled for Rhonda to come in. They rushed to the second bedroom, knelt on the rust and burgundy braided rug, and folded back a section. Starting her count from the closet, Tabatha pointed out the seventh floorboard. "Want the honor? It's your house."

Rhonda ran her hand over it before pressing one edge then another. "Can you see a way to get it up?"

Tabatha leaned in on her elbows. Up close, the jimmied planks were easy to distinguish from others. There were gouge marks and chips of old gray paint missing from the board's edge. "Do you have a screwdriver?"

Rhonda's brow furrowed as she stared at the section of flooring. With a brief nod, she jumped up, ran to the kitchen, and returned with a butter knife. "Closest thing I have."

"Good enough." Tabatha worked it into the area already chipped. With a little force, two boards lifted and a narrow six-inch wide section came into view. Several manila envelopes stood beside file folders. A camera, a micro recorder, four rolls of exposed film, a journal, and a small photo album filled the cramped area. They removed the items one by one.

Rhonda flipped through the album and started to sob all over again.

"What's wrong now?" Tabatha thought she'd never known anyone who cried as much as this girl.

Rhonda handed the photo album to Tabatha and rested her head against the bed. "It's pictures of me from when I was a baby until now. She had every school picture, birthday parties; she even has a snapshot of me in the hospital when I had my son. How did she get them?"

"I guess the woman who raised you sent them to her. You're lucky, you had two mothers who loved you very much."

"Yeah. Lucky." Rhonda dabbed her eyes with an edge of the tattered ecru chenille bedspread and took a deep breath. "Can I ask a question?"

"Depends. What's the question?"

"Now what? How do I get this stuff to them?"

Tabatha leaned against the closet door, scanning the hit list. Her name stood out in bold black letters against stark white paper. She glanced at the other names on the list, names of people these monsters considered beyond God's forgiveness. Her anger grew with each name. Who were these people to judge who was beyond redemption? Religious zealots, she surmised, who thought it righteous to kill or threaten women and children to get what they wanted. "What is your guarantee these cretins will let you and your son live after you've handed over this stuff?"

A tremor ran over Rhonda's body. "None."

"Look, why don't we pick up your son? You can stay with me. Let me handle these anal sphincters."

Rhonda's eyebrows crinkled, her head tilted a bit to the left. "Anal what?"

"Assholes."

Rhonda chuckled then sobered. "Your mother would never let me stay there. She thinks I'm trash."

"Hell, my mother thinks I'm trash. She'll get over it. There are seven bedrooms in that house. We can put your son in one and you in another, or you can have my grandfather's suite. It has two double beds, a sitting room and a private bath."

"Find out how the upper crust lives, huh?" Rhonda laughed, but fear laced her voice.

"It will be safer for you and Shane. I'd feel better if we took some precautions until I can stop these fanatics."

"You're going to try to fight these people? They'll kill you, Tabby." Rhonda's eyeballs bulged from their sockets.

Tabatha smiled. "No one but my daddy called me Tabby."

"I'm sorry. I don't know where that came from." Rhonda turned her eyes away.

Tabatha's attitude softened toward Rhonda. Her life had not been an easy one. She'd apparently not had a lot of money and no one to help her raise Shane. She reached out and touched Rhonda on her knee. "We had a rough beginning, but if we play this right, maybe we could become friends."

Rhonda's eyes narrowed. "Why would you want to be my friend?"

"Why not?"

Seven

Derek paced in front of his dresser, pausing to argue with his reflection in the mirror each time a new question surfaced. Who is she? *What* is she? Did she raise the dead or was it a ruse? How much did the other girl have to pay for this kind of information?

Who killed you, Dorothy McShayne? Tabatha's question reverberated in his brain. *John Phelps.* He knew the name but couldn't give it a face.

"Bainbridge, you're losing your mind. You didn't see what you think you saw. It's impossible. No one can raise the dead," he told the man staring back at him.

He turned away from his reflection at the sound of a knock. "Yeah. Who is it?"

"Come on, Derek, it's me, Frank. Let me in."

Derek paused, not sure if he should tell Frank what he'd seen tonight. He shook his head. No. He wouldn't tell anyone, yet.

Frank slammed his fist against the door. "Damn it, Derek, let me in."

Derek opened the door, blocking the entrance. "I'm getting ready for bed. What do you want?"

"What's gotten into you? You don't go anywhere. You don't do anything. You shut yourself in here, ignoring your friends. The boss is worried about you." He stood eye to eye with Derek. "They're going to force you to retire. Is that what you want?"

"I have to solve the kids' murders first, then they can do whatever they want with me." He stepped out of the doorway, allowing Frank to pass. "If I didn't have other cases, maybe I could find Elizabeth's murderer."

"Man, give it up." Muscles in Frank's jaw tightened then released. "It's been twenty years. The case is so cold it's going to give you frostbite." He dropped his gaze and rubbed his neck. "Derek, I didn't come to fight with you. Mary said to come over this weekend. Melita won't be there, but Mary's friend, Carla, is coming over. Her daughter just got into town. Don't worry. This isn't a setup."

Derek sat on the bed. "I don't know. Maybe."

"Mary isn't going to take maybe for an answer. Be there around eleven. Bring some beer." He paused before leaving. "Derek, let Elizabeth go. Find someone else. Life is too short, buddy."

"You ever heard of John Phelps?"

Frank met Derek's stare. His face paled and his Adam's apple bobbed several times. "Some big shot in New Orleans; old money. You met him at the Christmas party last year. Why?"

"Heard his name mentioned and I couldn't place it."

Frank pulled in a deep breath and eyed him a beat or two longer, then nodded. "Get some rest, man, and I expect to see you at the house on Saturday. With beer."

The door opened then closed, and silence once again ruled Derek's world.

"Let her go, he says." Derek closed his eyes, as an image flitted across his mind of Elizabeth's mutilated body exposed to the world, her bloody wedding dress, cut to shreds, surrounding her. "I can't until I give her justice."

The department deemed it a robbery/homicide. He didn't believe it. No one would mutilate a woman like that for a string of pearls and a half-carat diamond ring. This was personal. This was rage.

He stretched out across the bed. His eyes drifted to Elizabeth's side of the bed searching for her ghost, but this time her face eluded him. Fatigue finally took its toll, dragging him into a fitful sleep.

~

Elizabeth's back was to Derek as she busied herself with final preparations for the wedding. Derek called to her, begging her to stop, but she continued to walk away from him, vanishing into the food tent. His muscles felt weary, his feet refusing his demand to run. He crumpled to the ground and crawled, grabbing handfuls of grass to propel his fatigue-racked body forward. Entering the tent, he searched frantically for Elizabeth, calling out her name.

"Where are you, Derek?" Her voice drifted from the other side of the canvas.

He threw the stiff cloth to the side. Derek's heart shrank away from the sight before him; blood flowed freely and surrounded her decimated body. A breeze lifted her bridal veil, revealing her face.

"No." Derek shook his head and back away. Elizabeth's eyes opened and looked into his. Light, ice-blue eyes replaced her dark brown eyes. That couldn't be. He searched her face but found Tabatha's instead.

He breathed her name. "Tabatha."

Her eyes filled with tears. "I'm sorry, Derek."

He jerked awake, leaped from the bed and paced the distance of the small room. Blood roared in his ears. "Tabatha?" He shook his head violently. "No. I can't let you in. Elizabeth, where are you?"

He forced himself to remember her joy over finding their apartment and how she planned to decorate it in shades of green--green refrigerator, green sink and green range. He hadn't had the heart to tell her he hated green.

Shoving his hands into his trouser pockets, Derek discovered the notepad. He pulled it out and ran his finger over his words. "Physician's plate. New York."

He rushed out the door. "I'll find out who you are, Tabatha. You have to help me find out who killed those kids. You have to tell me who murdered Elizabeth. You have to explain to me what the hell you are."

Eight

Tabatha peered out the windshield, her gaze roaming over Gray Manor, checking shadows, trees and buildings for any movement.

Rhonda crouched in the car seat and hugged her son, Shane, closer. "Tabatha, I don't know about this. Your mom isn't going to be happy."

Tabatha pulled in front of the garage and got out. The night smelled of distant rain and jasmine in bloom. Looking up at the darkened windows of Carla's room, a pang of sadness twisted her heart. In Tabatha's memories of her mother, she could never remember a time when Carla was happy. Her mouth always turned down in a frown and her eyes narrowed in anger; there was never a kind word for Tabatha.

"She's in bed by now and won't know anything about it 'til tomorrow morning. I'll get up early to talk to her." Confident that they were alone, she strolled to the rear of the car to open the trunk. "Maybe we should put Shane in bed and come for the bags later. Or if you think he'll wake and be frightened in a new place, I'll fetch them while you put him to bed."

"Leave them. That way we won't have to lug them back when your mom throws us out."

"She won't throw you out, Rhonda." Tabatha reached for the kitchen door; at the same time, it swung open abruptly.

"Where have you been, young lady? I've been here all night waiting for you."

Tabatha rushed into the woman's waiting arms. She drew in a deep breath, savoring the smell of the old woman's scent. She'd always smelled of vanilla. "Bertha, I'm so glad to see you. Does Mom know you're here?"

A sprinkling of gray dusted Bertha's black hair and her dark eyes sparkled with mirth. Ebony skin, still smooth and wrinkle-free, glistened in the kitchen light. Her grandfather had hired Bertha when she was seventeen and she'd become family in short order, ruling the house with a simple word and a nod of her head. Everyone learned quickly never to argue with her.

"Good grief, I swear you look younger every time I see you. What's your secret, old woman?"

"Old woman, is it?" Bertha swatted her on the bottom and shooed her toward the kitchen table. "One question at a time." She turned and ambled toward the stove. "I'm here to take care of my baby girl. I'm glad to see you, too. My oldest son dropped me off. And, yes, the Queen knows I'm here." She smiled and gestured with a large ladle toward Rhonda. "Who is this?"

Tabatha placed her hand on her forehead. "Oh, I'm sorry. Rhonda, this is Bertha." She turned to her childhood cook. "This is Rhonda and her son, Shane. They'll be living with us for a while. You won't mind a couple more mouths to feed, will you? You *are* back to stay, right?"

"Who's gonna take care of you if I don't?" Bertha stirred the contents in the pot sending the scents of herbs, vegetables and beef into the air. Tabatha's stomach rumbled. Bertha turned her attention to the mother and son. "Lord, child, when was the last time you and that boy had a good meal? He looks half starved."

Rhonda's face reddened. "I don't starve my child. Shane's had his supper."

"Didn't mean any harm. I know good mommas from bad ones. They'll feed their children, even if they're starving themselves. Now, ain't that right? And you look about ready to fall over, so you just sit on down. I got a nice pot of soup made." She ran her black eyes over Shane. "Here, let me take the boy to bed. What room, baby girl?"

Tabatha noticed Rhonda's tight grasp on her son. "Bertha, I think Grandfather's suite would be best until Shane gets used to living here. It might be too scary for him to wake up alone in a strange house. We'll get their luggage while you take him up."

"No." Rhonda shook her head. "I'll take him. I don't want him out of my sight."

Tabatha laid gentle fingers against Rhonda's arm. "No one is going to hurt you or Shane while you're here. I promise. You're safe."

"Lordy, if anyone comes in this house that don't belong, I'll give them a taste of my iron skillet. Ain't nobody gonna hurt my family."

Rhonda looked from Bertha to her son. "Okay, but if he wakes and starts to cry, you come get me right away. You hear me?"

"Of course. Now give him here. He needs to be in a bed. Poor little thing."

As Bertha left, she gave Tabatha one of her, 'you're gonna tell me what's going on,' looks, and Tabatha knew she would get no sleep tonight.

"Rhonda, give me a second. I need to talk to Bertha. There are soft drinks in the fridge. Help yourself."

Tabatha rushed away, catching up with Bertha at the base of the stairs. "Can you toss my things in my old room? I don't want Rhonda knowing I gave up the suite for her and the boy."

"Baby girl, I already knew what you were up to. It'll be taken care of." Bertha touched her cheek to Tabatha's. "I always knew you had a good heart." She started up the staircase but turned and said, "Oh, I had my boy and his friends come drag some of the furniture down from the bedrooms to the living room.

It might not match, but at least you children have someplace to sit." She continued up the stairs.

Tabatha returned to the kitchen and gestured toward the back door. "Let's get your luggage. Sooner we get that taken care of, the sooner you can get back to Shane."

"You know this woman good?" Rhonda asked as they walked toward the car.

Tabatha nodded. "I know her very well. She came to work here when I was born and stayed until my mom sent me away. She's family, not a servant. Don't treat her as such and we'll get along fine." Rhonda nodded. "You'll love her and so will Shane. She'll spoil him rotten, though." Tabatha unlocked the trunk and handed Rhonda one of three bags, hefting the others herself. "Word to the wise--eat some soup, or you'll never get to bed. Now relax. Nothing is going to happen." Tabatha opened the back door, stepping away to let her pass. "Bertha wasn't kidding about the skillet. She may be old, but she's spry. And she doesn't take any guff off anyone, even my mom. This is a safe place."

"No such thing." After placing the luggage by the door, Rhonda sat at the table.

Tabatha retrieved bowls and filled them from the pot. "This is really hot, so be careful." She passed one to Rhonda.

Carla stormed into the room, her long black hair falling into wild eyes, spittle around her lips. She jabbed her finger toward Rhonda. "What is she doing in my house, eating my food?"

Tabatha groaned inwardly. "I knew the loving welcome was too good to be real."

Carla's face flamed. "How dare you? Who the hell do you think you are? Whose child is that and why is Bertha taking it upstairs?"

Tabatha turned from Carla's rage, sat and blew steam from her bowl. Using the only weapon she knew would deflate Carla's rage, she said, "Bertha brought the food, Mom. It isn't yours. And actually, the house isn't yours either. It's mine. Paw-Paw left it to me, remember?" Tabatha dared a glance in her mother's direction but turned away from the hate filling Carla's eyes. "The child is Shane, Rhonda's son. Their house is being renovated and I invited them to stay here until it's finished."

"This is my home. They go or I go," Carla screamed and hit the table with her fist.

"Well, Mom, I'll miss you. Let me know where you end up so I can forward your mail." Tabatha knew if she reached out and touched Carla at that moment she would be turned to ash by the heat of her mother's rage.

Rhonda pushed away from the table and stood. "I'll get Shane and we'll go. I don't want to cause trouble."

Tabatha grasped her wrist and pulled her back down onto her chair. "No, Rhonda. It isn't safe in that house right now. Sit and eat your soup. It's really good, don't you think?"

As if not sure what to do, Rhonda hesitated. She lowered her eyes and nodded. "Yes; very good." She brought a spoonful to her lips and blew away the steam.

Tabatha turned to look at her mother. Carla's face had grown pale and her lips were tightly pressed together.

"Would you like some soup?"

"How long?" Carla hissed.

Tabatha fought not to smile. "Oh, it won't take me but a second or two to fill a bowl for you."

Carla closed her eyes and gritted her teeth. "How long will they be here?"

"Not long, Mrs. Gray. I promise you that," Rhonda said. "I don't want to be here any more than you want me here."

Turning abruptly, Carla stomped away, mumbling incoherently.

Tabatha grinned at Rhonda. "God, I love my momma."

~

Tabatha's downward stroke with her hairbrush paused at the sound of a knock at her bedroom door. "Come on in, Bertha."

The older woman strolled into the room with an air of authority. "Okay, baby girl, why you come home after all this time?"

Tabatha dropped to the bed. "This has gone on long enough. Mom and I have to work things out. I didn't ask for the Gray magical powers. But I've got to learn to accept who and what I am, and so does she."

A small smile tugged at the corners of Bertha's lips. "And what brought that on?"

"I made a friend. Bobbie Luckman. She's a nurses' attendant at the hospital where I worked." Taking a deep breath, Tabatha looked Bertha in her big brown eyes and said, "Bobbie came to the morgue one night and saw a dead guy following me around like a puppy. I'll give her credit; she took it pretty well. She nearly tripped over herself trying to get out of the morgue, but I managed to calm her down and explain. Bobbie didn't care, Bertha. She still wanted to be my friend. Do you know what that means to me?"

"Of course I do, baby girl. We all need friends. Now, what about Rhonda and the boy?"

"They're in trouble and needed a safe place to stay for a while."

She patted Tabatha on the hand. "We'll talk later. You look like you're about to drop. Go to bed. Want some hot chocolate?"

"No, thanks. I'm sure once my head hits the pillow I'm going to sleep for a week. Good night, Bertha. Love you."

Bertha placed a kiss on her forehead. "Good night, baby girl. Welcome home." She took Tabatha's hand, pulled her up from the bed, turned down the covers and fluffed the pillows before leaving.

Tabatha slid between satin sheets and moaned with fatigue. "Sleep. No beeper. No patients. Just blessed sleep." She closed her eyes and drifted on the edge of a dream.

She didn't recognize the small apartment. In the bed, a man slept restlessly. His dreams floated above him with horrid reality. A child's funeral service was being held a mere ten yards away. His desperation to find the killer left a bitter taste in his mouth, a pain in his very core.

He sobbed in his sleep. "Where are you, Elizabeth?"

Tabatha wanted to soothe him, to give him rest from the pain.

"Hello, Derek," she whispered and touched his forehead. Her heart lurched as a vision ripped at her soul. A bloody wedding dress, a beautiful girl, mutilated almost to the point of dismemberment--Elizabeth.

Tabatha jerked away with a cry and bolted awake. Her fear, like cold water on a hot skillet, spewed in all directions, trying to escape. Sweat gathered between her breasts and trickled to her belly. Her breath came in ragged gasps.

"God, help him."

Nine

Derek stared out the window, picking plaque from the wrinkles of his brain, seeking ways to find the elusive Tabatha. He'd searched motor vehicle data for New York license tags that had been exchanged for Louisiana's, and found nothing. He'd checked with the few physicians he knew, asking if they'd heard of a new doctor in town. No one had. He asked uniform officers if they'd seen a Grand Am with New York tags. They'd seen nothing.

The telephone's trill pulled him away from his thoughts and back to his empty apartment.

"Bainbridge."

"Derek, it's Mary. I'm not going to listen to some bullshit excuse. This isn't one of Frank's setups. My friend, Carla, isn't interested in having a relationship with anyone, and her daughter is too young for you. So load your cooler with beer and get your ass over here. We're having a barbeque."

He closed his eyes and rubbed the back of his neck. "All right. I'll be there in about an hour."

"That'll do." A short pause silenced the phone line. "Derek?"

"Yeah."

"I worry about you."

His laughter felt foreign, as if it didn't belong to him. "I'm worried about me, too. I'll see you later, Mary."

He replaced the receiver on its cradle. Seconds later, he'd stripped out of his clothes and stepped into the shower. Hot water stung his skin, reminding him he was still alive, but only in spirit. Maybe Mary and Frank were right. It was time to move on. His heart clenched painfully, and his mind recoiled.

"No, not yet."

~

Facing Bourbon Street, Frank and Mary's front façade was nothing more than a rotting privacy fence. Beyond the gate, a whole new world emerged. Tropical plants draped over each other in a competition for light and attention; some appeared to be reaching for glistening droplets of water from a courtyard fountain. It was almost selfish in its privacy, as though Mary and Frank were afraid of invasion if anyone saw how amazing their oasis was. Derek felt more than saw Mary standing in the doorway watching him.

"You showed up. Will wonders never cease?" She strode toward Derek, her arms reaching out to embrace him. "It's been too long, Derek. I've missed you."

"I've been busy." He hugged her tightly then glanced around. "Guests arrive yet?"

She shook her head, the noontime sun casting her long auburn hair in licks of flames. "No, not yet. Wanted to talk to you before they get here."

"Uh-oh." Derek noticed the lines beginning to form on her delicate face, but more prominent was the hint of despair in her green eyes.

"Not to worry." She led him into the house. "My friend's been a widow for a long time and isn't in the market for another man. Her daughter . . . well, let's just say she's not someone you'd want to hook up with."

"Frank said the daughter's back now?"

"Yeah. She plans to set up a business here. She was a beautiful child, but different. She seemed very lonely back then."

"You knew her?" Derek watched Mary's eyes fog over with memory.

"Last time I saw her was at her grandfather's funeral. Something strange happened and she--" At the sound of the front gate opening, she glanced out the window. "They're here. Why don't you go out back with Frank? We'll find time to talk later." She looked at the cooler by his feet. "You need help with that?"

He snorted. "The day I need help from a five-foot-nothing girl, it's time to lie down and give up the ghost." He leaned over, kissed her forehead then grabbed the cooler and made his way to the small back yard.

Derek chuckled at the sight before him. Frank wore red Bermuda shorts, a black New Orleans Police Department t-shirt and a yellow apron with a crawfish and the words, *Suck My Tail.*

Waving a spatula over his head, Frank smiled and shouted, "Glad you could make it, buddy. Open one of those beers. This is hot work."

Derek pulled two bottles from the chest and handed him one then turned his bottom-up, nearly draining it, when he glimpsed three women walking across the lawn. Beer spewed from his mouth and nose. He coughed. He choked. The earth dropped from under his feet, leaving his stomach behind.

Frank slapped his back. "Wrong pipe there, buddy?"

Derek managed to utter one word, "Tabatha?"

Frank looked from him to Mary to Tabatha. "You two know each other?"

Tabatha grinned. "Sort of. Hello, Derek."

His knees weakened. His heart did a dance against his ribs. "You're a hard woman to track down."

"Not if you know where to look." She ambled toward him, looking as if she were stalking prey. "Nice to know I made a good impression. I've been thinking about you, too."

Derek tried to untangle emotions running amuck through his already muddled thoughts. "Thinking about me? Why?"

She brought herself up on tiptoes, wrapped her hands around his arm and placed her mouth close to his ear. "We need to talk, but not here."

"Tabatha," her mother said. "You're making a fool of yourself."

Tabatha stumbled as if her mother's words were a physical slap. "I am not a fool, Mother. I'm merely greeting a friend." She turned and retreated the way she'd come.

Derek started to follow her when Mary stopped him. "She's too young for you to go sniffing around." She leaned close to whisper in his ear. "You don't want to get mixed up with that girl."

Derek moved Mary's hand from his arm and stepped away. Before leaving, he faced each of them. Mary's face was a mask of . . . what? Disgust? Anger? Jealousy? Frank appeared to be confused but pleased. "Carla, it's nice to meet you. Mary, we'll be right back. Tabatha and I need a couple of minutes to catch up."

~

Tabatha leaned against her car and waited. He'd come; she had no doubt of that. She giggled at Derek's reaction when she'd appeared in the doorway. At first she thought he would choke to death on the beer spewing from nearly every orifice in his face.

"Derek." She liked his name, the way it rang sweetly in her ear. She closed off the world around her, letting his image form before dark curtains of imagination. He was tall, probably more than six feet, with muscular arms, broad shoulders, eyes the color of semi-sweet chocolate; everything a girl could want. And she did want.

"Sleeping?"

"No. Dreaming, though." Tabatha looked up to see her vision come to life. "Go ahead. Ask."

"Ask what?"

She breathed in, trying to taste the essence of his voice. Her fingers ached to reach out and touch him. Instead she closed her hands into tight fists at her side. "How much did you see?"

"Enough." His gaze ran over her, leaving behind a scorching heat. "How did you make it look like a corpse rose from the dead? How much did that girl pay you for that ruse?"

Tabatha pushed away from the car, drawing closer to him. "Rhonda paid me nothing. She needed my help and I gave it. The corpse was her mother."

He blew air between his lips and waved his hand as if to dismiss her comment. "Do you know who John Phelps is?"

She shook her head and waited, knowing he'd supply an answer.

"Rich entrepreneur, perfect reputation. Not the type to be accused of murder by a dead woman."

"The dead don't lie, Derek. He killed her and I have enough proof to put Mr. Phelps away for a very long time. Dates, places." She smiled at him. "Have you ever heard of the Guardians?"

"No. What is it?"

"Who, not what. Guardians Against Paranormal Sinners. People. Bad people. You need to talk to Rhonda. If she doesn't mind, you can look at what we have. Rolls of film need developing, but I'm not sure where to get it done. I'd rather no one see the photos until we know what they are."

"How do you fake raising the dead, Tabatha?"

She released a ragged breath. "My father was a telekinetic, my grandfather a necromancer. I inherited my . . . talents from them. I don't use them normally, but Rhonda was in trouble. I don't plan on doing it again." She took a step back toward the door when he stepped in front of her, blocking her way.

His eyes narrowed, the muscles of his jaw clenched and his stance became almost threatening in nature. "If this isn't some kind of con, then you *are* going to do it again."

Her heart sank to her toes. "This isn't a parlor trick, Derek. Who do you want raised and why?"

"I have six dead little girls. I need to know who's killing them."

Tabatha turned away, laying her head on top of her car. The summer's sun heated the rooftop to the point that it nearly scorched her forehead. She wondered if God Himself had turned it into a branding iron and when she lifted her head the title '*Witch*' would be burned onto her face.

"I am a necromancer," she whispered. The words were freeing, as most acceptance of truths were.

"Let me tell Mom I'll pick her up later. I need you to tell me what you know about the killer. How he works. How he kills the children." She shuddered with a vision of a child sitting against a rotting crypt. "Did you just think about one of the girls?"

"Selma Fortier. She was the last victim. Why?"

"I saw her," she said.

"When?"

She turned her back to him and closed her eyes, fighting to erase the sickening image. "When you remembered the crime scene just now, it appeared to me. I'm not sure how, but we're connected, Derek." She ran her hands over her face. "Did they suffer?"

He came closer, placing his hand on her shoulder. "No. The coroner said they were drugged and then suffocated. All but the last child was bled before the body was marked."

A heavy weight of fear pressed down on her, nearly stealing away her breath. "Something's wrong." Tabatha heard the sound of a speeding car and saw it racing toward them before screeching to a halt. A .44 revolver appeared in the passenger side window aimed at her. Everything seemed to slow to a crawl, as though she need only to walk over and take the gun away from the attacker.

"Get down," Derek shouted, shoving her to the sidewalk as he drew his .38 from under his pant leg.

Shots rang out. Derek flung himself over Tabatha as bullets pocked, then shattered the front windshield of her car. Another splintered the fence behind them, spraying them with debris.

The car sped away, its occupants shouting a warning, "Give us what we want, or next time we won't miss."

Derek drew her into his arms and brushed her hair out of her face. "You okay? How did you know they were trouble? What do they want from you?"

Mary ran toward them, gasping for breath. "What the hell happened, Derek? We heard shots."

Derek glanced at Mary then back to Tabatha. "Are Frank and Carla okay?"

"Yeah, yeah. Fine. You?"

"We're all right. Aren't we, Tabatha?"

She nodded, rubbing her face against his chest. The smell of his cologne surrounded her with a comforting, familiar scent. "Yes. Yes, I'm fine." Mary yanked her out of Derek's arms and shoved her aside. Tabatha stood, brushing dirt from her slacks.

Mary ran her hands over Derek's chest. "Did you get hit?"

Derek's face was a mixture of shock and rage. "Don't ever treat her like that again."

"She's okay." Mary straightened herself and glanced at Tabatha. "I didn't hurt you, did I?"

"No. I'm fine," she said, thinking Mary's question sounded more accusatory than concerned.

Derek grasped Tabatha's arm and led her toward a white Chevy Blazer.

Tabatha swallowed hard, trying to get her heart out of her esophagus and back to her chest. "I have to take Mom home."

"You don't have a windshield, woman," Derek barked.

She groaned. "My first scratch."

"Mary, call for a tow truck. Have them take it to Bossy's on Airline. And can you give Carla a ride home when she's ready?"

"Derek--"

"Yes or no. Simple question. Not hard to answer."

Frank leaned against the fence and crossed his arms over his chest. "I'll take her home. You two go ahead. She'll be fine."

"Shut the hell up, Frank." Mary hurried to Derek's side. "Think no one called this in? You can't just run off. They'll want to talk to both of you."

"If they do, give me a call. But there isn't much I can tell them. We didn't see who it was. We didn't get a plate number. It was an old van, primer-gray with shaded windows. I didn't get off a shot." He kissed Mary on the cheek. "I just want to talk to her. I'll be back later."

Mary nodded, her expression anything but happy.

Carla stood by the gate, hands clenched at her side, face etched with anger. Her gray eyes were cold and accusing. "What have you brought down on my friends? Why did you have to come back?"

A tear trailed down Tabatha's cheek. "I came home to make things right with you, Mom. Apparently, I've wasted my time." She settled into the passenger's seat and turned her back to Carla.

~

After starting the engine, Derek pulled away from the curb, turning left on Barracks Street then right on Burgundy.

"Where are we going?" Tabatha asked.

The muscles in his jaw worked frantically. "You said I should talk to Rhonda, so we're going to talk to her."

"Well . . . uh . . . you're going the wrong way. I live on St. Charles, Garden District." She pointed behind them. "That way."

He slammed on the brakes and turned to face her. "Look, I don't know what the hell is going on, but I'm damn sure going to find out. Before I talk to Rhonda, I want answers from you."

"In the middle of the street?" As if the drivers behind them agreed, car horns blared.

Derek pressed his foot on the gas pedal, turned onto Esplanade then west on Royal. "Can you raise one of the kids?"

"Did the killer take their tongues?"

Tongues? Now what kind of question was that? "Why?"

"If anything is missing from their bodies when they go into the grave, I can't raise them with the part. I can only raise what is there."

"Yes, they have their tongues."

He tried to understand how a woman as seemingly gentle as Tabatha could be so clinical about such a thing as raising a cadaver. She came across as calm, cool, almost detached from any emotion.

"How long since the last child died? Not when you found her, but time of death."

"Last one was about a week ago. Why?" He was already getting tired of having to ask why. She looked at him, her eyes red and shining with tears. He didn't like the emotion her tears evoked in him, but he was relieved that she wasn't so detached after all.

"If she had been dead less than three days, I wouldn't have to raise her, I could talk to her."

He pulled over to the curb. "Let's start at the beginning. You can talk to the dead without raising them, but only within three days of them dying. But after that you can raise their bodies and talk to them. Do I have that right?"

She nodded. "A person's soul remains with them for three days."

When he started to speak, she placed her fingertips over his mouth. A hot flow of power rushed through his body, awakening every nerve like an electrical current. He mourned the loss when she pulled her hand away.

"I know. You want to know why, right?"

He thought it best not to speak at that moment and nodded.

She shrugged. "Maybe they need to know everyone will be all right. Before I acquired skills to block their voices out, they would plead for my help. They'd asked me to talk to their parents, husbands, wives, children. Some wanted them to know it was okay to go on with their lives, others wanted to say they were sorry. I didn't understand this curse, or whatever you want to call it. I only knew I was different."

He wanted to put his arms around her and say it was okay, that he understood. But he didn't. This was way beyond his comprehension. This was the realm of fairy tales and ghost stories told around campfires. He put the car into gear and pulled away from the curb.

"Each child is found in a local cemetery exactly three days after her death," he said.

"Sounds like the killer may know something about the soul leaving after three days."

"Frank thinks the killer could be some voodoo practitioner gone bad."

"Can you show me crime scene photos? Share your field notes? I'm a psychiatrist; maybe I can do a profile. Think of something no one else has."

"I don't think the department would allow a civilian, even a shrink, to have access to that information."

Her gaze returned to the view outside the window. "You don't strike me as a man who would give a flip what the department thought."

She fell silent when he didn't respond to her summation of him. Derek mentally retraced each crime scene, trying to think of anything else to ask.

They crossed Canal Street and proceeded down St. Charles Ave. Traffic thinned, high-rise buildings and concrete walkways gave way to a tree-lined street and nineteenth-century homes. With every block, houses became increasingly grand, changing from wood clapboarded, middle-class homes to old mansions of bygone days; and from modest gardens to professionally kept lawns.

"White three-story on the corner," Tabatha said, bringing him out of his observations.

He slowed and turned onto the drive, stopping midway. He tensed, stared at the house and said, "Porch swing."

She ran her gaze over a prone body on the swing. She shrugged. "Probably Rhonda."

He rammed the gearshift to park. "Okay, who is that?" He pointed toward three men running from behind the house and getting into a nearby car. The car roared to life and sped by, nearly sideswiping them.

"Oh, God. Where's the boy?" Tabatha dashed from the car. "Rhonda, wake up. Where's Shane?"

The person on the swing jumped up, slinging a bag from her back. "Tabatha, what's wrong? What happened?"

Tabatha stopped on the bottom step and stared at her. "Bobbie? How on earth did you find me? Where's Rhonda?"

"I looked up your forwarding address at the hospital. Who's Rhonda? No one answered the door when I knocked." She glanced behind Tabatha and asked, "Who's that?"

Ignoring her question, Tabatha ran up the remaining stairs and into the house, followed by Bobbie and Derek.

"Rhonda!" The thunder of running footsteps ran its course across the second floor and down the stairway. Rhonda met them with baseball bat in hand. "Jesus, Tab, you scared the snuff out of me. What's wrong?"

"Where's Shane?" Her voice was no more than a raspy whisper.

"I'm right here."

The four of them looked at the innocent face of the boy staring at them from the second floor landing.

"Can I keep it?" he asked, hugging a teddy bear to his bare chest.

Rhonda wrapped her hands tightly around the neck of the bat. "I'm sorry. He found it in a closet. He didn't mean to--"

"Of course you can have it, Shane. Teddy's been looking for a new friend," Tabatha said before sinking to her knees.

"Tabatha!" the three said in unison.

"I'm okay."

Derek picked Tabatha up and carried her to a nearby chair. "We saw three men when we drove up. Someone go check the backdoor."

Rhonda ran out of the room.

"Detective Derek Bainbridge," he said, looking Bobbie over. Black, straight hair hung to her waist, accenting cinnamon-hued skin. Her lips were full with a childlike pout, the corners turned up in a perpetual smile. Derek didn't feel comfortable with this new girl. Her eyes darted too quickly, as if taking inventory. She wore dingy tennis shoes, tattered jeans, and a faded, washed thin, red t-shirt. "And you are?"

"My friend, Bobbie," Tabatha said. "We worked together in New York. She came here for her brother's funeral, right?" She smiled at Bobbie and gestured toward a chair. "Where are you staying?"

"Motel downtown. I know some people in the Rigolets. I may stay with them until I find something."

"You could stay here but someone is trying to kill Rhonda, Shane and me. Staying here might put you on their hit list, too."

Bobbie sat straighter in her chair. "I'm listening."

"Me, too," Derek said.

Rhonda returned, carrying the bat and a jimmy bar. "Found this. Looks like someone was trying to break in."

"Momma, can I have a pop?" Shane asked from the doorway.

"Ask Miss Tabatha."

"Of course. I bet there's a surprise in the cookie jar, too." She started to rise.

"I'll get it," Rhonda said. "Come on, son. You can take your pop and a cookie to your room if you're careful. Say thank you to Miss Tabatha."

He kicked the floor with the toe of his shoe, head lowered, eyes peeking through a fall of carrot-red hair. "Thank you, Miss Tabatha."

"Why don't you call me Tab, Shane? It's much easier, don't you think?"

He nodded.

"Let's go, son," Rhonda said, setting the bat against the wall and leading him away.

Bobbie scratched her head. "I need a shower desperately, but I'm not going anywhere until I know what's going on around here."

Tabatha sunk lower into her chair. "Rhonda will be back in just a second. She can tell her part first. Then I'll tell you what we've learned since I left here this afternoon."

Rhonda strolled through the doorway with a bottle of beer for each of them. "Thought we could use one of these." She handed them out, then sat at Tabatha's feet. "You think it was them?"

"Them who?" Bobbie asked. "Will someone fill me in?"

Derek sat on the fireplace inglenook, rolled his shoulders and leaned back. Answers at last.

Ten

John Phelps slammed his fist on the massive mahogany desk and stared with contempt at his stepson. "What do you mean you couldn't get in? How much trouble can it be to jimmy a back door?"

"Someone drove up. A man in a white SUV." The teenager kept his gaze on the thick burgundy carpet, never looking up. "You said not to get caught. So we ran."

"Did he see you?"

"No." The boy shook his head. "I don't think so."

"You don't think, or, no, he didn't?" Phelps' voice roared with such violence the boy jumped back with a yelp.

He swallowed, cleared his throat then said, "I'm sure he didn't see us." He fidgeted with the keys in his pocket and glanced at the doorway. "We ran behind the garage. He couldn't have seen us." He glanced up but quickly looked away again.

"Where was your car?"

"We . . ." He cleared his throat again. "We left it around the corner. Didn't want to take a chance anyone would see it."

"Did you recognize the man in the SUV?"

"No, sir. Never saw him before."

"You're dismissed."

He turned to leave.

"If I find out you've lied to me, boy," Phelps paused, "I'll kill you."

His face paled. "Yes, sir. I know."

"Did he see you?"

"No, sir."

"Go."

Phelps lifted the lid of the humidor, picked one cigar out of many, bit off the tip and spit it into a nearby trashcan. A light touch on the trigger produced fire from a .44 Magnum lighter. Smoke slowly escaped between his lips, its warmth mingling with savored flavors of his victim's fear still lingering on his tongue. Their so-called magic couldn't save them. They begged for their lives and pleaded for forgiveness. His grin evaporated. All but one. She didn't beg for herself, but for her child and grandchild. She had no concern for her own life. No matter how much pain he inflicted on her, she refused to give him what he wanted. Refused him his pleasure.

Ah, but maybe the girl and her son will give it to me. He'd never killed a child. Running the thought through his mind, he felt his pants strain against his growing erection. Slowly he rose from his chair and strolled to the bathroom, closing the door behind him.

Eleven

Derek gauged each person's reaction to the story as it was being told. He searched to find any semblance of truth or something he could accept as such.

Tabatha appeared calm, her demeanor guarded.

Rhonda wrung her hands and stole glances at everyone as if expecting them to turn on her and blame her for this whole mess.

Bobbie's face held a hint of disbelief. "Damn," she said, breaking the silence. "Who do you think told them about your gift, Tabatha? Who knew you were coming home?"

Tabatha ran her fingers through her hair. "Nyssa, my mom, Rhonda and Bertha. I think that's it."

Derek forced himself to keep his face neutral. He distanced himself from his feelings and remained detached, unemotional, realistic.

"How did you find out, Rhonda?" he asked.

"My birth mother told me about the list and I came here looking for Tabatha. Nyssa said she'd be returning in a few days." She drained the last of her beer. "But, I swear, I didn't tell anyone else."

He stood, collecting empty bottles. "When was this?"

"The date you mean?"

He nodded.

"Two days before she came home."

"And you--" He pointed at Bobbie. "When did you find out?"

"I told you. I worked with Tabatha. She said she was going home."

"When?"

She shrugged. "She told me about it on her last night at the hospital. I'm not sure when she left town."

Tabatha handed her empty bottle to Derek. "Going for fresh ones?"

"Yeah. Head me in the right direction."

Pointing behind her, Rhonda said, "Straight back. Can't miss it. It's this big white monstrosity of a room. Fridge to the left."

~

The last thing Derek remembered was crossing from the dining room into the kitchen, then he was on the floor with the worst headache he'd ever known. He stared into Tabatha's concerned expression. "What happened?"

"I'm sorry, young man, but how was I to know you were Tabatha's friend? I thought you were one of those men trying to break in."

Derek glanced toward the sound of the voice and was met by a tall mountain of a black woman, a cast-iron skillet in her hand. He pushed himself into a sitting position, the world spinning around him. His stomach lurched. He groaned, raising his hand to examine the lump on his head.

"You gonna die?" Bertha asked.

"No. I think I'll live." He bit back what he really wanted to say.

"Okay. Then I'll make enough dinner for one more. Now, get on out of my kitchen."

Tabatha helped him to his feet, wrapping his arm around her shoulders. "I'm sorry. I didn't know Bertha was here. I need to tie a bell to one of her tits."

Derek glanced at Bertha now that he was standing and able to look her over from top to bottom, instead of the other way around. "It'd take a hell of lot of string."

"That's okay, Detective. My man, he likes 'em big." Bertha laughed, her breasts bouncing. "Now, why you comin' into my kitchen in the first place?"

He couldn't remember.

"Beer," Bobbie said. "We needed beer."

Bertha placed her skillet on the stove, reached into the cabinet, and tossed Derek a bottle of aspirin. "Well, help yourself, then get out. I got cooking to do."

Tabatha led Derek into the living room, settled him in the easy chair and sat at his feet. "You sure you're okay? You want to go to the hospital? You were out cold for a few seconds."

He shook his head, regretting it instantly when fresh pain shot through his brain. "No. I'm fine. How well do you know these people?"

"Bobbie I've known for about two years; Rhonda most of my life. Bertha was my grandfather's cook. When I left to go to boarding school, she quit. Came back as soon as she heard I was home."

"What about this Nyssa you mentioned?"

Tabatha drew her knees to her chest and wrapped her arms around them. "She and her husband came to work for my grandfather before I was born. Her husband died in seventy-nine, I think, but she stayed on as groundskeeper. Nyssa was like a second mother to me, a best friend really."

"I can't remember. Didn't you say your father and grandfather are both deceased?"

She nodded. "My father died when I was nine. My grandfather died nine months later. According to the death certificates, both died of heart attacks. My grandmother died giving birth to my father. Mom's my only living relative."

Derek committed this information to memory, to examine later. "Do you doubt the cause of death?"

She shrugged.

Bobbie and Rhonda returned with an ice pack for his head, bottles of beer and potato chips.

"Bertha said this is all she's going to let us have. She ain't gonna have us ruinin' our dinner," Bobbie said, imitating the black woman's southern accent.

Tabatha reached for a beer. "Did she say what we're having?"

Rhonda grinned. "Gumbo, fried shrimp, and potato salad. I feel like I've died and gone to gourmet heaven."

Tabatha's heart broke for Rhonda. A meal Tabatha accepted as normal dinner fare was a treat for her. What must her life be like? she wondered.

"Girls, what are we going to do about these men after us?" Bobbie asked.

"They're not after you, Bobbie," Tabatha said. "They don't know you from Martha Stewart."

Bobbie huffed. "You're my friend. You're in trouble; I'm in trouble. We're in this together."

"Has everyone forgotten I'm here?" Derek grumbled.

Rhonda gently placed an ice pack on his head. "Nope. But you're a cop. You won't be no help."

For the first time in ages, Derek found himself speechless. He opened his mouth several times for a comeback, but each time he came up blank. "What the hell is that supposed to mean?"

Rhonda's face reddened. "You can't fight within the law with these kind of people. Sometimes you just have to kill them."

Derek grinned. "That's when it might be good to have a cop on your side."

Tabatha stretched her legs out in front of her and leaned on Derek's chair. "I have a New York permit to carry. How hard will it be to get one here?"

Bobbie nodded. "Yeah, I have one, too."

Rhonda huffed. "Well, I want one."

Derek rubbed his temples. "Don't you think you should check on Shane?" he asked Rhonda.

"Yeah, he needs to wash up before dinner." She set down her beer and left.

Derek waited a few moments before he spoke. "Do you really think that girl should be allowed to carry a weapon?"

Tabatha chuckled. "It's a scary thought."

Bobbie rolled her eyes. "Maybe she'd stop being such a crybaby. Gads, she makes Eeyore look jolly."

"Who's Eeyore?" Tabatha asked.

Bobbie chuckled. "The sad donkey in Winnie the Pooh."

"Sorry. Didn't have a lot of time to read children's books when I was a kid."

Derek sat up, eyeing the bat Rhonda had left behind. Where Rhonda had handled it, the wood was blackened and cracked. "Are those burn marks on that bat?"

Tabatha reached out with her free hand to bring it closer. "It's still warm."

They gathered around staring at blackened patterns on the grip, then at each other.

Bobbie took it from Tabatha, looking closer. "Am I crazy, or are those perfect hand prints burned into this thing?"

Derek shrugged. "Looks like it to me. What's it mean?"

"Could our little cry baby be a firestarter?" Bobbie asked.

Twelve

Derek watched Rhonda help Shane onto the box Bertha placed on a dining room chair for him. Her hands gently touched his face before ruffling his hair playfully. No sooner had a bowl of gumbo been set in front of him than he dug in.

"You hungry, son?" Bertha chuckled.

Shane giggled, allowing a trickle of roux-thickened broth to trail down his chin.

Derek sat back in his chair. *Firestarter. This was getting too strange to believe. But why? He hadn't believed in necromancers either. Why should anything else surprise him?*

"So, Rhonda," Bobbie said, "how long you been a firestarter?"

The room plummeted into silence. Rhonda paled; the veins in her face and neck stood out in stark relief against the pallor of her skin. "What?"

Bobbie pulled the baseball bat from between her legs and held it up. "These your hand prints?"

"No." Rhonda jerked her head side to side. "No, I don't know how they got there. I . . . I. . . ."

Bertha swatted Bobbie's arm. "You leave her be. You ain't no ivory walker, girl. You got power of your own. I can feel it sure as my own heart beats. Onliest one in here that's got no magic is Mr. Derek."

"Shane doesn't," Rhonda said in a hushed tone.

Bertha covered Shane's ears with her hands. "It's dim, but it's there. Remember how you tried to hide it? The shame you felt? Don't do that to the boy. And the rest of you, drop this firestarter stuff for now." She lifted her hands away and shrugged into a gauze jacket.

All eyes were on Bertha.

"What? You think I been living here all these years and don't know what goes on?" She faced Tabatha and smiled. Bertha's love for Tabatha warmed the old woman's gaze.

"Your grandpa, he was a strong voodoo priest. But he wouldn't do it just for fun." She clicked her tongue against the top of her mouth. "No. He used it for good. Now, Tabatha's daddy, he could move things around with just thinking about it. Why, I think he could've moved this house if he took a mind to do so." She kissed Shane's head.

Tabatha swallowed the food in her mouth. "You never told me any of this before, Bertha."

She shrugged. "That woman, Nyssa, she just a wanna be. Tries to do spells with her herbs, but she ain't never gonna be nothing. She loved your grandpa though. Did you know that?"

Tabatha sucked in a quick breath. "No."

"Yeah. Had it real bad for him. Thought the old man was gonna marry her. But he never got over Miss Ella."

Something in Bertha's tone surged Derek's cop instincts to life. "Do you believe he died of a heart attack?"

"I don't say nothing I can't prove, Mr. Derek. All's I say is it a mite funny that Mr. Dunnock and Mr. Raoul goes from being healthy to dead within nine months of each other and both of the same ailment." She picked up her purse. "You girls get it straight between you. Ain't none of you average. God gave you gifts. Use them the right way. I got to get home to Oscar. He'll be waitin' for his own dinner."

Tabatha stood and gave Bertha a hug.

"There's enough gumbo left for y'all. Take it home with you."

"You sure, baby girl? I didn't buy--"

"It's fine, Bertha. Just take the pot and all. You can return it tomorrow. And we need to talk salary."

Bertha waved her comment away. "Whatever, child." She lifted the gumbo from the stove top and turned, looking down into Rhonda's upturned eyes. "Don't try to deny what you are, girl. God's gifts don't come bad or evil. We make them good or bad with the way we use them." She circled the table and kissed each one of them on their scalps then left without another word.

Bobbie touched the tip of her head. "What was that all about?"

Tabatha said, "When I was a kid, she told me her kisses left a protective seal on me."

"I don't have any gift," Rhonda said, tears once again filling her eyes.

"Oh, for the love of rain, will you stop being such a damn crybaby?" Bobbie said. "What are you ashamed of? Tabatha's an animator. I'm a shapeshifter. What's the big deal?"

"Shapeshifter?" Derek's heart skipped a beat. "Damn. I've died and gone to Fantasy Hell. What else exists in this world?"

"Well," Bobbie said with a sly smile, "I know a werewolf or two."

Rhonda jumped from her chair. "Bobbie, that's enough."

"Momma," Shane whimpered.

"You're gonna scare him with that crap. Stop it." Rhonda picked Shane up out of the chair, hugging him close.

Bobbie stood. "Wait, Rhonda." She held up her left hand, forming the boy scouts' pledge and placed her right hand over her heart. "Shane, do you know what boy scouts are?"

He nodded.

"This is their sign that they're telling the truth. If I lie to you while I have my hands like this, the Big Boy Scout in the sky will get me. Do you understand?"

Again, he nodded.

"I swear to you, Shane, I was kidding. I don't know any werewolves. Okay?"

He looked from Bobbie to his mother. "What's that?"

"Werewolves?" Rhonda asked.

"Uh huh."

She thought for a moment. "Remember the big bad wolf in Red Riding Hood?"

He nodded, eyes wide.

"That's a werewolf. Just a made up story. Nothing more."

Shane nodded and laughed, his hair falling into his joy-filled eyes. "I like that story."

Rhonda sighed. "Son, you need a haircut. Come on, it's time for bed."

As soon as they were gone Tabatha and Derek stared at Bobbie.

"Is it just a story?" Tabatha asked.

She looked away. "Yeah."

Derek reached for his beer, letting all he'd seen and heard rummage for a sit-down place in his thoughts. "Okay. And the shapeshifting? Was that just a story, too?"

"Nope." Bobbie leaned against her chair, a slow grin lifting her lips.

"Aha!" Tabatha shouted. "No wonder you weren't overly freaked out when you walked in on me at the morgue. It's not a big deal for you. What do you shift to?"

"I can turn into a cobra, among other things."

Derek almost let that slip by him, then jerked his head up and glared at her.

She laughed. "Did I scare you?"

"You're trying to tell me that was you?"

She shrugged. "Believe what you want, big boy."

He growled. "What the hell did you think I was going to do? I just wanted to talk to Tabatha. I needed her help." He grumbled under his breath. The scary thing is he was beginning to believe this nonsense. But he had seen Tabatha raise the dead. He had seen a cobra in the middle of the cemetery. A cobra in New Orleans.

"Wait." Tabatha said. "You two have met before?"

Bobbie chuckled. "Sort of. The night you and Rhonda went to the cemetery, I followed you."

"Why?" Tabatha tilted her head to the side, her brow furrowed, her eyes narrowed. "Where have you been staying?"

Derek leaned forward, elbows on table. "Good question. Bobbie, why did you follow them? Why didn't you make yourself known?"

"I've been staying in a hotel on Canal Street." She turned her gaze to Derek. "Someone had to watch out for them. They just walked in there like the whole world would turn their heads and ignore what they were about to do."

"How did you know what I was going to do?" Tabatha asked.

"I saw you park your car by the cemetery and pull out a crate with a live chicken in it. What would you think?"

Derek filled a cup with coffee and sipped. "So, you hadn't seen Tabatha since leaving New York until she was at the cemetery?"

"I was on my way to get a burger and there she was. I was going to stop long enough to say hi, and then I saw the chicken. So I followed you in. On the way out, this big bruiser starts coming after you." She shrugged. "So I delayed him."

Tabatha leaned forward, her face within inches of Bobbie's. "How did you delay him?"

"I shifted."

"Don't be coy, Bobbie. Shifted how?"

"Cobra, wasn't it?" she asked Derek.

"I need something stiffer than coffee or beer. Got any whiskey?" He pushed away from the table.

Tabatha gestured with a nod to the highest cabinet by the back door. "Top shelf." She faced Bobbie again. "Okay. Is that all you can shift to?" Her voice held a hint of sarcasm.

"No. I can turn into a house cat, dog, or a panther. That's my favorite." She grinned.

"Is that it?" This time Tabatha's voice was breathy and her eyes had widened.

"It's all I've tried so far. Figured it was enough for what I needed to do."

Tabatha showed no hint of her thoughts. She slowly turned to look at Rhonda when she returned to the kitchen. She shifted her gaze to Bobbie, then to Derek. She burst into laughter. "Derek's Angels."

He chuckled. "More like Derek's Devils."

Thirteen

The next morning Tabatha made her way down the stairs and out the front door to pick up the Times-Picayune from the porch, unfolding it as she re-entered the house and closed the door. On the front-page, photographs of three teenagers stared back at her. She gasped and sat down hard on a nearby chair.

"What's wrong?" Rhonda asked from the hallway entrance. "You look like you've seen a ghost." She chuckled. "Well, maybe that's not a good description, considering what you see and do."

Tabatha slowly lifted her gaze away from the newspaper. "This kid. The one in the middle." She tapped her index finger on the photograph.

Rhonda walked across the room to stand at Tabatha's side. "What about him?"

The sound of heavy footfalls on the porch pulled their attention away from the photograph.

A knock at the door eased Tabatha's worry. Bad guys didn't knock.

"Who is it?" Rhonda asked.

"It's me. Derek. Open up. I need to show you something."

Rhonda walked over, flipped the lock and let him in.

Tabatha held up the newspaper before he could show them his copy. "I saw."

"I thought you didn't see their faces?"

"He was shooting at me, Derek. Of course I saw his face."

He paused, staring at her. "Wait. You're saying one of them is the one who shot at us yesterday?"

"This guy." She tapped his face with her finger once again. "He's the one. What are you talking about?"

He glanced at the photo then ran his fingers through his hair, causing it to spike. "These are the men in the car that raced out of the driveway--the men who were trying to break into your house."

"Who are they?" Rhonda asked. "Why are they in the newspaper? What happened to them?"

"They're dead. Daniel Ross, David Miller, Brian Smith. Miller is the only one with a rap sheet, and the one you pointed out as the shooter. The others are clean. Ross is the nephew of an Orleans Parish street cop. Smith was the stepson of John Phelps."

"Oh, hell," Tabatha moaned.

"They were found in a car parked by the French Market. All were shot in the head, except Smith. They found him in the trunk, hands duct-taped behind his back and his tongue cut out. Coroner thinks the kid drowned in his own blood. Looks like a professional hit."

"Why cut out his tongue?" Rhonda asked, her voice scarcely above a whisper.

Derek sat on the edge of the fireplace. "The kid either lied to someone he shouldn't have or ratted someone out."

"Phelps isn't going to be very happy about this," Tabatha said. "Maybe he'll turn his attention to this and leave us alone long enough to make our move."

"Don't count on it." Derek pursed his lips for a moment, his brow furrowing. "I have a feeling Phelps did this job himself. I wonder if he knows the 'what doesn't go in the grave can't come out' rule?"

Tabatha dropped her gaze. "Could be. No tongue, no information."

"He'd kill his own son?" Rhonda shook her head. "I can't fathom such a thing. I'd die to save my son."

"Stepson," Tabatha reminded her. "Why would he kill him, Derek? What could he have done that was so bad?"

"He got caught. We saw them."

Their silence hung heavily in the air-conditioned room. Tabatha's heart ached for the boys in the photograph. So young, she thought. She tried to visualize David Miller the way he had been that day. His face was a torment of emotions; fright, anger, reluctant determination. "The only reason I'm not dead is because he didn't want to shoot me."

"Why do you think that?"

"His eyes. Miller didn't want to do it." She leaned forward, resting her face in her hands. "You said he had a rap sheet. For what?"

"Simple assault and battery, misdemeanor theft, didn't like to pay to gas up his car."

"Breakfast," they heard Bertha yell from the kitchen. "Come on, French toast ain't good cold. You, too, young man. I heard you in there."

They rose and started toward the kitchen. Tabatha stopped, resting a hand on Derek's chest and Rhonda's shoulder. "Not a word to Bertha about this. I don't want her worrying any more than she already is. Understood?"

"What about Bobbie? She's really not mixed up in this, yet."

"We're a team, Derek. She needs to be told."

He nodded and sniffed at the air. "Yeah, you're right. But can it wait until after breakfast? I'm starved."

In spite of the dark situation they were in, Tabatha chuckled. "Yeah. We can wait."

They filed into the kitchen and took their places. Bobbie was already sitting at the table.

"Morning, Bobbie," Tabatha said.

"Morning."

Tabatha noted Bertha filling a tray at the counter. "Where you going with that?"

"Takin' it to your mother."

"Bull. Let me have that. This has gone far enough." She pushed her chair back and took the tray from Bertha.

~

Tabatha knocked on Carla's bedroom door and waited for permission to enter.

"Come in Bertha, and be quick about it. I told you I wanted breakfast at seven not seven-thirty."

"Well, Mother, if you want breakfast at seven, then I suggest you get your prim little fanny to the kitchen and fix it. This will be the last meal brought to you. Bertha is not your personal servant." Tabatha set the tray roughly on the bed. "Enjoy." She turned on her heels and walked away, slamming the door behind her.

She heard her mother screaming all the way down the stairs and into the kitchen. By the look on the faces of the others, she guessed they did, too.

"Lordy, baby girl, I bet she's spitting fire," Bertha said.

Tabatha felt her face heat with her own anger. "I'm sorry you overheard that."

The room fell silent when Carla stormed into the kitchen. With a crash, the tray flew across the room and onto the floor. French toast, syrup, orange juice, and coffee flew in all directions. "I will not eat this. Bertha, fix me a decent breakfast." She lifted her nose in the air and turned to leave.

"Pick it up, Mother." Tabatha's voice, a hiss of fury, warned of danger.

Carla laughed, but it held no humor. The tray tore through the air and landed against the wall with a clang of metal and a violent spray of plaster.

"Pick . . . it . . . up."

Bobbie and Rhonda inched away from the table toward the door. Derek came to stand behind her. "Tabatha, calm down."

She stepped away from his heat, his voice. "Not now, Derek. Not a good time."

Carla's eyes widened in fear as Tabatha approached her. "You're crazy. Just like them. Satan's child, not mine. I told them, but no one would listen. Didn't want to have you, but they said they'd leave me without a dime if I had an abortion."

"Pick it up, Mother. I won't ask again. You will behave like the lady you think you are. We have no servants. We take care of ourselves. Do you understand what I'm saying? Bertha cooks for us, but that's all."

Carla fell to her knees, crying as she cleaned the mess she'd made. She screamed and crawled away when Bertha tried to help her. "Get away from me. Bad. All of you." She scanned the eyes watching her. She slowly pulled herself to her feet and straightened her housecoat. Drawing in a deep breath, she seemed to transform from the frantic woman of moments before to the persona of the lady of the manor. "I'm returning to my room, Bertha. I'll have my lunch at noon, please." She walked away without another word.

"Man," Rhonda said. "That was creepy."

Bobbie nodded. "Uh huh."

"Tabatha?" Derek said softly and touched her arm. "What just happened? How did that tray take off like that?" He drew her closer. "You're shaking. Are you all right?"

Bertha come to stand beside her and said, "Very impressive, little girl. How long you been holdin' that in?"

"A long time, I guess," she said and leaned against Derek. "I'm sorry. When I lose my temper, my power . . . erupts."

Her warmth seeped though his shirt and into his body. He raised his arms to hold her but thought better of it. "Remind me to never piss you off." She stepped away from him, leaving behind a sensation of emptiness in her wake.

"Yeah," Bobbie agreed.

"I'm glad Shane wasn't here to see that. He'd have loved it though." A schoolgirl giggle trickled out of Rhonda but soon turned into a full body-shaking laugh. "Did you see Bobbie's face when that tray flew in the air?" Rhonda crumbled into the chair, holding her stomach.

Bobbie turned to look at Tabatha, a crooked smile on her lips. "Well, at least she isn't crying." She laughed, drawing Tabatha into the giggles.

Soon everyone but Derek was laughing and holding their sides in pain. He had no idea what was so funny and wondered if they'd lost their minds.

"Baby girl, I've never seen you laugh like that," Bertha said, drying her eyes.

"I don't remember if I ever have." She reached for a paper towel, wiped her eyes and blew her nose. "What the hell are we laughing at, anyway?"

"I'm going to check on Shane," Rhonda said, leaving the room.

"I have a job interview this morning, so I'd better go get dressed." Bobbie hugged Tabatha. "Will you be home when I get back?"

"I don't know. But Bertha had keys made for everyone last night. They're by the front door on the coffee table."

She nodded. "I'll call if I'm going to be later than noon. See ya."

Bertha clicked her tongue. "I better get a mop and clean this mess. What got into that woman?"

"Do you have to go to work today, Derek?" Tabatha asked.

He nodded. "I don't want you out by yourself. You or Rhonda. They probably don't know about Bobbie yet."

"I'm not going to be a prisoner in my own home. I'll keep my gun in the car. You don't have to have a permit in Louisiana for that, do you?"

"No." He released a sigh, knowing he was wasting his breath. "Can you raise one of the murdered kids tonight? The sooner I find the killer, the quicker I can concentrate my attention on who is trying to kill you."

She looked away. "What time?"

"Around six."

She walked him to the door. "I'll be ready."

Fourteen

Tabatha met Derek at the door and led him immediately away from the house. "What's wrong?"

She remained silent as she directed him toward the garage.

In blood-red lettering across the driver's side of her car were the words:

Your world will darken.
Your soul cry out.
Your friends can't save you.
Have no doubt.

His heart jumped to his throat. "When did you discover this?"

"I went to the grocery this afternoon, came home and unloaded the car. After the last trip in, I unpacked the bags and returned to close the trunk. That's when I first saw it." She shrugged. "He'll never be a poet, huh?"

"You saw who did this?"

"No. Didn't see or hear a thing."

Derek drew his cell phone from his jacket.

"What are you doing?" She placed her hand on his arm.

"I'm going to call this in. Tabatha, someone was within a few yards of the house while you were running back and forth bringing in groceries. He could have been hiding beside the garage or in the trees the whole time, watching. He could have killed you."

"What are you going to say? 'Hey, boss, Saturday I met a girl. Today, someone wrote a poem on her car. Oh, and by the way, she can raise the dead.'"

"You want to let it go? There could be fingerprints. Have you looked in the car? Maybe he left something behind."

She rapped her arms around her waist. "Do you have someone you can trust to keep his mouth shut? Another detective?"

"Frank."

"No," she shouted, then calmed her voice. "You saw how his wife reacted to me. I don't know what my mother told her, but Mary doesn't like me at all." She shook her head. "No. Anyone but Frank. He'd tell what happened Saturday just to make his wife happy."

Derek recalled how Mary reacted to her presence at the cookout. She'd made it clear she didn't like or trust Tabatha.

"Who returned your car?"

"What?"

"The shots shattered the windshield. I had it towed to a garage I do business with. Who brought it back to you?"

"Oh. He said his name was George. Tall, lanky, brown hair and had one finger missing."

Derek exhaled. "Yeah, that's George's description. Who was with him?"

"No one. He brought it on the tow truck. After I paid him, he drove off."

He flicked open his phone, clicked through his list and pressed the call button. "George in?"

He was silent for a moment before saying, "Hey, George. The black Grand Am I sent over there. Is it ready to be picked up?" He paused. "Who told you to deliver it to Miss Gray?" Silence again. "No, no. That's fine. It's no problem. Thanks, George." He returned the phone to his shirt pocket.

"Frank?" she guessed.

He nodded.

"What did he have to say today?"

"He took a sick day." Derek tried to make sense of Frank's actions. Derek had never known him to behave like this. "Maybe we should do this another night. If someone is watching you, they may--"

"See me work my magic?" she interrupted him. "I'll know if anyone is close."

"You didn't notice I was watching you raise Rhonda's mother."

Tabatha smiled. "I knew you were there."

"We'll go with you and stand guard a few feet away."

Rhonda's voice caused them both to jump and Derek to reach for his gun. He released a breath and dropped his hand. "Good way to get yourself shot, girl."

She grinned. "Nah. You're one of those perfect record types--no mistakes. You always think before pulling the trigger."

"What do you mean by 'we'?" Tabatha asked.

Bobbie and Bertha stepped out of the kitchen door. Bertha's wide grin glistened in the sunlight. "If anybody tries to get past me, I'll sit on 'em."

Rhonda nodded. "I'll think of something to stop them."

"What about Shane. Who'll take care of him?" Bobbie asked.

"We can drop him off at Momma's. She'll keep him safe. Besides, it's only for a couple of hours."

"Rhonda, if someone wants to use Shane to get what they want, your mom couldn't stop them from taking him," Tabatha said. "She could get killed trying."

Bobbie stepped onto the stoop, joining them. "Bertha, you want to help, right?"

"My baby girl needs me, I'm there."

"Okay; Derek, can you get us a roll of crime scene tape?"

He tried to figure out what crazy idea she was cooking up, but came up blank. "I have some in the back of my car."

Bobbie paced back and forth in front of the porch. "Let's see. Do you think Shane would be safe with you, Bertha?"

Bertha snorted. "I got my skillet." She gave Derek an embarrassed grin. "And I got my man's double barrel. We can lock ourselves in his room and play games. God help anybody who tries to get in that door."

Bobbie stopped to stare at Derek for a second. "You think we could get away with roping off the area and saying we're looking for evidence? Something you might have missed?"

"The cemetery where Selma Fortier is entombed was never a crime scene."

"Damn." She paced some more. "What about the cemeteries where the others are buried?"

He shook his head. "No."

She sat on the stoop and tapped her finger on her chin. "Okay, what about this?" She paused. "No." She stood and paced again. "Where is Selma's grave?"

"Greenwood Cemetery," he answered.

"Greenwood?" Tabatha said.

"Yeah, it's at the end of Canal."

Tabatha shrugged and glanced away. "That's where my family is buried. No one will question my going there. I come and go all the time. What's your plan, Bobbie?"

"We can tape it off. Rhonda and I will walk the perimeters and keep anyone from coming near while you do your thing."

Derek scoffed.

She shrugged. "Got a better idea?"

He couldn't believe he was going along with this, but desperate cases require desperate actions. "No tape. It would call too much attention to us. All you have to do is keep your eyes and ears open. If we can hide from someone, they can hide from us. Those crypts are too tall and too close together to see anything until you're right up on them. But sounds carry. If you listen, you can hear someone coming."

Tabatha shoved her hands into her pockets. "Let's do it."

"Chicken?" Bobbie asked.

"In the pet carrier sitting under the shade tree."

Bobbie shook her head. "Where do you get these chickens?"

Tabatha shrugged. "Bertha raises them."

Derek jogged to the carrier and picked it up, then stopped as something caught his attention. "What's that mound behind the garage?"

"It's been there as long as I can remember," Tabatha answered. "Mom said it was dirt grandfather had brought in to level off the yard, but never had it spread. Trees and ivy have turned it into an impossible mass of roots."

Something about it didn't feel right. It was too perfectly formed for a forgotten pile of dirt. He brushed it away from his thoughts to focus on more important issues. He was going to find out who killed Selma Fortier tonight.

"Derek? You still with us?"

He smiled. "Sorry. Dreaming of putting away the killer."

"My car?"

"Sure. That poem isn't conspicuous at all."

Her shoulders slumped. "Well, yours screams 'cheese it, the cops.'"

Derek chuckled. "Cheese it?"

"Get down, run, hide."

Bertha disappeared into the house returning with keys in hand. "Here, take the Oldsmobile. It's nearly an antique, but it runs good."

Rhonda stood from the stoop. "Bertha, take care of my boy, you hear? He's all I got."

"Child, you worry about yourself. That boy is safer with me than a plate of grits at a Yankee wedding."

"Let's get this over with," Rhonda said and slipped into the front passenger seat.

"Well, well. Look who's gone all brave on us," Bobbie teased.

Bertha gave Bobbie a slap on the rump. "I'm gonna take a switch to you if you don't stop pestering her."

Bobbie laughed. "Yes, ma'am. I'll behave."

"You better."

"Let's go raise the dead and kick some killer ass," Bobbie said. She opened the car door and ushered them inside. "I'll even share the back seat with Tabatha."

Fifteen

Phelps saw the car pull to a stop in the drive and opened the door before the passenger walking to the front entrance could ring the bell. "I told you I didn't want to be disturbed. My wife is mourning her son. She wants silence. What's so important that it can't wait?"

"The fellowship needs your expertise on a little matter."

"Who?" His heart began to pound, his body reacting to the adrenaline racing through his system. "Ahhh, epinephrine; the perfect after dinner cocktail."

Phelps waved her in, closed the door, and led his visitor into his private office. Phelps went behind his desk and sat, then said, "Who? When?"

"The 'who' is Rhonda Meads. We don't give a shit when. But no body this time. Went out for a pack of cigarettes kind of thing." She paused as if rethinking her next comment. "I hired your stepson to do the job, but he screwed it up. Dumb bastard didn't have sense enough not to do it in broad daylight and in the residential area of Bourbon Street."

"I'd watch your mouth if I were you." He reached into the box of cigars, offering one to his guest. "Why are you so afraid of this girl? What's so special about her?"

"She's dangerous. Got information she shouldn't." She leaned in close. "Two other girls with her. A girl named Bobbie. Don't know her last name. And Tabatha Gray. Leave the Gray girl to me."

"What the Gray girl do?"

"She's hooking up with that cop, Bainbridge."

"Hooking up?" Phelps lit a cigar and blew the smoke in the woman's face.

The visitor frowned and waved the offending haze away. "One of my informants told me that whore was all over him. You know about her power?"

"Power?" Phelps took a slow, long draw on the cigar. "You know I don't believe in that hoodoo shit. I believe in brute strength and the element of surprise. Now, give me the particulars. Description? Where does she live? Where does she work? Why do you give a damn that she's interested in Bainbridge?"

She flung a snapshot and a folded piece of paper onto Phelps' desk. "That's Tabatha Gray's address and where they're staying." She handed him two photographs. "The one on the right is Rhonda. The one in the center is Tabatha. They don't work right now. And we don't need that damned detective sniffing around. Maybe you could use your charms on her."

He stretched out his legs and rubbed his crotch. "Is that what I use, darlin'?"

Phelps watched with great amusement as the woman stood abruptly, walked out of the office and to her car. He heard the car door slam then tires screeching out of the drive. After glancing at the paper, he refolded it and placed it in an inside pocket of his jacket.

"Tabatha Gray," he whispered and gazed upon the photograph. "Such perfection. Too beautiful for your own good, I fear. Why would you want Bainbridge? I could give you the world. I could give you life."

Sixteen

Tabatha reached over the seat, grasping Derek's shoulder when he started to veer the car toward the gate off City Park Avenue. "No. Go around to the Canal Boulevard entrance. Where's the grave site?" She looked out the back window searching for the forest green pickup truck that had been behind them since pulling into traffic at South Claiborne Avenue Overpass. It was nowhere in sight.

"Not far from the sales office," Derek said as he maneuvered his way around the cemetery's borders. After a quick survey of the area, he parked the car at the rear of the building and out of sight from the street. "Last chance, Rhonda. Sure you want to do this?"

Rhonda swallowed hard, the sound loud in the quiet car. She turned to face Tabatha then Bobbie. Her complexion had lost its color and her eyes were round with fear. "I'm okay. Let's get this done."

They managed to get twenty feet away from the car when a man opened the door of the office building and shouted, "Hey! You can't park here."

Derek drew his wallet from his jacket and flashed his badge. "Police business."

The man waved and closed the door without another word of protest.

Bobbie chuckled. "How on earth do you people not get lost in this maze of white? Kind of creepy to think someone is just on the other side of that wall." She pointed toward the closest crypt.

Tabatha eyed the area as they passed each crosswalk, reaching out for any sense of being followed. "I used to take a bus here when I was a kid. I'd come after school and stay until Bertha would come find me."

Rhonda brushed a strand of hair out of her face. "Why? I'd think the last thing you'd want to do is come to a cemetery. I mean being able to hear the dead."

"I missed Daddy and Paw-Paw." Tabatha's heart raced with the slightest touch of Derek's fingers brushing across her hand. She allowed herself one quick glance and discovered his gaze upon her. She grasped tightly to the warmth in his smile of encouragement.

The hum of nearby traffic surrounded them as all conversation faded away. Their footsteps echoed from one crypt to another, vocalizing in rhythmic whispers of warning to Tabatha's ears alone.

"Anyone talking to you now?" Rhonda asked, breaking the haunting murmurs.

"No."

Bobbie turned her attention to the scene around her. "Thank God. This place has its beauty, but still, it gives me the creeps."

Derek stopped at a marble crypt, topped with a prone sculptured angel. He sat the animal carrier at his feet. The chicken clucked and pecked at the side of its cubical. "Don't be in such a hurry to get out of there, chicken," he warned.

"Where's your family buried, Bobbie?" Rhonda asked.

"My kind are cremated and our ashes scattered on sacred ground."

"Why?"

"Well," Bobbie said slowly, "if we aren't cremated we can return, and we aren't very nice our second time around. We turn into soulless monsters. Sacred ground because that's how it's been done for eons."

"I'm ready," Tabatha whispered. "Get away from here." She pointed to her left. "Don't come any closer than three rows away until I call for you."

Rhonda and Bobbie agreed. Their eyes darted about the cemetery in what Tabatha prayed were healthy doses of fear and caution. She turned to Derek, hoping she'd frightened him enough that he'd leave also. Unfortunately, there was a determined set to his jaw.

"I'm staying."

She couldn't think of anything she could do to change his mind. "Then you have to promise to stay inside the circle. No matter what happens, you must not leave the protective area."

He released a heavy sigh. "Whatever you say."

She turned her head slowly, seeing Rhonda and Bobbie still standing next to her. Their images began to blur and falter. "Go. Do *not* come until I call you. Spirits can harm you if you get too close."

"Wait," Bobbie said. "What spirits?"

"When I call the dead, restless spirits come to the beckoning as well. Evil within a person does not always die with them. They don't want to be dead, so they search for a conduit, a person to live through. Do you understand what I'm telling you?"

They stared wide-eyed, but said nothing.

"If you hear someone coming, warn Derek and run, but do not run toward us." Tabatha faced Derek. "Do not speak to me until I acknowledge you. Do not break my thoughts. I'll try to call her without blood. She's been dead such a short time, and I can already feel my power drawing her to me."

"You're the boss." Ever on the watch, he moved two steps back.

"Go." Tabatha began to chant and form the circle with the contents from a slender glass vial.

Rhonda and Bobbie glanced at each other for a split second then ran until they reached an area Tabatha deemed safe.

Tabatha's voice pleaded with the spirits in a monotone and eerie whisper. A strange glow materialized as the circle joined. With each symbol she formed, sounds faded. Lifeless silence soon enveloped them.

The power grew with a tingle of expectation. The sighs of wandering spirits called out to her, seeming to choke the life from the air. Sounds of drumbeats thundered in her ears, and she realized it was Derek's heart reaching out to slow her heart's rhythm, to match it to his own steady pace.

"Selma Fortier, live. Come to me."

Locks clicked open and sounds of scraping stone broke the eerie silence. "Come, Selma Fortier."

Tabatha inhaled slowly, fighting dark fear and panic. The smell of chloroform burned her nostrils. Her mouth lost its moisture. "Selma Fortier, I command you to live."

With a moan the doors swung open and a child stepped into the dying sunlight. A golden scarf wrapped around her head glowed like a halo. She wore a white dress that fluttered in the slight breeze, brushing against her thin legs. One arm held a teddy bear tightly against her chest, the other hung at her side.

Tabatha forced herself to move, making her feet take each step to join Selma on the small marble entryway. Tabatha lowered herself to her knees. "Selma, I need to ask you a few questions. Is that all right with you?"

Selma tilted her head and stared at Tabatha with empty eye sockets. "Why is it so dark?"

"It's night," Tabatha said, choking back a sob. "Selma, who hurt you?"

"I don't know," she said in an innocent, little girl voice.

Tabatha's heart sank. "Can you tell me what happened?"

"I was playing with my new doll in the yard. Someone put a smelly rag on my face. I felt sick. I tried to call my momma but I went to sleep."

"Do you remember anything else?" Tabatha asked.

"I tried to wake up, but my head hurt. My tummy burned. Then I smelled the bad rag again."

Tabatha turned her head to look at Derek, saw his Adam's apple bob in his throat and knew he was fighting tears. "Anything else you can think to ask?"

"No. I think you asked them all."

"Someone is coming," Rhonda hissed.

Tabatha reached out to touch Selma's arm and tell her to return, but with a brush of her fingertips on the child's arm Tabatha was transported to a backyard and heard footsteps behind her. She turned to see who was there. Roughness of a chloroform-soaked cloth on her mouth stung, the smell choked her, and she struggled to cry out, to breathe. She saw an arm, a wristwatch.

"Tabatha," Derek said, jerking her away from Selma. "Send her back. Someone is coming."

She gasped for air. "Return to your resting place, Selma Fortier. Rise again only when God calls for you."

Selma turned away, returning to the elaborate crypt, doors swung closed, and sounds of the real world once again filled the space around them. Voices in the distance called back and forth.

Derek drew his gun and moved to leave.

"Stop!" Tabatha shouted. She rushed to destroy the protective circle, scattering salt and ash as she spoke the words to send the spirits back to the next realm. One by one, symbols were ground into the soil and the air once again became fresh, breathable. With a wave of her hand she called Rhonda and Bobbie over, and whispered one word, "Run."

The four of them sped by crypts, glancing down each empty row before continuing to the next. Men's shouts became distant, buffered by stone and marble. As they cleared the last row of tombs she saw that Bertha's Oldsmobile had been blocked by a black Cadillac and green truck, beat up past recognizing its make or model.

"Oh, hell," Tabatha swore. "Now what?"

Rhonda said, "Give me the keys. At last, something I can do to help."

Derek tossed the keys to her and guarded their backs as she jumped into the driver's seat. The car roared to life and moved forward, slowly at first until bumpers met. She floored the accelerator, using the Oldsmobile's muscle strength to push the nameless truck. Tires screamed in protest, their acrid smoke leaving behind the heavy scent of burnt rubber.

Rhonda slammed on the brakes and backed up. "Get in," she yelled.

They piled in, barely getting doors closed before Rhonda sped away and charged into traffic. Cars braked and swerved, tires squealed. Everyone gripped anything they could get their hands on to keep from being tossed about. Tabatha leaned out the window and looked toward the cemetery before Derek forced her back down into the car. She saw three men exit. Two men dressed in jeans and t-shirts drew their guns and aimed. The one dressed in a suit and tie stopped them with a wave of his hand. Her eyes met with Mr. Suit's. His lips curved into a smile before he brought his fingers to them and blew her a kiss.

Tabatha knew she'd had her first encounter with John Phelps. She returned her thoughts to the gravesite and fought to understand what she'd experienced upon touching Selma. Noticing the gun she didn't remember drawing, she engaged the safety and tried to return the .38 to its shoulder holster.

Derek took the weapon away. "What happened back there, Tabatha?"

She slowly turned to face him. "What happened?"

"With Selma. Your eyes rolled into your head. All I could see were their whites. What happened?"

"Grandfather warned me. I forgot. I didn't think. I just wanted to comfort her."

Bobbie turned to look at them. "Is she going to be all right?"

Derek wrapped his arms around Tabatha, holding her close. His warmth warred with an unbearable cold trying to seep into the marrow of her bones. "He warned you about what? Talk to me."

"Never touch them. Too much for the living to take on their memories." Tabatha tried to get closer, needed to know Derek was real. "The killer."

"What about him?" Rhonda asked, risking a quick glance into the backseat.

Derek kissed the top of Tabatha's head. "We'll find him. One of the children had to see something."

She shook her head, rubbing her face against his chest.

"It's not a he. The killer is a woman."

Derek's silence was like a vacuum sucking life from the air. "A woman?"

Tabatha released a weary breath. "When I touched Selma, I was in her body. I . . . she didn't see the woman's face, but she saw her arm. A watch."

"Could you tell type or style?" he asked.

"Gold metal band. Real gold, I think. Square black face, Roman numerals. Her arm is thin with black hair. I saw a sleeve, faded denim or chambray, rolled to her elbow. Her breath smelled of sage." She hid her face in his chest again. "She laughed, Derek. She laughed at the child's fear."

An uncomfortable silence ruled the ride home. The atmosphere was palatable, leaving a bitter taste behind. Derek rolled his shoulders, fighting the tension knotting his muscles.

"You're home, baby."

Tabatha straightened, drawing herself away, her eyes darting about, searching for perceived danger.

Rhonda shut off the engine and leaned her head against the seat. "They didn't follow us."

Bobbie snorted. "Why should they? They know where we live."

"I don't know what to do." Tabatha leaned her head against the front seat. "Do we tell Bertha what happened? I shouldn't have let her stay. She's in just as much danger as we are, now. Bobbie, you should have gone on your way, too."

Bobbie scoffed. "Those assholes are after anyone who has talents they don't understand. They would have gotten around to me eventually. For the last time, Tabatha, I'm your friend. We're in this together. Hell, look at Rhonda. She's scared shitless, but she was there for you, for us." With a nod, she seemed to make an important decision. "Derek, keep your mouth shut and your mind open. I'm going to let everyone in on something important."

"I'm a good listener," he said. "Whether I'll believe it or not, I can't say."

Rhonda slammed the steering wheel hard with her fists. "What do we have to do? Shove it up your nose for you to smell the truth? This is our real life. This is what we are. We've had to hide our whole damned lives. I made sure everyone knew about Tabatha. Want to know why?"

Tabatha held her breath, waiting for Rhonda's answer.

"It kept their attention away from me. I didn't want anyone to know I had this problem. I didn't want to be seen as a freak." She turned her eyes to meet Tabatha's. "I'm sorry. I wish I could take it back."

"It's okay. If I'd thought of it, I'd probably have done the same thing," Tabatha said. "Now, Bobbie, what's so important?"

Bobbie turned away, staring out the window. "Remember I said my brother needed his ceremony?"

"Yes, I remember. That night in the morgue."

"His name was Elsu Luckman. He was the leader of the shapeshifters. I'm the last of my bloodline, so the burden has fallen to me."

Derek held up his hand. "May I ask a question?"

Bobbie rolled her eyes. "Yes, you may."

"How much of what's going on now did you know about before you arrived?"

"I knew nothing about the children being murdered, but I knew about the Guardians. It's another reason I was asked to return. We've had six of our people murdered in two months. Everyone is scared."

"They're expecting you to find the killers?" Derek asked.

Bobbie shrugged. "Yes, I guess they are. Maybe not me actually doing the hunting, but they expect me to do what has to be done to stop them. Too many of my people have lost their powers or they have weakened. My brother and I come from a very powerful line of shamans. We held the strongest sorcery. But now, it's only me."

"Does this have anything to do with you fastening yourself to Tabatha?"

"Yes, again. Once I found out about her talents and that she was coming here, I knew she'd be in danger of being discovered."

Rhonda gave an unladylike grunt. "Well, someone made sure they knew about her. The list is extensive. I don't know if your name is on it or not."

"It is," Tabatha said, her voice slightly above a whisper. "I checked the list again this morning. I didn't think to look before because as far as I knew, she wasn't here."

Derek shifted in his seat. "Rhonda, Tabatha said you had some things your mother left behind. If you don't mind, I'd like to have a look."

"Yeah, I have it inside."

They filed into the kitchen and came face to face with Bertha and her shotgun.

"Well, it's about time y'all got home. Shane's had his dinner and he's already in bed for the night." Bertha ran a loving gaze over Tabatha. "Girl, you look like you've been chewed up and spit out."

"We had a bit of trouble. But no one got hurt," Derek said, rubbing Tabatha's back. "She just needs rest."

"Sit. I got your dinner in the oven."

"I'm not hungry, Bert," Tabatha said, starting toward the stairway.

"I ain't hearing it, baby girl. At least have some soup. Not good to go to bed without eating for half the day."

Derek guided her toward a chair and sat down next to her. "Eat some soup, then you can rest while I look at what Rhonda has."

She rubbed her tired eyes and yawned. "Rhonda's mother apparently had a camcorder set up. There are also audiotapes."

Bertha moved rapidly about the kitchen, bringing each of them a bowl of crawfish corn chowder. "Hush up and eat, baby girl. I'm not leaving until that bowl is empty, and you know how Oscar is about me being late."

~

They sat on the sofa in Rhonda's sitting room, shuffling through papers. Derek picked up the micro recorder, pressing rewind. The tape whirled backward with a near-silent hum. At the end, he pressed play.

"What are we going to do about Dorothy?" A deep masculine voice asked, followed by sounds of chairs scraping against floorboards.

A second voice was that of a woman. *"She's one of them and we've got all we can from her. I don't trust her. Don't trust any of them."*

"Shit, Dana, you don't trust anyone. I sometimes wonder if you trust us." The man laughed.

"They call that one 'Dub' later in the tape," Tabatha said.

"I trust whom I must, but only so far. I've warned you from the beginning about her. She's got something on us. She won't tell me what, but I've got that much out of her. Stupid bitch thinks I'm going to help her bring us down."

"Our man downtown is going to cover for us. Suicide," Dub said.

Clothing rustled and then footsteps ended their conversation.

"Pardon me, Mr. Phelps, but your wife is on the phone. Insists on speaking to you."

"Thank you, James. Tell her I'll be right there."

Footsteps faded before they once again spoke. *"Yes, it's all taken care of. Poor Dorothy was so distraught. Everyone knew it. The Women's Club was very worried about her,"* Dana said and snickered.

"Better go talk to your wife, Phelps," Dub said.

Sounds of movement, a grunt, then Phelps answered. *"Getting meddlesome, always wanting to know where I've been, with whom."*

Dana spoke again. *"Is it still set it up for Friday night?"*

Dub said, *"Late. After the girl and kid have gone to bed."*

"Why don't you let me get rid of the kid, too? He's bound to have some magic in him," Phelps said.

"We don't kill until we're sure. We're not animals," Dub shouted.

She laughed. *"Yeah, but some of them are."* A chair scraped against wood. *"Where you going, Dub?"*

"Home. Do you mind?"

"Good idea. Time for all of you to get out," Phelps said. *"Where's Dorothy now?"*

"She went home an hour ago. Said she has things to do," Dana said, her voice now farther away. *"Later, alligator."*

The tape fell silent, matching the quiet of the sitting room.

"Well?" Rhonda finally asked.

Derek sat back, sinking into the overstuffed sofa. "We have a man they called Dub, a woman by the name of Dana. Phelps was there. I'll bet James is a houseman. And they have a dirty cop or someone with power covering their murders."

"The names in these files are coded, calling themselves Agent Red, Agent Falls," Rhonda said. "The film isn't any help. The camera is set at the rear of a meeting room and everyone has hoods covering their faces. They talk about jobs completed and yet to be carried out, but no names."

"Like the Klan?" Derek asked.

Tabatha stretched and yawned. "No. Black hoods with angel faces, gold halos painted around their heads. Guess they think they're some kind of saints."

Bobbie raised her arms over her head and groaned. "I'm going to bed, kids. I can't keep my eyes open any longer."

"I'm really tired, too," Rhonda said. "Doors and windows locked?"

"Yeah. I took care of that," Tabatha said. "Turned on the alarm system, as well."

"If it's all right with you, I'll sleep on the couch downstairs," Derek said. "I feel better staying close for now."

Tabatha rose and stretched again. "There's another bedroom. Luckily, Mom hasn't started selling furniture up here yet. Come, I'll show you where it is, then I'll find some clean linens." She waved at Rhonda and Bobbie. "Night, girls. Don't let the boogie man get you."

Derek followed her down the hallway. "How come your mother has such a big place? Seems strange to have so many bedrooms for one person."

"It was my grandfather's house. His thinking was that family stayed together. He added onto it when Mom and Dad married. Thought they'd fill it with kids, I guess." She smiled. "Grandfather used to tell me that when I grew up and had my own kids, he'd build more bedrooms for them." She pointed to her left. "This is my room. Yours is next door."

She opened the door, letting him in. "I'll be right back. The linen closet is down the hall."

He ran his hand along the wall until he found a light switch. Bright light from a chandelier brought the enormous room into view. It smelled of cedar and furniture polish. Hardwood floors were buffed to a perfect dark sheen, and moldings stained the same darkness as the floors edged a high ceiling. The walls were covered with garish red brocade. A fireplace sat in one corner flanked on each side by Queen Anne chairs. In another corner a small table had been set with a fine silver tea set. The double bed touted what looked to be a hand-carved mahogany headboard. At the foot rested a matching chest.

"Will this do?"

He jumped at Tabatha's voice. "Fancy."

"It was supposed to be Mom and Dad's room, but she had a fit and said she wouldn't stand for it. She expected a suite and wouldn't stay here until she got one."

"I guess she got it."

"Yeah, Paw-Paw gave up his until he could turn three bedrooms into a suite of his own. Then she had the nerve to say she wanted the new one." Tabatha whipped open a blue fitted sheet, stretching its corners onto the mattress. "She didn't get what she wanted that time. Grandfather told her she could sign annulment papers the next day. She shut up."

Derek shook his head. "So she was a spoiled rich . . ." He thought better of finishing his thought.

"Rich bitch?" Tabatha laughed. "Not by a long shot. My mom came from the Irish Channel. Poor as dirt. But she planned on making up for it." She sat, elbows on knees, face in her hands. "Stay with me tonight."

His heart lurched. "Tabatha, I--"

"Most of my life I've been alone," she said, interrupting him. "I've had no one to call my own. You're the only man, except for my dad and grandfather, who knew about me and still accepted me. You didn't run away. All I ever wanted was to be like everyone else. Normal. But for just this moment in time, I'm happy I have this magic. I can help you. All I ask is that you help me. I don't want to be alone tonight."

"Tabatha, I can't."

"Elizabeth?" she asked, her voice choking on what he thought may have been a suppressed sob.

He nodded. "I have to give her justice before I can go on with my life."

"You mean before you can let her go, don't you? She's dead, Derek. She'd want you to be happy."

He wanted to believe Tabatha was right, but he couldn't. "Tabatha. . . ."

Standing abruptly, she walked past him. "When we find the children's murderer, I'll raise Elizabeth and ask who killed her. Will that please you?"

He grabbed her by the arm and turned her to face him. "I need to know. You don't understand." He swallowed hard and forced himself to look her in the eyes. "It was our wedding day."

Tabatha's mouth formed a hard line. "From the time I saw you in the cemetery, I knew I wanted you." She pulled her arms out of his hands and walked away. "Life goes on, leaving those behind who don't react quickly enough." She closed the door behind her.

The room lost its spirit; silence cooled the space where her voice had warmed the air just moments before. In retrospect the light wasn't as bright as it had been; her absence drained it of life.

The door hit the wall with a crash as he swung it open. "Tabatha!"

Derek hesitated at her bedroom door not at all sure he was doing the right thing. He filled his lungs with air then slowly breathed out; counting the reasons he should return to his own room. She deserved a man who could give her his heart. His had been claimed twenty years ago. She was too pretty, too rich. Too good for him.

He heard the knock and stared at his hand in disbelief. He didn't remember raising his knuckles.

"Come in," he heard Tabatha say, her voice muffled by the wooden slab separating them.

Derek wiped his sweaty palms on his pant legs before turning the doorknob. He swallowed hard at the sight of her sitting on the bed, brushing her hair and dressed in a long white t-shirt. He tried not to stare, but Tabatha's erect nipples pressing against thin material were hard to ignore.

"Tabatha, I. . . ."

"Still love Elizabeth," she finished for him.

"No. Yes. I mean, a part of me will always love her, but it's not that." He sat next to her, folding his hands in his lap. "I swore I'd find Elizabeth's killer and justice for her."

Tabatha started to place her hand over his, but pulled away at the last minute.

"You can touch me. I won't bite, I promise."

"That's all I'm asking, to be touched and held. I'm afraid, not so much for me, but for my friends, for you." She rested her arms on the nightstand and lowered her head into the crook of her elbows. "I shouldn't have let Bobbie stay here."

"Didn't you hear what she said? Those fanatics are killing her people. Her name is on that list. They knew about Bobbie and it has nothing to do with her staying here." He placed his hand on the center of her back. "No, you did right for both Bobbie and Rhonda."

"What about my mother? Am I doing right by her?" When Tabatha turned to face him, her eyes were filled with tears.

"Hell, from what I see, she rarely leaves that bedroom of hers. They'd have to burn the house down to get to her."

Tabatha giggled and wiped her eyes. "You don't have to stay, Derek. I'm a big girl."

He wrapped his arm around her waist, drawing her closer. "If it's okay, I'll stay."

She kissed him softly on his shoulder. "It's okay; and thank you."

He stood and crossed to the other side of the bed. After slipping out of his shoes he stretched out, fully dressed.

Tabatha rolled her eyes. "I'll look away, then you can strip to your skivvies. All right?"

"I didn't want you to think--"

"I won't think anything. You can't sleep in your clothes and leave here tomorrow looking like a rumpled ragamuffin." She turned her back to him. "My eyes are closed." She yawned and snuggled under the covers.

Derek undressed quickly, placing his folded jeans and shirt on a nearby armchair. He slid his revolver under the pillow, pulled back the sheet and stretched out, staring at the ceiling. "When did you know you were . . . that you had your family's. . . ."

Tabatha rolled over, facing him. "First recollection I have is around the age of four. I heard a baby crying. For two days I heard that child cry. Such a sad sound. Lost. Scared."

He faced her. "What did you do?"

"I asked my mother where the baby was and why it was crying."

"And?"

"At first she was confused. Didn't know what I was talking about. I didn't understand why she couldn't hear it." Tabatha turned her face into her pillow. "I'll never forget my mother's face when she realized I was born with the Gray curse. Her expression took on that same dark disdain as when she saw a cockroach. Like she wanted to squish and discard me like unwanted vermin."

Derek twirled a lock of Tabatha's hair around his index finger, rubbing his thumb over the silky strands. "She didn't try to explain why you heard the baby?"

"No. My grandfather walked in while I was talking to her. When Momma hissed at me, he gathered me in his arms, took me to his room. He explained everything as best he could to a four-year-old. Then he told the baby everything would be all right and to stop crying. She did. Then he reassured me, saying I wouldn't hear the voices again for a long time."

"Your mother hissed at you?" He didn't know if he should laugh or be angry.

Tabatha lifted her face out of her pillow and laughed softly. "Like a snake."

"Good grief."

"She was never right after that. I think she took a step over that thin line of sanity into insanity. She got worse as time passed. She even seemed happy when Daddy died."

"Mary said you thought your mother killed your father and grandfather. Is that true?" He hoped he didn't sound as much like a cop as he felt at that moment.

"Yes."

"Why?"

Tabatha rolled onto her other side, turning her back to him. "I saw her put something in Dad's wine. A powder. A couple of hours later, he died. Same thing happened to my grandfather, though I didn't see her do it that time."

"Jesus. Did you tell anyone?"

"Hell, yes. I told everyone I knew. But no one would listen." She sighed heavily. "It doesn't matter any more. Look at her. She's being punished more than any court could have penalized her. She's a broken woman. Scared to leave the house. I was surprised when she said she was going to Mary's that afternoon. Even more surprised that she wanted me to go with her." Tabatha turned her head to smile at him. "I'm glad she did though, or I'd have had to come up with a way to meet you."

Derek rubbed her arm. Tabatha seemed to take that as an invitation and scooted across the space separating them until her back was flush against his chest and her bottom against. . . .

He groaned then slid his butt backward, forcing space between her backside and his hardening erection. *Keep your mind off of her body. Think of something else.*

"When did the voices start again? You said your grandfather managed to quiet them."

"When I was ten years old I was playing tea time with my dolls. I heard Paw-Paw calling me. When I tried to find him, he told me I'd never see him again. I ran crying to my mother and told her Paw-Paw had died. She told me I'd just had a bad dream. But about ten minutes later she got the call."

"Your father's spirit called for you after he died?"

"No. But I got to talk to him right before he passed away. He told me to be brave and take care of Momma. I promised him I would."

Suspecting she wanted to talk this out, he waited until she took a deep breath and spoke again.

"I was so scared of death, sure that it must be a terrible place,--a lonely, dark nothingness after the souls were hushed. I'd been taught it was the start of a new life, one that would never end. But I wasn't sure about that. Too many unanswered questions filled my mind. Did life halt when their pleadings silenced? Was death nothing but a black void, or a never-ending sleep? I just didn't know enough to have any answers."

"You do now?" He'd always hoped for Elizabeth's soul that there was more after this life.

"Faith is a strange thing, Derek. If you ask for strength, God gives it to you. He's like this great big, beautiful gift-wrapped package. But if you want the gift, you have to take the whole package. You can't pick and choose what parts you want to accept."

"Is it really that simple, Tabatha?"

"It is for me." She paused. "Is there something else you want to know?"

"Mary said something happened at your grandfather's funeral." He felt her whole body stiffen. "She didn't say what it was. If you don't want to talk about this, it's okay."

"No. I'll tell you. I don't want any secrets between us. You need to know everything about me. I need to know you can accept me as I am. No matter what that is."

"I already do. I don't need to know any more than I know now."

Tabatha closed her eyes and let that day return like an old black and white movie.

~

"Get up and get dressed. It's time to go to the funeral." Carla poked her finger painfully into Tabatha's shoulder. "Don't play games with me. I know you're not asleep." She sat on the edge of the bed and shoved a tangle of hair out of Tabatha's eyes. "I expect you to be dressed and downstairs in ten minutes. I don't want no sniveling brat, either. Wipe away those tears."

"Yes, ma'am." Tabatha rose and walked to the bathroom. Seven minutes later she stood by the door while Carla appraised her appearance.

"Can't you do something with that stringy hair? And did you sleep in that dress?"

Heat of embarrassment rushed up Tabatha's face. She ran her hand over the faded black cotton dress, trying to smooth nonexistent wrinkles.

Her mother released a huff of breath between her cherry-red lips. "You'll have to do. We don't have time for you to change now."

The drive through New Orleans to Greenwood Cemetery didn't take long. Carla rolled her dark eyes when mourners tried to express their sorrow. Tabatha sat on a hard metal chair, legs crossed at the ankles and hands folded in her lap, trying to escape her mother's scrutiny. She kept her eyes downcast, never showing any sign of hearing an unknown soul talking to her from within a crypt a few feet away.

Nyssa hugged Tabatha tightly. "Everything will be all right, baby. Don't cry."

"Get away from my daughter, voodoo witch."

Tabatha cringed at the hurtful words Carla spewed toward her only friend. Nyssa had been there when she needed comfort or someone to talk to and had patiently explained the strange power that enabled Tabatha to hear voices no one else heard. It became a daily lesson to learn how to keep it under control until she was old enough to understand the magic born to her and its dangers.

Carla put her face so close to Tabatha's she nearly tumbled backward. "What the hell are you daydreaming about? Don't you embarrass me, Tabatha Gray. You keep your mouth shut and pretend to be decent."

"Yes, ma'am," she whispered and pulled in a fortifying breath to calm her anger.

Her mother seized Tabatha's arm in a painful grip. "What did you say? Are you back-talking me?"

She swallowed hard. "No, ma'am. I said I'd be quiet."

"You'd better well, or you'll pay."

Tabatha gritted her teeth and tried to diminish dangerous powers building within her. She brought her eyes up to look at her mother. Wind sent long tendrils of hair spiraling around her head, resembling black snakes rising to strike any who dared come too near. Carla's red painted lips were turned down in a disapproving grimace. Her gray eyes were rimmed in black and green, giving her the look of an enchantress from one of Tabatha's fairytale books. Carla's was the face of pure hatred staring back at her.

"She has such beautiful eyes," a bystander said and smiled at Tabatha.

"Cursed with her father's eyes is more like it," her mother spat and turned to the gathering crowd. "Now that the old man is gone, I'm sending her to a boarding school in New York."

Tabatha's heart thudded painfully against her ribs and tears stung her eyes. She couldn't believe what she'd heard and turned to listen more closely.

"I can't have her underfoot anymore. I have a life and she isn't part of it."

Tabatha jumped from her chair, ran to her mother's side and grasped at Carla's red silk skirt. "No, Mommy. Don't send me away. I'll be good. Please. I want to stay here."

Carla's eyes narrowed. "I told you to sit still and be quiet. You can't even do something as simple as that." She shoved Tabatha away with one hand while calmly smoothing wrinkles from her skirt with the other. "You are your father's daughter," she said as if it were an insult. She took long angry strides toward the casket holding Raoul Gray's remains. "I hope you rot in hell, you old bastard. You can't protect her now. And you can't keep me from my money."

Grandpa Raoul's lawyer, Dan Langton, stood beside her. "The reading of the will is tomorrow, Carla. You might be surprised what the 'old bastard' left to whom."

She swirled around, facing the man no older than herself. "What will?" The second word escaped in a low growl of anger.

A slow grin of satisfaction lifted Langton's lips. "He left everything to Tabatha except the caretaker's house." He turned and nodded a greeting to Nyssa. "You can live there for as long as you desire, and I'm to see to it that your salary and utilities are paid."

"I'm Tabatha's mother. She's just a child. I'll have control of the money."

Langton shook his head in a slow glide from side to side. "It's in a trust until she turns eighteen. You cannot touch it. Only the executor can decide how the money is spent."

"Whom did the old man give this power to?"

"I'm not at liberty to divulge that, but I can assure you, Carla, it's not you."

Carla spun around facing the crowd. "Ten years I put up with his son. Ten years! Then he up and dies on me, leaving me with this devil child. I earned that money. All of it. It's mine!" She looked around wildly, her angry gaze finally settling on Tabatha and Nyssa. "You!" she hissed. "Why should you have any of it? What have you ever done to earn it? They'll know what you are! I'll tell them! Everyone will know." She rushed forward.

Nyssa stepped closer to Tabatha, pulling her into her arms. "Get away from her!"

Nearby men restrained Carla, but she continued to scream and claw at the air. "I'll kill you!"

"It's okay, baby," Nyssa cooed. "She can't hurt you."

A rush of icy air swept up Tabatha's back. *"Be careful, Tabatha,"* Raoul's voice warned. *"She rid herself of your father and now me. She will not stop until she has it all."*

She twisted herself out of the old woman's arms, whipping around to face her mother. "You killed him!" Hurt, fear, and rage built one on top of the other, each emotion stronger than the last, making Tabatha feel like a pressure cooker about to explode. "No one would listen. I tried to tell them you killed Daddy. Now you've killed Paw-Paw."

Carla wrenched one arm free, and the force of her slap sent Tabatha to the ground. A wail of unbridled fury roared though Tabatha's clenched teeth as her eyes slowly rose to meet her mother's.

Carla struggled to free herself from tight grips holding her arms again. Her howls of anger quickly turned to choked and gargled moans of pain and fear. Her body stiffened and trembled with violent spasms. The crowd gasped as Raoul's casket began to shake, nearly tumbling from its stand.

"Tabatha," Nyssa shouted, "no!"

She spun around coming face to face with Nyssa, then let the power go. Carla fell limp.

Tabatha's rage slowly subsided and Raoul's casket stilled. A sorrowful cry escaped her throat. Mourners' faces filled with horror as they stared at her. She closed her eyes, wet with shameful tears. Only when she heard her grandfather's voice did she look up again.

"You must learn to control the magic, or evil will claim it and control you."

~

Tabatha gradually let go of the past and turned to face Derek. "Do you see why I wanted to tell you? This thing, this magic I have inside me can be evil. I've fought against it, nearly mastered it. Rhonda came to me needing my help. Then you and the children. I see now, that it can be used for good; but Derek, like sanity and insanity, evil and good is divided by a thin line. I fear what I'll become if I ever cross over that line. I could lose you forever. I could lose me."

He pulled her into his arms. "There's no evil in you, Tabatha."

She brushed her lips over his, then across his face to his ear. "Sometimes it's easier to be alone, but it's never better. I've been waiting all my life to find you. And you don't want me. What am I to do?"

Derek hesitated for a long moment. She ran a soft trail down his arm with her fingertips, taking his hand and with gentle persuasion, guided it to her breast.

This time he didn't hesitate.

Seventeen

Derek woke before sunrise to find himself in a strange bed with Tabatha in his arms. The night before came rushing back in a flood of memories. The warmth of her touch on his body, the sound of her voice, the smell of her skin once again filled his senses.

He brushed a lock of hair away from her face and marveled at her beauty. "Why, Tabatha? You could have anyone you want. Why me?"

Tabatha stirred against him, her fingertips trailing over his chest, and her breath brushed against his neck. "Because we were meant to be together. I knew it when I felt your presence in the cemetery that night. I knew it before I saw your face."

He released his pent up emotions in a rush of breath. "I don't know how this can work. I'm a cop, Tabatha. Always have been, always will be. I've seen what the job does to relationships. Their women worry about them, nag them to quit. Cops get killed every day."

She lifted her head off his shoulder and smiled. "I'll just raise you from the dead." She giggled and turned to look at the clock. "Damn, Derek, it's four in the morning."

He drew himself to a sitting position. "Where's the john?"

Tabatha pointed to a door in the corner of the room. "It's only a half bath. If you're looking for a shower, it's down the hall on the right."

"This will do." Derek pulled on his briefs before making his way to the bathroom, shutting the door behind him. He turned on the light and frowned at his reflection in the mirror over the sink. "What the hell are you doing, Bainbridge? She's just a kid. You can't do this. An affair with Tabatha is out of the question." He'd tried to go on after Elizabeth's murder, but he was a failure at relationships. He glanced back at his reflection in the mirror and shook his head. "It's too late and you know it. She's got you by the balls." He chuckled at his choice of words. He relieved himself, flushed the toilet and washed his hands, giving himself one more look. "Stupid son-of-a-bitch."

He walked toward the bed, glancing out the window when he heard a car screech to a halt on the street below.

Tabatha screamed his name and dove toward him. She hit him with a full body slam as a bullet blew out a window and lodged in the ceiling, spraying them with plaster and glass.

He landed with a thud, Tabatha on top of him. He fought to regain the breath knocked from his lungs. The world slowed to an easy spin, sounds of shouting drifted from the hallway, followed by the door swinging open with a crash.

"What's going on here? Tabatha, you little tramp, get some clothes on!" Carla's expression contorted with shock and confusion. She stumbled a few steps away from them. "Wait." She placed her hand on her forehead, her face drained of all color. "No. You're not supposed to be in here. Where are that girl and her son?"

"I gave her Grandfather's suite." Fear and suspicion twisted Tabatha's gut. "Why, Mother?"

Carla shook her head as if trying to gather her thoughts before speaking. "Tabatha isn't supposed to be with you, Derek. Frank said. . . ."

"Mother, what have you done? What are you mixed up in?"

Carla's eyes filled with red-hot hatred, her mouth forming a hard line. "Whore! I want you and the rest of this trash out of my house. I don't want you here."

Tabatha stood, pulled her robe from the foot of the bed and slipped it on. "Mother, I'm going nowhere. This is my home. I own this house. My friends can stay as long as they please. If anyone's going to leave, it'll be you. I'll buy you another house, something smaller and easier to take care of if you'd like."

"I'm not the one leaving. That's the end of this conversation."

"No, Mother, it isn't. We are staying. You're the one who has to make a decision."

Derek raised his hand. "Hold on. Mrs. Gray, what did you mean, she wasn't supposed to be here? What do you know about this?"

Carla ran her tongue over her bottom lip. "I'm going back to my room. I'll not be treated like this."

"You won't like the holding cell downtown, ma'am. You really need to answer my questions."

She grasped her throat. "You wouldn't. You can't. I--"

"I would, I can, and I will."

Tabatha watched Derek's face turn hard as stone and his brown eyes darkened to near black. "Derek?"

"Not now, Tabatha. Mrs. Gray?"

"They want that girl." Her eyes darted from Derek to Tabatha. She swallowed several times before speaking again. "All I did was tell them what bedroom she was in. They said they'd kill all of us if they had to." She raised her chin in the air, glaring down her nose at Tabatha. "You see what you've brought down on us? You and your demon friends? I don't want you here. Why won't you leave me alone?" Carla twisted the sash of her robe into a tight knot and mumbled incoherently.

Police sirens neared. Derek quickly pulled on his pants and shirt and ran his fingers through his hair. "I'll meet them downstairs. You two put this off until later. The cops don't care about your personal problems." He fixed Carla with a scowl of anger. "I'm not finished talking to you. Do you realize Tabatha could have been killed?"

"But she wasn't, was she? Why is that, Tabatha? Magic?" Carla scoffed. "Evil. Evil magic. Just like them. I should have taken care of you before you were born." She glared at Derek. "Has she told you about her curse? Do you want to be with a witch? She'll pull you down to Hell with her, Derek. Even I would make you a better wife." A strange smile lifted her lips.

He laughed before he could stop his reaction. "Mrs. Gray, that wouldn't have happened even if I'd never met Tabatha."

Carla's smile vanished as she turned to leave. "Oh, I don't want you. It's just that Frank said you're only using Tabatha. You're still in love with a dead woman. But Tabatha already has a spell on you. You just don't realize it."

"Mother."

Carla stopped with her back to Tabatha.

"What's it to be? New house or accept that I'm not leaving? Your choice."

"This is *my* home. It's mine." She stomped her foot like a spoiled child. "You cannot take it from me. I'll kill you before I let that happen."

The look she gave Tabatha caused a shiver of dread to run down Derek's spine. Carla hurried down the hallway, slamming the door to her bedroom behind her.

Derek draped his arms around Tabatha's shoulders. "I have to go downstairs. Are you going to be okay?"

"I'm fine. I grew up with her outbursts. We haven't seen the worst from her yet. I fear we will, though." She stepped away and smiled, but he saw the tears in her eyes.

He kissed her softly. "We'll face it when it comes. Together."

"Together." She grasped his arm as he walked away. "Twenty-nine," she said.

"Twenty-nine?"

"I'm twenty-nine years old. Not a kid."

He trailed his fingertips over her cheek. "We'll deal with that, too. Get dressed and meet me downstairs. They'll want to talk to all of us."

"Derek?"

"Yeah?"

"You might want to zip up."

Bobbie and Rhonda ran into her room as Derek left.

"What happened, Tabatha? What was that explosion?" Rhonda asked.

Tabatha pointed to the ceiling above the window, noticing how her hands shook.

"Oh, my," Rhonda said in a tiny voice. "That's a bullet hole. A big one at that. What kind of gun makes that kind of crater?"

Bobbie's voice trembled with her reply. "Some kind of rifle. A 30.6, maybe. Looks like someone's been hunting for bear."

"Okay, I'm ready." Tabatha tried to calm her nerves. "Derek said the police would want to talk to us. Just tell the truth; you were sleeping and don't know anything."

Bobbie shook her head. "I wasn't asleep. I saw the car. It was the same Caddy that was at the cemetery."

Tabatha thought for a few seconds. "No. You were asleep and saw nothing. We don't know which cops are helping Phelps and it's best we keep this to ourselves until we do."

Bobbie and Rhonda agreed.

"Where's Shane?" Tabatha asked.

Rhonda smiled. "He's still sleeping. It takes more than a mere gunshot to wake that boy. I think an atom bomb could go off and he'd sleep through it."

Tabatha noticed the corners of her mouth quiver. "It's going to be all right. Just stick to your story. You didn't see a thing. And look scared."

Rhonda shrugged her shoulders. "Won't be hard for me. I didn't see anything, and I'm terrified."

Bobbie took a few deep breaths. "I'm ready if you are."

Tabatha, Rhonda and Bobbie entered the great room as Derek opened the door and greeted the men.

"Come on in," Derek said, stepping away from the doorway, letting two officers pass.

"What are you doing here, Detective Bainbridge?" one officer asked.

"Detective Bainbridge is here because I invited him. Do you have a problem with that?" Tabatha glared at the cop, daring him to say anything.

The blond-haired officer cleared his throat and shook his head. "No, ma'am. I just wasn't expecting it." He cleared his throat again. "Now, someone want to tell us what happened here? How about you, Detective?"

He shrugged. "Someone shot out our bedroom window."

"Guess that's why you're bleeding," the other cop noted.

Tabatha and Derek glanced at each other.

"Derek?" Tabatha's voice shook.

"It's both of us," Derek said, guiding her to a nearby chair. "Let me see. Your robe is all bloody."

"It's just small cuts. Must have been when the window splintered. A few shards hit me. Where are you cut?"

"My right arm. Nothing serious."

"Any idea who would want to harm you or Detective Bainbridge, Miss? I'm sorry, what is your name?" the blond officer asked.

Frank walked through the doorway and answered his question. "Her name's Tabatha Gray, Officer Wayne. Evening, Officer Dillon."

Wayne turned to acknowledge Frank. "Detective Panner."

Frank faced Derek, mouth turned down in a hard frown. "What are you doing here, Bainbridge?"

"Why do you care why Derek is here, when you should be trying to find out who shot at us?" Tabatha jumped from the chair, putting her face so close to Frank's she could smell stale cigarette smoke on his breath. "I know you wanted to pair Derek up with some cop's whore, but we have other plans. Live with it."

He smiled. "Let's see if you can live with it, witch."

It appeared to Tabatha that Frank leaped up then backward, but she quickly realized he was dangling from his shirt collar which was twisted in Derek's fists. "Did you just threaten her?"

Frank struggled to free himself as he demanded, "Let me go, damn it. You don't know what you're doing. She's not a normal person. She's a witch. She's evil."

Derek glanced at Officers Wayne and Dillon. "Do you have need of a homicide detective in this case, officers?"

"Anyone dead?" Dillon glanced from one to the other. "Nope. Don't see a stiff."

"Go away, Frank. You're not needed." Derek stood him on his feet and pointed toward the door.

"I can't believe you'd give up more than twenty years of friendship over this slut."

Derek eyes turned cold and when he spoke his voice held an icy calm. "I've warned you once . . . one more word against Tabatha and you won't be leaving on your own power."

Tabatha's stomach tightened at Frank's glare. His mouth lifted in a grin. She returned his smile, conjured enough power to lift him from his feet and sent him flying out the door.

"Shit!" Officer Dillon said.

Officer Wayne scratched his head. "What the hell did he trip over?"

Derek shrugged.

Wayne chuckled. "I'll make a report, but you've got to come in today and file your statements. Did anyone see who shot at the house?"

Derek shook his head. "Wasn't time. Everyone was in bed. By the time Tabatha and I got to the window they were gone." He turned to Bobbie and Rhonda. "Did you two happen to see anything?"

They shook their heads.

"We'll have a look around the property," Officer Dillon said.

Derek nodded and ran his hands over his face. "The sun's going to rise soon and I'm willing to bet none of us are going to get any more sleep."

"What's going on here?" Bertha's voice bellowed from the doorway.

Every eye shot toward the black woman staring back at them.

Derek grumbled under his breath. "Bertha, one of these days you're going to give me a heart attack."

Bertha rested her fists firmly on her ample hips. "Is anyone going to answer me?"

Bobbie moved front and forward. "Someone shot out Tabatha's bedroom window. The cops are here to check it out, but they were just about to leave."

"Baby girl, you're bleeding; you, too, Mr. Derek. Get on into the kitchen. I'll bandage you up and fix breakfast. You officers look hungry."

"No, ma'am. We need to be going," Wayne said.

Bertha crossed her arms under her breasts and glared down her nose at them.

Tabatha tightened the sash around her housecoat. "Don't even bother to argue. When she says go, you go, so you might as well wash your hands and get ready for breakfast. After you eat, you can take a look around."

They filed into the kitchen and sat around the table. All heads turned when Carla came to the doorway and stomped her foot. "No. I won't have it. No more people moving into my house."

Eighteen

Derek walked officers Wayne and Dillon to their patrol car, chatting with the usual ease of one cop to another. "Ever been on a call like this before?"

Dillon smiled. "No, sir, I haven't. That's some girl you have, Detective. Does she have a sister?"

Wayne punched him on the arm. "Boy, have some respect."

"Didn't mean no disrespect, Detective."

"None taken, Dillon. And, no. No sisters. I don't know if the world could take more than one Tabatha Gray."

Dillon ran a keen gaze over the house. "If you'd like, we can run by here a few times a night during our rounds. Keep an eye on the place."

Derek batted the idea about in his mind. How much should he tell them? "How long have you been on the force?"

"Dillon is a rookie, less than one year. Me, I've been a cop for three years."

"You boys clean?" Derek asked, knowing they would understand his meaning.

Dillon's face showed his resentment. "Hell, yes, I'm clean. I became a cop to fight crime, not become part of the problem."

Derek nodded, giving his attention to Wayne.

Wayne returned Derek's hard stare, his face stoic but open. He searched Derek's face intently. "Detective, I don't know why you're asking, but I'm clean as they come. What's going on? Are you in trouble?"

"This is the second time Tabatha and I have been shot at. The first time we didn't report it, for reasons of our own. You boys ever hear of the Guardians?"

Wayne's eyes flashed angrily. "Man, if you're one of them, I don't want anything to do with you. And if you got them on your ass, you're in deep shit. No one knows for sure who they are, but everyone knows you don't want to piss them off."

"Do you know their convictions? Their agenda?"

Wayne and Dillon glanced at each other before Wayne answered. "Killing."

Derek nodded. "If the Guardians have reason to believe you're different, they view you as expendable."

Dillon rubbed his chin. "What do you mean by different?"

Derek ran a glut of explanations over in his mind but wasn't sure which one to use. "Remember the Salem Witch Trials?"

They nodded.

"The Guardians have the same mentality. If they believe you dabble in the arts, so to speak, you're given the death sentence. They set themselves up as judge, jury and executioner."

"Shit," Dillon said under his breath. "They think you're a warlock?"

"No. They think my girl is a witch."

"Tabatha? Hell, that girl doesn't have a mean bone in her body," Dillon said.

"It's her hair and eyes. She looks a bit different, so to them, she is different." Wayne hiked his gun belt higher on his hips and shifted his weight to his other foot. "What is it you want us to do, Detective?"

"Call me if you see anything out of place or anyone hanging around. I expect what I've said will remain between us."

"Of course." Wayne nodded.

Dillon copied his partner's actions and hiked his gun belt higher. "I have no problem with that."

"Wayne, you're looking to move up in the department, aren't you?"

"Yes. Why?"

"You two stick with me on this and I'll make sure everyone hears good reports about you."

Dillon puffed up his chest. "You can count on us, Detective, but not because we want a leg up. This whole thing is wrong. Just let us know if or when you need us. We're your men."

"You boys have first names?"

"Travis Dillon."

"Hal Wayne."

"Derek Bainbridge." He shook their hands before pulling two business cards out of his wallet. "My home, cell and office numbers are on these. Use your first names, no last names. We've been told the Guardians have one or more cops on the payroll. Am I getting across to you?"

Travis gasped.

"How do you know we're not with the Guardians?" Hal asked.

Derek remembered the flash of anger at the questioning of his honesty. "Instinct."

Travis hooked his thumb toward a crowd gathering across the street from them. "Want us to talk to them? See if they saw anything."

Derek ran his hands over his face. "Yeah. It won't look right if I do it."

~

An hour later Derek watched them drive away, hoping his gut reaction was correct and that he'd done the right thing. He scanned the neighborhood. Several groups of people still huddled in clusters, pointing, staring, and whispering behind their hands. He'd started to walk away when a woman's voice rang out clearly, heavy with resentment.

"This is a nice neighborhood, mister. We don't want a whorehouse in it. Get your girls out of here."

He crossed the street and flashed his badge. "Ma'am, I can assure you this is not a whorehouse. But you can file a complaint if you think it necessary. First, though, I'd look up slander or defamation of character if I were you. My officers will want to question you fine folks further. Make yourselves available." When they quickly scattered, he pocketed his wallet and made his way to the backyard.

He checked the garage locks and windows, then studied the lay of the gardens. Tall shrubs separated the homes on St. Charles Avenue from the houses on Carondelet Street. He knelt, looking beneath lower limbs to find a cedar fence blocking any entry. His eyes once again strayed to the mound behind the garage. An old oak tree had made its home on the peak of the soil amid a thick mat of English ivy that draped itself down and across the gardens below. He ruffled through the groundcover, running his fingers along the surface of the hardened soil. Knotted tree roots wove in and out, tangled with the ivy's thinner but equally embedded root system. His eyes traveled over the mass, noticing it butted against the garage, forming the back wall of the structure.

"What you looking for?"

He turned to see Bertha standing in the doorway watching him. "You wouldn't know where the key to the garage is, would you?"

"Why, sure I do. Ain't nothing in this house I don't know where it is. Why you wanting it?"

"Just curious."

"Well, Mr. Derek, you know what they say about curiosity, don't you?"

"Yeah. It solves a lot of crimes." He smiled when she laughed. "Bertha, if we're going to be friends, can you drop the Mister? Derek will do."

"Whew. That's a relief. I thought you were going to ask me to call you detective."

"That's my job, not my name. Now, about that key."

"Okay. Okay. I'll get it for you. Tabatha went to shower and dress. You need to do the same, son. You look like a grizzly bear, all that hair on your face. You be needing a razor?"

"Yes, ma'am. You happen to have one around here?"

"Humph. Been more than one man lived in this house. I think I can come up with a razor and some fresh blades. Be right back with that key."

He returned his attention to the mound and walked its edge, end to end. "This isn't just a pile of dirt. I'd bet my life on that."

"Who the hell are you? Get away from there."

Derek turned to find himself face to face with a very angry woman pointing a very big gun.

Nineteen

Tabatha switched off her hair dryer and placed it on a shelf above the sink before pulling a t-shirt over her head and slipping on a pair of jeans. She let her mother's latest episode of *As Carla's World Turns* do a rerun through her thoughts. Carla's frustration over finding two more people making themselves at home around the kitchen table had been too much. She'd ranted. She'd shattered dishes. She'd stomped her feet. In short, she'd thrown an old fashioned tantrum. It had taken Derek and both officers to subdue Carla and convince her they were only there investigating the shooting, not moving in.

Carla had straightened her back, tipped her nose in the air and muttered, "Well, okay then. See to it you don't stretch it out any longer than absolutely necessary."

"Thank heavens Officers Dillon and Wayne have a sense of humor," Tabatha muttered.

The bathroom door burst open with a crash, frightening Tabatha so badly she stumbled backward and landed on the toilet. Bertha filled the empty doorway, breaths ragged and gasping.

"You scared the life out of me," Tabatha said. "What's wrong?"

"Lordy, baby girl, that crazy woman has Derek in the backyard with her dead husband's big ol' pistol aimed at his heart."

"Momma?" she said with disbelief.

"No. Nyssa. Nyssa is gonna shoot your man if you don't get your skinny butt out there and stop her!"

Tabatha ran past Bertha, never stopping or slowing until she'd exited the backdoor and maneuvered her way in front of Nyssa.

"What are you doing?" she asked as calmly as she could manage.

"Going to shoot a prowler," the older woman whispered, never taking her attention away from Derek.

"Nyssa, honey, that's no prowler. That is my friend, Derek." When Nyssa showed no sign of lowering her gun, Tabatha said, "*Detective* Derek Bainbridge."

Nyssa's eyes locked onto Tabatha. "You have a cop snooping around my place? Why?"

"No, Nyssa. Listen to me. He's looking around because there was a drive-by shooting. He wants to make sure everything is as it should be. No hiding places for bad guys." Tabatha glanced at Nyssa's hand. "You've got a gun aimed at me. Would you mind putting it away?"

Nyssa dropped her gaze to the gun then back to Tabatha's face. Slowly she lowered her arm to her side, dangling the weapon from her fingertips. "I don't want him around here."

Snatching the gun away from her, Derek jammed it under his waistband. "I'm beginning to think the only sane one among you is Bertha." He pointed his finger within inches of Nyssa's nose. "If it's legal, you'll get it back. If not. . . ." He shrugged.

Nyssa's reply came in an angry rumble. "That's my late husband's gun. You can't take it."

"Ma'am, you just pointed a loaded gun at a New Orleans Homicide Detective. I could do a lot worse than take it. Be grateful that I don't arrest you." He strode across the yard and into the house, slamming the door behind him.

Nyssa clenched her fists at her side. "I want it back. Do you hear me?"

With all of Nyssa's anger directed toward her, Tabatha swallowed hard and drew a greedy breath. In all the years she'd known Nyssa, Tabatha had never seen her so irate and couldn't understand the reasoning behind it. "I'll do what I can, but you screwed up, Nyssa. What were you thinking?"

"You're taking his side on this? I'm your friend. I was more of a mother to you than that woman who lives in m . . . your grandfather's house."

Tabatha caught the near misuse of 'my' when Nyssa referred to the house, but let it pass. "I'm not taking anyone's side. I'm saying you went a little overboard drawing a gun on someone before you knew what was what." She ran her hand down her friend's arm. "I'll do what I can to get your gun back. But you have to promise me to put it away, and be smarter about pulling it out next time."

Nyssa turned away and pulled a ring of keys out of her pocket. She entered the garage and slammed the door behind her.

Tabatha cupped her hands around her face and peeked through the window into the dark enclosure, trying to see what the old woman was up to. Nyssa was grabbing lawn chairs, old barbecue grills, lawnmowers, anything she could move, and stacking them against the back wall of the garage.

"Baby girl, she's been like this for a long time now. She won't let anyone in there," Bertha said. "I snuck in there one night, but I didn't see anything out of the ordinary."

"When did you do this? I thought you hadn't been back since I left."

Bertha rolled her eyes. "I couldn't leave your momma to fend for herself. I'd come once a week and make meals, put them in the freezer so all Miss Carla had to do was pop them in the microwave. Your momma ain't well, Tabatha. And I'm not talking about her mind. I don't know what's wrong, but she started looking worst for wear about a month ago." She wrapped her arm around Tabatha and forced her away from the building. "You ain't seen her in a long time. You see how she done lost a lot of weight and I don't think she sleeps good."

"I'll see to it she goes to the doctor."

"Good luck with that, baby girl. I've tried to get her to go for a while."

"Maybe she'll let me examine her." Tabatha ran her gaze over the house. "Why didn't you call me? Tell me about her health, the condition of the house, about her selling everything."

Bertha breathed in deeply, exhaled, and looked away. "She made me promise not to call you. She ain't been getting the checks, Tabatha. She thinks you cut her off."

"I didn't stop her checks. I'll call Mr. Langton. Find out what happened."

"She's been getting strange notes. I saw one of them on the back door one day." Bertha visually searched the yard as if expecting to find someone listening. "Someone wants to know about your magic, baby girl. They want to learn how to harness it. The note threatened if she didn't tell them what they wanted to know, they'd kill her."

"Derek and I are taking care of it, Bertha. I'll make sure Momma gets her money."

The sound of breaking glass and a string of profanities streamed from the kitchen. "Lordy, now what?" Bertha mumbled.

Tabatha glanced from the garage to the house. "What now indeed."

Twenty

Derek strode past Frank's desk to his own. At once he noticed the bare space where his crime scene photographs had been the day before. He hitched his eyes in Frank's direction. "What's going on here? Where are my snapshots?" Then he noticed his files were AWOL as well.

Frank shrugged. "Lieutenant said to send you in when you got here. I'm sure he'll tell you."

Frank's smug demeanor irked Derek, but he kept his expression neutral as he made his way to the office. He swung the door open with a little too much force causing it to slam against a chair behind it. "Where are my photographs? My files?"

Lieutenant Mason looked up from his paperwork, his green eyes bloodshot and fatigued. "Have a seat, Detective Bainbridge."

"You're not taking me off this case."

"Wasn't planning on it. The case is still yours for now, but you've got to find the killer quick. You know Selma was brought across the Mississippi state line. The governor got a call from the Feds. He's keeping them at bay for a few more days, but I wouldn't count on too many." Mason leaned back in his swivel chair, scrubbed his bald head with his hands, and sighed. "Another blond-haired girl has come up missing. Got the call around six this morning."

"Damn." Derek closed the office door and sat hard on the chair. "Name?"

"Missy Lynn Blythe."

"Age?"

"Eleven," the Lieutenant said, leaning forward. "The kid went out to get the newspaper. Just like that," he snapped his fingers, "Missy's gone. Parents are coming in at ten. Be ready."

Derek nodded solemnly then stood to leave.

Mason pulled his six-foot frame from his chair. "Bainbridge."

"Yeah?"

"You can have two men from this list. They've approved the overtime. I'm working on the go-ahead for three more. You're to work on nothing but this case. I want him caught."

"I'd rather pick my own men." Derek reached for the doorknob.

Pointing toward Derek's hand, Mason said, "What happened to you?"

Derek lifted his bandaged hand and shook his head. "Dropped a glass in the sink. Cut myself trying to clean it up."

"Stitches?"

"No, sir. Bandage was my girl's idea." He felt his lips lift in a half smile.

"Your girl? Well, well. It's about time. But don't let your mind wander. I want this bastard caught. Understand?"

"We're on the same page, Lieutenant."

Derek had taken two more steps toward the door when Mason spoke again. "Are you and Panner having problems? Jackman asked where you were and Panner damned near bit his head off."

"Let's just say he doesn't like my choice in women, and leave it at that."

"Still trying to hook you up with that Potts girl?"

Derek raised his eyebrows. "That will happen the day New Orleans gets snow in July."

Mason chuckled. "Within the hour I want to know who'll be working with you. Two for now. I'll try to get more reassigned in a few days. I'm going to get them in here for a meeting at nine-thirty. I'll tell Panner he's off the case. I can't spare both of you."

"He's gonna howl."

Mason shrugged. "Life's a bitch, then you become a cop."

"By the way. Where are my files and photos?"

"In conference room two. It's yours for the investigation. It's to be kept locked when you aren't in there. No one is to enter without you or me knowing about it. Make sure the men you choose can keep their mouths shut."

Derek nodded. "Do you know two street cops named Travis Dillon and Hal Wayne?"

"I know Hal, he's on the list. Comes from a long line of cops; father, grandfather, great-grandfather. Good man." He pursed his lips and furrowed his brow. "Isn't Dillon a rookie?"

"Yeah. But he comes across as eager to learn. Won't try to be the hero. I like the kid."

"He isn't on the list, but I'll okay it if you want him. Who else you want?"

Derek rubbed his chin. "I'll have to give that some thought."

Mason reached into his desk drawer, pulled out a notepad and pen and wrote down the names. He reached for his phone and punched in a number. "Sergeant, I need you to round up Officers Wayne and Dillon and send them to my office immediately."

"They're answering a call, but he'll have them come in as soon as they're free," Mason said as he replaced the receiver.

Derek closed the office door behind him and returned to his desk.

Frank leaned forward and smiled. "They took the case away from you, huh?"

Derek fought to keep a straight face. "No, not exactly. He's taking all my other cases away so I can concentrate on the voodoo case. The Feds are breathing down his neck."

"It's about time they let us loose with it."

"Panner," Mason yelled. "Come in here."

Frank's right eyebrow rose sharply. "What's up, partner?"

"Damned if I know."

After Frank walked away, Derek waited for the drama to begin. It didn't take long.

"No. I won't stand for it. That's my case as much as it's Bainbridge's. You can't take it away from me."

He heard the door shut and their shouts became muffled, albeit just as angry. Derek glanced across the bullpen toward the other detectives. All had stopped what they were doing to listen to what was going on in Mason's office. All but the rookie, Detective Jackman, who sat at his desk reading a folder, minding his own business. Dressed in a new black double-breasted suit, he looked uncomfortable and unsure of himself. As if feeling Derek's eyes on him, he looked up.

"Jackman, got a couple of minutes? I need to talk to you."

"Sure. What's up?" He walked over to Derek's desk, turned the suspect's chair around and straddled the seat, crossing his arms over the back of the chair.

"The lieutenant is putting me on the Voodoo Killer case full time. I need someone to take over my other cases. Can you handle it?"

"Well, yeah. But why did the lieutenant pick me? I've been a detective less than a year. What about Panner?"

"Panner won't be on the case." Derek turned back to the paperwork on his desk. "And the lieutenant didn't pick you, I did."

"Why?" he asked, straightening his suit. As if in afterthought, he ran his fingers through his blond hair.

"You think outside the box and don't mind bending the rules if it'll find the perp. Got a first name?"

"Troy."

Derek handed him a stack of folders. "Ask if you have any questions."

Troy cleared his throat. "I'll do you proud, Bainbridge."

"I know you will, or I'll have your butt in a sling." He softened his words with a smile.

"I have no doubt about that." Troy chuckled. "I heard another kid came up missing."

Derek slammed his fist on his desktop. "Where did you hear about that?"

To his credit Jackman didn't react to his outburst. "Uniforms were talking about it when I came in."

"The only talk I want is behind closed doors, with only our men. If you hear anyone else talking, make it clear it's to stop. If they give you any lip let me know. I don't want the press to hear a damn thing from anyone. Nosy bastards don't care about anything but getting a story, and they don't give a shit if they blow a case doing it."

Derek glanced up when he noticed Travis and Hal in the squad's doorway. "I need to talk to those guys. Can you make decent coffee?"

"Yeah, if I do say so myself."

"Conference room two. Make enough coffee for say . . . six or seven people. And stay in the back of the room. I want you to hear everything. If I'm allowed to have another detective, you'll be caught up with what's going on."

"You got it." Jackman jogged toward the stairway.

Detective John Karney strolled over to Derek's desk, slapping a folder against his thigh. Dressed in a brown mismatched suit, white shirt and a green tie stained with yesterday's lunch, Derek considered him a disgrace to the department. "What's the kid so excited about? Ran out of here like you told 'em he'd won the Power Ball."

Derek gritted his teeth to keep from telling the slob it was none of his affair, instead saying, "Running an errand for me."

Karney nodded. "All those kids are good for. Takes years to be a good homicide detective." He nodded as if agreeing with himself. "Anyway, tell Panner I gathered the information he wanted."

"What information is that?" Derek reached for the folder and read the label. Heat baked his face and blood rushed to his brain. The label read *Tabatha Gray*.

"I'll see to it he gets it, Karney." When Karney walked away, Derek flung the file into his top drawer and locked it away.

Twenty-one

Tabatha sat on the front porch watching the sunset paint the sky in bands of coral, red, and turquoise. The hum of traffic slowed as rush hour diminished. The Saint Charles streetcar rolled by, its clang and low rumble making her feel at home. Tabatha had missed New Orleans and especially this neighborhood. It was steeped in the sounds of children playing, dogs barking with joy, welcoming their families return--the sounds of normal people with normal lives. She envied their normalcy.

She steeled herself for what she knew was to come. "Mother, I know you're there."

Carla appeared at the corner of the wraparound porch and came to stand behind Tabatha. "Bertha said you wanted to speak with me. Before you start, I'm not moving out. This is my home."

"I'm not kicking you out. All I'm asking is that you treat my friends and me with respect. They've done nothing to you and are doing no harm staying here." She glanced up at Carla, but the anger and contempt in her mother's face made her heart twist with regret, and she turned away.

"Why did you have to come back, Tabatha?"

"I don't know." She swallowed hard. Sadness tightened her throat. "I wanted to make things right between us, but I know that's not possible. I think most of all, I just wanted to come home."

"Why did you tell Bertha you wanted to talk, instead of coming to me? Am I not worth that much effort?"

Tabatha gritted her teeth. "I didn't tell her I wanted to talk to you. I think she's trying to play peacemaker. Do you realize she's not been paid since I left? The meals Bertha made for you all these years, she paid for. But you treat her like a common servant. That's going to stop. Bertha is my friend. From now on you'll eat at the table with everyone else or do without. Maybe if you'd get to know my friends, you'd like them."

Carla snorted.

Tabatha glanced over her shoulder. "That was ladylike."

"It's hot out here. Will there be anything else?" Carla asked.

"I'll let you know when we're finished. Now, let's talk about Derek."

"What about him?"

"Did you actually believe you and he would be a couple?" Tabatha held her breath.

Carla released a cross between a sigh and a growl. "No. Frank and Mary asked me to keep him away from you. They don't want their friend mixed up with someone who practices voodoo."

"I don't practice voodoo. Who told them I did, Momma?" She glanced back and was surprised to see a hint of shame on her mother's face.

Tabatha changed the subject. "Bertha told me about the notes. The Guardians are doing the same thing to Rhonda. Said they would kill her son if she didn't do what they wanted. These people are true evil, Momma. Not me."

"What about that other girl? What's her problem?"

"What girl, mother?"

"That dark one."

"Her name is Bobbie and I worked with her at the hospital in New York. She received letters about people in her clan being murdered and then her brother was killed, and she had to bring him home." Tabatha massaged the back of her neck, trying to soothe the tension. "We don't know if the Guardians are responsible for her brother's death, but we're sure they are responsible for the others."

Tabatha stretched her back and rolled her shoulders. "Momma, I've inherited the Gray legacy. There isn't a damned thing I can do about it. I've spent my life fighting it and it hasn't done one whit of good. Now, I've accepted that it has a use for good, but I'm also aware it can be evil. I promise you, I didn't come home thinking I'd become a professional necromancer."

"Is that all? Anything else you want to unload from your conscience?"

Tabatha's back stiffened. Her heart raced with anger-fed adrenaline. She wanted to tell her mother she was being a bitch, but instead she said, "When did you get your last check?" She heard Carla's sharp intake of breath and the tense atmosphere became thicker with the strain.

"You should know," Carla spat.

"No. I don't. I had no idea you weren't getting them." Tabatha patted the step beside her. "Sit. My neck is killing me."

Carla sat, back stiff, jaw stubbornly set, teeth gritted.

"The best way for me to find out what happened is to know when your checks stopped."

"More than a year ago," Carla said flatly.

"For the love of God, Mother. Why didn't you call me or at least write?"

"I called that lawyer of yours."

"Dan Langton?"

She nodded. "He never had time for me. Said I wasn't going to pull that stunt on him, and he wasn't going to give me one more dime than I was allowed." She turned her face away. "I wasn't going to beg for your chump change handouts."

"Chump change?" Tabatha resisted the urge to grasp Carla by the shoulders and shake her. "You get more in two months than some people make in a year. What did you spend it on? You live here free. Mr. Langton pays the utility bills. Bertha was supplying your food. Then I come home to find our furniture gone. All the things Paw-Paw treasured. What would have been next? His bedroom? Or maybe mine? I'd venture a bet everything's intact in your suite."

Carla darted from the steps and ran toward the front door. "Stay out of my room. It's all I have left that you haven't taken control of. Leave me alone. It's mine. Stay out!"

The sharp slamming of the door gave a feeling of finality to their mother-daughter talk.

"Well, that went well," Tabatha sighed.

~

As Derek pulled into the drive, he saw Tabatha sitting on the top step of the porch. His heart thudded against his ribs and his mood worsened. *Someone shot at her from a passing car, and only this morning someone shot out her bedroom window, but she thinks nothing of being out in the open? She might as well send out a written invitation. Shoot me.*

He slammed the car door and stormed toward her.

"What's wrong?"

"What are you thinking? You're not invincible, Tabatha. Bullets will kill you."

She glanced around the neighborhood then shrugged. "They won't try anything with so many people out and about. That's not what got you started. Bad day?"

"Another missing girl. Went out to get the newspaper for her dad, same as any other day, but this time she vanished." He slumped down beside her. "And I don't have any more of an idea who the killer is than I did when we found Mandy Green's body."

"She the first?"

He nodded.

Tabatha inhaled deeply several times. "What's the missing girl's name?"

He rubbed his face with both hands. "Missy Lynn Blythe."

Tabatha's body visibly relaxed and the world around them grew silent and still.

Derek stared at her for long moments, watching the changes in her expression and her complexion fading to white. "Tabatha?"

Her body trembled. Her breathing became labored. He grasped her shoulders and shook. "Tabatha, talk to me. What's wrong?"

When she faced him, her pupils had dilated to abnormal proportions with only a hint of blue surrounding them. "What?"

"You scared me, Tabatha. Don't ever do that again."

She tiled her head to the side. "I can't find her. She doesn't answer."

"What does that mean?"

"She's not dead."

Derek's frustration reached his tolerance level as he asked, "Who's not dead?"

She smiled. "Missy Lynn Blythe."

Chills ran from the top of his head to his toes. "How do you know?"

"I can't feel her presence when I call for her. She doesn't answer me."

"So. Does every ghost answer you?"

"I don't talk to ghosts, Derek. I speak to the lingering soul. When people die free of worry or regrets, they may not speak, but murder victims want to talk. They've been robbed of their normal life span. They have things they want to say. Most of the time, it has nothing to do with the murderer. They simply want to say goodbye to their loved ones."

"So you think Missy is still alive?"

"I'm sure of it." She paused. "Derek, I want to see the crime scene photos and any evidence you've gathered."

He ran his fingers through his hair then glanced down at this watch. "The lieutenant should be gone by now. I could probably get you into the task room. What do you expect to see?"

"I just know I need to see them."

Twenty-two

The conference room didn't come across as special in any way. Windows ran from wall to wall, facing the Broad Street entrance. Harsh fluorescent lighting made the brown folding tables stand out in sharp contrast to the stark white walls and off-white linoleum flooring.

Twenty-four metal chairs surrounded the table, nine of which had a file folder placed before them on the table. At the far end stood two bulletin boards; one filled with photographs of the children alive and happy, the second, photographs of their tortured bodies.

Tabatha leaned against the edge of the table and one by one, searched each girl's face. "They all look the same."

"Yeah. Blond-haired, blue-eyed. That's the only link between them we've found so far. They're from all over the New Orleans area, except for one. She's from Mississippi. Some come from wealthy families, others have next to nothing."

"Why would a woman kill children like this?"

"What makes you think it's a woman?"

Tabatha glanced toward the sound of the voice that was definitely not Derek's. She came face to face with a tall, bald, green-eyed man, his features stern but not unkind.

"Detective Bainbridge, would you please introduce us?" the man asked.

"Lieutenant Mason, Tabatha Gray."

"Dr. Tabatha Gray," she corrected.

Mason lifted his brow. "Doctor?"

"Psychiatrist."

He looked at Derek and raised his eyebrows in a high arch. "Ahhh, looking for a profile?"

"Yes, sir."

"Good idea. What did you come up with so far, Doctor?"

Tabatha returned her attention to the bulletin board and said a quick prayer for guidance. "You asked why I think it's a woman. I'll start there."

She pointed to each crime scene photograph. "Look at the side of the crypt where the killer wrote her message. It's been washed of mold and stains. Then notice the bottoms of each letter have been wiped clean to a neat edge. No running of the blood." Tabatha pointed to Mandy Green's head. "A man would take the hair, not the scalp." She moved her finger down to Mandy's torso. "The death circles carved in their stomachs are neat and again cleaned of blood. Detective Bainbridge informed me there was no sign of sexual abuse."

Mason nodded. "That's right."

"Okay, let's look at the wording on the crypt." She lifted one of the photographs and read. "Ogou La Flambo, Lieutenant of burning battlefields. Gorge with this blood. Grant me my revenge."

Tabatha turned to offer Mason a cryptic smile. "A man would never ask for help, not openly anyway." She pointed to the last word of the message. "A man gets even, a woman gets revenge."

Mason came to stand at her side. "Why take the eyes?"

Tabatha raised both hands palms up in front of her. "Anonymity. Makes her feel invisible, invincible, maybe even godlike. It's hard to second guess a twisted mind."

"Godlike?" Derek spoke for the first time since the lieutenant had arrived.

"Think about it. Can you see God? No. But you know he's there by his works." She paced to the windows and looked out at the traffic below. "Did she take the eyes or just remove them? And were they removed postmortem?"

"Selma Fortier's were left lying on a note, the others she took. Their eyes were removed before death." Derek reached for a folder and pulled out a paper, handing it to Tabatha.

She stared at the short, one line note. "This handwriting. . . ."

"What about it?" Derek asked, coming closer to glance at it.

"A woman's handwriting." A tug of recognition worried her conscience, but stayed too far away to grasp. "*She has to pay.*' Notice she says 'has', not 'had'. I think she's trying to kill the same person, over and over. For some reason I think the killer's afraid of the person she's trying to kill, so she chooses substitutes." Tabatha walked back to the photographs. "I'd say she's older. Someone who's worked hard all her life for what she has and wants to keep it."

Lieutenant Mason stirred, pulling her out of her thoughts. "Can you think of anything else?"

"Do you have any evidence from the scene?"

Derek shook his head. "The bodies had been scrubbed. Fingernails clean. Not a hair, not a speck of dirt other than that from the cemetery."

"The children's bottoms all have freezer burns," Mason added.

"The killer keeps them for a few days, then?"

"Three," Mason said.

Tabatha nodded. "So she usually kills them right away."

"We're not sure. It's hard to pinpoint the exact time of death when the body has been frozen. Little or no decomposition."

"Did any of the children's parents miss anything, like jewelry?"

Derek shook his head. "A couple of them had hair barrettes missing, but that's it. Each of the kids was found naked. No clothing left behind."

"Dr. Gray, maybe you should be careful," Mason said.

Tabatha's heart skipped a beat. "Why?"

"All these girls look like you."

She smiled. "All but one thing."

"What's that?"

"I'm a big girl. I can fight back."

Mason smiled. "Yes, ma'am. I bet you could. I don't have to remind you not to speak of this outside this room, do I?"

"No, sir, you don't. I want her caught as much as you do. There's something unspeakable about killing defenseless children. It's cowardly and unforgivable. I hope I was a little help to you."

"You have been, Dr. Gray. Thank you."

"Tabatha."

He smiled. "Tabatha it is. Now, if you wouldn't mind waiting outside the door, I'd like to have a few words with Detective Bainbridge."

"Don't mind at all. I'll wait for you by the car, Detective. Nice meeting you, Lieutenant Mason. I wish it could have been under more pleasant circumstances."

Tabatha pulled her purse onto her shoulder, walked out of the conference room, and didn't stop until she'd made it to the parking lot. She leaned against Derek's Blazer, closed her eyes and drew in a deep breath. She heard footsteps coming toward her and opened her eyes expecting to see Derek.

"Well, well. Isn't this just too damned easy?"

Twenty-Three

The blade of the hunting knife glinted in the streetlights. Slowly, Tabatha raised her gaze to the man standing at her side, his face hidden by a black satin mask. A halo embroidered with golden threads decorated the top and slanted holes cut in the material revealed menacing green eyes staring back at her.

"You're coming with me, witch." His voice held a low rumble of hatred.

Without thought she swiped at the mask and pulled it free. "Hello, Frank."

"It'll do you no good. You're not going to live long enough to tell anyone." He clutched her arm in a painful grip and pressed the tip of the blade to her throat. "Make a noise and I'll kill you where you stand. Come on."

She covered her forehead with her free hand as if she were about to faint, then connected her knee with his groin. He squealed like a frightened girl and sunk to the ground.

"I don't think going with you is quite what I had in mind, Frank."

"What's going on over there?" a uniform cop yelled from the station house steps. "You need help, ma'am?"

"I think I have everything under control, officer. Can you tell Detective Bainbridge I'd like to talk to him? He's inside."

The policeman hooked his thumb toward the door. "He's on his way out now. I'll send him right over."

Frank swore under his breath and quickly tossed the knife into the back of the Jeep parked behind Derek's Blazer. "Stay away from Derek, bitch. You're a walking corpse. Don't take him down with you."

"I'd save my energy for things like standing up straight if I were you."

"Just remember, if I don't get you, someone else will." He leaned against the wall. With a few deep breaths, he managed to paste a smile on his face.

Derek sidled up to Tabatha, twined his fingers with hers and looked at Frank. "What's going on? You're looking kind of flushed, buddy."

He shook his head. "Nothing. Came to look at some files and saw Tabatha standing out here. Not safe for a woman out alone these days, even on police property. Never know what could happen."

Tabatha chuckled. "Never know what could happen to a man who picks on the wrong woman, either."

"Was he harassing you, Tabatha?"

Her gaze drifted toward Frank's face and she saw defiance in his eyes. She smiled. "No more than a pesky mosquito. If he gets too close, I'll just swat him."

"I've been swatted by bigger and much better." He pulled himself away from the wall, wincing in pain. "Here kinda late, ain't you, Bainbridge? They find the kid?"

"No. Not yet. I was speaking with Mason about the case and the men who'll be working it with me."

"I wanted to talk to you about that again. You've got to get me back in. This is my case as much as it's yours. Insist that Mason put me back on. We're a team, Bainbridge."

"I can't insist anything, Frank. Mason said he couldn't afford to have both of us tied up on the Voodoo Killer."

"Did you tell him--?"

"Damn it, it's out of my hands."

Frank swung his fist, knocking Derek to the asphalt. Shaking his fist in Derek's face, he snarled, "Detective Bainbridge, the big hero. You're always hogging all the glory. It's my case, you son-of-a-bitch. I won't let you take it away from me."

Tabatha gasped and stumbled backward, stunned that a so-called friend would react so violently. As she righted herself, she noticed a folder on the front seat of the Jeep. She quickly averted her eyes to keep from attracting Frank's attention.

His attack didn't keep Derek down for long. He jumped up and moved toward Frank, fire in his eyes. "I've put up with your ego and bad temper all our lives. No more. Stay away from Tabatha. While you're at it, stay away from me. I've had enough."

Frank's back was to her, so Tabatha glanced at the folder again. An embossed, unconventional crucifix decorated the cover. Instead of the usual cross, Jesus hung with hands over head, nailed to a stake. Circling the crucifix, mother-of-pearl lettering read *Guardians Against Paranormal Sinners* and stood out in stark relief against the blood-red background.

Tabatha's breath caught. Disappointment in Frank flooded over her, then shame for jumping to conclusions. The folder could be evidence. He could be innocent of everything but bad judgment.

"Only the very best for you," Frank roared. "Elizabeth couldn't see past your charm. She would have been happier with me. But we both lost her, didn't we? I got over her and went on with my life. You play the long-suffering lover. I'm sick of it."

"Leave Elizabeth out of this. She warned me about you, Frank. Said you weren't the friend you pretended to be. I guess she was right."

Taking advantage of the commotion, Tabatha grabbed the folder and dropped it into her bag. She spotted Mason coming out of the building and started toward him, speaking over her shoulder to the arguing men. "You boys better call an end to this." Hoping to keep Mason's attention averted from Derek and Frank she yelled, "Lieutenant Mason, can I speak to you a moment?"

"A pretty woman can talk to me any time." He grinned. "What can I do for you?"

"I hope I didn't get Detective Bainbridge in trouble. I'd read about the case in the newspaper and mentioned it to him. I thought I could be of help. I wasn't thinking straight, I guess. I'm sure you have your own profiler. I didn't mean to step on any toes."

"Ma'am--"

"Tabatha," she said.

"Tabatha. I'm not going to turn down help. Bainbridge should have talked to me first, but I did tell him he had free rein over the case."

"Tabatha," Derek called. "Ready to go?"

She nodded. "Thank you again, Lieutenant. I hope you find your killer soon."

Mason walked at her side, continuing to talk. "Do you have any other ideas? Something that might give us more of a clue."

"I'll work on it tonight. Maybe I can come up with something else."

Frank's face twisted with rage. "You're letting her work the case? She's a goddamned witch, Lieutenant. She talks to the dead."

Mason glanced at Derek, raising one inquisitive eyebrow. "Like a medium?" He shook his head. "Frank, you need a vacation."

"No, I need you to give me my case back. I've been working on the Voodoo Killer since the beginning. It's mine."

Mason's expression hardened. "I dole out the cases around here. I. . . ."

Tabatha rolled her neck and closed her eyes, shutting out the argument. She relaxed, lowered her barriers and listened for Missy's voice, hoping she would find welcomed silence again. Tabatha clasped her hands over her ears and gasped. Missy's cry of sheer terror gripped at her soul.

"Tabatha?" She didn't know when Derek had moved close enough to cup her face with his hands. "What is it?"

She looked up at him, tears stinging her eyes. "She's killed her."

"Who killed--" Mason stopped mid-question. "What's she talking about?"

"Our Voodoo Killer has killed again," Derek said, his voice heavy with fatigue.

"What makes her think she's killed Missy?"

Derek shook his head slowly, his face a mask of resignation. "She doesn't think she's dead. She knows it."

Frank grabbed Mason's shirt, his face aglow with delight. "See, I told you. She's a witch. The dead talk to her."

Tabatha watched the lieutenant's knuckles turn white as he squeezed Frank's hands, dislodging them. "I don't give a damn if she grows fangs and sprouts batwings. If she can stop any more kids from being killed, I'll listen to anything she has to say. Go home, Frank." He returned his undivided attention to Tabatha. "Let's go back inside. I have a few more questions."

"I have a better idea." She inhaled several times, hoping to stop the quiver in her voice. "Why don't you come to the house? We can talk there without worrying about anyone eavesdropping." She glanced at Frank. "I have a lot to say and I don't want the world listening."

"Okay. I'll follow you over. But could we stop off for some burgers or something? I'm starving."

Derek grunted. "I wouldn't if I were you. Bertha would be fit-to-be-tied if you brought burgers into her kitchen."

"I'm sure there's a hot meal waiting for us." Tabatha tried to calm her shaking fingers as she retrieved her cell phone and dialed home. "Bertha, one more for dinner. We'll be home in about half an hour."

She paused, listening. "When?" Again a moment of silence surrounded them. "Damn. Is Shane there?" She sighed. "We'll be there in fifteen."

"What's wrong?" Derek asked as she disconnected.

"Rhonda left two hours ago, saying she'd be back in about thirty minutes. She's still not home."

"Shane?"

"Bertha has him."

Frank's chuckle drew their attention. But his humor was short-lived as Tabatha's fist cold-cocked him, knocking him to the ground. She shoved her foot against his throat.

"Where is she? Where do they have her? I swear, if they do anything to her, you'll be the first I come looking for."

"Fuck you."

Tabatha felt a gust of wind, then as if by magic Frank vanished from under her foot. When she looked around to find him, Mason had him by the neck, feet dangling off the ground.

"She asked you a perfectly polite question. I expect a perfectly polite answer. What's going on? Who has whom? And where?"

"Give me back my case," Frank croaked. His face grew bluer by the second.

Mason released him and stepped back.

Frank dropped to his knees, gasping for air. "I'll have your badge for this."

Mason looked over his shoulder at the officers standing by the door. "Detective Lewis, place Detective Panner under arrest. Charges will be attempted kidnapping and use of a deadly weapon, for starters."

Frank snorted. "You have no proof."

"Frank, Frank, Frank. As long as you've worked here, have you never noticed that my office window faces the street?" He reached down, picked up the black mask from the ground, and waved it in front of Panner.

Derek's face paled. "What happened, Tabatha? Why didn't you tell me?"

"I figured I could handle him on my own."

"Detective Bainbridge, you may want to get the weapon out of the Jeep. Looked like an eight-inch hunting knife. Am I right, Panner?"

"Go fuck yourself. I ain't saying nothing. And you," he pointed toward Tabatha, "you better keep your mouth shut if you want to see your friend alive again."

Detective Lewis trotted over from the base of the steps to where they stood. "Stand up, Panner. You're under arrest. You have the right to remain silent," Detective Lewis began.

Tabatha massaged her temples. "Let it go, Lieutenant."

Mason glared into Frank's eyes. "One last chance. Where are they holding the girl? If you know, tell us and this could go away."

"I'd be in more trouble if I told you." He glanced at Tabatha. "Thou shalt not suffer a witch to live." He shot his gaze to Derek. "Whosoever lieth with a beast shall surely be put to death."

Mason shook his head. "What the hell are you babbling about?"

Tabatha turned away, opening the car door. "Exodus chapter twenty-two, verses eighteen and nineteen." She got into Derek's Blazer and closed the door, shutting out their voices.

Leaning her head against the seat, she allowed Missy's voice to reach her once again. "Missy, my name is Tabatha. Do you know where you are, honey?"

No, she sobbed. *I'm so afraid.*

"Tell me what happened. Did you see who took you?"

I went to get Daddy's newspaper. A woman in a blue car stopped and asked if I knew where the Johnsons lived. I told her I didn't know. Then she opened the door and pulled me in. She put a rag on my face and I don't remember anything after that.

"Can you tell me what she looked like?"

She had black hair, but she had on a hat. She was real skinny.

"Did you see the color of her eyes, Missy?"

Brown. They were mean. She looked like she was mad at me. I didn't do anything, I swear.

Tabatha swallowed a sob. "I know, baby. None of this is your fault."

I woke up once. I was in the ground. I could see tree roots over me. It smelled like dirt and rotten meat. I heard someone talking real loud outside, but when I tried to yell, the woman put the rag on my face again.

"You said she had on a hat. Do you know what kind?"

Like boys wear all the time. My daddy has some, too.

"Baseball cap?"

I guess. Are you coming to bring me home? It's dark here. I'm scared.

"Yes, we're going to find you. Missy, don't be afraid. She can't hurt you anymore."

Promise?

"I promise."

Tabatha turned her face away when Derek slid onto the driver's seat and started the engine. "You all right?" he asked.

"She's skinny, black hair, brown eyes and drives a blue car." She drew a deep breath and faced him. "Missy said when she woke she was underground. What could that mean?"

"What exactly did she say?" Derek asked, shifting in his seat to look at her.

Tabatha repeated the child's words verbatim.

Derek seemed to sink into the seat with the release of a deep breath. "When we find her, do you think if you touched her like you did Selma Fortier, you could see what Missy saw?"

A cold chill ran down Tabatha's spine, remembering the fear and pain Selma experienced. The idea of going through that again terrified her.

Tabatha, are you still there?

She jumped at the voice's intrusion. "Yes, Missy, I'm still here."

Derek's head snapped back. "You're hearing her right now?"

Tabatha nodded. "Don't be frightened."

"I'm not." He took her hand in his. "Ask her to describe what she saw. Was there anything there? Was it dark?" He shook his head. "No, don't ask her that."

There are chairs, a desk, and a shelf with lots of big bottles. There's a light hanging from a wire, but it's not on now. It's dark. I'm afraid.

Tabatha swallowed the tears in her throat. "Missy, can you hear Detective Bainbridge?"

Yes.

The moisture evaporated instantly from Tabatha's mouth. "She can hear you, Derek. I've never known that to happen."

His Adam's apple bobbed. "I'm sorry, Missy. I didn't mean to scare you."

Is he going to help you find me?

"Can you hear her, Derek?"

He shook his head.

"Try, Derek. Relax, shut out the rest of the world. Shut me out. Listen for her."

"Tabatha, I'm not--"

She shot to her knees on the seat, drawing so close she could feel his breath on her face. "Concentrate. If she can hear you, you should be able to hear her.

Close your eyes." She ran her fingertips gently over his forehead to his temples. "Relax. Think only about Missy." Tabatha continued her caressing trail over his face.

"Missy, say hello to Derek."

Hello, Derek. Will you come get me?

Tabatha watched his face flush and his expression change to shock and disbelief.

A tapping on the car window jerked them both back to reality. Derek drew in a deep breath and opened his eyes. He rolled down the window. "What?"

"What's the hold up? I'm starving."

"We're leaving now. Just follow me there." He rolled up the window and put the car into gear.

"Derek?" Tabatha sat down and pulled the seatbelt across her chest.

"What?" His voice was a growl.

"Did you hear Missy?"

He was silent for a long moment. He ran his fingers through his hair. "Yes."

Twenty-four

Bertha sat at the kitchen table, her legs working off nervous energy in a jogging bounce from the balls of her feet. "Baby girl, if I'd known something like this would happen, I'd never have let Rhonda go out alone." She jumped from her chair and wiped away the tears streaming down her cheeks with the back of her hand.

Tabatha pulled her into the chair again and knelt down in front of her. "None of this is your fault. Rhonda knew it wasn't safe going out alone, but she did it anyway." Tabatha patted her knee. "We're going to find her. Don't worry."

"Oh, lordy. I almost forgot dinner. You kids sit down. I'll have it ready in a few minutes." Bertha stood then seemed to notice Mason for the first time. "Ain't you new? I don't remember meeting you before."

Tabatha smiled. "Lieutenant Mason, this is my friend Bertha. Bertha, this is Lieutenant Mason."

Bertha began to sob again. "Lieutenant, it's all my fault. I shoun'ta let her go."

Mason placed his hand on the black woman's shoulder. "Now, ma'am. It's no one's fault."

Derek leaned against the doorframe, staring out at the backyard. "Did she say where she was going?"

Bertha reached into her bra and produced an embroidered handkerchief, dabbed her eyes and blew her nose. "She got a phone call from her momma, I think. Was goin' to take Shane with her, but I wouldn't hear of it. He was taking his nap and you know how babies are when you wake them up before they get their nap out."

"Yes, ma'am, I do," Mason said. "I have eight brothers, all younger. Does anyone know her mother's phone number?"

They looked to Tabatha. She shook her head. "She didn't tell me, but I'm sure we can find it in the phonebook."

Derek moved away from the door, shutting it behind him. "Lieutenant, there are some things I'd like to show you. Rhonda's mother left behind journals, tapes and a home movie about the Guardians before she died. I think you'd find them interesting."

Mason held up his hand as if asking permission to speak. "I'm a bit confused. You say Rhonda's mother called, but then in the next breath say her mother died."

Tabatha answered. "Rhonda was adopted, but a few months ago she found her birth mother. That's what we mean when we mention her mother. Her adopted mom she calls Momma."

"Confusing, but I think I got it." Mason nodded once.

They heard the front door slam shut and rushed toward the foyer. Seconds later, Bobbie walked past them and flopped onto a chair. "Hell."

Bertha hurried to her side. "Did you find her? Did you find Rhonda?"

Bobbie shook her head. "Her mom said Rhonda's boss called. Said if she didn't come to work today, he was going to fire her. I went to the Coffee Joe's and her boss said it wasn't him who called. In fact, he'd given Rhonda three weeks vacation time she had coming to her. So the call was a set-up to get her out of the house."

Tabatha's heart sank. "Why would she go out alone like that? Why didn't she ask you to go with her? She knew it was dangerous."

"I'd say that's why she went alone." Bobbie glanced at Mason and held out her hand. "Hi. Bobbie Luckman."

He took her hand in his. "Lieutenant Mason."

She returned her attention to Derek. "I heard you telling this guy about Rhonda's things." She hooked her thumb toward Mason. "What about the film? Did you get it developed?"

Derek nodded. "I was just about to show them to the lieutenant."

Bobbie huffed. "Lieutenant, hell. We're all in this together. There's none of this show-to-one-person bullshit. Whip them out, big boy. There could be some hint as to where they took Rhonda."

Bertha stood, wiping her hands on her apron as she headed for the stove. "Supper's gonna burn if I don't get busy. I bet you kids are hungry."

"Ma'am, I'm so hungry, I could eat your shoe." Mason chuckled. "Now, what about these photos?"

"I want to ask you a question, first," Derek said, standing by the kitchen window staring out at the back yard again.

Tabatha came to his side. "What are you looking at out there?"

"What exactly does Nyssa do around here?" he asked.

"Mostly yard work." Tabatha glanced out the window and saw Nyssa pulling a garbage bag behind her before lifting it into the trunk of her car. "She tends the flower gardens, stuff like that. Why?"

"Does she take away trash or yard debris?"

"Sometimes. I'm not really sure what she does in that garage." Tabatha reached up, taking bowls out of the cabinet and carried them to the table. "She's probably cleaning up from trimming bushes or something."

Derek watched the older woman get in her car and drive away, making a mental note to check out the garage later. It was probably nothing, but no one was above being a suspect until they were cleared. "Lieutenant, do you know John Phelps?"

Mason frowned. "Yeah, I know him. He's a big-mouthed entrepreneur that likes to flaunt his money. I've heard talk he has political big boys in his pocket, but no one's been able to prove it. He looks clean, but I'm not so sure. Why?" The scowl on his face deepened. "You think Phelps is involved with Rhonda's disappearance?"

Tabatha's frustration mounted with every wasted moment of talking. "His son and a couple of his friends took a shot at me on Bourbon Street. I'm pretty sure Phelps was behind it and I'd be willing to bet he has Rhonda. He'll do anything to get her mother's stash. There's enough evidence to put a lot of people away for a long time."

Mason turned a chair around, straddled it and crossed his arms over the back. "Okay. I want the whole story. I'm getting bits and pieces, here and there. Start again at some semblance of a beginning."

"The beginning started a long time ago, Lieutenant," Tabatha said. "And right now we don't have time for me to tell it. Our friend is out there waiting for us to find her."

He raised his brow. "What about Missy?"

Bobbie stepped in front of him, planting her fists on her hips. "Who is Missy? Why should she come first?"

Tabatha sighed. "The killer took another little girl. She's dead."

"Well, I don't mean to sound apathetic here, but Missy is dead. Rhonda isn't." Bobbie glanced at Tabatha. "Is she?"

"No. Not yet."

"Then the living takes precedence over the dead." She returned to her chair and sat. "Now, let's see those pictures."

They gathered around as Derek laid out photographs one next to the other. "Look at the surroundings. See if you recognize anything. Maybe a landmark, or a room you've been in before."

Bertha tapped one photograph. "That's old man Finch's warehouse out on River Road. I think it's an architecture recovery company now. They go in and save mantels, gates and such when old homes are torn down."

Tabatha picked up the photograph and studied it. "This guy." She placed her finger on the man's image. "I've seen him before."

"Where?" Derek moved to her side.

She concentrated. A vision flashed in her mind of the man leaning against a building. It came and went before she could fully grasp it. She tried again. Sounds of tires screaming, gunshots, and yelling filled her head.

"He was on the corner that Saturday we were at Frank's. He saw the shooting."

"What shooting?" Mason asked.

Derek held his hand in front of Mason in stop-sign fashion. "Can you think of anything else, Tabatha?"

Tabatha leaned on the table with both hands, chin lowered to her chest. Memories twisted and righted themselves again. "They tossed the gun from the van's window. He snatched it up and put it in his waistband, then turned the corner and vanished."

Derek leaned closer. "Why didn't you tell me about this before?"

"I didn't remember it until now."

Mason looked from one to the other. "Will someone fill me in? What shooting?"

Bobbie shrugged. "Last Saturday Derek and Tabatha were at Panner's house. When they were about to leave there was a drive-by shooting. No one was hurt. No one saw anything that could help the cops find who did it. Did I miss anything, Tabatha?"

Tabatha shook her head. "No, not really."

"Detective Bainbridge, did you file a report?" Mason paused. "No, of course you didn't. Damn it, Bainbridge, one of these days I'm going to fire you."

"Not until I solve the Voodoo Killer case, I bet." Derek's tone held no disrespect or malice.

Just the facts, ma'am, Tabatha thought.

Mason rubbed his head and groaned. "There isn't enough here for me to get a search warrant. If they have your friend at that warehouse, I've got to tell a judge something besides I have a hunch."

"Screw a search warrant." Bobbie stood so quickly, her chair turned over. "I'm going to get Rhonda out of there. I can get in and look around without anyone seeing me."

"How do you plan on doing that?" Mason asked.

Bobbie's body slowly crumpled toward the floor as if her bones had turned to putty. Joints popped and became misshapen. Her skin changed from her usual cinnamon hue to gray-green, her eyes narrowed, her face blended with her neck, her neck into her body. Clothing fell away and she slithered toward Mason before pulling her new form to an upright position in front of him. Her tongue lashed out as if to taste him. Her eyes held a hypnotic stare with his.

Mason's pallor grayed. "Mother of God. What the hell? Shit!" He drew his gun, but his hand shook so badly the gun slipped from his grasp. His lips turned a frightening shade of blue and his eyes rolled into his head. A second later he crumpled to the floor.

A clatter of chairs scraping the floor and Bertha's shouts broke the stunned silence.

Bertha slid her arm under his shoulders. "Oh, lordy. You didn't give the poor boy a heart attack, did you?"

Bobbie's snake form slithered into her clothing. Her body thickened, her tail split and formed legs. Arms coiled from newly shaped shoulders. Bones popped as a human face sprang from the flattened head of the cobra.

"He'll be all right," Tabatha said, checking Mason's pulse.

Derek snorted. "Yeah. Guess we should've warned him about Miss Cobra's bag of tricks."

Mason groaned and opened his eyes. His eyes widened, wild with what Tabatha could only describe as terror. Slowly he began to regain some color. She gently touched his hand and whispered a soothing chant. His breathing slowed and the muscles in his body relaxed. Mason pulled in a deep breath, released it slowly and drew in another. He glanced around the room, before rubbing his face. "I told you I was hungry. Can't go without eating all day. I knew better."

Bertha patted his cheek. "Come on, son. You're gonna lie down, while I fill a big bowl with gumbo for you. You're gonna eat every bite. You hear me?" She glanced at Bobbie and shook her head. "Little girl, you do that in my kitchen again, I'll take a broom to you."

Mason helped them lift him from the floor. "What were we talking about? Oh. Oh yes. Rhonda. We were going to find your missing friend." He froze for a long moment, and if it were possible, his face paled even more, before his eyes shot to Bobbie.

She smiled and shrugged her shoulders. "Look, dude, I'm sorry I scared the shit out of you, but this is kind of an emergency. Talk just didn't seem the right way to explain how I could accomplish getting in and out of the warehouse without being caught."

He gave his head a severe shake. "No. It's lack of food. Blood sugar's too low."

Bobbie's eyebrows rose sharply. "Shall I show you again?"

Mason's hands flew out in front of him. "No. No, I've had enough for one night."

Tabatha stepped between them. "That's enough, Bobbie."

She shrugged. "Worked, didn't it?"

"Take him into the living room, Derek," Tabatha said. "He's better sitting up than lying down. Bertha, bring the gumbo."

Derek guided Mason through the hallway to the living room. Tabatha and Bobbie followed closely behind, and Bertha brought up the rear with a large mixing bowl filled to the rim.

Tabatha chuckled. "I hope you don't expect him to eat all of that."

"He's gonna eat all I can get down his gullet. Son, you scared the wits out of me, fainting like that."

"Ma'am, I did tell you I was hungry."

"My girls tell me they're hungry, but they don't make a point of it by keeling over."

Tabatha placed a TV table in front of him and gestured for Bobbie to follow her out of the room. As they returned to the kitchen she glanced back to make sure Derek wasn't following them.

"Now's our chance. Let's go find Rhonda." Tabatha grabbed her keys from a hook by the door, and they slipped out into the night. "Hope you don't mind being seen in my car. I haven't had a chance to get it repainted since someone used it as a notepad."

Bertha stood in the doorway and tossed Tabatha the keys to her junk-heap. "Take mine. I'll keep them busy. Now, hurry." She rushed back into the house.

"Maybe we should push it to the street first. Derek will hear the engine if we don't," Tabatha said.

She slid into the car and put it into neutral. She glanced to Bobbie leaning in the passenger side. "Ready?"

Bobbie nodded.

Tabatha stepped out and grasped the steering wheel. "Once we get it moving, jump in. The drive slants enough that we'll keep going once we get it rolling."

Tabatha took a deep breath and pushed. The Oldsmobile was slow to move at first, but once they cleared the flat section of the drive the car began a steady increase in speed. Tabatha jumped in. Bobbie soon did the same. Tabatha braked when they reached the end of the drive. Once she saw the street was clear of oncoming traffic, she popped it into park and turned the ignition. The engine roared to life.

Twenty-five

Tabatha drove down Saint Charles, turning right on Leak Avenue. A few minutes later, at the Jefferson Parish line, it became River Road. It had changed little since she was a girl. The levee to her left was all that protected the businesses and middle-class homes on the right that lined the narrow road, from the Mississippi River.

Her thoughts returned to peaceful days, horseback riding on the hillside while watching ships lumber past. The camaraderie between her and one particular horse had been strong. Strider would start to neigh as soon as Tabatha stepped from Bertha's car and took off for the stables. She'd spent many hours sitting on the embankment, telling Strider her dreams with the certainty that he wouldn't laugh or belittle her. Even in the darkness she could see the stables were gone now. A few new businesses had cropped up along the roadway, in accompaniment to shrimp and vegetable stands. Each structure formed its own shadow in the moonlight, moving, twisting, forming ghostly shapes. Each phantom whispered of danger.

"How much farther?" Bobbie asked, drawing Tabatha out of her reverie.

Tabatha rolled her shoulders. "Not far. If it hasn't changed since I was there last, we'll have to find a place to ditch the car. The building has a large, but open parking area--nowhere to hide." She pointed to her right. "There. At least this hasn't changed."

The warehouse loomed before them, a white goliath sitting in a sea of blacktop. A light glowed dimly in a lone opening, while the rest of the building slumbered in darkness.

An uneasy feeling of being watched washed over Tabatha in a frigid bath of fear. Her skin turned to gooseflesh and cold adrenaline rush through her veins.

Bobbie reached for the door handle. "Let me out here."

"No. I'm not letting you go in there alone." She turned a corner and found an empty space in front of a vacant house.

"Look, Tab. I can get close without being seen. You can't. The minute I find out where Rhonda is, I'll come get you."

"No."

"You'll get us caught, damn it. Ten minutes." Bobbie jerked her arm out of Tabatha's reach and glanced at her watch. "Come after me at seven minutes after eight." She closed the door softly, making no noise and stuck her head through the open window. "Not before." She vanished into the shadows.

Tabatha sat watching the dash clock tick away minute after minute. Every sway of tree limbs appeared a threat. Each breath of the wind whispered her name. Sounds intensified, movements exaggerated. Thoughts of Phelps and his henchmen waiting in the dark made her nerves twitch. Her mind worried over dangers Bobbie was putting herself in, while she sat in the car, safe. Three minutes later she'd had enough and made her way toward the warehouse.

She dropped to a crawl as soon as she was in sight of the building, knowing if she could see it, anyone near could see her. At the wall she pulled herself up, sliding along it to the lit view port. Tabatha peeked and saw Phelps in the office with his feet up on a desk, hands behind his head. His eyes were closed, a sardonic smile lifting the corners of his mouth. He's enjoying himself, she mused with disgust.

Tabatha looked around the room. All four walls were covered with architecture magazine clippings of antique moldings, mantels, wrought iron fences and gates. At last she found a door to the far right.

She jerked away when Phelps opened his eyes and glanced in her direction. Drawing deep breaths, she tried to slow her heartbeat to a normal pace but quickly realized she was hyperventilating.

She moved farther along the building to peer into each opening until, at last, she saw Rhonda tied to a rocking chair, gagged, her eyes wide with fear, with a half-formed snake writhing at her feet. Within seconds, Bobbie stood before her naked.

Tabatha turned the corner of the building hoping to find a door, but found only a solid wall. She removed one of her shoes, turned her face away and with all the force she could muster hit the window, creating a loud thump, but the glass didn't break.

Bobbie rushed toward her, her bronze beauty naked to the world. "Think you could make a little more noise, girlfriend?" she asked after sliding the window open. "What were you planning to do, crawl over the jagged edges?" She helped her through the opening before rushing back to Rhonda's side.

Tabatha placed her finger to her lips. "Shhh." She took off her linen duster and handed it to Bobbie. "Phelps is in the front office."

"Shit!" Bobbie fumbled with the knots. "We gotta hurry."

"Hello, darlin'."

Their collective gasps echoed in the quiet room.

Tabatha didn't have to look behind her to know whose voice it was. "I'm not your darlin', Phelps." She didn't falter in her attempts to undo Rhonda's imprisoning knots.

"Mine or nobody's."

She swallowed hard. He'd made his intentions clear in three simple words.

When the rope fell away from Rhonda's wrists, she grasped the bandana around her mouth and tugged it down to her neck. "Is Shane all right?"

Tabatha nodded. "He's with Bertha. No one's going to get to him."

Rhonda struggled with the ropes at her ankles. "He's going to kill us."

Tabatha faced Phelps. "He wants something from us and dead, we're useless to him. What is it, Phelps? What are you and your fanatics after? Is this all a game to you?" She huffed. "Guardians Against Paranormal Sinners. GAPS would be a better tag for a bunch of men with nothing but space between their ears."

"You don't want to make me mad, darlin'. It wouldn't be pretty." He leaned against the doorjamb and lit a cigarette. With a flourish of his hand he sent a plume of smoke sailing in front of his face. His eyes narrowed, his lips thinned to a mean line. "What do you want with Bainbridge? He's got to be ten, fifteen years older than you. Now us, we're a better match. With your power, my strength, we could rule the world. I would be a king, you my queen. You didn't come for this weakling. You came because you knew I'd be here."

Tabatha stared at him in disbelief. He'd hooked his thumb in the waistband of overly tight jeans and his fingers toyed with a gun resting in its holster. His slender face proudly touted dominance. She judged him to be thirty, maybe thirty-five. A big man, he moved slowly, but with a purpose to each action. Wisps of black hair fell over his brow to dark brown eyes that held no warmth.

He smiled. "Like what you see?"

"I see a monster."

The last of the ropes fell away and Rhonda scurried behind Tabatha. "He's not gonna let us go. He can't. We know who he is."

"Come with me, darlin', and they can go free." Phelps took another drag on his cigarette. "No one will bother them again. I promise."

Bobbie laughed. "That ain't gonna happen, little man. We stand as one. We're family."

"What's a half-naked squaw gonna do to stop me?" Though his words were for Bobbie, he continued to gaze into Tabatha's eyes. With a slow, purposeful shrug, he moved away from the doorjamb and started toward them.

A hurricane-strength power grew inside Tabatha's body, no matter how hard she fought to force its dangerous effects down and stop the inevitable storm that would erupt.

"Stay away, Phelps."

His laughter fueled her anger.

Glass rattled in the sills. She struggled for air, closed her eyes and willed the energy to lessen.

"You can feel it can't you? You can't deny me."

She opened her eyes as he reached out his hand, his slow steps closing the space between them. The power burst free in a blinding flash of light and heat. Glass shattered and flew at Phelps in a controlled spray like bullets from a rapid-fire machine gun. He roared with fury as the razor-sharp fragments tore at his body, face and hands.

Screeching tires and Derek's shouts for Tabatha infiltrated the room.

"Better run, little man. Deputy Dog is here." Bobbie smiled.

Phelps faced Tabatha one more time, pointing his finger toward her. His eyes burned with rage. "Remember what I said. If I can't have you, no one will." He took one more draw on his cigarette, flinched in what Tabatha hoped was pain, then flicked the butt onto the floor at Rhonda's feet. "Tell that cop, he touches Tabatha and he dies. She's my woman."

Rhonda nodded, speechless.

Tabatha cringed at the carnage that had been his face. "What about your wife, Phelps? I'm sure she'll be happy to hear that little tidbit."

"I'll take care of her." He glanced toward the beam of spotlight searching outside. "I'll be back for you, Tabatha." He wiped blood from his face, kissed the air and retreated into the dark warehouse.

Rhonda cried out for Derek while trying to clamber out the window.

Bobbie glanced at Tabatha and chuckled mirthlessly. "To hell with us, she's gonna save herself."

Tabatha grasped Rhonda's blouse and pulled her back inside. "You're not to tell Derek anything. We fight our own battles."

Rhonda opened her mouth, then slammed it shut, saying nothing.

"Too bad that glass didn't cut his damn throat," Bobbie said, echoing Tabatha's thoughts.

They crawled out the window and came face to face with two angry men. Derek stood before Tabatha, his ire evident in his popping veins and red face.

"What the hell were you thinking? You could have been killed. Why didn't you wait for me?"

She shrugged. "You were busy; and as you can see, we're fine."

Mason gestured toward the warehouse. "I'll check out back." He jogged away.

Derek ran his hands over his face and released a heavy sigh. "If I were a violent man, I'd give you a spanking you'd never forget."

Bobbie chuckled. "Oh, that sounds exciting."

"I'm in no mood for jokes." He glanced at Tabatha then jerked his attention back to Bobbie. "Where the hell are your clothes?"

Bobbie grinned before taking a few steps away and retrieving her clothing from the ground alongside the building. She slowly glided her jeans up one leg and then the other, and turned her back to Derek before sliding the waistband over her rear. She turned to face him once again and slipped out of Tabatha's jacket, baring her breasts. In a seductive slink, she tugged her shirt on and dangled her bra and panties in Derek's face before shoving them into her pockets.

"Better?"

The sound of Derek's teeth grinding wore on Tabatha's already frayed nerves. She rolled her eyes and huffed a sigh of disgust. "Good grief, Bobbie."

"This was a stupid thing to do," Derek roared. "You girls could be in deep shit. You broke into a building outside of Orleans Parish. I can't do a thing to help you."

Mason turned the corner of the building, rejoining them. "That won't be a problem. I know the owner. He'll just want someone to pay for damage."

Tabatha nodded. "Done."

"Now," Mason said. "What happened? Who had Rhonda?"

Rhonda rushed front and center. "Those men from the cemetery grabbed me right off the street. When they brought me here, Phelps was waiting. He only wanted her." She pointed to Tabatha. "He thinks she's his. Said he'd kill you, Derek, if you touch her. He called her his queen."

Tabatha threw her hands in the air in a gesture of hopelessness. "Remind me to keep her away from state secrets."

Mason scrubbed his head with tight fists. "I just walked the perimeter. I didn't see anyone leave. No cars. Nothing. Are you sure it was Phelps?"

Rhonda's stomped her foot. "Yes, I'm sure. Before Tabatha got here he kept repeating, 'Mr. John Phelps requesting the audience of Ms. Tabatha Gray. Paging Tabatha Gray.' I tell you the man is nuts."

Tabatha raised her hand as if asking permission to speak. "When you find him, his face is going to be a bit . . . bloody."

"Bloody from what?" Derek asked.

Rhonda jumped in once again. "Glass went flying. He got it right in the face."

"What glass? Did someone shoot out a window?" Mason asked.

"No." Tabatha's mind raced for a believable answer. "I knocked it out trying to get in. Phelps just happened to be in the way."

Mason shook his head. "This just keeps getting better and better. I'll put out an APB." He turned to leave. "You want a ride, Bainbridge?"

"No, I think I'd better stick with the girls. Phelps may be watching."

Mason nodded before flipping open his phone and clambering into his car.

Derek turned his full attention to Tabatha. "You got some explaining to do, woman."

Twenty-six

The silence was thick as peanut butter and just as dry. Derek's hands ached from grasping the steering wheel in an effort not to pound it through the dash. He clenched his jaw and ground his teeth.

"Don't ever do that to me again, Tabatha. Phelps wouldn't think twice about killing all three of you." Turning, he gave a cold stare of warning to Bobbie and Rhonda, sitting in the back seat. He glanced out his side widow, then to the rearview mirror, anything to keep from looking directly at Tabatha. He'd had years of practice keeping his expression neutral, but with her attention on him, it was difficult to maintain his composure. Sparks of rage warmed the usually cool blue of her eyes, and her lips were pressed into a firm, white line. "You will leave Phelps up to me. That's an order."

"You have no right to order me to do anything. I'm a big girl, Bainbridge. I don't need you."

His breath hitched and a jolt of pain stabbed at his heart. "Maybe I need you, Tabatha."

Her expression softened. "For what? To raise Elizabeth? I've already told you I would. To help find the serial killer? I want that as much as you do. When I've completed those tasks, then what? What could you possibly need from me?"

Good question. What was it a man needed from a woman? A warm smile when the world turned cold? A tender touch when life became too difficult to bear? To hear the words 'I love you'?

"Just to be there," he said under his breath.

He guided the car toward the garage and turned off the engine. Rhonda and Bobbie quietly got out and made their way to the house. When Tabatha reached for the handle, Derek grasped her arm. "Wait."

"I think we've said enough tonight, Derek."

He dropped his hand away. "I didn't ask you to resurrect Elizabeth. You're the one who offered. I need to know who killed her, but I'll do it on my own. I don't want you to raise her, Tabatha. Not if it will come between us."

"She's already between us. You kiss me, you think you're being disloyal to Elizabeth. You touch my hand and feel her disapproval." She looked away and shook her head. "No. If we have any future at all, Derek, I have to do this. You'll never let her go otherwise. I'll give you the closure you need. Then you're going to have to decide. If you choose me, you have to be sure you're ready to give all of yourself to me. When . . . if we're together, I will not share you. I will not play second fiddle to a dead woman."

He cupped her cheek in his palm and turned her to face him. "Maybe Frank's right."

Her mouth turned down hard. "I can't imagine Frank being right about anything where I'm concerned."

"He said I've spent so much time living with Elizabeth's ghost that I've forgotten what it's like to have a real woman love me."

"I'm real. I'm here, and I love you. But it doesn't mean a thing, does it?" Tabatha leaned forward, kissing him on the cheek. "Tomorrow night we'll raise Elizabeth and then you'll have your answers." She stepped out of the car, closed the door and walked away.

Derek watched as she entered the house without him. "It means everything," he whispered, the sound hollow in the empty car.

~

Tabatha came face to face with Bertha, arms crossed, looking down her nose at her.

"Where is Mr. Derek going?"

"Home." Tabatha wanted to cry, could feel the tears pressing against her bottom lids.

"Sit down, baby girl. We need to talk."

Tabatha wanted to scream. The last thing she needed right now was to talk. "Whatever it is, can it wait? I'm tired. I want to go to bed."

Bertha pulled out a chair and waited until Tabatha plopped onto it, then took the one next to her. She pushed a cup of tea into Tabatha's hand.

"Your grandpa. . . ." Bertha paused as if searching for the right words. "He wanted to tell you about your abilities when you were older, but someone got in the way of that. So, I'm gonna tell you. You're the first daughter to be born in the Gray family in many generations. The gift has always been passed from father to son. When you're momma found out she was going to have a baby, she was afraid you would be like your daddy and grandpa. Raoul told her you were a girl and it wouldn't pass to you."

"That's why she didn't have an abortion?"

Bertha shook her head. "No, baby girl. She didn't have it because your daddy told her if she did, he'd leave her without a penny. You're momma was terrified of being poor again. Still is."

"So, why am I the way I am if it can't pass from father to daughter?"

"Oh, your grandpa knew the truth of it. You see if you'd been a boy, you would've gained one power. But being the first girl in hundreds of years, you gained them all. That's not happened since before Jesus, baby girl."

Tabatha's heart skipped a beat. "All?"

"You are a true sorceress, Tabatha Gray. There isn't an ability you can't call upon. If your grandpa had lived, he would have taught you. What he didn't know, he'd have found out from someone who did. Child, if you could have seen the way he cried the day you were born. He knew what a hard life you'd have."

Tabatha fought to breathe. "What do you mean any ability? Rhonda's a firestarter. Are you saying I could draw on that power as well? Or shapeshift like Bobbie?"

A thoughtful expression stilled the old woman's face. "I don't think so. I think he meant all the Gray family abilities. Your grandfather's, your father's and so on back up the line. He said his great-grandfather had power over the weather and another could call animals to him and charm snakes. Mr. Raoul said you could be the most powerful sorceress in the family, and it was our job to make sure you grew into a good person and used them for good not evil. He had a set of family journals he was going to leave to you, but they've vanished. Said they would explain everything."

"What do you think happened to them?"

She looked away, saying nothing.

"Bertha, you told Derek you thought--"

The old woman's back stiffened. "Thought ain't proof. I ain't saying nothin' about nobody with no way to back it up."

"Then tell me what you think and I'll try to find proof. What is it you're hiding from me?"

"Baby girl, your momma didn't kill your grandpa or your daddy. She had to force them to take their medicines by putting it in food or a drink. Someone tainted their medicines, I think. Someone who thought they had something to gain from their deaths."

"What kind of medicines?"

"Your grandpa and daddy both had been sick for a while. Your grandpa had a bleeding ulcer and your daddy was well on his way to having one. I don't remember what they were takin' now. Some kind of powders."

"Who switched the meds?" When she saw Bertha's reluctance, Tabatha reworded her question. "Who do you *think* switched them?"

Bertha stared down at the table and fidgeted with the salt and pepper shakers. "She loved him, but when he didn't marry her, she got mad."

"Stop it. Who?"

Bertha raised her soulful black eyes to stare unblinkingly into Tabatha's. Suddenly, Tabatha didn't want to know the answer.

"Nyssa."

Tabatha wanted to run--to go anywhere but where she was. The air thickened, making breathing difficult. Tears refused to be held back and washed her face in a rush of moisture. "No." She shook her head. "You're wrong. She's my friend."

"No, baby girl, Nyssa is no one's friend. Has she ever talked to you about makin' out a will?"

She fought to talk past the growing lump in her throat. "All of her letters were filled with her worry about what would happen to the estate if something happened to me. She thinks Momma would squander everything."

"I bet she said you should put her in charge of the money to keep your momma from blowing it all, right?"

"Yeah," was all she could manage to utter.

"She said the same thing to Raoul. He told her he'd changed his will, and two weeks later he was dead. Only problem was he'd only told Nyssa that so she'd hush about it. He had no intention of leavin' her in charge of his family or his money. So when the will was read, she was fit to be tied. Started in on tryin' to convince you that your momma killed them both."

Tabatha remembered her grandfather's last words. *She rid herself of your father and now me. She will not stop until she has it all.* It was Nyssa at her side. Nyssa who tried to comfort her.

A choked sob escaped before Tabatha could censor the sound. "No. I don't believe it. It can't be."

Bertha drew her into her arms. "I know, baby girl. I didn't want to hurt you, but you needed to be warned. She won't be satisfied until she gets what she wants." She lifted Tabatha away, placed her hands on her shoulders. "Don't eat or drink anything she brings here. Do you understand what I'm tellin' you?"

"Are you sure, Bertha? Could you be wrong?"

"Could be, but I ain't. I've known Nyssa all my life. We grew up in the same neighborhood. Her house was the one that ended the white neighborhood and mine the first of the black's. She was a little shit even back then. Used to throw poisoned meat over the fence just to kill my dogs. When I cried, she called me a ninny nigger."

The first cold encroachment of belief began to touch Tabatha's mind.

"Your man knows. He sensed it from the beginning. Ever notice how he watches her like a hawk?"

Tabatha waved her hand in dismissal. "That's because she pulled a gun on him."

"No. Mr. Derek may not have the gift, but he's a smart man." Bertha lowered her hands. "One more thing. He loves you, he just don't know it yet. Men, they slow about these things. He carries this weight on his shoulders. Guilt and grief are heavy loads, baby girl. He needs an end to it. Only you can give that to him."

"I'm going to. Tomorrow night he'll know who killed Elizabeth. Then it's in his corner. He can walk away or choose to be with me. But I'll not make the next step. He has to reach out to me."

"Baby girl, just be there for him. He'll reach out."

Tabatha stood to leave, but turned back to face her friend. "Bertha, do you have the gift?"

Bertha laughed. "Child, I'm just a simple cook."

Somehow, Tabatha didn't believe that.

Twenty-seven

Derek stood at the back door watching Tabatha toy with a bowl of cereal. Her eyes were red and puffy, her face swollen. He knuckled the window a couple of times and smiled when she waved him in.

"Are you okay? You look like you've--"

"I lost my blouse." She choked on a sob.

"Blouse? What's it look like? There's some outside on the clothesline."

"It's pink, with embroidered flowers on the collar. Bertha made it for me."

"Tabatha, you're not crying over a blouse. What's wrong?"

She drew a deep breath and straightened her spine, but the breath rushed out in another sob. "Bertha thinks Nyssa killed Daddy and Paw-Paw."

Her statement was blunt but filled with emotion. The cold, analytical cop inside him took control, turning the world to black and white. "Why does she think that?"

Tabatha returned her attention to her bowl of cereal, lifting one "O" at a time, as if counting them. In a slow, deliberate tone she repeated what Bertha told her the night before. "Nyssa took care of me when Bertha wasn't here. She taught me to control the power. She cried when Momma sent me away."

He sat in the chair next to her, leaned back, stretched his legs out under the table and folded his hands over his stomach. The memory of that morning by the garage ran through his mind. He remembered Nyssa's strange reaction to his looking around the back yard and the fear and rage when Tabatha told her he was a cop.

"What do you make of it, Tabatha? Do you think there could be any truth to it?"

She shrugged and dabbed her eyes with a paper towel. "Why would Bertha lie to me? She honestly believes what she said. But why would Nyssa kill them? Why would she want to harm me?"

Derek took her hand in his. "Money. Sounds like she thinks you stole what she considers hers. People have killed for much less than what you have, Tabatha." He leaned forward in his chair and brushed a strand of hair away from her face. "Did you know she was a pharmacist before she came to work for your grandfather?"

"You ran a check on her?" She sounded incredulous.

"Yes. I did checks on all of you."

"All of us? Me?"

"It's my job, Tabatha. I'm neck deep into a murder investigation. And I've had reservations about Nyssa from the get go. Now that I think about it, all the while she was stacking up mowers and coolers against the back wall, she was mumbling about something being hers. I thought at the time she believed I was going to take her tools."

"What else did you find? I mean if she's in the system at all, it had to be more than her being a pharmacist." She pulled her hand from his and lifted her face to look at him.

His heart skipped a beat. Her eyes were filled with unspoken accusations.

"She was arrested for killing animals when she was seven and again at nine. In high school she was convicted of breaking into lockers, stealing money, clothes and jewelry. She got into a fight with another girl in her senior year and pulled a knife. If a teacher hadn't forced her off the girl, Nyssa would probably have killed her. When she left for college, she seemed to straighten out. Didn't have any more brushes with the law. Her record was sealed once she turned eighteen."

"If her records were sealed, how did you get them?"

He slouched down in his chair and thought about his answer, then decided to be blunt and truthful. "I'm a cop in the middle of a murder investigation. That overrides any damn judge's rule to seal a person's record."

Tabatha pushed the bowl of cereal away. "I'm sick of this, Derek. I don't know who to trust."

"You can trust me."

Tabatha offered a thin smile. "I know." She rose from her chair and went to the sink, filling a glass with water. "What time do you want to go to the cemetery tonight?"

He sat against the chair and tried to gather the facts into a coherent stream of thought. The Guardians are trying to kill Tabatha because she's different. Nyssa may want her dead because of greed. But what did Tabatha focus on? Helping him find a child killer and Elizabeth's murderer.

His cell phone rang, pulling him out of his thoughts. "Yeah?"

"Bainbridge?"

"Who else would it be, Lieutenant? It's my damned phone. What ya got for me?"

"I don't know who it was at the warehouse last night, but it wasn't Phelps."

"If Tabatha says it was Phelps, then it was. What's this about?" Tabatha came to stand at his side.

"Phelps is in ICU at Ochsner Hospital. He was in a one car accident ten minutes before he was allegedly in the warehouse with the girls."

"Was his face covered with broken glass?"

"Hell, yes. His face, his hands, his chest. The window blew out when he hit the light pole. And before you ask, there were several witnesses."

"How did the girls know his face would be cut up, Lieutenant?" Derek ran his fingers though his hair as he tried to think what to do next. "Call the hospital and tell them I want the glass analyzed. I don't like this, Lieutenant. Where was the wreck?"

"Higgins and Magazine by the Contemporary Arts Center. He couldn't have gotten that far even if they had the time wrong by a half an hour. It wasn't him, Bainbridge."

"Humor me. Have the glass checked."

"Yeah, all right, but it's a waste of time. Oh, one question. How did that girl, Bobbie, pull off that trick? She had me going there for a minute or two."

"Trick?" Derek asked, confused at the sudden change of subject.

"How did she make herself look like she was turning into a snake?" He chuckled. "She must be a real hit at parties."

Derek flipped his phone shut when the line went dead. "The bastard has witnesses who swear he was in an accident clear across town the same time he was at the warehouse."

She sighed and emptied the glass of water into the sink. "It doesn't matter. I know it was Phelps. And you believe me, that's all I need." She leaned against the cabinets. "You do believe me, don't you?"

Derek breathed a heavy sigh. "Of course, I believe you."

Her whole body relaxed. "Is he in the hospital?"

"Ochsner. Must be in bad shape. They have him in ICU."

She shrugged. "Well, at least he's out of commission for now. One less worry."

Her calm acceptance of the situation didn't sit well with Derek. "You don't seem upset that Phelps made you look like a liar. I'm not sure what the lieutenant thinks."

"I'm going to take a nap. I'll see you tonight. Around six, okay?"

He'd been dismissed. "Yeah. Fine. Six."

He leaned down to kiss her, but she walked away, leaving him staring after her.

~

The drive to the precinct seemed longer than usual as the distance between him and Tabatha grew. He tried to figure out what he could have done or said to upset her. From the moment they'd met she'd been affectionate, showering him with attention, listening to his every word. Now, she made no attempt to touch him and avoided any eye contact. When Tabatha walked away from him, her shoulders were slumped as if her soul had deflated; leaving her with no support for the shell that remained.

"She'd found out her best friend may want her dead and may have killed her family. That's what it is."

You're losing her, Derek.

The soft, delicate whisper was so clear that Derek turned to check the back seat, expecting to find someone there. But he was alone. His chest was tight and painful, his lungs felt as if they had forgotten how to function. He was losing Tabatha. He'd pushed her away once too often.

He pulled into the parking lot and shut off the engine. How did he feel about that? It's for the best, he thought. She's better off without me.

But are you better off without her?

This time the voice came from the vacant passenger seat. "I'm losing it."

He got out of his car and entered the stationhouse, climbing the stairs to homicide. Before he reached his desk, Mason motioned for him to come into his office.

"Close the door," Mason said when Derek entered. "We need to talk."

Derek sat in the chair facing Mason. "Tabatha isn't a liar, Lieutenant."

Mason looked up, a look of confusion crossing his features. "Who said she was?"

"No one. But you--"

"I said it couldn't have been Phelps. Who it was, I don't know. Maybe someone wants us to think it was him. That warehouse wasn't well lit, Bainbridge. She could have been mistaken."

Derek didn't believe it but let it slide. "Will that be all?"

"No. That's not why I called you in. It's Panner. He bonded out. I thought maybe you'd want to tell Tabatha. I don't think he's stupid enough to go after her again, but hell, I'd never have thought he'd do it the first time."

"Did he talk?"

Mason picked up his coffee and took a sip before answering. "Lawyered up from the start." He drained his cup and went to fill it again. "Want some? It's mine, not that slop out there."

Derek declined.

"It's none of my business, but if Tabatha was my girl, I'd be stuck to her like flies to shit until this is straightened out. She's a keeper, Bainbridge."

"She'll make some man a good wife someday." A vision of Tabatha in another man's arms flashed across his mind, and his body stiffened with anger.

"Some man? You're going to walk away from something like that? Are you nuts? Do you know what Panner's problem is?"

The change of topic jarred Derek. "Problem?"

"Yeah, big problem. You were accepted into the force when he had to wait for the next session at the academy. You passed the sergeant's exam--he failed it three times. You almost married a wealthy girl half the men in the state of Louisiana would've cut off their dick to have. And now you've found someone, a second someone, as great as the first. He's jealous of you, Bainbridge."

"You're crazy. Frank has nothing to be jealous about. He's got a great wife who, by the way, came with a good amount of wealth herself. He made sergeant; it just took him a little longer. He made detective a month after I did."

"Yes, after you. He feels like he has to follow in your footsteps for everything he gets. Like you're holding him back somehow. I didn't know you'd dated his wife before you met Elizabeth."

"How do you know all this?"

"Panner lawyered up, but he talked, all right. Talked about how the world hands everything to you on a gold shield. It irks the shit out of him that you're finally settling down with another woman. A woman that's a few years younger than you, while Mary is older than him."

Confusion clouded Derek's thoughts. "What's that got to do with anything?"

"He can't stand the thought of you having anything or anyone better. Not that Mary isn't great, you understand. He has to best you, Bainbridge." He came around the desk and sat on the corner, crossing his legs at the ankle. "Don't let him mess this up. Tabatha is the best thing to happen to you in twenty years. Elizabeth wouldn't want you to give up on life. You did that on your own. I don't care that you spend the department's time going over and over Elizabeth's case. I hope you find the bastard who did it. But I do care if you throw away a chance at happiness. Tabatha is that chance."

Derek slumped down in the chair. "I think I've already blown it."

When Mason said nothing, Derek turned to see that he was staring into the bullpen area. Derek saw Detective Jackman pointing to the phone, then at him. He held up two fingers.

"You have a call on line two." Mason moved to the other side of his desk and handed him the receiver.

He placed it against his ear and waited for Mason to connect him. "Detective Bainbridge."

"I left a gift for you on the levee. Orleans and Jefferson Parish line. Better hurry before someone takes it."

The electronic generated voice stunned him at first but piqued his cop's intuition. "Who is this?" The caller's laugh squeezed his heart with fear. "I'm not going anywhere until you tell me what this is about."

"You'll know when you see it. It's the closest thing to a clue you'll get." The line went dead.

Derek reached across the desk and dropped the receiver in place.

Mason's brow furrowed. "What was that about? You look like you're trying to come up with the final Jeopardy question."

"Something about evidence on the levee at the parish line."

"Evidence for what? Who was it?"

Derek shrugged. "The voice was distorted. Could have been female or male."

Mason picked up the phone. "Brenda, find out if there's a unit near River Road. I'll hang on."

After a few moments of silence he glanced at Derek. "Dillon and Wayne are a couple of blocks away. I'll send them to check it out."

Ten long minutes later, Mason's intercom came to life. "Lieutenant?" the voice of Brenda, the dispatcher rang out.

"Yeah, what you got?"

"Officer Wayne thinks Detective Bainbridge ought to see what's out there."

"Did he say what it was?"

"No, sir. Just said to get Bainbridge down there *now*."

Derek jumped from the chair and started toward the door.

"Hold on, Detective. I'm going with you."

~

Topping the rise of the levee, Derek's heart nearly leaped from his chest.

"It's only a doll, Detective," Officer Dillon said.

On the grass, a life-size rag doll sat facing the river with black voids instead of eyes. It wore faded jeans and the lost blouse Tabatha had described that morning. A hello tag had been placed on her right shoulder with Tabatha's name printed in block letters. The doll's blond hair drew his attention before he glanced down at the unbuttoned blouse framing a blood-red death circle decorating the stomach.

Derek's knees nearly buckled. His breath caught. He rummaged through his jacket pockets to retrieve his cell phone.

"Bertha, is Tabatha home?"

"No, she went out a little while ago. Didn't say where she was going. Call her cell phone. Got the number?" When he said he didn't, there was a moment of silence before she gave it to him. "You coming to dinner tonight, Mr. Derek?"

"Later, Bertha." He severed the connection and keyed in the number she'd given him. He slammed his phone shut when he got the away message. "Where the hell are you, Tabatha?"

Twenty-eight

"My name is Dr. Tabatha Gray. I'd like to see John Phelps, please." Tabatha waited as the woman sitting at the desk checked the visitor's list of names.

A tall, bleached-blond, fortyish woman stormed to Tabatha's side. "You're not his doctor. Who are you and why do you want to see my husband?"

"I'm his psychiatrist, Mrs. Phelps." Tabatha held out her hand and waited.

"Piffle. My husband doesn't have a shrink, nor does he need one."

Tabatha lowered her hand. "I assure you--"

The nurse cleared her throat. "Yes, Doctor, Mr. Phelps has requested to see you as soon as you arrive."

Tabatha's mind recoiled. No one knew she was coming here. How could he be expecting her?

"She's not going in there without me." Mrs. Phelps stormed through the ICU doors into her husband's room before anyone could say a word. It was a matter of seconds before Phelps' bellow penetrated the silence and Mrs. Phelps came running out in tears. She sat on the visitors couch and turned her back on Tabatha.

Tabatha stepped up behind her and gently touched her shoulder. "Mrs. Phelps, it's normal for a man not to want his wife in the room when he's talking to a psychiatrist. It's not a slight on you, nor does it mean what you're thinking." Mrs. Phelps slapped Tabatha's hand away. Tabatha chuckled to herself. "Let me put it another way. If Mr. Phelps were Adam and I were Eve, there would have been no human population." She smiled. "Get my drift, sweetie?"

"My name isn't sweetie, it's Cookie. And before you ask, yes, it's my real name. My mother thought it was cute. I think it's dumb." Mrs. Phelps blew her nose on a tissue.

"Well, Cookie, go to court and change it. While you're at it, change the last name, too, and get the hell out of Dodge. That son-of-a-bitch will end up killing you when he grows tired of you."

Cookie's brown eyes locked onto Tabatha's. "My John would never hurt me."

"Your John is a killer, Cookie. A hit man. The ringleader of a band of cutthroats. He doesn't care who he hurts to get what he wants."

Cookie shook her head. "I don't believe you."

"You'd better. Think about how your son died and whether you want to end up the same way." Tabatha held Cookie's gaze. "Go change that name, Cookie. Start a new life."

Tabatha went to Phelps' room. She held back a laugh at the sight of him. One leg dangled from pulleys, the other lay on the bed in a cast from his toes to his knee. His swollen face was covered with contusions and stitched lacerations, and contorted into a gruesome mask when he smiled.

"I knew you couldn't stay away, darlin'. Don't worry about me. I'll be fine. But, you see now, I'll do anything to get my way. Even sacrifice myself. Now, come over here and give me a kiss."

She did laugh then. "You look like a filleted blowfish."

"Darlin'--"

"Shut your mouth and open your ears." She reached into her purse and pulled out a .38 snub-nosed Smith and Wesson. "This is my friend, Bruce. I'm well trained to use him and I will if you come near my friends or me again. You're delusional if you believe I have any feelings for you. You're not even worth the effort to hate." She sauntered over to his bedside and ran the cold gun barrel from his knee to the top of his thigh before shoving it against the outline of his hardening penis under the sheet. "I want you to make like a magician and disappear."

"Why don't you close the door? The nurse won't let anyone in. I have something for you." He gyrated his pelvis, rubbing his groin against the gun.

Tabatha forced a grin. "Yes, the nurse. I believe you'll need her assistance soon enough." She returned the gun to her purse, leaned over and looked into his eyes, wanting to see the pain in them. Then she released the traction cords supporting his broken leg. With a satisfying thud it hit the mattress. Phelps screamed in pain then swung his fist toward her, but she quickly ducked out of reach.

"If you hurt my friends, this is only the beginning of your pain."

The nurse rushed in. "What happened? Oh, Mr. Phelps, why is your leg down? I told you it has to stay suspended."

Tabatha placed her hand on her forehead and sighed. "I believe Mr. Phelps will be needing his pain medication a little early, nurse."

Spittle spewed from his mouth as he yelled, "I'm going to kill you, bitch."

Tabatha spared him a glance. "Get in line."

~

Traffic on River Road slowed to a crawl. Tabatha thought of taking a different route home, but she was so close to Saint Charles, it didn't seem worth the effort. She cringed at the memory of what she'd done at the hospital, but at the same time she was awarded with a thrill of satisfaction. A chuckle escaped when Tabatha thought about what Derek would say when he found out.

As she inched closer to her turn, she saw several police cars on the side of the levee, their blue lights flashing. Atop the hill stood Lieutenant Mason and Derek, staring down the river side of the slope. As if feeling her gaze on him, Derek glanced over his shoulder. Motioning in her direction, he spoke to Mason and trotted down the hillside. Tabatha pulled out of traffic and onto the grass before getting out of the car. Her heart picked up velocity sending adrenalin through her bloodstream.

"Is it Missy?"

When Derek didn't answer quickly enough, she ran past him to the top of the levee, stopping so suddenly that her feet slipped out from under her. She slid down the embankment coming to a halt at the side of what she thought was a body. She gazed into the hand-painted face and blank eyes staring back at her.

"What is this?" she asked when Derek helped her stand. Her mind whirled in confusion. The nametag caught her notice, then the cryptic pattern cut into the belly of the doll. "Wait, that's my blouse."

"Come on, Tabatha. You shouldn't be here. They're still searching for evidence." He tried to pull her away.

"No." She jerked her hand from his. "The hair. Look at the hair." She dropped to her knees and gently separated the strands. The putrid stench rushed up her nostrils. "Oh, God." She gagged, crawling a few feet away before vomiting.

"Come on, baby. I'll have someone take you home." Derek reached down, drawing her into his arms.

"It's the children's hair, Derek." She drew a deep breath, trying not to gag again. "Someone sewed the children's hair onto that thing. Where did she get my blouse? Who is doing this?"

Bertha's warning stabbed through her brain. *I didn't want to hurt you, but you needed to be warned. She won't be satisfied until she gets what she wants.* Derek's words followed closely behind, reinforcing their validity. *Sounds like she thinks you stole what she considers hers. People have killed for much less than what you have, Tabatha.*

In a sudden moment of lucidity, she knew the answer.

Twenty-nine

Tabatha arrived home within minutes of leaving the crime scene, if it could be called such. No real crime had been committed on the levee. A doll had been left behind--a doll with a complex message. Her best friend wanted her dead. That realization shot an arrow of pain into her heart. The woman she'd loved and trusted had more than likely murdered her father and grandfather.

A knock sounded at the door. She crossed the room expecting to find Derek, but instead Officers Dillon and Wayne stood on the threshold, their expressions grim.

She offered the best smile she could conjure and asked, "Would you like to come in? I'll make some coffee."

Wayne removed his hat and ran his fingers through his hair. "No, ma'am. Detective Bainbridge wants us to keep an eye on Mrs. Bouchard. He said to tell you as soon as he can get everything squared away with that business on the river, he'll be here." Wayne toyed with his hat and glanced toward Nyssa's property.

Dillon spoke. "Ma'am, we didn't want to worry the detective with this, but we have no idea what this Bouchard woman looks like."

Tabatha motioned them in and led the way to the window. She pointed to the small white cottage. "She's standing at the back corner of the house, looking in this direction. I would imagine she thinks you're here to tell me about the doll. Should I go over there and confront her with what I know?"

"No, ma'am." Dillon hiked his gun belt higher on his hips. "Detective Bainbridge said you're to act normal toward her. If she knows you suspect anything she might bolt, or worse, she might. . . ."

"Kill me?" Tabatha snuffled.

Wayne patted her on the back. "Ms. Gray, please don't cry on us, now. It won't look good if the detective or lieutenant catches us blubbering all over each other."

She tried to laugh. It didn't work. "Didn't Derek say we're to use first names?"

"I'm Hal," Wayne said and gestured with a nod toward Dillon, "and he's Travis."

"Yes, I remember. Are you sure you don't want coffee? It wouldn't be any trouble to make it."

"No, ma'am." Travis said. "Detective Bainbridge said for us to sit out front in the unit. When he gets here, if he says it's okay, coffee sounds great."

She smiled. "Go to your unit and I'll bring it out to you. How's that for a compromise?"

Travis looked to Hal. "What do you think?"

Hal nodded. "Sounds good to me. I've not had lunch and coffee would tide me over for a while. If you're sure it's no trouble, Tabatha."

She squared her shoulders, trying to appear brave. "No trouble at all."

They let themselves out as she pulled the carafe to fill it with water. Tabatha glanced through the glass and saw that Nyssa was still watching the officers. Noticing the window lock was broken she peered around the room, feeling insecure in her own home. Had anything been tampered with? She wondered if she'd ever feel safe again.

She set the carafe down and picked up the coffee canister, then dumped the contents into the trash and went to the pantry to open a new can. After measuring out the right amount, she filled the carafe with water. While the machine gurgled, Tabatha checked for something to make sandwiches with. There were two cans of chicken spread in the pantry and a loaf of bread in the freezer. She popped four slices into the toaster. The only sounds in the house were the coffee dripping into the carafe, the toaster heating up, and the intake of her own breath. She'd never felt more alone in her life.

Tabatha leaned her head on the cool marble counter. With a sudden release of pent up emotions she wept. She cried for the lost years with her mother, for giving her love to the woman who had taken what she held most dear in life-- her family.

A hand gently touched the middle of her back, its warmth swallowing her whole.

"Why are you crying? What's wrong?" Carla asked, her voice soft but tentative.

"She killed Paw-Paw and Daddy. She told me you did. She said--"

"I know."

Tabatha turned into her mother's arms and held her tight. "Can you ever forgive me?"

"There's nothing to forgive, Tabatha. Nyssa was able to help you when I couldn't. I didn't understand you. I didn't understand any of you. All I wanted was to feel safe and to never do without again. Your father gave that to me for a while. After he and Raoul were gone, I was terrified. I had no idea what to do with you. If you'd only been. . . ."

Tabatha pulled away. "Normal?"

Carla sighed. "So you see, we both need to forgive."

Tabatha looked into her mother's face and saw fatigue had stolen her youth. Her gray eyes were bloodshot and the sparkle of life had vanished. Deep lines framed her mouth, and her color was wrong. Bertha's words shouted in her brain, 'She poisoned my dogs.'

"Mom, I want you to go see a doctor."

Carla turned away. "After this mess is over."

"Mom, I don't know how long this is going to drag on. I want you to go now. If you won't let me take you, what about Bertha? One way or the other, you're going. You might as well call your doctor and tell him you're coming in today."

Carla waved her hand in the air. "Oh, your dashing detective won't let it continue much longer. He reminds me of your daddy, you know. Dunnock was my knight in shining armor. He rode into my heart in his white convertible and whisked me away from a drab world of poverty to this." She waved her hand around the kitchen. "I loved your father." She glanced behind Tabatha. "Your toast is burning, dear."

Tabatha ran to the toaster and hit it on the top. The bread popped up, blackened and smoking. "Hell."

"It's not acted right since you came home. Let me get mine. I'll be right back." She left the kitchen and went upstairs.

Tabatha grabbed the toaster and threw it out the back door, using it to vent all her frustration and anger. It hit the ground with a crash of metal against hard soil. She thought about going out and stomping on it, but Carla returned.

She handed Tabatha an old two-slice toaster and smiled. "It's old and ugly, but it works."

"Thanks, Mom. I've got two hungry officers sitting outside. Want to help me make the sandwiches?"

Carla glanced at the loaf of bread. "Where did you get that?"

"Freezer. Did you know it has a lock on it? The wrapper looked like it's never been opened. I checked."

"Bertha bought the freezer a while back and wouldn't be happy with anything without a lock. I think she's known all along what happened. How did you open it?"

"She put some keys on my ring. I kept trying them until I found the right one." Tabatha smiled to herself. "That old woman has more power than I do, I think."

Carla laughed and Tabatha's heartbeat quickened at the true sound of happiness it held.

"I love you, Momma."

"I know, honey." Carla closed the distance separating them, embraced Tabatha and kissed her on the forehead. "When did you get so brave?"

"Brave? Momma, I'm scared spitless." Tabatha wrapped her arms around her mother's shoulders. "I know you are, too, but I'll do the best I can to make you feel safe again. I promise."

Carla stepped out of Tabatha's embrace and a small, sad smile lifted her lips. "I called Dr. White while I was upstairs. He can see me at nine tomorrow morning. Is that soon enough for you?"

Tabatha smiled. "Thank you."

"Your Prince Charming just pulled into the drive. I'm going back to my room. Be careful, Tabby. That woman has taken everything dear to me. She's got it into her head that the estate should be hers. And I fear she'll not stop short of death to get it."

Tabatha slathered the bread with mayonnaise and chicken spread. "Don't worry about Nyssa, Momma. Derek's going to see to it she never breathes the fresh air of freedom again. If he has his way, she won't live to see her next birthday."

Carla's hand flew to her chest. "He's going to kill her?"

"No. He's going to prove she's the Voodoo Killer. We believe she's the one killing the children. Juries aren't all that lenient with people who torture and kill kids." Tabatha drew a deep breath, releasing it with a whoosh. "She's trying to kill me, Momma. Those children were supposed to be me."

"She's been trying to kill me for years." Carla chuckled. "She's not very good at it, it seems." She ran her fingertips over Tabatha's cheek. "Maybe we should get to know each other, Tabby. We're not the same people we were nineteen years ago."

Derek appeared by the back door and reached for the knob. Carla crossed the room to let him in. "Come in, Detective. We've finished our talk. I was just going to deliver these sandwiches to the policemen out front." After placing the sandwiches on paper plates, she poured two cups of coffee and arranged it all on a tray.

Carla glanced at Derek. "Do you know what you're getting into? Are you sure you're ready to take on all this and a crazy mother-in-law to boot?"

"Momma!"

"Oh. Sorry. Jumping the gun." She left them slack-jawed and staring after her.

"What's gotten into her?" Derek asked.

Tabatha lifted her shoulders in a shrug. "She saw me cry and realized I'm human."

Thirty

Tabatha dropped onto the chair, her legs refusing to support her another second. "I'll understand if you want to walk away from me. I'll let you go if you want."

Derek lifted the coffee pot and filled two mugs. After setting one in front of Tabatha, he pulled out a chair and joined her at the table. He stared down at his coffee.

"What brought that on?"

Tabatha tore open a packet of sweetener and dumped it into her coffee, the clanging of her spoon against the cup raged against her already frayed nerves. "In Nyssa's sick mind. . . ." She forced back a sob. "This is all my fault, Derek. Those children are dead because of me."

"Bullshit. The fault lies with one person. Nyssa Bouchard."

She brought her eyes up to meet his, fearing the rejection she'd see in them. "You've not said if you want to go. Do you?"

He slowly shook his head. "You'd be better off if I said yes, but I can't."

"How would I be better off? I've been alone most of my life. How can it possibly be right to return to a life of solitude after finding someone who makes me feel whole? To be alone again would be unbearable."

Tabatha nearly jumped out of her skin when the door was flung open and Bertha rushed in. "Nyssa's on the way over here with a soup pot in her hands. Don't you eat nothing that woman brings in this house."

"Wouldn't think of it." Tabatha toyed with her coffee cup. "We have to act normal toward her. Derek doesn't want her to know we suspect her."

"Suspect her?" Bertha rolled her eyes. "Wring her neck like a chicken is what I want to do. Killing my dogs is one thing, trying to kill my baby girl is quite another matter."

Derek pointed to the chair. "Sit down. She thinks I'm here to tell Tabatha about the doll, so let's talk about it."

Bertha remained standing, her arms crossed under her breasts. "Doll? What doll?"

Derek filled her in, starting with the phone call. "Forensics is going to check the sections of scalp sewn to the doll's head to see if it matches the children's. Other than that, there really wasn't any evidence."

They turned their gazes to the door when Nyssa tapped it with the pot.

Bertha pressed her lips into a thin angry line. She opened the door and asked, "What do you want? What's in that pot?"

"Nothing for you, old woman. I brought my girl some chicken soup. Thought it'd make her feel better."

Tabatha forced a smile. "Feel better?"

"I saw the cops sitting out front and then your detective friend comes running in, I figured something happened."

Derek leaned back in his chair and took a swig of his coffee. "No, not really. We found a doll on the riverfront, but it meant nothing to Tabatha. Just some kid's prank."

"Kid's prank?" Her brow rose sharply.

Derek shrugged. "Yeah. We tossed it in the garbage."

"The garbage?" Nyssa's face reddened and she stammered a rush of guttural sounds before pulling herself together. "Did you see this doll, Tabby?"

Derek tapped the toe of his shoe against Tabatha's heel. She shook her head. "No. Why would I? It had nothing to do with me."

Nyssa glanced from one to the other. "Then why are the cops sitting out front like they're guarding the place from marauders?"

"They're waiting for me," Derek said before lifting his cup to his lips.

Bertha took the pot from Nyssa's hands and placed it on the stove. "We'll have this for lunch. Too early to be eating soup now."

Tabatha's back stiffened when she realized she'd not seen the girls or Shane since the night before. "Where is everyone?"

Bertha pointed over her head. "When I left to go to the store this morning, they were still asleep. I guess they still are. Though it's strange for Shane not to be up and about by now." She glanced at the clock on the range. "It's almost ten o'clock. I'll go rouse them."

Tabatha watched her leave the room before turning her attention to Nyssa. "Thanks for the soup. That was kind of you."

The old woman's eyes darted to the pot then back to Tabatha. "I best be going. I've got some weeding to do in the front beds. And the sprinkler system needs flushing out." She nodded curtly to Derek. "Detective." She waved goodbye to Tabatha and closed the door behind her.

Derek leaned close. "Do you have a container?"

"A container? What do you need it for?"

"I want to take some of that soup to the lab before Bertha pours it down the disposal."

"Under the sink." Tabatha watched as he ladled out a large portion of the soup and fastened the lid onto an old mayonnaise jar.

Bertha's wail trailed down from the second floor followed by thunderous footfalls on the stairway. She rushed into the kitchen waving a piece of paper. "They're gone. They took them. They took the baby."

Derek grabbed her shoulders and shook. "Who took the baby?"

"I don't know." She handed Tabatha the note. "What does it mean? What do they want?"

"They who?" Derek's voice dripped with impatience.

Tabatha's face paled. "Phelps."

"How do you know?" Derek asked.

She read the note aloud. "It's me or no one." Her heart raced. "He said those exact words to me at the warehouse last night."

Tabatha's cell phone rang. She reached for it, but Derek beat her to it. "Unknown caller." He looked at her for a long moment before handing her the phone.

"Dr. Gray," she said.

"Hello, darlin'."

She glanced at Derek and nodded. "What do you want, Phelps? I'm busy."

"Oh, you're never too busy for your friends, are you? I have them, you know."

"Where are they?" She turned the note over and mimicked writing. Derek handed her the pen from his pocket.

"Can't tell you that."

"Okay, where are you?"

"You know where I am. I'm in the hospital. Good alibi, I think."

She worried her bottom lip with her teeth. "Seen Cookie lately?" She glanced at Derek and smiled at his frown. "Hello. Phelps, you still there?"

"Cookie isn't your problem, darlin'."

Tabatha laughed. "No, she's your problem, darlin'." Saying the endearment nearly choked her. "Cookie knows about her boy. She knows you killed him and his friends."

"She can't. No one knows."

"I know." She wrote on the paper. *He admitted it!*

Phelps' voice came in a hiss of fury. "Come to me, now. If you don't want your friends to end up like the boy, you'll be here in twenty minutes."

White noise filled the receiver.

She smiled. "I think I hurt his feelings."

Derek's face twisted with anger. "Why did you tell him that? He's not going to let you go now."

"He wants me to come to the hospital."

"No! I forbid it."

Tabatha stood from her chair and kissed him softly. "I'm going. You can wait outside the room. Listen. Maybe you should get someone else to be there as a witness."

"Witness to what? Your murder?"

"He won't harm me in such a public place." She chuckled. "But, I bet I can get him to do a lot of talking. He wants me. Thinks we're two of a kind, he and I."

"Well, he can't have you."

"And why is that, Derek?" She saw his Adam's apple bob.

"Because you're mine."

She swallowed the laughter of joy that threatened to bubble from deep within her. Instead, she placed her hand over his heart and smiled. "Yes, Derek, I am."

Thirty-one

Visiting hours were over when Derek and Tabatha met up with Hal and Travis at the hospital. With a flash of a badge and a few discreet words to the hospital administrator, they were allowed to advance to Phelps' room. Derek and Hal positioned themselves to the left of the door and Travis to the right.

Tabatha steadied her breathing, rolled her shoulders and tried to appear calm. She looked at Derek and nodded. She was ready.

She pushed the door until the hydraulic mechanism froze it in an open position. Vases of flowers lined the windowsill and every tabletop. Tabatha listened to Phelps' slow, deep intakes of breath and watched the movement of his eyes under closed lids. Nightmares she hoped.

She moved closer, but still out of Phelps' reach and shouted, "I'm here, Phelps. Now, where are my friends?"

He jerked out of sleep, looked around the room as if not sure where he was. He turned his attention to her and smiled. "Hello, darlin'. It's good of you to come see me. Shut the door and come closer."

She ambled toward him, clenching her hands into fists at her sides. Visions of choking the life out of the bastard flashed across her mind. "The door stays open."

"No need to be afraid. I won't hurt you. Like my new room? No more dangling leg."

"Too bad. I rather enjoyed the toy myself."

His expression hardened. "That wasn't nice of you, Tabatha. You need to be spanked for being so mean to me."

"Enough of your games, Phelps. Why did you take my friends?"

"Why, darlin', I'm in the hospital. How could I have anything to do with the disappearance of your friends?"

"Do you really think I'm so stupid as to think you're not powerful enough to have them taken? What I don't understand is why."

"I warned you, Tabatha. It's me, or no one. They were taking up too much of your time. Bainbridge will be next, but since he's a cop, it'll take a bit of planning. Not like that scared little girl, Rhonda. Such a cry baby, that one."

Tabatha held her temper at bay. "What do you want from me?"

"Just you, darlin'."

"Why should I trust you? I don't even know you. I know nothing about you. Why would I choose to be with a complete stranger? Especially one with so many secrets."

"What do you want to know? I'm an open book, if you'll only turn the pages and read."

Tabatha counted to ten, pulled in a calming breath and sat on the bedside chair. "Tell me about the Guardians. When did you form your little club?"

Phelps laughed. "My little club? The Guardians aren't my creation. I'm just their enforcer."

"Who is in charge of it then?"

"Few people know, and I'm not one of them."

A rush of disappointment surged to Tabatha's brain. "Then how do you get your assignments?"

"I have contact with one member. He comes to me with who and when. Your lover would be surprised to hear he's a cop."

"Cold and calculating; no feelings toward your victims at all. Killing is just a job to you."

He shot a glance toward the open doorway. "Who said I killed anyone?"

When she stood to leave, Phelps reached out and grabbed her hand. "Where do you think you're going? I haven't said you could leave yet."

Unbidden anger burst in her brain. "You do not say when I can leave or stay. I am my own person. No one tells me what to do."

"Not even Bainbridge?"

"No one. Let go of my hand. Now."

"And if I don't?

A vase of roses flew through the air and landed with a crash above his head. He released her hand and yanked the covers up to protect himself from the flying glass. "Son-of-a-bitch, Tabatha. Shit like that is why they want you dead." He flung the sheet off the bed with a clatter of broken glass falling to the floor. "But I can keep you safe. I'll take you away where they'll never find us. If you stay here and I don't kill you, they'll find someone to do it."

"Where are my friends?" Tabatha asked.

"Darlin', my terms must be met. Me or no one. Me, and your friends go free. Choose Bainbridge and you all die. It's on your shoulders. How much do you love your friends?"

"Where would we go?"

He smiled and relaxed against the pillows. "I have a chateau in Switzerland. Ever been to Europe, darlin'?"

Tabatha nodded. "Where are they?"

"They will be released when we are on our way."

"No. I get them back now or no deal."

Cookie rushed into the room, her face livid with rage. "You son-of-a-bitch. I'll kill you."

A growl erupted from deep within Phelps' chest. "What the hell are you doing here, Cookie? Why aren't you at home?"

"You lying bastard. You're going to run off with this bitch and leave me with nothing? She warned me but I didn't believe her." She covered her face and wept into her hands.

"Cookie, you know I'd never leave you. I needed her help, that's all."

Cookie dropped her hands from her face. "Go to hell, John. I'm leaving. You can have this bitch."

Tabatha saw Derek reach out and grab Cookie as she ran from the room. Tabatha quickly stepped in front of the door, blocking Phelps' view. "Oops. Sorry about that. Didn't mean to mess up your love life."

He shrugged and snorted. "Good riddance. I'll be out of here in two days. Be ready to leave, Tabatha."

She crossed her arms. "My friends?"

"They'll meet us at the airport."

Tabatha walked to the door, giving him no answer. "Goodbye, Phelps."

"Do we have a deal?"

She tugged at the door, letting it shut slowly behind her. His bellow followed her down the hall.

Travis walked at her side. "Cookie handled her role in this really well but broke down when she got to the waiting room. I think she's ready to talk."

Tabatha nodded. "A broken heart is a lethal weapon."

Thirty-two

Tabatha and Derek sat outside Phelps' house watching shadows move across the shaded windows of the second floor. Cookie had said that Rhonda, Shane and Bobbie were in the left front corner bedroom. Dana and Dub, friends of Phelps' she said, were keeping watch.

Tabatha broke the silence. "Dana and Dub are two of the voices on the tape. This proves Phelps is ass deep in this."

Derek nodded. "I couldn't have phrased it better myself. I still think you should have gone home and let us--"

"No. They're my friends. I got them into this; I'll get them out. Besides, Phelps' goons won't hurt me. They're scared of Phelps and what he'd do to them if they harm me. There's no such protection for you and your men." She glanced out the back window to the car parked behind them. "They waiting for us?"

Derek turned to look behind them. "Yeah. I told them to let me go first. I'd signal when I had the place figured out. Cookie said the patio doors were unlocked."

"You shouldn't trust Cookie completely. She loves Phelps and love is an unreliable witness."

Tabatha reached for the door and was out of the car before Derek could stop her. She ran across the yard to the back, sliding along the house until she could peek through the patio doors. A wall-sized aquarium supplied the only source of light in the room, casting shadows from the furniture onto the walls. A large yellow cat lay on the coffee table, its eyes peering through the darkness, its tail moving in time to the old grandfather clock ticking off the seconds.

Tabatha jumped, grasping her throat when Derek came up behind her. "You scared me," she hissed.

His eyes were aflame with anger. "I told you to stay in the car."

"And I told you they're my friends."

"Can you two do this later," Hal whispered from the corner of the house. "The lights went out upstairs."

Derek glared at Hal. "You're no better at following orders than she is."

Hal shrugged.

Derek edged closer before inching his head around the doorframe.

Tabatha reached out and tested the door. It slid open about an inch when the cat's head snapped around and the overhead lights came on. Tabatha jumped back but stayed close enough to see inside.

A man and woman strolled into the room. The woman sat on the leather couch, leaned back and put her feet on the slab-style coffee table, kicking the cat away. "Filthy animal."

The man stooped behind the bar and reappeared with two beers. "Cookie should be home any time now. I wouldn't be kicking Sinopa if I were you."

She snorted. "When Phelps gets rid of that bitch, I'm going to send that cat to hell." She glanced over the back of the couch toward the bar. "Dub, are you going to stand there until those beers get hot?"

He walked over, handed her one and flopped on the couch. He reached for the remote and turned on the TV. Sinopa jumped up beside him and curled up on his lap. Dub scratched the cat's head.

The sound of ESPN filtered through the opening into the night. Derek chanced another look into the room then pulled back. He dug his fingers into Tabatha's arm and forced her to follow him to the corner of the house.

"What's wrong? You look like someone sucker-punched you," Hal said.

"It's John Karney," Derek hissed. "Karney is Dub."

Travis appeared out of the darkness. "Who's Karney?"

Derek released Tabatha's arm and raked his fingers through his hair. "Damn it! Doesn't anyone obey orders any more? I told you to stay in the car."

"Mason's on his way. Said to wait for him." Travis hiked his holster higher on his hips. "Who's Karney?"

"Homicide detective."

Hal shook his head. "There's your link to the department."

"The lieutenant isn't going to be happy. They're tight."

Tabatha slunk along the wall until she reached the patio doors again. She pulled her loose blouse above her waist and drew her snub-nosed .38, inhaled and kicked the latch, sending the door sliding open with a crash of glass and metal.

Dub and Dana jumped to their feet reaching for weapons, but with a shout of warning they froze.

Derek rushed in, his own gun aimed. "We're gonna have a long talk about this later, Tabatha."

Dana's eyes widened. "You're that witch. You're worth a lot of money dead. A lot of money."

"Sorry to disappoint you, Dana, but I'm very much alive and plan to stay that way." She took her eyes off of the woman long enough to find Travis. "Go get my friends."

Travis looked at Derek. "Detective?"

Derek nodded. "Both of you go. There may be more of them upstairs. I've got a call to make."

"Bainbridge," Dub said, then swallowed so hard it had to hurt. "I'm working undercover. You've blown my cover, damn it."

Dana snorted. "Lying son-of-a-bitch. He's second in command. The big guy bites the big one, Dub here takes over."

"Shut the fuck up, Dana."

"Who's the big guy?" Tabatha asked, ignoring Dub. "Phelps?"

Dana laughed, a loud grating sound. "He ain't anything but a hired assassin. Should have done you myself. Phelps was always soft for pretty women."

Derek motioned with his gun. "Weapons on the floor." His eyes bored holes into Dub. "Both of them." He gestured to the cop's ankle.

Dub and Dana dropped guns from their waistbands then Dub reached for his ankle weapon. Tabatha saw the gun leap from the leg holster as if of its own accord and the world slowed, frame by frame. The gun spewed flames from its barrel moments before more gunshots roared in her ears.

Dana flung herself to the floor, retrieved her gun and aimed it at anyone who was in her line of fire. Another shot, louder, closer, sounded and a neat, round hole wept red tears from Dana's forehead. She collapsed to the floor.

A thin trail of smoke twisted from the barrel of Tabatha's gun. Her heart clenched painfully. She had fired the bullet that killed Dana. She frantically searched the room for Derek, praying he would tell her she hadn't done it. That it was all a mistake. But when her eyes met his, she saw the pain in them. Her gaze raked down his body but stopped at the spreading red stain covering his right leg.

Dropping to her knees in a near faint, Tabatha wailed and scrambled toward him on all fours.

Derek slid down the wall, dropped his gun to the floor, never taking his eyes off of her. "Are you hit?"

She shook her head violently. "No. Oh, God, no! Don't you die on me, Derek. Don't you dare." She reached out snatching an embroidered table runner from a nearby table and tied it around his upper thigh. She struggled to contain the sobs forcing themselves from her chest. This was her fault. She caused this. "I need to see the wound. I have to cut off these damn jeans."

Mason and a barrage of police officers charged into the room, aiming guns at anything that moved. "What the hell happened here?" He looked from Tabatha to Derek. "Detective."

Derek drew a shaky breath. "Lieutenant."

"Tabatha, get out of the way and let me take care of him." Mason grasped her by the arms and settled her beside Derek. Mason ripped Derek's jeans at the bullet's entry. He withdrew a two-way phone. "Officers down. Send an ambulance and the coroner." He gave the address and clipped the phone on his waistband. "Don't worry, Tabatha. It's still there. Just a leg wound."

"It?" she asked then felt the rush of heat flame on her face once she realized what he meant.

Mason patted her shoulder. "He won't walk right for a while, but he'll live." He reached into his jacket's inner pocket and slipped a paper to Derek. "I told you to wait for me. Here's the damn search warrant."

Tabatha glanced at Derek's blood on her hands then at Mason. "It wasn't his fault. I started it. I wanted my friends out of here." A sob tore from her throat. "I could have gotten him killed."

Mason nodded. "Yes. You could have, but you didn't." He shouted orders to his men, sending them through the house looking for anyone else who might be hiding, then held his silence until the three of them were the only ones in the room.

Derek gestured toward one of the bodies. "It's John, Lieutenant."

"John who?" He stood and strode to the man's corpse, rolling him over on his back. "Oh, hell. What am I going to tell Vera?" He faced them. "Vera won't get the dependent's check if . . ." He sighed. His whole body went limp and he dropped to the couch.

Tabatha touched Derek's arm. "He's dead. No harm to us now. Let his wife remember him as a good man."

Travis and Hal came into the room and knelt at Derek's side.

"What's going on?" Hal asked.

Tabatha wiped the blood from her hands onto her jeans. "We could say he was part of the raid."

Hal shook his head. "He don't deserve it, but I know Vera. It'll kill her. She worshiped him."

All eyes turned to Travis. "I won't say a thing."

A harried police officer rushed from a side room into the den. "Lieutenant, those girls are threatening to do us bodily harm if we don't let them come down here. They want to see that Tabatha and Derek are alive."

"Let them out. It's safe."

Tabatha cleared her throat. "One more thing, Lieutenant. I don't have a permit for my gun yet. Not here in New Orleans anyway."

"Oh, hell." He leaned his head back on the couch. "Where's the gun?"

She handed it to him.

"It's legal to have a concealed gun in the car. You took it out because you heard shots in the house. You feared for your life and the life of your friends. You saved a police officer's life, Miss Gray. I think I can clear this." He jerked his head up and looked at her. "You didn't kill John, did you?"

"No."

Derek raised his hand. "That would be me."

"Drop gun or department issue?"

"I don't normally carry a drop, Lieutenant, and you know it."

"But?" Mason asked.

"I got it off a drug-bust-gone-bad perp. Never got around to turning it in."

"Thank God for small favors. Give me the gun."

When Derek handed it over, Mason wiped it clean and put it in Dana's hand. "I don't want to know, Bainbridge."

Mason sighed, the sound heavy with fatigue. "Tabatha, you wouldn't consider working for the department, would you?"

Tabatha shrugged. "I'll think about it, Lieutenant."

Rhonda rushed into the room first, a sleeping Shane on her hip. Her eyes looked like muddy holes peering out of her pale face. "You hurt?"

Tabatha shook her head. "Derek got shot."

Bobbie sauntered into the room, arm in arm with one of the officers. "My, my. You southern boys sure know how to make an entrance."

Thirty-three

Tabatha sat amidst a sea of uniformed and plain-clothed police officers in the waiting room of the hospital surgical wing. On her right sat Hal, on her left, Travis. She stared straight ahead at the door, waiting for the doctor to return with news of Derek's condition. Her head hurt. A lump of lead sat in the pit of her stomach. She wanted to cry but refused to let these men see her break down.

With every new officer joining them, the same question was asked. "Who's the girl?"

All but two or three had reacted with jaw-dropping disbelief to Travis' reply. "Derek's girl. Leave her alone."

Tabatha looked up expectantly when Mason knelt in front of her. "Honey." He swallowed hard. "Phelps has vanished. His guard was found unconscious in the room, so we're thinking someone got Phelps out."

Her gaze frantically searched the room. "Where's . . . .?"

"I sent them home. The girls were about to drop and Shane needed some rest." He patted her hand. "I just checked up on them. They got there safely and I've got a car stationed in front of your house and men out back. No one is going to get to them again. I promise."

Tabatha released a shaky breath. "Thank you." She looked up when silence enveloped her surroundings.

A doctor walked in garbed in green scrubs. He ran his fingers through his dark brown hair before nodding to the officers. "Bainbridge family?"

Mason stood. "This is his fiancée. I'm his lieutenant."

Tabatha knew her face showed her shock. Where did Mason get such an idea?

"I'm Dr. Vissman." He looked Tabatha in the eyes. "And you are?"

"Dr. Tabatha Gray."

His brows shot up, but he didn't comment on her declaration. "Detective Bainbridge is resting comfortably. There was minimal damage to his leg. No main arteries, no nerves involved; the muscle was torn pretty badly, and he's going to be sore for a while. But it's nothing that won't heal soon enough." He shifted his attention to Mason. "He won't return to work for a few days. I want him to keep off his feet and his leg elevated. I'm keeping him overnight. After which time I'll decide if he can go home."

Tabatha nodded. "What time will you see him in the morning?"

"I start my rounds at seven."

"I'll be here at seven to take Derek home." Tabatha knew she sounded arrogant, but she didn't care. She wanted Derek out of this hospital and home where she could look after him.

He frowned. "Dr. Gray, it will depend on his condition whether I release him or not."

"Dr. Vissman, if you did your job well and didn't leave any leaking veins, you can release him to me. It's not as if you're sending him home with a fretful wife. The doctor in my name isn't an honorary title. I'm medically trained and I know how to take care of an injured man." She returned his hard stare. "I'll be here at seven. Please have the necessary papers signed for me to take Detective Bainbridge home. Now, may I see my fiancé?"

"He's resting. I'd rather he not have any visitors this late."

Mason gently placed his hand on the doctor's shoulder, drawing his attention away from Tabatha. "We'd appreciate it if you'd give us a few minutes with Detective Bainbridge."

Vissman's jaw clenched.

Tabatha drew a breath. "Dr. Vissman, I know I'm coming across as a hard-ass, but we've been through an awful lot tonight. I need to see with my own eyes that he's as well as you say. I need to touch him."

The doctor's expression softened. "Five minutes."

She fought not to weep with relief. "That's better than nothing. Thank you, Doctor."

Derek lay in bed with his leg propped on a stack of pillows. His ashen complexion concerned her, but his breathing was deep and even. Tabatha touched his forehead and smiled when he opened his eyes and looked at her.

"Hi, baby," he whispered in a hoarse voice. "I knew you'd be here."

"I've been here the entire time. I wasn't about to leave without seeing you. The doctor's going to release you in the morning. You're going to stay with me. No arguments."

He nodded. "I'm too tired to argue about anything."

She laughed softly. "Good. We only have about five minutes and I don't want to waste it."

Lieutenant Mason leaned over the bed. "You look like shit, Detective."

Derek chuckled. "Thanks."

"You're welcome." He walked to the door and glanced out, then returned to Tabatha's side. "We need to talk about what happened. Internal Affairs will be here in the morning as well. We need to get our stories straight."

Tabatha turned the sheet down to Derek's knees and removed the bandage from his leg. When he and Mason looked at her questioningly, she shrugged. "Just checking the doctor's work. If you didn't notice, he's a bit young."

"No younger than you, I'd guess," Mason said.

She smiled. "Yes, but I don't cut people up. I just mess with their heads."

Mason laughed. "Point taken."

Derek ran his hands over his face. "Okay, what's our story?"

Tabatha replaced the bandage and covered Derek with the sheet again. "Make it as close to the truth as possible. I'm not a good liar."

Mason sat in the only chair in the room. "Actually, you won't have to lie. You ran into the house. That's the truth. You saw Dana Tally aim her gun at Detective Bainbridge and shoot him. Again, that's the truth. The closest thing to a lie is when you entered the house. You came running when you heard a shot. Detective Karney was already on the floor when you got there."

"Why was Tabatha with us on a raid in the first place?" Derek asked.

"I overheard you talking. Knew you were going after my friends and followed you. You didn't know I was there at all."

Mason didn't say anything for a long moment. "That might work." He looked to Derek. "What do you think?"

"After Tabatha heard the shot, it would take her longer to get from her car to the backdoor than it would take Dana to shoot Karney and turn to shoot me."

"Okay. I waited until you disappeared around the house then got out of the car. That's when I heard the shot, then reached into the car and retrieved my gun."

"Why didn't we have our guns drawn?" Derek's voice was laden with fatigue.

Mason stood. "Look. Internal Affairs won't be here first thing in the morning. Get some rest, and I'll meet you at the house. Let's sleep on this. Give me time to think this thing out." He patted Tabatha on the back. "I'll leave you two alone."

"Thanks, Lieutenant. I'll be right out."

She waited until the door closed then gently slid into bed next to Derek. Leaning on her elbow she gazed down into his face. "You scared the hell out of me, Derek. I thought I'd lost you."

"I'm tougher than that." He pulled her close to his chest and breathed deep. "You smell like spent gunpowder."

"Turns you on, does it?"

"Oh yeah. Better than fancy toilet water." He kissed the top of her head. "I'm fading fast, kid."

Tabatha glanced up as he closed his eyes. "Get some sleep, baby."

When she moved to get out of bed, his arms tightened around her. "Stay."

"I can't. They frown on girlfriends staying the night. I'll be here early in the morning. I promise."

Mason rushed into the room. "Internal Affairs is here."

Thirty-Four

Tabatha repeated her story for what felt like the hundredth time, rolled her shoulders and sighed with fatigue.

"And where was Lieutenant Mason while this was going down?" Larsen asked.

She ran her gaze over him. He was a balding, short, stocky man, with small, close-set, jade-green eyes. His nose had apparently been broken more than a few times and slanted to one side.

"The lieutenant was out front. Detective Karney, Detective Bainbridge, and two police officers went to the back of the house. I had parked my car two houses down from Phelps' place. When I saw them running toward the back, I got out of my car and made my way to the back. They were rushing in when I got there. There were shots. When I arrived I overheard Detective Bainbridge tell the woman to put her gun down. She tossed it down. The detective told her to lay face down on the floor. She bent over, reached under her pant leg, drew another gun, and aimed it at Bainbridge. I shot her, Mr. Larsen."

Kenyon, the second Internal Affairs officer, leaned back in his chair, stretched his feet out in front of him, shook his head and sighed. "It's Detective, Miss Gray. You do understand you are not allowed to carry a concealed gun in Louisiana, don't you?"

"I have a permit to carry in New York, which is where I've lived for the past nineteen years. I just moved here. And it's Dr. Gray." If he wanted to play the name game, she could play as well. Tabatha met his stony stare without flinching. "Let me see if I understand. You have a dead woman who kidnapped my friends Bobbie, Rhonda and her son, Shane. This woman, Dana Tally, shot one officer dead and another in the leg; but I'm the one having to explain why I shot the bitch?"

Kenyon leaned forward, clenching the arms of the chair in a white-knuckle grip. "Now, Miss Gray--"

"It's Dr. Gray. Get it straight."

He stiffened his spine, stood, towering over her. Bull, from the old TV show Night Court came to mind. Kenyon could pass for his double.

"Ma'am . . . *Doctor*, we're only trying to get to the bottom of this. There's no need to get testy with us."

"Fly that by me again. Who is the one sitting here giving you a blow-by-blow breakdown of what happened? Who has been here for hours telling the same story over and over?" Tabatha stood from her chair and brought her breast so close to Kenyon's chest he took a quick step back. She poked his ribs with her index finger. "Arrest me or let me go. I'm tired. It's nearly time to take Detective Bainbridge home, and I've had no rest."

"Not until we speak to him." Kenyon smiled as if he'd won a debate. "Alone."

"Well, bully for you, Kenyon. But I'll not stand for you taking as much time with him as you did me. He's been wounded and the last thing he needs is for the likes of you wearing his strength down."

"What is Detective Bainbridge to you, Miss--" He held up his hand. "Sorry. Doctor."

"I'm going to marry him."

Larson laughed. "Know what you want and go after it, huh?"

"I'm a strong woman, Larson, and an honest one. You can check my references. Talk to anyone who worked with me. I started carrying a gun after some gang kids kidnapped me at gunpoint to treat a friend of theirs who'd been shot during a botched robbery attempt. I was able to fight my way out of that one, but didn't want to take a chance on the next time."

"You fought off a bunch of gang-bangers? Bullshit." Kenyon snorted.

She smiled. "I can take care of myself. If I'd been there when that bitch took my friends, this whole thing would never have happened. She wouldn't have gotten past me."

"Think a lot of yourself, don't you?" Kenyon said.

"Am I free to go?" She glanced at her watch and yawned. "It's a quarter of seven, and I told the doctor I'd be there to pick Derek up on the hour."

Larson nodded. "Don't leave town. We may want to talk to you again, after we speak with Detective Bainbridge."

"I'm not going anywhere. I have a home here. I'm starting a private practice in a few months."

Kenyon held up his hand. "Hold on. I thought you said you were from New York."

"My mother sent me to a private school when I was ten. I went to college and med school after that. Had my internship and residency in New York. I've lived there for years, but New Orleans is home."

Kenyon mumbled under his breath, "One of those rich bitches."

"No." She lowered her gaze away from his for the first time. "An unwanted bitch. After my father and grandfather died, my mother had no time or need for me. Anything else about my private life you'd like to know?"

Kenyon's face flushed. "Didn't want to know that much."

Larson chuckled. "You're free to go. Give us a few minutes to talk to Detective Bainbridge, and then you can take him home. If his story jibes with yours, I doubt we'll need to talk again."

Dana's voice drifted into her consciousness. *"Hey, bitch, you listening to me? Tell them it's all a mistake. Tell them I'm not dead."*

Tabatha grabbed the back of the chair and sunk to her knees. Larson rushed to her side and lifted her into his arms. "Dr. Gray, are you all right?"

The realization of what she'd done hit her like a dump truck of garbage. A sob escaped her throat before she could block it. "I killed her."

Kenyon jerked the door open and shouted for help. Dr. Vissman rushed in, took one look at Tabatha and groaned. "I knew it would hit her sooner or later. Shock and exhaustion," he said. "You men should be ashamed of yourselves. You don't give a damn who you hurt as long as you get your facts."

Orderlies rushed in with a gurney and Larson laid her on it. "You're going to keep her for a while?"

"Twenty-four hours."

Tabatha looked up at Dr. Vissman and said, "No, I've got to take Derek home."

Vissman shook his head. "Neither one of you are going home today, Dr. Gray.

Thirty-five

Tabatha opened her eyes to an overly bright, white room. She moaned and drew the covers over her face to block out the sunlight.

"Tabatha. You awake?"

Derek's voice made her forget her headache, replacing it with memories of the night before. She jerked the blankets away and sat up. Derek sat in a wheelchair beside the bed; he reached out to touch her hand.

"Are you all right? Are you in any pain? What time is it?" she asked.

Derek glanced at his watch. "I'm fine. A little pain but nothing serious. Ten."

"I've been asleep for three hours? Why didn't you wake me?"

"Dr. Vissman said to let you sleep. And you slept a bit longer than three hours."

"No. I distinctly remember it was seven o'clock when he made me lie down."

Derek nodded and grinned. "Seven o'clock yesterday morning."

It took a few moments for what he'd said to sink in and make sense. She mentally counted off the days since Missy's death and felt the tears welling up. "Missy has been dead four days. I won't be able to talk to her. I failed her."

"She was dead already, Tabatha. You couldn't have saved her."

She was about to reply when Dr. Vissman entered.

"Well, I see the patient finally decided to join us. How are you feeling?"

Like a failure. "Fine. Can I go home?"

Dr. Vissman took the stethoscope from around his neck and placed it against her chest, listened for a few moments, then shoved the stethoscope into his pocket. He next checked her blood pressure and pulse. He patted her on the head. "Get dressed, Dr. Gray. You can go home."

"What about Detective Bainbridge? I'm not leaving without him."

Vissman laughed. "The detective was released at eight this morning. He's been hanging around waiting for you. You gave him quite a scare."

She grinned. "We're even."

Dr. Vissman's face turned serious. "The lieutenant told me you're looking for the child killer, but I have to insist that Detective Bainbridge not overdo. We don't want infection . . . ."

"I know what to watch out for, Dr. Vissman. I may be a psychiatrist, but I've had the same medical training as you. I'll make sure he behaves himself. If there is any sign of trouble, you'll hear from me immediately."

He nodded. "Good enough." He stared at Tabatha as if formulating a thought. "Where do you work, Dr. Gray? What hospital are you affiliated with?"

"I've not had time to take care of the legalities. When I do, I plan to set up a private practice."

"Let me know. Maybe I can send some work your way."

"That would be great. Thanks."

He glanced from her to Derek and offered him his hand. "Take care of her, Detective."

Derek grasped his hand. "I'll do my best, Doc. Thanks for everything."

Turning to look at Tabatha one more time, Dr. Vissman nodded and left the room.

Derek snorted. "I think our friendly doctor has a crush on you, Tabatha."

She felt laughter bubble up from her chest but held it down. "Jealous?"

He frowned, saying nothing for what felt like an eternity. "Hell, yes. It's hard for an over-the-hill cop to compete with a young handsome doctor."

She slid from the bed, walked behind him and hugged him close. "First, you're not over-the-hill. Second, you're much better looking than Dr. Vissman. Third and most important, I love *you*, Derek."

He placed his hands on her arms and leaned against her body. "I love you, too, kid."

Tabatha wanted to cheer, but she simply kissed his cheek. "Let's go home. Bertha must be pacing the floors by now."

~

Tabatha shook her head as Bertha ran from the back door and threw the passenger car door open.

"Mr. Derek, I swear, I ought to give you a whippin'. Goin' off and getting' y'self shot. You come on, now, and let me get you to bed. You listen to what I say, and you'll be up and around in a couple of days."

Derek's laugh boomed in the car's small interior. "You might be biting off a bit more than you can chew, thinking you can spank me, woman. I'm not ready to go to bed, and I'm up and around now."

Bertha made a noise between a grunt and growl. "I ain't seen you movin' yet. You're still sittin' your butt in that car." She shook her head and clicked her tongue against the top of her mouth. "Put your arm around my shoulders and I'll help you get up."

"I can get up just fine, Bertha." He turned in the seat, placed one hand on the roof of the car and the other on the door. He tried to lift himself up on his feet but failed.

When he tried again, Bertha's arm reached under his arm and around his back. With one movement he had been lifted to his feet and was being led toward the door. "Young man, you best learn not to argue with me. Didn't your momma tell you to respect your elders?"

He smiled. "Yes, ma'am."

Rhonda, Shane and Bobbie stood at the door.

Shane ran to his side and wrapped his arm as high up on Derek's body as he could reach. "I'll help you, Mr. Derek."

"Thank you, Shane. That's down right manly of you. Did you take care of our women while I was gone?"

Tabatha watched as the young boy's chest swelled with pride. "Yes, sir. I wasn't afraid of them people. I told her you'd come get us. I'm Momma's brave little man. She said so."

Tabatha's heart lurched and tears threatened. She glanced at the others and noticed there wasn't a dry eye among them.

Bertha said, "You too, baby girl. I want you to get some rest."

"Bertha, I just slept for twenty-seven hours straight. I'm not in need of any more rest."

The look Bertha gave her nearly singed her hair. "You ain't too big for a whippin' either, baby girl. You don't have to go to bed, but I don't want you gallivanting about looking for the bad guys. They'll still be around in a couple of days."

Tabatha followed them through the kitchen and into a small room to the left. "I made up the servant's room. Thought with Mr. Derek's leg being all messed up, he couldn't do too well with the stairs." Bertha turned down the covers and started to unbuckle Derek's belt.

He battled with Bertha's insistent hands. "Whoa, woman. I can undress myself."

Bertha frowned. "Mr. Derek, I've seen it all before."

"You ain't seen this particular 'all.'"

Tabatha sidled up to Bertha and smiled. "That's my job."

Bertha giggled like a little girl. "Yes, I guess it is." She took a few steps before turning back. "I'll give you ten minutes, then I'll be back with some food. I'm sure that hospital didn't feed you like I do."

"No, ma'am," Derek said with a chuckle. "No one has ever fed me like you do."

Bertha's face glowed with his praise. "No hanky-panky. Ten minutes." Her laughter trailed behind her.

Derek unbuckled his belt then paused and turned toward the door. Rhonda, Shane and Bobbie stood there watching. "You girls looking for a free show?"

"Oh!" they said in unison.

"Sorry. We'll let you get settled," Bobbie said. They turned to leave.

Shane stood his ground.

"What is it, son?" Derek asked.

"I'm not a girl. I can stay and help, can't I?"

Tabatha pleaded silently for him to let the boy stay.

"Yeah, you can help. Shut the door, okay?"

Shane pushed the door closed and walked to Derek's side.

Tabatha waited until Derek had unbuttoned and unzipped his jeans before she helped him sit on the bed. She carefully pulled the pants down until they were past the wound. "Okay, Shane, help me take Derek's jeans off."

He nodded his head vigorously. "Yes, ma'am." He grasped the bottom of the pant leg on the good leg and pulled. Tabatha did the same to the opposite side. Once the jeans were off, Shane folded them carefully and placed them on the chair. "Now what, Tab?"

Derek took off his shirt and handed it to the boy. "Hang this on the chair back, then go tell Miss Bertha I'd like to have an icepack. Can you remember that?"

"Yes, sir." He hung the shirt and raced away. "I'll knock when I come back, okay?"

"You're a good man, Shane." Derek settled on the bed with a sigh.

Tabatha sat on the bed beside him, placing her hand on his forehead. "You're a little warm. After you eat, I think you should get some sleep. I'll wake you if Mason calls."

"Don't look so worried. I'm fine."

She rose from the bed and stared out the window. "I'll have to let Dana talk, Derek. She tried to talk to me that night but I . . . well. . . ."

"Went down like a brick." He chuckled.

"Yeah." She drew in a deep breath. "The dead are usually freer with their information. Maybe she'll give up names."

"You going to do it now?"

Tabatha saw his reluctance and shook her head. "Not here, not now. You need to rest. Later. Besides, Bertha will be here in a minute. There won't be any peace until you eat."

There was a light knock on the door. Tabatha pulled the blanket over Derek and said, "Come in, Shane."

"How'd you know it was me, Tab?"

"That's your special knock. I'd know it anywhere."

He giggled. "Here's your icepack, Derek. Where you want it?"

Derek reached out and took it from the boy, placing it on his knee. "Ah, feels better already. Thank you, son."

He kicked at the scatter rug. "Momma said I have to take a nap. Can I sleep in here?"

Derek patted the side of the bed. "We'll take one together."

Shane jumped onto the bed and scurried under the blanket. "I'll be careful. I won't hurt your leg."

Bertha returned with a bowl of soup and a tall glass of iced tea. "Dr. Vissman said no beer."

Tabatha waited until he'd cleaned his bowl and drunk his tea before leaving him and Shane to their nap. She closed the door and made her way out to the back stoop where she dropped her shields and waited. The voices came in a jumble, making it impossible to know whom they were or what they were saying. "I need to talk to Dana, first. Dana, are you there?"

There was a moment of silence before a timid voice broke the quiet. *Tabatha, are you coming to find me?*

This was impossible. "Missy?"

Thirty-six

Tabatha ran through the days since Missy's death, re-counting, and trying to understand how she could possibly still hear the child.

I'm not afraid anymore, Tabatha. I have a new friend with me.

This had never happened before. Who could be with her? Another soul? The angel of death come to take her? "I'm glad, sweetheart. Derek and I are going to find you. We got held up for a while."

Oh, no. I ain't going for this shit. Dana's rough voice replaced Missy's calmness. *This is my time.*

"Dana!" Tabatha warned. "Keep your tongue civil, or I won't talk to you at all."

I have a question and I want it answered pronto. You got it?

Tabatha sighed. "I'll be right back, Missy."

All right. Missy's voice held such patient peacefulness that Tabatha wondered what had changed in the last twenty-four hours. She had to force herself to pay attention to Dana's roar of anger.

Are you going to listen to me or not, bitch?

"One more profane word and the answer is no."

Am I dead?

Tabatha swallowed hard. "Yes."

You killed me.

Tabatha was shocked when she heard herself laugh. "Live by the gun, die by the gun. You shot Detective Bainbridge and would have shot me. I made a choice between us. Guess who won?"

No remorse?

Tabatha refused to answer that one. "Do you have any remorse for the people you killed?"

I didn't kill people. I killed monsters.

Anger speared Tabatha's gut. "Is that what you think I am? A monster?"

Frank turned the corner of the house. She flung herself to her feet as he came closer.

"Talking to the dead again, woman?" he asked.

"Hello, Frank."

Oh, hell, someone else butting into my time, Dana said.

Tabatha studied Frank's face. His cool, green eyes held no emotion, revealing nothing of his intentions.

"What are you doing here? What do you want?" Tabatha despised the quiver she heard in her voice.

He chuckled. "You don't have to worry. I didn't come here to harm you. Believe me, when you come to your end, I'll have a good alibi for my whereabouts."

Her heart pounded against her ribs and she struggled to calm her anger. "You didn't answer my questions?"

"You stole evidence. Give it back, or I'll see to it you go to jail."

"What are you talking about?" It took a few seconds for Tabatha to remember the folder she'd taken from the seat of his car.

"Don't play coy with me. You have the Guardians' initiation folder. You took it that night at the station. I want it back."

The back door swung open and Derek stood with a crutch in one hand, his revolver in the other. "Get out of here, Frank. Leave her alone."

Frank glanced at the gun in Derek's hand and smiled. "Heard you got yourself shot. Should choose your friends a bit more carefully."

"I've told you a million times, Frank. I don't have any friends."

Frank's face reddened. "I want my folder back. Hiding evidence is a crime. I could arrest her."

"You'd have to be a cop to arrest someone, Frank. Last I heard you got canned."

Tabatha moved toward the door.

"Where do you think you're going, witch?" When Frank's hand grasped her upper arm, Tabatha's instincts kicked in and with little effort she turned, twisted from his grip and landed a solid jab of her elbow into his ribs. He went down holding his side, gasping for air.

Tabatha strode up the stairs and past Derek, not stopping until she was in her grandfather's study. She slid open the desk drawer and breathed a sigh of relief. The original folder lay atop several copies. "Thank you, Bertha," she whispered.

She removed the folder and closed the drawer. When she drew close to the kitchen she heard Derek's anger-filled voice.

"If you ever come near her again, I'll personally send you to your grave."

Tabatha stopped at Derek's side and opened the folder as if she were planning to read it. "What do you think, Derek? Think I should give it back to him? Or would you like to see it first?"

"No!" Frank reached for the paperwork, but she pulled it out of his reach.

Derek ran his fingertips over it. "Do I need to look at this, Tabatha?"

"Not really." She flung the folder toward Frank, hitting him in the middle of his chest. The papers fluttered to the ground in disarray. "There's your file. Now go away."

He fell to his knees and nervously gathered the scattered papers. His eyes narrowed. "Did you read it?"

She shrugged. "Not really. I've been kind of busy. Glanced at it a couple of times. Saw a filled out application form." She smiled at the alarm in his eyes.

His eyes scanned the yard. "I'm not any part of the Guardians. I was investigating them."

"Bull." Tabatha laughed, the sound mirthless. "You're in it up to your eyeballs. Go away, Frank. You have what you came for."

Tabatha, Missy's voice cut through her anger. *Elizabeth said you shouldn't make Frank mad.*

The air rushed out of Tabatha's lungs. She felt the blood drain from her face. She glared at Frank and placed her hand on her forehead.

Frank's face paled. He ran his tongue over his bottom lip. "What? What's wrong? You look like you. . . ." Fear filled his eyes and panic added force to his words. "Did you see something about me? Can you see the future? Can you read minds, too?"

"I . . . I'm . . . not feeling well. I need to. . . ." Tabatha staggered against the doorjamb and drew hard, deep breaths. Could Missy's new friend be Derek's Elizabeth? And why was she worried about angering Frank? Oh, God. Could he have. . . .?

Tabatha's stomach tightened. She'd have to tell him. But how could she? How could she tell Derek that Elizabeth was with Missy? Tabatha pushed herself away from the doorframe. "I need to sit down for a few minutes. Goodbye, Frank. Not that it hasn't been a fun visit, but I'd like you to leave now." She ran her fingertips over Derek's arm. "Don't stand here too long. You need your rest."

Derek searched her face, concern coloring his expression. She must have hidden her reaction well, because he nodded before turning his attention back to Frank. "You have what you came for. Why are you still here?"

Tabatha shut out Frank's reply as she stumbled toward the living room. She collapsed onto the couch and lowered her head to her hands. "Missy, who is your new friend?"

Her name is Elizabeth. She said she's a friend of Derek's. When are you coming, Tabatha?

"Soon, baby. I promise."

Damn it, woman, Dana roared. *You said it was my turn. I want to be heard.*

"And I told you if you didn't stop swearing in front of the child, I wouldn't listen to you at all."

What child?

Confusion seemed to be a constant diet for Tabatha lately. "You can't hear Missy?"

Bertha sat beside Tabatha and pulled her into her arms. "Honey, you know they can hear thoughts directed at them. You don't have to speak aloud."

Tabatha met Bertha's loving caress with one of her own. "Paw-Paw never told me that. I thought..." She shook her head. "Makes sense. I hear them in my head."

"Baby girl, you look like day-old grits. Stiff, gray and . . . ."

"Hard to clean up after." Tabatha chuckled as she wiped tears from her cheeks. "I remember you telling me that when I was a kid. If I remember right it was when I had the stomach flu. Threw up on everything in sight."

I've had enough of this. Who are you talking to now? I know it ain't me.

"Dana, what do you want from me?"

"In your mind, baby girl," Bertha reminded her.

What do I want? Dana's laughter sounded manic, grating. *I want to be alive. I want my life back.*

"I can't give that to you, Dana. I'm not God. Is there anyone I can talk to for you? Anything I can do for you?" Tabatha's whisper was barely audible.

You're going to come get me. I'm not dead. If I'm dead how can I be talking? If I'm dead how can I hear you? You owe me.

"Last chance, Dana. Tell me what you want, or I will rescind my link to you. Your remaining time will be spent in silence."

You listen to me, bitch. Ain't nobody going to shut me up. You owe me.

"I beseech the curtain of silence to descend. No words shall pass between us."

No! I won't let you leave me. You did this to me. I'll . . . .

Silence swirled around Tabatha's head like an over-active Jacuzzi. She sighed with the release it offered and curled into Bertha's inviting arms.

Bertha patted Tabatha on the back and kissed her forehead. "I'm going to go fix you kids something special for dinner tonight. Mr. Derek needs to get his strength up, and you need to be alone for a few minutes. There's someone else needs your attention, isn't there?"

Tabatha looked away. "Yes. Someone I need to talk to." She waited until Bertha left the room before speaking again. "Elizabeth, will you talk to me?"

Yes.

Tabatha sighed. Even in death, her voice was innocent and alluring. "Did Frank kill you?"

Thirty—seven

Tabatha curled up into a tight ball, burying her face into the musty overstuffed couch. She longed for the days when this, her grandfather's favorite place, held his comforting scent; a mixture of cherry-blend pipe tobacco and aftershave.

How was she going to tell Derek that Elizabeth was with Missy? For that matter, how could she explain that Missy was still talking to her after the three-day grace period had lapsed? Could she have been wrong about the day of death? But how could she have heard Missy talking to her if she hadn't been dead? And how could Elizabeth, dead twenty years, be talking to her?

"Elizabeth? Are you still there?" Tabatha whispered.

Yes. I'm here.

"Are you going to answer me? Who killed you?"

You can't raise my body, Tabatha Gray. It will be too painful for Derek. He needs to let me go.

"I agree, but he's not going to. Finding your killer has become his life goal. Derek will never let you go until he solves the case. I love him, Elizabeth, but I'm selfish. I will not share him with your ghost."

Who is this Dana you were talking to? What is it you need from her?

"Information. She probably knows who the head of the Guardians are and where I can find him. Maybe details about the organization that could help me bring it down." Tabatha straightened on the cushion and leaned back. Her head felt like it would explode from questions trying to force their way out.

What do the Guardians have to do with you and Derek?

Tabatha tried to laugh but it sounded more like a sob. "They want to kill me and my friends. They think powers like ours come from Satan and that we should be destroyed."

You closed Dana out. Can you reverse that? Can you still talk to her?

"Any time within the three days since her death. After that, not usually."

Usually?

"It's been four days since Missy died, and I can still hear her. Do you have something to do with that?" She swallowed hard. "And you've been gone a lot longer than that."

Never mind about me. You need to try again. Ask Dana what you need to know. Give her one more chance.

Tabatha noticed Elizabeth had avoided her questions again but lowered her shield and drew in a drink of cool air. Dana's sobs drifted across the void of death. "Dana, you've got one more chance. Will you talk to me?"

Dana's answer held a hint of fear along with her anger. *Go away. You can't help me. You killed me. You can't change that.*

Tabatha swallowed the bitter taste of guilt. "Who is the leader of the Guardians?"

Go to Hell.

Dana. Elizabeth's warning tone threw the atmosphere into a cold silence.

Who is that, Tabatha? Fear chilled Dana's voice. *Who is calling to me?*

I am Elizabeth Ann Morrie. Answer her questions, Dana.

I'm not falling for that trick, Tabatha. Elizabeth has been dead a long time. I ain't telling you a damned thing.

A loud screech of terror filled Tabatha's head. She covered her ears. A foolish move, she knew. You can't close out what is coming from inside you.

"What was that? What's going on?"

Tabatha, make her go away. I don't know anything. I swear. I don't know who the leader is. I only knew what Dub told me. No names. Dana's sobs grew louder. *No. No. Get her away from me.*

Dana, if you're lying, Tabatha will raise your soulless body and command you to talk. It's not a good feeling. You'll have no control over what you do or say. You'll be her puppet. Now. Who is the lord of the Guardians?

I don't know! Dana screamed. *I swear, I don't know.*

Tabatha batted away her building guilt and pity for Dana. "Do you want me to do anything for you, Dana? Anyone you want to say anything to? Any last regrets?"

There was a long silence before Dana answered. *I had no one close enough to care what I have to say. And it's too late to have regrets. God is through with me. No reprieve.*

Tabatha ran her tongue over her dry lips. "Maybe that is the true purpose of the three-day grace period, Dana. Talk to Him."

Dana sighed heavily. *She's gone now. Thank you.*

"Who's gone?"

Elizabeth. Goodbye, Tabatha. I'm not mad at you anymore. It's better this way.

"Goodbye, Dana. I'm sorry." Tabatha's attention returned to the other problem at hand. "Talk to me, Elizabeth. Who killed you?"

Don't raise my body, Tabatha. It will do more harm than good. It will be too painful for Derek to know. Love him and in time, he will move on.

"I don't want to wait. I want him now."

"Who are you talking to, Tabatha?" Derek asked as he limped into the living room.

She's doing it right under your nose, Tabatha.

A silence only a necromancer could know filled Tabatha's conscience when Elizabeth closed the link between them. What had her last comment meant? Who was doing what under her nose?

"Tabatha? Are you all right?" Derek slowly made his way to her side and sat on the arm of the couch.

"I'm fine. Just a little tired." She looked into his concern-lined face and tried to give him her best smile. "Where did you come up with that raggedy robe?"

"Don't try to change the subject. That was more than tired I saw out there. Something frightened you, Tabatha. Now, start talking."

"When I flung the file at Frank I saw a photograph I'd not noticed. I thought I'd seen the person before."

"I can't believe you gave him the file before I got a look at it. I could skin you alive for that."

"I had Bertha make copies. They're in the desk. I'm going to go lie down for a few minutes. You need to do the same. The doctor made me swear I'd make you rest. Then we'll look at the files."

A slow smile lifted the corners of his lips. "I will if you join me."

"We both can't fit in that twin bed. And you can't make it up the stairs yet. Besides, isn't Shane still in there?"

Derek nodded. "Sound asleep. That boy needs a daddy."

"Well, don't get any ideas, buster. Rhonda can find him one. I'll give you all the kids you want." She chuckled. "Now who's turning pale?"

Bertha stomped into the living room, her fists on her hips. "Mr. Derek, why aren't you in that bed? Am I gonna have to treat you like a child? Get. Get." She waved her hands toward the hallway. "Off with both of you."

"Yes, ma'am," Derek said with a sigh of resignation. "A short nap; then I want to see that damned file."

"Your wish is my desire, master."

"Yeah, right. If it fits into your plans." He shook his head and grasped her hand. "Come on. I'll walk you as far as the stairs."

As they brushed past Bertha, Derek glared at her. "After this is over, we're going to get a double bed for that room."

Bertha's laughter trailed behind them.

Thirty-eight

Tabatha stretched across the bed and placed her forearm over her eyes. Elizabeth's warning repeated itself over and over like a mantra. "Under my nose. A hint?" She jerked her arm away from her face when she felt the bed give with the weight of someone sitting on its edge.

She released a pent-up breath. "Bertha, you scared me to death."

"Sit up. We need to talk." Bertha brushed her hands nervously over the skirt of her blue uniform. "You know, I'm nobody's fool. I know you're upset about something. Come out with it, baby girl."

"Why are you wearing that uniform?"

"Your momma threw a hissy fit. Said she wasn't going to have her servants running around looking like part of the family."

"Damn it. I thought she'd straightened up. I'll put a stop to this. If you wear that thing again, I'll fire you."

Bertha snorted. "You ain't been paying me, so trying to fire me would be kinda silly, wouldn't it?" A deep frown creased her brow. "Now, stop trying to change the subject. What is goin' on with you?"

Tabatha swallowed, released her breath and started again. She fought tears but couldn't understand why she was to the point of bawling. "I called my lawyer; he's sending you back pay and regular checks will come each week. If I'd known you were still working here, I'd have made sure you were being paid. He can't explain what's happened to Mom's checks, but he's reporting their disappearance to the police. He's taking my word on the fact they're missing at all."

"Tabatha." Bertha's tone held a warning. "I'm not talking about money and you know it."

"Elizabeth doesn't want me to raise her body. She said Derek doesn't need to know who killed her."

Bertha shot up from the bed, her dark chocolate skin fading to milk chocolate. "Are you saying you been talking to a woman that's been dead for a long time?"

Tabatha nodded. "Twenty years dead."

The old woman wrung her hands and swept the room with her gaze. "Has this happened before?"

Tabatha shook her head.

"What this dead woman wantin' from you?"

"Just to be left alone. She says it feels bad when a person is raised; like being a puppet, having no control. She said it would hurt Derek if he found out who killed her."

"Baby girl, she ain't restin'. She roamin' the earth with no peace. She wantin' somethin'."

"That's not all."

Bertha raised her chin and clasped her hands tightly in front of her. "Tell me."

"Missy has been dead for four days." She paused trying to come up with a way to say it without sounding silly. "She's still talking to me and Elizabeth's with her."

"Oh, lordy. I don't know what to make of this. You sure it's been four days?"

Tabatha wiped away a tear. "Positive. I don't know if I should tell Derek any of this or not. How is he going to handle the fact that Elizabeth is talking to me and doesn't want me to raise her? That she doesn't want him to know who killed her? Want to hear what I think?"

Bertha nodded, but said nothing.

"I think Frank killed her."

Bertha groaned. "I wouldn't want to be in your size sevens."

"I thought Frank didn't like me because of the curse. I didn't realize he was trying to keep me from finding out the truth."

"Now, you stop calling your gifts that. God don't curse people from birth, and you've been like this since I've known you."

Tabatha waved away her words. "I thought once he saw I was doing good with my . . . gift, he would start to understand and accept me. But I'm not so sure now. If he killed Elizabeth, could it be he . . . Oh hell, I don't know. Maybe I'm going down the wrong skunk hole."

"What skunk hole would that be?"

Tabatha and Bertha both screeched, jumping away from Derek's voice.

Bertha stomped her foot. "Mr. Derek, you scared the fool out of me. You shouldn't be up here. How'd you climb those stairs? You pop those stitches and I'll whoop you good."

Derek's face was hard, his eyes determined. "Who do you think killed Elizabeth?"

Tabatha stood from the bed. "I'm not saying until I have something to back it up." She paused before going to his side and helping him to the bed. "Bertha, can you find some pillows to put under his leg? Looks like he'll be staying up here for a while."

Bertha and Tabatha's eyes met, a silent agreement of silence passing between them. "I'm sure I can find some pillows." She left the room, her back ramrod straight.

Derek sat, then raised his leg onto the mattress. "Start talking, Tabatha."

"Missy is still talking to me."

"How is that possible? You said three days was the limit. It's been . . . ."

"I can count." Tabatha cringed at the anger in her voice. If she could have gotten her hands on Elizabeth right that moment, she'd have choked her. "I don't know. Some people refuse to leave. Maybe she won't let go until she knows the killer is caught."

"What's this got to do with Elizabeth?"

"Tell me about the wedding day, Derek. Where were you? Where was Elizabeth? Frank was your best man, right?"

"No. My brother, Garth, was best man."

"I didn't know you had a brother."

Derek shrugged. "He lives in Dallas; married with four kids."

She sighed. "Go on."

"Frank and I went to the same school, but he was Elizabeth's friend. That's how we came to hang together. Seemed every time Elizabeth and I went out, he showed up. It was like a damn threesome. After her death, I guess he clung to me because I reminded him of her. He loved her in his own way, I guess."

"But he was at the wedding, right?"

Derek's brow crinkled. "Yes. I remember seeing him. He was sitting in the back row of chairs. I think he was already half plastered before he got there. The wedding was in Jackson Square. It took some doing to get permission to close it off for the private affair. But since it was on a Tuesday, the city gave in and took the money."

Tabatha swallowed hard before asking the next question. "Who found her?"

"I did." He stared at the ceiling. "There were canopies all along the fence. The food and drinks were being readied in most of them. The others were lined up with tables and chairs. I remember seeing her in the area where they were putting out the cake, giving orders like she always did." He chuckled. "I turned toward her father when he said something about it being bad luck to see the bride before the wedding. When I turned back she was gone."

Bertha returned and tossed four large feather pillows onto the foot of the bed. "I'm going to fix Carla a snack. I'll be back in about twenty minutes." She pointed her finger at Derek. "I don't want to see you on that leg again today. Do you understand me?"

"Yes, ma'am. Only when I have to go to the can."

Bertha snorted. "Don't get cute with me." She glared at Tabatha. "Don't you go keeping him awake all day."

Tabatha rose to leave, but Derek grasped her wrist and drew her beside him. "If you want me off my leg, she stays."

Bertha shook her head but left without an argument.

Derek settled himself against his pillow. Tabatha thought he'd decided to take a nap and had settled beside him when he continued with his story.

"When it was time for the wedding to start, her father went looking for her. A few minutes later he came back saying he thought Elizabeth had run off. He was joking, but it scared me. Here we were in the heart of New Orleans. Not a safe place, really. But she wanted to be married in the park just like her mom and dad. I went to the car to see if she was there. I checked the portable toilets. I asked everyone if they'd seen her. I started checking all the stands. I noticed something smeared on the drape of the farthest one away from the main group. When I lifted the cloth I found her." He shivered as if a chill had run the length of his body. "She had been mutilated. Her dress ripped to shreds."

"What did you do?"

He snorted. "They tell me I went nuts, but the best I can remember, it was Frank that went crazy. Before Elizabeth's father could cross twenty feet, Frank was across the park and trying to put her back together. He was drenched with her blood by the time the cops got him off her." Derek's eyebrows collided above his nose. "Frank seemed to appear out of nowhere."

"The police questioned everyone, I'm sure."

"It was after midnight before anyone was allowed to leave. No one saw a damn thing. She was there one minute; the next she was butchered without a sound." He faced her. "Who do you think did it, Tabatha?"

"Can you visualize the scene? I mean before you went to look for her. Where was everyone?"

He sighed and looked away. "Who?"

"Start with her father."

"He was right beside me. Her mother was rearranging flowers by the altar."

"Just rerun it in your head. I don't know everyone. Where were they? You don't have to tell me, just think about it. Was someone there, then wasn't? Or were they one place, then all of a sudden close to the scene?"

"I can't remember everyone. There were caterers, off-duty officers, a lot of people I didn't know. Homicide said it could have been a homeless man who had been begging for food earlier, but I don't believe it. Who killed her, Tabatha?"

"I don't know who killed her, Derek. I'm doing the same thing you did back then. Trying to think of anything that would add up to a good answer." She opened her mouth, and the next words flew out before she could stop them. "Elizabeth doesn't want you to know. She said for me not to raise her."

Thirty-nine

Derek's mind rearranged Tabatha's words like a jigsaw puzzle, trying to make sense of them. He dissected the sentences, his brain rejecting all the possibilities.

Elizabeth is talking to her? No. That wasn't what she said. He sucked in deep greedy breaths, nearly hyperventilating. He didn't care. Why wouldn't his psyche allow him to think? *Okay. Stop. What exactly did Tabatha say? 'Elizabeth doesn't want you to know. She told me not to raise her.'* He rubbed his face with his hands before running his fingers through his hair. He reached for Tabatha. She wasn't next to him. His gaze swept the room, finding her in the corner close to the door.

"Run that by me again. I'm sure I didn't understand you." Derek forced the words past his throat. His voice sounded gravely, grizzly almost. He came across as dangerous, even to his own ears.

When Tabatha spoke again, her words were quiet, plain and to the point. "She's with Missy. Maybe that's why she can still talk to me." She swallowed hard before looking away.

"How? How can this be?"

Tabatha shrugged.

"That isn't an answer, woman," he spat.

Tabatha shrunk deeper into the corner; her eyes glistening with unshed tears.

Derek released a sigh of exasperation and seized one of the bed pillows in a death grip. "What are you saying, exactly? Spell it out for me. I'm having trouble wrapping my mind around it."

"How do you think I feel? I was talking to Missy and she up and tells me she's not afraid anymore because she has a friend with her. I thought maybe it was the Angel of Death coming for her. Then she tells me her friend's name. I still didn't want to believe it was your Elizabeth." Tabatha shoved away from the wall and strode to the window, turning her back to Derek. "I went to the living room to be alone while you and Frank talked. I came right out and asked Elizabeth if she would talk to me. She did. It's her, Derek." She turned to face him, tilted her chin up and glared at him with a defiant stare. "Simple enough for you?"

Derek jumped to his feet, gasping with pain when the foot of his bad leg hit the floor. Tabatha started toward him, but he gritted his teeth and flung his hands in front of him. "Stay away from me."

He saw the hurt in her eyes, but it wasn't enough to squelch the anger burning in his soul. "Why didn't you call me? Why wouldn't you let me talk to

Elizabeth? Are you so jealous of her that you'd deprive me of that one pleasure?"

"Yeah, I was going to run right out there and tell you in front of Frank, that Elizabeth would like to have a word with you. And let me set you straight, jackass. You want Elizabeth, fine. I'll not stand in your way. Go lie with her. You try to find out who killed her. I'm finished."

She reached for the doorknob, but Derek slammed his hand against the door. "I'm not finished. I want to talk to her. Now."

"Derek, it doesn't always work like that." Her voice shook. Whether it was from fear or anger, he wasn't sure. "I'd like to talk to Dub; find out the leader of the Guardians. For reasons beyond me, some dead choose not to talk. Maybe they're being stubborn. Maybe they're finished. Maybe they're glad it's over. Maybe some of them go straight to where we go when we leave here. I don't know. All I know is I've never had a twenty-year-gone soul talk to me before. This is as new to me as it is to you. And whether you like it or not, I can't make her talk on command."

"What's the difference in raising the body and asking questions?"

Tabatha sighed raggedly then walked away from him to sit on the edge of the bed. "No soul. They can tell you what the memory stored, nothing more. A soul can tell you what they think, feel."

Derek hobbled over to stand in front of her. "I want to talk to her."

"Well, good luck."

He grasped her by her upper arms and drew her so close her nose touched his. "Now."

A force like a solid wall striking him, forced him away from Tabatha and flat on his back in the center of the bed. His head spun from lack of oxygen, his lungs forgetting how to breathe. "What the hell was that?"

"Anger," she said between clenched teeth. She stepped away from the bed and stared off into the distance. "Elizabeth, will you talk to Derek?"

"Well?" Derek's heart ached. His head throbbed. The waiting was torture.

Tabatha shook her head. "Nothing."

His mind recoiled from her answer. "Nothing? She won't even talk to you?"

"Missy, can you hear me?" Tabatha looked into Derek's eyes when he closed his hand around hers.

Yes, I can hear you.

"Is your friend, Elizabeth, still there?"

Yes. But she said she's mad at you for telling Mr. Derek that she's here. She won't talk to him. She says she doesn't want to be inter . . . interrogat. . . .

Derek grunted. "Interrogated? When did I ever interrogate her? I only want to find the man who killed her. I need that satisfaction."

He needs revenge, Elizabeth whispered.

Derek froze. His eyes darted to Tabatha's. "That wasn't Missy."

He heard me? Elizabeth screeched.

"When we touch he can hear what I hear." Tabatha jumped and glanced at Derek. "She just slammed the door in my face. She's got a bit of a temper."

Derek's insides shook. "I need a drink, and I don't mean tea." He limped to the door, flinging it open.

"You shouldn't be going up and down those stairs. I'll bring you something."

"No. You women aren't going to coddle me to death. I'm fine. I need to work the soreness out. It's just a bullet hole. I've had them before. I'll probably have them again. I'll get my own damned drink."

"How old did you say you were, Derek?"

That stopped him in his tracks. "Forty." She smiled sweetly at him and Derek knew he was going to get a smart remark.

"Oh, I thought maybe it was four."

He grumbled under his breath as he made his way to the staircase. He leaned his full weight on the polished mahogany banister, threw his good leg over the top, and lifted his injured leg. He slid down to the first floor. "Where there's a will there's a banister. Now, if you'll help me get off this thing, I'll go get my drink."

"You mean you need my help with something? Imagine that." She took her time coming down the stairs, leaving him to straddle the wood for as long as she possibly could. He knew he must look ridiculous.

As they walked toward the kitchen Derek smiled. "I loved doing that when I was four, too. But our banister wasn't as long as yours."

"You know Bertha isn't going to let you go back up those stairs, don't you? She's going to fuss about you being down here again as it is."

"Bertha and I need to have a long talk. I'm not going to put up with being babied."

"Lord, I wouldn't want to be around when you tell her that. She's already laid claim to you. What her baby girl wants, she makes damned sure baby girl gets. And she knows I want you. So you are now part of her family. She will kill to keep you safe. Might as well accept that."

They found Bertha sitting at the kitchen table, staring into her empty teacup. Her lips moved in a slow chant, her eyes fixed and glazed over. Tabatha cleared her throat.

Bertha sat up suddenly, dropping the cup to the table with a clatter. "Mercy. baby girl, you caught me daydreamin'." She shifted her attention to Derek. "Boy, what am I going to do with you? I told you to stay put. You gonna tear that leg open again, and it's gonna get all festered."

"I came down to get a drink." When the old woman opened her mouth to comment, he raised his hands in front of her face. "I don't need anyone waiting on me. I'm a big boy now."

Bertha rose from her chair and planted her fists on her hips. "But the doctor said you're to rest, and I intend for you to do just that."

"He meant not to go to work for two days. Not to stay in bed for two days, old woman."

"Old woman, is it?" Bertha's eyebrows darted up. Her mouth thinned to a fine line. "I'll show you old woman. You ain't drinkin' no alcohol. There are pain pills on the counter over there. Take one of them. But I ain't lettin' you have no booze. I done called the doctor and he said no. Not a drop. So get that idea out of your fool head." She picked up her teacup, refilled it and placed it back on the table.

"I'm not taking pain pills. They knock me out."

Bertha clapped her hands. "Bingo, baby boy. Just what the doctor ordered. Rest."

He glanced at Tabatha and frowned at her smug expression. "Go ahead and say it."

She smiled. "I told you so."

Derek raked his hair away from his forehead. "Okay. You win. I'll take one pill. Take a nap. Then Tabatha and I have a job to do tonight. After that, I'll rest for two days. Deal?"

Bertha shook her head. "Where do you think you're going tonight?"

He looked at Tabatha. "The cemetery."

Forty

The flash of lightning and the sounds of thunder and rain hitting the windows woke Derek. His brain, still in a fog from the effects of the Demerol, was lethargic and confused. Something played with his subconscious, wanting to come to the forefront of his thoughts, but it jerked away each time he tried to grasp it. He needed to be someplace, but where? He glared at the clock on the night table. Seven minutes after five. He turned his gaze to the window, trying to decide if it was morning or evening, but with the storm brewing outside it was impossible to tell.

Drawing several deep breaths, Derek fought to clear his head, then rolled over and snuggled his face into the pillow and drifted between wakefulness and sleep. Bertha handing him that damned pill and a glass of iced tea flitted across his dreams. Tabatha and Bertha were arguing. About . . . what? He groaned and rolled over on his back again, blinking several times to clear his vision.

"You okay?"

Slowly, Tabatha came into view, a cup of steaming coffee in her hand. "Am I alive?"

"I'm afraid so." She set the coffee on the nightstand and went to stand in front of the window. "The Weather Channel says the rain will be out of the area by six. We can leave then, but I don't know how we'll get into the cemetery. They lock that cemetery up at three."

The cemetery. That was what they'd been arguing about. The memory of Elizabeth's voice returned, and with it a moment of indecision. She didn't want him to know who killed her. Didn't want Tabatha to raise her. Something about a puppet. The room began to spin and his stomach lurched. Derek shot out of bed and crumpled to the floor.

"Sick. Going to be. . . ."

Tabatha grabbed a nearby trashcan and reached him just in time. Derek snatched the can away and turned his back to her, sure his stomach was trying to tear itself from his insides. His whole body seized with each gut-wrenching expulsion. After a few moments of calm he felt a tap on his shoulder and looked around.

Tabatha held out a glass of water. "Rinse."

Derek did as ordered, pulled himself back onto the bed and breathed deeply. His head began to clear. He grasped the cup of coffee with shaking hands and swallowed one large gulp, waiting several seconds to see how his stomach would react to this new intrusion. So far, so good. He took another gulp. The coffee's warmth soothed his throat, then made a hot trail all the way down to his gut. Things were looking up.

He ran a gaze over the room to figure out where he was. The servant's room, he decided. "Where's the nearest bathroom?"

She pointed to his right. "It's only a half bath. If you want a shower, I'll help you up the stairs and wrap the leg so you don't get the wound wet."

Derek stood slowly. The world remained on its axis. He nodded, letting Tabatha put his arm across her shoulders to support some of his weight. Step by step they made it to the second floor and to the large bathroom down the hall from the bedrooms.

"Pull your shirt off." Tabatha unbuttoned his jeans and slid them carefully down his legs.

Derek tossed his shirt to the floor, sat on the toilet and lifted his legs so she could pull the pants away. As she wrapped the thin sheet of plastic around his thigh, the warmth of her hands spread to his groin. He grew hard and his heart began to race. "Shit."

Tabatha lowered herself onto her knees. She looked into his eyes and leaned in to brush her lips across his. "Before or after?"

He swallowed hard. "Before or after what?"

"You want me now or later?" She kissed him again, but this time her mouth was demanding, her tongue teasing his into action.

"My leg," he said between gasps.

She jerked away. "Did I hurt you?"

"No. I meant I don't think I could . . . you know." He felt a flood of heat rush to his face. It was bad enough that he'd lost any hint of self-respect having to have a woman undress him. Hell, now he was suggesting he couldn't make love to her.

Her eyes strayed to the bulge in his underwear. "Oh, I think you can. I'll get on top," she whispered and slowly maneuvered between his legs again.

Her mouth slid down his neck, kissing a trail to his collarbone. With each touch of her warm lips on his throat, tremors traveled over his entire body. She worked her hand under the waistband of his briefs, finding her target. Her hot hand surrounding him, her lips playing their game of seduction, combined to drive him mad. He gritted his teeth.

"Jesus! Tabatha, stop."

She glided her head back and forth while she trailed her lips across his taut nipple. "You only have two options; before or after the shower. Stopping isn't a choice."

"Here? On the toilet?" This just was too surreal.

Tabatha smiled seductively, removed her hand from his briefs and stood. "My bedroom."

His mind racked up reasons why this wasn't a good idea. "What about Bertha? Rhonda? Bobbie? Shane?" He sounded and felt more frantic with each name.

"Bertha went home. Rhonda took Shane to her mother's house. Her mother is taking him to Disney World for a week. Rhonda won't be back until later tonight. Bobbie went out. Said she had business to take care of and that she'd be home before midnight. She called Travis to take her, so she's safe." Tabatha smiled down at him. "We're alone."

Derek groaned, a desperate sound even to his own ears. "Tabatha . . . ."

She placed her finger over his lips and shook her head. "Shhh. It's what I want. No strings. I don't expect forever. Just here. Just now."

He found the strength to push himself up, using his one good leg to stand before her. Still on her knees, her lips pressed against his hardness, only the thin material of his underwear separating him from her mouth. He grasped her arms and pulled her to her feet. All reservations melted away. Her body pressed against him, her hungry eyes staring into his was all that he could think about. He wanted her more than he'd ever wanted anyone or anything. His groin cramped with his need.

Tabatha stepped away and placed his arm over her shoulders, leading him out of the bathroom and to her bed.

"Lie down." Her voice washed over Derek like a caress. He lowered himself onto the bed and drew her close. With shaking fingers he released the button and pulled down the zipper of her jeans, ran his hand under the denim and panties, cupping her bare bottom. He snuggled his face into her firm belly and inhaled her scent, soft and warm, calling out to him. Slowly, Derek forced the jeans and panties down to her knees.

Tabatha braced herself on his shoulder with one hand while working her clothing off with the other, first the jeans and panties, then t-shirt and bra. She stood before him naked, breasts heaving with each breath, her eyes boring into his.

"Touch me, Derek."

Though his body shook with need, he forced himself to slow down, be gentle, when all he wanted to do was throw her down on the bed and devour her, bury himself so deeply into the hot, wet core of her passion, he'd make her scream with pleasure. Instead, he gently brushed his fingertips over her breasts. She released a shivering sigh. His tongue slid over her lips, leaving behind a simmering moistness he longed to feel against his own lips. Derek made a hot, wet trail to her belly, darting his tongue into her belly button.

"Lie down, baby." There was so much passion, need and trust in her eyes. Derek thought of stopping but knew it had gone too far. He maneuvered himself onto the bed, positioning himself at her hipbone. He kissed it gently.

"Open up for me, Tabatha. Let me taste you."

She did as he asked, and Derek lowered himself between her legs, thrusting his tongue against the swollen nub of her womanhood. She whimpered, clawed at the sheet with white-knuckled desperation, and screamed his name. He slid his finger into her and felt her hot, wet grip, trying to draw him deeper. Back and forth, he worked in and out of her. Tabatha's whole body tightened as she rose from the bed. Her inner muscles grasped his finger. She screamed, and her orgasm flooded her with wetness.

Derek kissed a sensual trail up Tabatha's body before she rolled to her side to face him. He poured every emotion and need he'd been withholding, into their embrace. When he drew away he gazed at her. The blue of her eyes had darkened to the color of the Caribbean Sea and held an intensity that almost frightened him.

"Tabatha?"

"Shut up." She kissed him, leaving him breathless and his body screaming for release. With slow deliberate movements she worked her lips down his throat. Her wet tongue lashed out to each nipple, before sucking it into her mouth and biting gently, sending shocks of pleasure coursing through his bloodstream.

Tabatha slid lower, down to his bellybutton, darting her tongue in and out in a seductive mockery of what was to come.

She rolled from the bed, looking down on Derek. He protested and tried to pull her back down beside him, but she shook her head and whispered, "No," before walking to the foot of the bed. She lowered her mouth to his ankle, kissing first up one leg then the other until she stopped just short of reaching his throbbing need. She wrapped him in her hand, gently caressing and massaging. Smiling, she touched her lips to his erection and allowed him to glide slowly past her lips. The moist heat of her mouth was nearly his undoing. He gasped for air as a tingling numbness gripped his whole body, sure that he would faint like a silly girl if he didn't fight it.

Tabatha released her hand from him and drew him in deep, deeper. Sucking with her lips, licking and probing with her tongue, she sent him to the edge of bursting.

"Tabatha, please."

In a lightning quick move he slid from Tabatha's mouth, pulled her on top of him and guided himself into her. She was wild with her own passion and took all of him in one hard, quick action. She moved with urgency, bringing him out nearly to the tip of her entry then thrusting him deep into her once again. He met her every downward stroke with an upward movement of his own.

She threw her head back and gasped before the walls of her body tightened around him. "I'm going to . . . ."

He answered her unfinished statement with his body's own explosion. The world darkened and stars burst inside his brain. The climax seemed to last forever and not long enough at the same time.

Tabatha collapsed atop him, breathing hard, her heartbeat thundering against his chest. "Are you trying to kill me?" She giggled.

He pulled in several breaths before trying to answer. "Me? I was going to ask you the same thing."

As Tabatha lay against him, their bodies still joined, he felt himself begin to harden and groaned. With a slow gyrating movement of her hips, the heat of passion began to build again.

A beam of sunlight broke through the clouds and past the windows, bathing them in a golden glow, adding to the warmth of their lovemaking. At that moment, his world was perfect.

Forty-one

Tabatha closed her eyes and desperately tried to hold onto the glow of peaceful happiness surrounding her. The memory of making love, of Derek's soft declarations and promises were still fresh in her mind.

"Are you listening to me, baby girl?" Bertha's voice cut through Tabatha's reminiscences like iced coffee on a winter's day. "A chicken won't be a powerful enough sacrifice. It's got to be something more . . . ."

Tabatha nodded. "Elizabeth's only been dead twenty years, not a century."

The old woman expression hardened with disapproval and her mouth turned down hard. "I don't see why this can't wait until tomorrow night. Derek shouldn't be out wandering in no graveyard. Just look outside. The rain may be over, but it's left behind a terrible fog, and it's thick as my gumbo roux out there. He's going to catch his death."

Looking out the kitchen window, Tabatha knew Bertha was right. It wasn't a fit night for the dead or the living.

"What can you be thinking?" Bertha asked.

"It's the eve of the full moon. My powers are at their peak for the next three days and the dead are drawn to Luna's power on nights like this." Tabatha glanced up when Derek entered the kitchen. He held a black leather backpack out to her. "This will work better than that canvas satchel you've been carrying."

Her heart skipped a beat. It had been years since a man had given her a gift, and then it had been her grandfather. "Thank you. It's beautiful." Swallowing hard past the lump of emotion in her throat, Tabatha said, "Your choice. If you want to wait until the weather is better, it's okay with me."

Derek shook his head. "No. Now. Tonight. I'm ready."

Bertha huffed before flinging open a nearby cabinet door and taking out two gallon jugs filled with a dark red substance. "Take this. If it don't work, you can kill another chicken."

Derek took the containers from her and hoisted one to eye level. "It's warm. What is this?"

"Goat's blood," Bertha whispered as if afraid someone would overhear.

Derek quickly set the jugs down and wiped his hands down the legs of his jeans.

"Don't get squeamish, boy." Bertha clicked her tongue at him. "You want Miss Elizabeth raised, somethin' gotta give blood. To raise a body gone twenty years, it's got to be--"

"He doesn't need to know, Bertha," Tabatha interrupted her. "Derek is ready. I want to get this over with. We need to be concentrating on the child killer, finding Missy. I want to break up the Guardians. I want to find Phelps." Pausing, Tabatha stared hard at Bertha and hoped she was getting her point across. "This is what you've wanted, too, isn't it?"

Bertha's eyes widened. "Why would I want Elizabeth. . . .?"

"No. But you want me to use the magic. You want me to build on my powers, to become strong like Paw-Paw and Daddy were. I understand that now." Thinking hard, she began figuring things out as questions came to her. "Can I pick and choose how I use it? Yes. Can I turn down Derek? Yes. Should I? I don't know. I love Derek. If this will make his life easier and give him the chance to move on, then I have to do this. Not only for him, but for me."

Bertha's eyes filled with tears before she turned away. "I wish I had the power to help you, child. But I don't."

"What power do you have, Bertha? I know . . . I feel some kind of energy flowing from you sometimes."

Taking a deep breath, Bertha faced her. "Another night, baby girl. Now go. And, Derek, you take care. You hear me?"

"Yes, ma'am. I have a jacket in the car." He hugged her tight. "Nothing's going to happen to me. I promise."

She pushed out of his arms, grabbed a dishtowel from the fridge door and wiped angrily at the counter. "Don't tempt the fates, baby boy. And don't make promises out of your control. Now, run on. I'll be waiting for you when you get home."

Tabatha opened the door and made her way down the stoop. Derek followed closely behind.

"It's going to be tough driving in this mess." Derek's voice sounded muted in the thick mist. "We'll have to take it slow and easy. Don't want to end up at the cemetery in a hearse."

Tabatha stopped so suddenly that Derek nearly knocked her to the ground. The sense of another person in the fog surrounded her with cold fear.

Derek grasped her arm, steadying her. "What's wrong? Did you forget something?"

"We're not alone." Dread closed around her throat like a fist trying to choke the life from her. She drew a deep breath and searched the wet blanket of air around them.

"Sorry, Detective, but that's my girl. I'd appreciate it if you'd get your hands off her."

For the first time in her life, Tabatha understood the old saying 'my blood ran cold.' A shiver ran down her spine then back up to her brain. She searched the fog-shrouded yard for the owner of the voice, though she recognized it instantly.

"Where is he? Can you see him?" Derek whispered frantically.

She shook her head. "What do you want, Phelps? I don't have time for your games."

"Not a game, darling." Phelps' endearment, spoken with a low hum of anger, rushed over her with sandpaper roughness. "You've played hard to get long enough. I've got a plane waiting and you're coming with me." He stepped out of the fog dressed in combat camouflage and strange looking goggles shoved up to his forehead, a gun in his hand. "Don't make me force you, Tabatha. I've grown tired of waiting for you."

Derek stepped from behind Tabatha, putting her to his back. "You'll have to go through me, Phelps. Tabatha is mine." He shifted his weight from his good leg to his injured one and back again, rubbing his back against Tabatha.

She started to move away but realized, with the scrape of the butt of Derek's gun against her stomach, that he was trying to tell her to arm herself. Tabatha had no idea what kind of gun it was, only that it was big. She lifted it out of his holster and took a step away. "Drop it, Phelps. I don't want to shoot you, but I will."

He laughed and cocked his pistol. "Shall we die together, darling? Is that the game you want to play with me? Recreation time is over. Or is this a diversion to give your cop time to--"

With a howl of rage, a sleek black cat leaped from the fog and onto Phelps. Her claws tore into his face and throat, sending a geyser of blood from his wounds. Screams filled the air as he tried to escape from the razor-sharp teeth tearing his skin away.

Tabatha shot, the slug hitting the pavement close to the commotion. The recoil of the gun knocked her to the ground and its roar nearly deafened her. The cat jumped into the air and rushed away a few feet before turning to look at Tabatha.

Tabatha jerked her attention back to Phelps, but he had managed to crawl way. The sound of a car door slamming shut, the roar of an engine, then the crunch of tires moving quickly down the drive told her he was gone.

Derek stood looking down at her, his legs spread slightly, his arms crossed against his chest. "Why didn't you kill him when you had the chance? He'll be back, you know."

Tabatha fought for air. "I was aiming for the bastard's head. What the hell is that thing? A cannon? Shit."

He grasped her hand and pulled her to a sitting position. "It's a .45."

A nude Bobbie stumbled out of the fog and smiled. "Guess we showed him."

Derek shook his head and tossed her a jacket. "Bobbie, will you put some damned clothes on?"

Tabatha chuckled. "So that's your so-called housecat disguise?" She ran her fingertips over the lump on Bobbie's forehead. "You're hurt."

Bobbie fluttered her hand through the air as if to brush away Tabatha's concern. "It'll be gone within five minutes. We shifters heal quickly." She sat cross-legged at Tabatha's side. "Where are you two going in this soup?"

Tabatha brushed her hair out of her face. "To the cemetery."

"You should be safe from Phelps. I'm pretty sure I took out an eye. He's going to be a regular pirate; one eye, peg leg." She chuckled, but sobered quickly. "If he does come back though, his anger will be a quagmire of madness. I felt his anger. He's crazy, Tab. Stone, brain rot, nuts." She tugged the jacket closer around her nude body. "Want me to go with you?"

Tabatha shook her head. "This is something Derek and I need to do on our own." She smiled. "Closure."

Bobbie nodded. "I understand. Be careful, woman. Rhonda and I need you. You're our cornerstone, our strength." She stood, tossing Derek's jacket back at him and waggled her bloody fingers. "Bye-bye, Derek." With an exaggerated model's walk, she sauntered away.

"I hope all her kind aren't exhibitionists." He shook his head and said, "She's right, you know. Without you, we'd all be screwed. We're all counting on you."

The weight on Tabatha's shoulders pressed heavier. "God, please give me the strength to hold us all up."

Forty-two

The cemetery reminded Derek of an old black and white horror movie. The dense fog made breathing difficult and his vision could only penetrate the wetness a few feet in front of him. The mist swirled around them as if dancing a morbid ballet of excitement at their arrival.

The clanking of tools as Tabatha hoisted her bag onto her shoulder seemed out of place in the silence. "Thanks again for the backpack. It's really nice, especially in weather like this."

"You're welcome." No matter her façade of bravado, Derek knew she was afraid. Not of the ceremony, but of what his reaction would be to facing Elizabeth once again. He looked away, shocked to discover a sharp edge of apprehension cutting into his own bravado.

"How are we going to get in? This place has been locked up for hours."

"I called and arranged for the gate to be left unlocked. Told them we had gotten an anonymous tip that the Voodoo Killer would be disposing of a body here tonight."

Tabatha nodded. "Good thinking, but don't you think they'll call the department to check on your story?"

"I doubt it. The caretaker has known me for twenty years. We've talked about the killings. And with three kids of his own, he wants this bitch caught as much as we do." Derek grabbed the two jugs of blood, walked to the entrance, and after setting one of the jugs on the ground, lifted the latch. The gate swung open with a groan of hinges too long without oil. Derek picked up the jug from the ground and they walked through and closed the gate. Crypts reached skyward like miniature, windowless skyscrapers. The sheer number of them nearly overwhelmed him.

"Creepy, huh?" Tabatha asked with a shudder. "I keep expecting to see Lon Chaney pop out from behind something."

"He isn't buried here is he?"

She giggled. "No."

"Whew."

"Lead the way, Derek. Let's get this done and get out of here. I knew there was a reason I always did this at sunset."

He began walking through the maze of crypts. "What do you mean?"

"Ever get the feeling you're being watched?"

"Yeah, why?"

"At sunset, the feeling is there, but it's like a light touch of interest. Right now, it's as if in each tomb we pass someone is grasping for me, pleading with me to bring him or her back. I can feel their touches, cold but not quite lifeless. It's not a bad feeling, just unsettling."

"We're here." Derek set the jugs on the ground, settled himself on the concrete graveside bench and once again withdrew a mini whiskbroom from his pocket. He brushed away the dirt from the top of the sarcophagus-style tomb. "Hi, Lizzie. I know you're going to be mad as hell, but I've got to do this. Please try to understand." He straightened and faced Tabatha. "Where do you want me?"

She ran her gaze over the area. "Step away for a minute. You can return to the bench after I make the circle. Until I have Elizabeth in front of me, do not move toward her. I've heard stories of the re-animated attacking if they think someone is going to hurt the one who raised them."

Derek forced his mouth down hard and raised his eyebrows sharply. He stood and walked backward in long exaggerated strides. "Is that where they get the term 'death grip'?"

Tabatha smiled. "I don't know." The sound of the backpack's zipper ripped the silence. She placed a long blade at her side and removed the container of salt, glanced skyward, then started to etch the circle in a clockwise direction, keeping her footsteps outside the circle. Stepping into the ring, she bowed as if in prayer. Raising her head, she took a deep breath, her body straight, facing the tomb. Stardust-speckled light shimmered on everything surrounding her. "Well, that's new," she whispered. "Come back into the circle, Derek. Sit. Do not say a word."

He swallowed so hard the noise of it hung heavy in the mist. The second he stepped into the area, he felt the magic. Hot and yet cold at the same time, it surrounded him. Knees shaking, stomach rolling, heart thumping so hard he worried it would fight its way out of his chest, Derek collapsed so firmly onto the bench that it jarred his teeth.

"What's the knife for?"

"Like I said, sometimes the dead can attack. Conventional means don't stop them."

Tabatha took the bottles of blood, pouring them around the grave. It exited the jar in a mixture of coagulated clots and separating liquid. Tabatha's mouth moved in a silent chant before her voice grew forceful and loud, "Rise, Elizabeth Ann Morrie. I command you to live."

A clump of soil flung from the side of Elizabeth's tomb, landing at Derek's feet. It startled him so badly he cleared the bench in one swift tumble, landing on his feet on the opposite side. He stared at the soil for a moment then returned his gaze to the tomb. The concrete slab covering the casket trembled and slid to the side. The casket swung open, and Elizabeth's body floated upward and hovered. Eyes slowly opening, Elizabeth looked at Tabatha and drifted to stand in front of her. Derek fell to his knees, gasped for air, and fought not to weep. She was still as beautiful and youthful as on the day she was taken from him. He let his hungry gaze sweep over her. When he looked into her eyes his heart ached. Though this may be Elizabeth's body, her eyes held no warmth, no life. The bright light of her soul was gone. This wasn't the woman he'd loved. Only her shell remained. Pain washed over him in hot waves of regret. Drawing a deep breath, he walked to Tabatha's side.

"Elizabeth, I am Tabatha Gray."

Elizabeth's head tilted to one side then the other. "I know who you are. Why are you here?"

"There is someone who needs to ask you some questions. I want you to give him answers." Tabatha reached out, grasping Derek's hand, drawing him closer. "Elizabeth, I'm going to step away. I'll not be far." She looked into Derek's eyes. "She isn't real. It's just the shell. Don't expect emotion. Just ask your questions and be satisfied with the answers she offers." Tabatha took a step away before Elizabeth's hand grasped her wrist.

The coldness of her grip raced through Tabatha's body. "I'm only going over there, close to the edge. I won't leave you here, Elizabeth. I promise." She pulled Elizabeth's grip from her arm and stepped away.

Derek cleared his throat. "Hello, Lizzie."

She once again tilted her head and stared at him. "Hello."

"Do you know who I am?"

A look of confusion crossed her face. "Yes, I know who you are. Derek Timothy Bainbridge, but I don't understand why you're here."

He felt himself flinch at the use of his middle name. Lizzie had used it only when she was angry with him. "That's right. I hate to bring up bad memories, but I need to know who hurt you." He cleared his throat. "Who killed. . . .?"

A gust of hot wind knocked Derek to the ground and a screech of anger nearly burst his eardrums. His gaze darted over the area, finally finding Tabatha crawling on her belly toward him. "What is going on?"

Tabatha gasped. "Her spirit has taken over. I've lost control of her. She'll not obey me now."

Their attention was jolted back to Elizabeth when her corpse fell to her knees, drawing a deep breath before slowly rising to her feet again. Her face was twisted with anger and disgust.

"I told you not to raise me, Tabatha."

"It's not her fault. I made her do it."

The wind died and Elizabeth's features softened. "There's nothing to worry about, Tabatha Gray. I mean no harm and I do not want to stay." Elizabeth returned her attention to Derek. "You were always hardheaded. Why couldn't you leave it alone? God will take care of my killer. His judgment will be much harsher than anything you could do."

Derek said, "I have to know. Who killed you, Lizzie?"

"No!" The shouted denial came from the darkness like a blast of thunder. Frank moved from behind a nearby crypt, stumbling toward the circle. When he met the edge, a surge of power kept him from entering. "Let me in, Elizabeth. Please, let me in. I love you. Don't leave me again." His sobs racked his whole body.

Derek stormed toward him.

"Don't step out of the circle," Tabatha and Elizabeth said as one.

Stopping short of leaving the protection, Derek stared at Frank while clenching his fists at his sides. "Did you kill Lizzie, Frank? Was it you?"

Frank fell to his knees. "I'm sorry. I didn't know. I loved her. It was my fault."

"Did you do it to keep me from having her? Is that it?"

A trill of laughter surrounded them. "I love you, Elizabeth. Don't leave me, Elizabeth. You can't marry Derek, Elizabeth." The taunting voice bounced from one tomb to the next making it impossible to discern from what direction it came. "Perfect Elizabeth. Couldn't be satisfied with just Derek. No. You had to have Frank worship you, too. What about me?" The voice dissolved into a wail.

Frank crumbled into himself, sobs still racking his body. "I tried. You pushed me away. I wasn't Derek. I wasn't good enough."

Derek listened to the feminine timbre, so familiar but not quite grasping whom it was. "Who are you? What do you want here?"

"Derek, why? You were supposed to come back to me. Was her memory better than my arms? I loved you more than she ever did. Why did you abandon me?"

Derek's heart skipped a beat. "Mary? Oh, God, no. Why, Mary?"

"You were going to marry her. Frank begged her not to do it. It broke his heart that she'd chosen you over him. He's loved her since the first grade." Mary moved out of the darkness and toward Derek. "I loved you, but you tossed that love aside like it was so much garbage. I thought if I said yes to Frank you'd see what you were losing and come for me, but you didn't. I had to marry this," she gestured toward Frank, "this whimpering idiot."

"Derek," Frank choked on a sob. "I'm sorry. I'm sorry, Elizabeth."

"Derek? Elizabeth? What about me? I've spent too many years married to a man who cries out in his sleep for another woman." Mary reached into her handbag and withdrew a snub-nosed .38, aiming it at Elizabeth. "Why won't you die, bitch? Do I have to kill all of you?" Mary pulled the trigger before Tabatha knew what she planned. The bullet slammed through the shield and into Elizabeth's middle section. Her body jerked with the force of the slug, slumping, then straightened. She opened her mouth, emitting a horrifying screech. A light blue mist escaped and the corpse stilled. The mist formed into a glowing transparent form that surrounded Derek and Tabatha.

The sounds of feet striking the hard soil intensified. "Drop the gun, Mary," Mason shouted. "Drop it, or I'll shoot."

Derek saw Travis Dillon, Hal Wayne and Troy Jackman work their way around Mary until she was surrounded.

"I've got her covered," Mason said. "Go check the area. Make sure she's alone."

Travis darted to his left, Hal to his right, and Troy directly behind him.

Mary turned her gaze to Derek. "This is all your fault, you know. If you'd only loved me." She raised the gun toward Mason. Before she could pull the trigger, Derek fired. Mary sank to the ground, dead.

"No," sobbed Frank. "No. Mary, don't die. I'm sorry. I do love you. Please don't leave me."

Mason placed his hand on Frank's shoulder. "Come on, Frank. It's over."

Frank jerked away from his touch, bared his teeth and snarled like a rabid dog. "Get away from us! We don't need you." He picked up Mary's gun and hugged it to his chest. "If I'd only loved her more, none of this would have happened."

Tabatha took a step toward him but stopped abruptly. "Let me go, Elizabeth."

The power lessened around Derek then returned when Tabatha walked away. With a kick at the soil, she broke the circle of power, knelt down in front of Frank and reached out for the weapon. "Let me have the gun, Frank. You don't need it. No one is going to hurt you."

His eyes met hers. "Bring her back to me. I'll love her more this time. I'll make her forget Derek. You can do it."

"No. I can't. It wouldn't be her, Frank. Look at Elizabeth. Is that really the woman you loved?"

He did as she said and then shook his head. "No, but I don't care." He leaned close and whispered, "I know who the Lord of the Guardians is. If you bring her back to me, I'll tell you."

Mason took three quick steps forward before Frank raised the gun toward him. "Stop where you are."

"Detective Panner, you've had a terrible shock. You don't want to do this. Put the gun down." Mason inched closer.

Frank grasped Tabatha's blouse and pulled her closer. "The Guardians' Lord is . . . ."

"Frank!" Mason yelled. "Let her go. Now."

Frank jerked his arm out straight, the gun never wavering from Mason.

Derek fought to get to Tabatha, but Elizabeth's cloak of power refused him release.

A single shot rang out. A small hole formed between Frank's eyes and he slumped against Tabatha.

Screaming her name, Derek tore himself away from Elizabeth's grasp. When he came to Tabatha's side he frantically wiped away the blood splatters on her face and arms. "Did he hurt you? Are you hit?"

"No. I'm fine."

He rounded on Mason. "You son-of-a-bitch. You could have missed. You could have killed Tabatha."

" She's fine. I wouldn't hurt Tabatha. You know that."

"I ought to rip your balls off and shove them down your throat."

Tabatha opened and closed her mouth several times before sound finally came out. "Derek, I'm okay."

"See," Mason said. "No harm done."

Derek raced toward him, his face a mask of rage as he grabbed his boss by the shirtfront. "Frank could have jerked at the last minute and that bullet would have been in the back of her head instead of his."

Mason jerked out of Derek's grip and dropped to Tabatha's side. "I'm sorry if I frightened you. But he was going to kill me. I had to do it."

She nodded. "I know. Maybe he'll talk to me. Maybe I can still find out."

Mason shook his head. "He's dead, Tabatha; and even if he could still tell you, he'd regret it. His mother is still living. If Frank had been in his right mind he'd have thought of that. The Guardians would have killed her if he talked. Still could. They're a bad bunch."

Derek returned his attention to Elizabeth's body. Her once silky skin had begun to rot, her fingers decayed to the bone. Thin strands of sinew held the flesh that remained together, and her eyes had disintegrated to black holes.

Mason gasped. "Who or what the hell is that?"

"Send her back, Tabby." Derek fought to keep his emotions out of his voice. "I don't want to remember her like this."

A single tear trailed down Tabatha's cheek. "Return to your resting place, Elizabeth. Rise again only when God calls your name."

The corpse rose into the air and hovered over the tomb for a moment, then descended. The concrete slab returned, covering the shell that had been Elizabeth Ann Morrie.

"Holy Mother of God," gasped Mason.

Troy Jackman ran toward them, Hal and Travis trailing behind him. "We heard the shots. What happened?"

Mason nodded but never let his stare leave Tabatha. "What did I just see?"

She cupped his cheeks with her hands and drew his ear close to her mouth. A thick gray mist surrounded them for a short fragment of time. Derek leaned close enough to hear her whisper, "You will not remember seeing Elizabeth. Derek and I were here because of an anonymous tip that the killer was going to bring Missy's body tonight. You saw nor heard nothing more." She then mumbled a phrase Derek didn't understand.

She released Mason's shirt and walked away.

He took a step back and shook his head. "Come on boys, we need to call the coroner and the crime scene guys. We need to clean this up before the reporters and public see this mess." Mason never looked back at Elizabeth's gravesite.

Derek gathered Tabatha into his arms. "Are you sure you're okay?" She crumpled into his arms. "No, damn it, you're not okay." He searched for one of the officers. "I need an ambulance."

"No. I just need rest. My magic is empty. I'm exhausted." She shoved against his shoulder. "Look. Elizabeth is waiting for you. Go to her. This is your chance to say goodbye."

Elizabeth's spirit smiled back at him. "Are you sure? I don't need . . . ."

"Yes you do, and so does she. I'll be fine."

He stood before the spirit, not sure what to do or say. "Lizzie, I wish it could have been different. I had no idea Mary could do such a thing."

"Shhh. None of this is your fault. You can't make someone love you, nor could you make her not. You have to let me go, Derek. I'll go happily, knowing you have someone to watch over you. Someone who loves you as much as I do."

"She's so young, and I'm so. . . ."

"She's had a tough time of it. You are the first glow in her life since her grandfather and father died. I know you love her, Derek, and I'm okay with that. She needs you as much as you need her."

"I'll always love you, Lizzie. I'll always carry you in my heart."

"You'll always be a part of me." She raised her hand and touched his cheek, her fingertips nothing more than a warm wisp of air against his face. "Be careful, Derek. Someone you hold trustworthy is not what he seems. Tabatha is in danger. You must keep her close, safe from their harm."

"I promise."

Elizabeth's voice weakened, blending with the breeze. "The children's killer works in her own back yard. Stop her before it's too late for Missy." She smiled. "Goodbye, Derek."

Derek swallowed the lump of emotion threatening to choke him. "Goodbye, Lizzie."

Her spirit began to fade; then with a flash of blinding light she returned. In a shriek of terror she warned, "Tabatha's house is on fire! You must hurry. They're inside!"

Derek's heart raced. "What?"

"Hurry," she whispered into the wind and was gone.

Forty-three

"Hurry," Tabatha pleaded with Derek. Panic seized her in a vise-like grip as her lungs struggled for air.

"I'm going as fast as I can, Tabatha. If I drive any . . . ."

Derek's voice faded, the forward motion of the car froze and the scenery around Tabatha vanished. Blackness flowed over her before an explosion of light threw her back against the car seat, and sounds and sights assaulted her senses. Strange laughter drifted into her ears. Images of the upstairs hallway of Gray Manor flashed across her mind, and the overpowering scent and taste of kerosene burned her nose and throat.

The walls rotated around her, stopping long enough for her to see piles of rags at the foot of the bedroom doors. The sensation of bending at the waist while walking backward threw Tabatha into a momentary state of vertigo. She felt herself reach into her pocket and withdraw a box of matches, watched the match grate along the striker and a flame spark on the end of the wooden stick. She brought the match up to eye level and marveled over the colors-- yellow, red, and streaks of blue.

"So pretty," a voice said in a half-whisper.

Not her voice, Tabatha realized.

The match fell from her fingers and trails of flames raced toward the bedroom doors before igniting in a scorching flair of heat.

"No," Tabatha shouted. "Who are you? Why are you doing this?"

The intruder shrieked, then hissed, "Get out! Get out of my head."

Tabatha felt as if a door had been slammed in her face, and the scene was gone. She found herself back inside the car, staring into Derek's worried eyes. "Hurry," she whispered, feeling more exhausted than before. "Someone is trying to kill them."

Once again she was slammed against the seat, a thunderous crash of sounds rushing over her. Tabatha felt herself jerk forward and when she opened her eyes, she was looking out of someone else's eyes again. She watched the cup of tea in her hand as it tumbled to the floor. Smoke. She smelled smoke. Panic threatened to pull her into darkness. *I have to get out.*

Her mother's voice was a comfort at first. Then Carla's panic struck Tabatha full force.

Carla's mind rebelled against the smoke drifting under the door. Excruciating pains shot through her head, confusion tried to make her deny what she was seeing. Carla's hand reached out for the doorknob, then she hesitated and peered around the room at her belongings.

"No," she cried. "I can't lose it all. I won't. It's mine." The window was thrown open and Carla leaned out. "No. Too far down. Everything will be ruined." She ran her fingers through her hair, and her thoughts were a jumble again. *The money. The jewelry.* She stilled for a moment and a memory played across her mind. Her panic rose by notches. "The girls; the child. Oh, God! I've got to let them know. I've got to get them out!"

The backdrop spun in front of Tabatha's eyes like a movie on fast-forward, stopping in another bedroom. Suddenly, Tabatha was jerked from actor to observer, active perpetrator to horrified witness. Instead of looking out of another's eyes, she was watching the scene unfold from a distance that forbade participation. Their thoughts were as if spoken aloud. Tabatha could hear but couldn't speak. She couldn't help. All she could do was watch helplessly as her friends fought an unseen foe for their lives.

~

Rhonda lay on the bed, sleep fogging her thoughts. A strange glow permeated the front room of the suite, growing, then dimming. Cigar? *Maybe Derek's back.* But why would he be in her room? Besides, she'd never seen him smoke. She coughed. No cigarette or cigar could smell that bad.

Wakened by the furious beating of her heart, Rhonda shoved her fear behind her, stood and forced herself to enter the other room. Her breath caught and terror gripped her by the throat. Flames licked at the base of the door and smoke hovered along the ceiling. Her magic began to build inside her, a heat that thickened her blood. Though she'd not felt it since she was a teenager, she recognized it instantly. Did she start this fire? Had she dreamed of doing it, causing the magic to escape? She shook her head in answer to her own questions.

Reverse the magic, Rhonda.

Rhonda stumbled into a nearby corner. "Tabatha?"

Pull the power in. Take the fire away. Reverse the magic.

"I don't know how." She waited for a reply but none came. She slid down the wall and curled into a ball. She concentrated on the magic, trying to push it away, force it back down to the pits of Hell where she was sure it had been born. The door groaned, its wood buckling. Rhonda stared at it but kept her thoughts on reversing the magic. The flames shot up the door, and as if blown out like a birthday candle, vanished.

Rhonda jumped to her feet, raced to the door and grasped the knob.

Tabatha reached out her hand, placing it between the knob and Rhonda's hand. She cried out. Scorching pain seared the palm of her right hand. Blisters instantly formed, and began to burst and weep.

"Damn, Tabatha, what happened to your hand? How. . . .?"

"Oh, God, Derek. I'm seeing everything they see. Feeling their pain, their fear."

He gunned the engine after turning onto Saint Charles Avenue. "If you can feel them, they're still alive. Have you seen everybody?"

She leaned back, closed her eyes and pulled in a deep breath. "The killer. Momma. Rhonda." She bolted forward, eyes wide. "Bobbie!"

~

As if in answer to Tabatha's call, Bobbie switched off her hair dryer and raised her nose into the air. "Shit. The damn house is on fire." She ran to the connecting door to Rhonda's room, flinging it open. "Rhonda," she screamed, "get the hell out. Run." Following her own advice she ran to the exit, getting within a foot of it as it crashed open. Bobbie and Rhonda came face to face with Carla.

"We have to get out of here," Carla told them.

Bobbie ran her gaze over the floor length, royal blue silk robe, stopping at the flames licking the hem of the garment. She ran back and snatched a damp towel from the floor, and began to beat the flames away.

"Carla, you're burnt. Get out. Go."

"Have to save you." Carla slumped against the shattered and smoldering doorjamb. "Tabatha would never forgive me."

The snake side of Bobbie began to recoil from the flames. She allowed the fear, anger and desperation to feed her leopard until the fur lay just under her skin, waiting to escape, but held it at check. She couldn't shift in front of Carla. It would send her over the edge. Still, her leopard allowed her to move at incredible speed to Carla's side, catching her before she hit the floor.

"Rhonda's right here. Hurry." No other words were necessary. They ran, not stopping until they jumped off the porch and landed on the front lawn.

Carla lay gasping for air. "Where's Shane. Where's the baby?" Before Rhonda or Bobbie could stop her she rose and raced back into the house.

~

Horror cut through Tabatha like chainsaw. "No, Momma!" she screamed, and the sight was taken away.

Derek squeezed her arm. "Tabatha, we're here. The firemen are talking to Bobbie and Rhonda."

"Momma went back for Shane. She doesn't know he's not here. I have to get her out, Derek. I have to save her."

Derek pulled right up to the house, and Tabatha jumped out of the car before it came to a halt. She got within a few feet of the front door before a fireman stopped her. "You can't go in there, ma'am."

"My momma's in there!"

"No. Look. Johnson has her. See?"

Tabatha fought a crush of emotions at the sight of her mother's limp body in the arms of her rescuer. "Is she dead?" she whispered.

"No, ma'am. She'll live, but she's gonna hurt for a while." The fireman placed her on the grass and shouted, "Where's the damned ambulances?"

"ETA two minutes," answered another fireman.

Bobbie and Rhonda rushed to her side. Rhonda's eyes were round and glazed over with shock. Mild burns glowed red on her chin, arms and hand. Bobbie's burns, though less in number, were more severe, skin peeling from the calf of right her leg and arm.

Rhonda grasped the wrist of Tabatha's injured hand. "You're hurt. How did you do this?"

Tabatha ignored her question and lowered her gaze to Carla, choking back a sob. Her face was blackened, her hair singed, and the silk of her robe had fused to the skin of her legs. Carla's breathing was labored, fluids gurgled in her throat and choking coughs tore from her chest.

"I'm so sorry I wasn't here. This is all my fault," Tabatha said between sobs.

"No." Rhonda shook her head. "But someone did this, Tabatha. Someone tried to kill us. They set rags on fire in the hallway."

Derek came up and looked them over. "The ambulances are here. Tabatha, why don't you go with your mother?" He put his hand on Rhonda's shoulder. "You and Bobbie go in the other. I'll follow in the car."

Bobbie backed away. "I can't go to the hospital, Derek. I'll heal too quickly. And if they take blood from me, there'll be too many questions."

Tabatha glanced at Bobbie's burns and realized they'd begun to heal already. "Derek, take her. . . ." She didn't know where Bobbie could stay.

"I'll take her to the apartment. She'll be safe there."

"No. I need to shift. Change to the leopard. I'll be healed when I shift back to my human body." She glanced around. "Those trees by Nyssa's cottage--I'll go there. Derek, come back for me in a couple of hours."

He nodded. "Why leopard? Why not the snake?"

"The snake would want to shed its skin to rid itself of the wound. That saps me of strength and leaves my skin raw. Sort of like a micro-dermabrasion from hell." She glanced around at the scurrying firemen. "How will you explain my leaving?"

Derek nodded. "I'll think of something. Don't call attention to yourself."

She gave him a cocky smile. "Yes, sir." She strolled to the back of the house and out of sight.

Tabatha climbed into the ambulance with Carla, choking back her tears. "It's okay, Momma. I'm here. You're going to be okay."

"My duster. It's ruined."

"I'll buy you another one. Hell, Momma, I'll buy you a hundred more. What were you thinking going back into that house? You could have been killed."

"Shane. I didn't get Shane out," she sobbed, trying to sit up, but the paramedic gently pushed her back down. "I let it happen again."

"Momma. Shane is with his grandmother. He wasn't in the house." Tabatha swallowed hard. "I'm proud of you. You did a good thing saving Bobbie and Rhonda. Thank you."

Carla closed her eyes and released a deep breath. "Not enough."

"What do you mean 'happen again'?"

"My brother. We were only four years old. We were playing with matches and the curtains caught fire. I ran away and left him. He died. I couldn't let that happen again."

"Momma, you were a baby. You didn't know better. Let it go."

The female paramedic looked Rhonda over. "There's another ambulance waiting for you, honey. Don't worry. You're both going to Ochsner and will arrive within seconds of each other."

"I'm staying with my mother," Tabatha said. "I'm not leaving her."

"That's all right, but you'll have to stay out of the way." She placed an oxygen mask over Carla's nose and mouth and opened a bottle of saline, emptying it on the burns.

The paramedic from the second unit dashed over. "Who am I here for?" Rhonda glanced in Tabatha's direction as if waiting for her permission to leave.

"Go ahead. I'll see you at the hospital."

She lowered her gaze to the ground and cleared her throat. "I don't have insurance, Tab."

"Don't worry about it. I'll cover the cost. Now go." Rhonda turned and limped away.

Derek came to the back of the ambulance. "Is she okay?"

Tabatha choked on a sob. "She's hurting, Derek, and I can't do anything to help."

"Just let her know you're there."

"Baby girl! Where's my baby girl?"

Tabatha and Derek turned to find Bertha running from one fireman to the next screaming for Tabatha. The fireman Tabatha knew only as Johnson directed her to the ambulance. Bertha rush toward them with hands over her mouth and tears wetting her cheeks.

"Tabatha is fine, Bertha," Derek assured her. "It's Carla and Rhonda that got the worst of it."

"Oh, Miss Carla, you gone and burnt yourself up. Just look at you. Don't you worry; I'll take good care of you."

Mason walked up behind them and nodded once to Derek. "And how did you know about the fire, ma'am?"

"Everybody in the parish knows about the fire."

"Maybe, but the roads are blocked off. How'd you get here?"

"My usual path." She turned away from him, cooing and whispering over Carla.

"And just where is that?" Mason persisted.

Bertha raked her dark eyes over Mason. "What you trying to say, young man? You think I had something to do with this? You think I'd hurt my baby girl?"

"'Baby girl' wasn't in the house. But her mother and friends were."

"Stop it," Tabatha screamed. "Bertha had nothing to do with this. What the hell is wrong with you?"

Mason shrugged. "Wouldn't be the first time hired help . . . ."

"Bertha isn't hired help. She's family." Tabatha fought the magic building in her gut. "Why are you doing this?"

"As I was saying, people decide all the time to end a grudge with murder." He returned Bertha's once over with one of his own. "I hear you got magic of your own. Voodoo Priestess or something, isn't it?"

Bertha's back stiffened and her voice lowered to a hard-edged murmur. "What or who I am is no concern to you as long as I don't break any laws. Next time you fall on your face in Miss Gray's home, see if I take care of you. I'll just sweep you out with the rest of the trash."

The paramedic clicked her tongue. "We're leaving now. This patient doesn't need to hear this. Take your conversation elsewhere." She slammed the door shut in Mason's face.

Tabatha watched out the back window as they drove away. Derek took Bertha by the arm and led her to his car.

"Voodoo priestess?" the paramedic asked with a chuckle.

Tabatha shook her head. "Good grief." She couldn't think about this now. "I'll worry about that tomorrow."

"Scarlet," Carla whispered.

"What about her, Momma?"

"You're starting to sound like Scarlet." Carla smiled, a flash of white from her smoke blackened face. "Is your heart set on Derek, Tabby?"

"I love him, Momma. Have from day one."

Carla closed her eyes. "Be cautious then, Tabby. People you think are least likely to present a threat are the ones you need to beware of most."

"Your friend, Mary . . . ."

"Yes, her for one."

Tabatha told Carla what had happened in the cemetery, leaving out Elizabeth's rising and ghost. "It was self defense; they had to shoot her." When Carla opened her eyes, they were filled with questions. Tabatha nodded. "She's gone."

"I always suspected she was the one who killed Elizabeth. She was obsessed with Derek." A shiver ran over her body. "It hurts, Tabby. Make it stop."

The ambulance came to a stop and the back doors flew open. "I'll do everything I can." She laid her hand on her mother's thigh and felt Carla relax. "I promise."

Forty-four

Derek led Bertha to his car and opened the door for her.

"I can't believe that little shit, thinking I'd set fire to Tabatha's home." Bertha puffed up her chest and released a growl of anger.

"If I may be so rude as to ask again, how did you know about the fire?" Mason asked from behind her.

She slid into the car and shut the door without answering. Derek joined her and opened the windows. "Want to tell me?"

Mason got in the back.

"Oscar, my husband, is a retired fireman and still has a scanner sitting in the kitchen. He had it on listening to the dispatcher. Then the call went out for a fire at Tabatha's address. I didn't even stop to change. Look at me." She waved her hand over the simple housedress she wore. "I never go out in public dressed like this."

"You look fine." Derek turned the key in the ignition and buckled up. "You want to go to the hospital?"

She shook her head. "Take me home so I can change. You can just drop me off and go on. Tabatha needs you. My car's in the shop, but I can take Oscar's."

"How'd you get here?" Mason asked.

"My son dropped me off at the road and I came down the path. I figured I'd stay with my baby girl. Guess I wasn't thinking how bad it could be."

Mason nodded, seemingly satisfied with her answer. "I'm going to see what the firemen found. I may want to talk to you again, Bertha."

She raised her shoulders and dropped them with a flourish. "Suit yourself. I ain't got nothing to hide."

"What's your last name?"

"Monroe. Maiden name, Cuvier. But you know that already, don't you, Lieutenant? Voodoo priestess? Where did you hear that one? Nyssa Bouchard and her gossip?" Her nostrils flared. "Maybe you should check *her* out. Her halo ain't as straight as she pretends. No, sir."

The lieutenant stepped out of the car and walked away without comment.

"Get me home, son. Our baby girl needs her man there with her, not sitting here talking to no old woman." She lowered her voice and mumbled, "Or some puffed up, full of himself asshole."

It took all of Derek's self control not to laugh out loud. He looked behind them then pulled away from the curb and made a u-turn toward the river. "Bertha, you will never be old. You'll probably outlive us all."

She shook her head, her expression saddened. "No, son, I won't. I'm old. I just needed to make sure Tabatha was going to be taken care of." She glanced out the window. "You know where I live?"

Derek chuckled. "Yes, ma'am. Oscar and I have known each other since I was a rookie. But, I didn't know he was your husband until you said he was a retired fireman and told Mason your last name."

"Well, you ain't got time to catch up on things. Just drop me off. Maybe I'll bring Oscar with me to the hospital."

"Can I ask you one more question?"

"Shoot."

"You have some kind of magic like Tabatha, right?"

She inhaled deeply releasing it in a slow stream of breath. "Some call it reading tea leaves. I can look into them and see things. Sometimes it's the future or a warning. I'll never be like Tabatha, son. She's special among the special." With a pause and a nod of her head, Derek knew she had made a decision.

"Let me tell you the story of the Gray Legacy," she began. "You need to know."

~

Tabatha sat with elbows on knees, head in hands, one of them bandaged, her hair hanging down her arms to the calves of her legs. She rocked slowly. Derek's heart ached at the desperation in her body language.

"I'm here." He sat beside her and pulled her into his arms. "They're going to be all right, sweetheart."

Tabatha nodded but said nothing.

"Have you heard anything since they were brought in?"

"No. The doctors and nurses keep running in and out but don't stop to talk to me." She released a combination hiccup-sob. "Surely we'll hear something soon."

He rubbed her back and kissed the top of her head. "What was it like back there in the car? You scared the hell out of me. You went into a trance or something. Your eyes dilated so much there was no color left to them."

She cradled her face into the crook of his neck. "Imagine you can see something happening but from inside the heads of the people it's happening to. Like you're looking out of their eyes. You've got your own emotions and theirs to wade through, while trying to keep your sanity. You lose the sensation of being you. You become that other person for a fleeting moment. Feel their emotions. Smell their surroundings. Taste the air they breathe."

"Shit, that must suck."

Tabatha snorted with laughter. "Yeah. It sucks."

"Ma'am, are you Dr. Gray?"

She stood abruptly, facing the nurse. "Yes. Is my mom okay? My friend?"

"Miss Meads will be released in a day or two. But the doctor wants to keep your mother for a few days."

"Can I go to her?"

"Dr. Rider will be out soon. I'm sure he'll let you see her, but she's going to be sedated and may not make a lot of sense."

Tabatha swatted away the tears trailing her cheeks. "I just want to make sure she's okay. I need to see for myself."

The nurse smiled and patted Tabatha on the arm. "I understand, ma'am. I'd feel the same way if it were my mother." She glanced behind her. "Here comes Dr. Rider now. Everything is going to be just fine. You'll see."

"Thank you." Tabatha leaned against Derek.

"Dr. Gray?" The doctor's silver-gray, short-cropped hair stuck up in disarray. His blue eyes found hers and demanded her attention. "I'm Dr. Rider. Your mother has told us all about you, young lady."

"Is she going to be all right?"

"Second and third degree burns on her arms and legs, made worse by the fact that the robe she wore melded with her skin. We had to peel away the material and the skin came with it. She's in a lot of pain, but the Demerol will take effect soon. I'm concerned about the other symptoms she's exhibiting. Has she complained of feeling ill before the fire? Tired? Nauseated? Listless?"

Tabatha nodded. "She had an appointment to see her doctor about it. Our friend Bertha would be more apt to answer your questions. I've been gone for a while, but Bertha sees Mom on a regular basis. I'll have her come to see you, if you'd like."

Dr. Rider nodded. "That might be a good idea. I'll let you go in and see Mrs. Gray, but make it short. She needs her rest."

"Thank you."

Derek stayed at Tabatha's side as she started toward Carla's room.

"Hold on. Are you family?" Dr. Rider asked Derek.

"He's with me."

Rider shook his head. "Only family right now. Sorry."

Derek flashed his badge. "I'm going in."

The doctor bristled, his mouth turning down in a hard frown. "The patient isn't up for questions, Detective. I won't allow it."

Derek nodded. "I won't say a word. I'm not leaving my girl's side, though. I just want to be there in case she needs me."

Dr. Rider's eyebrows shot up. "Ah. So that's it. Very well. But, mind you, no questions."

As they walked to the side of the bed, Carla looked at her daughter. Tears streamed over her temples into her hair. "I hurt, Tabby. Make it stop."

"It will soon, Mom. Try to sleep."

"The house? Is it gone?"

"No. The firemen doused the flames pretty quickly. Mostly smoke damage they said. You shouldn't be worrying about that right now."

"My room? Is my room gone?"

Tabatha sighed deeply, and Derek felt it down to his toes. "Carla, we've not been in your room, so don't worry. And the firemen were in and out after the fire was extinguished. Nothing will be missing."

"Derek?" She reached out her hand to him. "I'm so sorry about Mary. How is Frank taking it?"

"Mom, Frank was killed, too."

"He tried to love her, but she'd never let him forget he wasn't Derek. Never good enough." Carla grasped Derek's hand tighter. "I wanted to tell someone, but I couldn't be sure. It was just a feeling. No proof."

"It's okay, Carla. Rest. It's not important now. It's over."

"No." She shifted her gaze to her daughter; more than pain shown in her tense expression. "Go in my room. It's okay. You'll find everything you've been looking for. Save what you can."

"I don't understand, Mom. What are you so afraid of?"

"I can't be poor again, Tabby. I couldn't bear it. When Nyssa told me that your will left her in control of the money, I was afraid I'd end up with nothing."

"Mom, if I died today everything would be yours."

Carla gasped. "Don't say that."

The corners of Tabatha's mouth quivered. "It's just an expression, Momma. Nyssa and Bertha will be taken care of if I should die before them. But you will be the main beneficiary. I'd never cut you out of my life or my will. And you don't have to worry about money. Paw-Paw invested well. None of us will ever hurt for money. So relax. You'll never be poor again. I promise."

Carla sighed, closed her eyes and smiled. "I'm safe?"

"Yes, Momma. You're safe. We'll take care of you."

Carla's breathing slowed; her grip on Derek's hand relaxed, and he pulled away. Tabatha and Derek readied to leave but turned back at the sound of Carla's gasp for air.

"Stay out of the garage. Something terrible. She's got too many secrets and bad ways. Don't trust her." Her hands flailed for theirs.

Derek brushed her hair away from her face. "Relax, Carla. I'm here. I'll make sure you're both safe. No one is going to hurt my girls."

"Your girls," Carla whispered. "Safe." Then she slept.

Tabatha slipped her hand into his as they walked down the hallway. They'd nearly made it to the elevator when he heard angry voices coming from the waiting room.

She groaned and buried her face against Derek's chest. "It's Nyssa and Bertha. Stay here. I'll put a stop to this."

Derek drew her closer, his arms tightening around her waist. The idea of Tabatha alone with Nyssa made his heart freeze in fear. "No. I'm coming with you."

She drew a deep breath before stepping out of his embrace and walking to the waiting room. She stood in the doorway staring at the two women standing toe to toe.

Nyssa bared her teeth, her voice escaping in a low rumble of hatred. "I want you out of my house, nigger."

"Nyssa!" Tabatha strode toward the two women, her soles striking the tiled floor echoed in the sudden silence. "When has Bertha ever been in your house?"

"This is between Bertha and me. Nothing for you to worry about." Nyssa smiled and reached out to touch Tabatha's face, but she stepped out of her reach. "Tabby. What's wrong? Why are you looking at me like that?" She jerked her gaze back to Bertha. "You. You've poisoned her against me." Her fists came up claw-like, ready to attack. Her breath escaped in a gushing gasp as she flew backward, landing on the leather sofa.

Tabatha brought her face close to the old woman's and stared her into the eyes. "If you come anywhere near my family or friends again, you will pay for your sins, Nyssa. Paw-Paw figured out your game, didn't he? He was going to cut you out completely."

Nyssa's chin lifted, her jaw jutting out in a defiant point. "He loved me. It was Carla and this . . . this nigger that poisoned his mind against me. It should have been mine. He was going to change the will. He promised me."

"Watch your mouth, Nyssa." Tabatha backed away from her. "Come on, Bertha. It's time to go home. The doctors want Mom to rest tonight."

"You can't choose her over me." Nyssa's voice was incredulous. "I'm the one that raised you. I taught you everything you know."

"The choice has been made. Do not step foot on my property again. Stay out of my life. Stay away from my garage."

Nyssa's face paled and she swallowed several times. "All my tools are in there. How can I take care of my gardens? No. It's mine. You can't do that."

Derek stepped between Nyssa and Tabatha. "You'll be served with a restraining order within the hour. You'll be allowed, for now, to remain in the caretaker's cottage, but you will not come any closer. Do you understand?"

"You can't put me out of my house. Raoul said it was mine until I died."

Derek felt a smile lift the corners of his mouth. "If you believe nothing else believe this. I will find proof of your guilt, Nyssa. You're going down."

Forty-five

Daybreak, still an hour away, draped the house in a melancholy blackness. Soot-encrusted windows allowed enough of the streetlamps' glow to enter and form shadows that took shape and danced like living entities on the walls. Water seeped through the ceiling, drop by drop, as if the house cried for its injuries. The heavy smell of kerosene and scorched wood permeated everything. Humid, smoke-choked air stung Tabatha's nose with every intake of breath. The atmosphere reminded her of a steaming vat of crab boil.

Tabatha ran her fingertips over a soaked armchair and for an instant saw her grandfather sitting in its comforting softness. He shrugged his shoulders, smiled and said, "So what? It's just a chair. Time to pick your own furnishings, sweet face." And with those words touching her heart and mind, he vanished, leaving behind the soft scent of cherry-blend tobacco and Old Spice cologne. Tabatha released a startled yelp when a bright light sliced through the darkness.

"Derek, you scared me." She placed her hand over her heart and exhaled.

"Sorry. I remembered I had a flashlight in the trunk of my car. Department issue. Stronger than anything you can buy at Home Depot." Derek ran the beam of light over the immense room. "Didn't think there would be this much damage down here."

"Mom's suite is directly overhead. The rest of the bedrooms run the length of the hallway and dining room. Maybe the kitchen was spared, since no one was staying above it." Tabatha shrugged her shoulders in a slow roll of tense muscles. "I'll have to find a place for us to live."

"What about my apartment?" He pulled a handkerchief from his pocket and wiped sweat from his face. "It's not Gray Manor, but it is dry and cool."

The thought of living in what should have been Derek and Elizabeth's home didn't set well. She shook her head. "Mom will need a place to go when she gets out of the hospital. And I'm not leaving Bobbie and Rhonda to fend for themselves. I need to find a place large enough for all of us."

Derek wrapped his arm around her waist and drew her close to his side. "Think you can handle staying there until we find a place? You may not find anything today."

She turned into his arms, accepting the comfort he offered. "We'll talk about this later. I want to see the rest of the house."

He ran his hands over her back and lowered his face into her hair. "We both need rest, and you'll not be able to see much in this darkness."

Bertha stepped over the threshold and clicked her tongue. "Lord have mercy. Look what that bitch done, baby girl. What was she thinking? She claims to love this house then tries to burn it to the ground." She stormed past them and headed toward the kitchen.

Derek glanced from Bertha back to Tabatha. "She's convinced Nyssa is the one that did this?"

She shrugged. "You know, she's right about one thing. It doesn't make a lot of sense. Why would Nyssa try to burn down the house?"

"One thing I've learned in all my years in law enforcement is not to discount anything. The minute you do, it'll jump up and bite you on the ass."

Tabatha rubbed her stinging eyes. "I've got so many people trying to kill me, I'm beginning to feel like public enemy number one."

She took a step away from Derek when the overhead light came on. Bertha appeared in the doorway and smiled. "The firemen turned the power off at the breaker box, I can't see what it would harm to turn them on long enough to check the place out. What you think, baby boy? I flipped off everything but the necessities. The icebox is unplugged, the water heater and air conditioner is off."

Derek shrugged. "Enjoy it while you can. The power company will be out soon to turn it off at the pole. Just make sure we throw the switch when we leave. Don't want to risk finishing what someone started."

They made their way through the dining room into the kitchen. The arsonist had trailed a stream of kerosene to the back door leaving a blackened streak of cracked tile, soot-covered cabinets and appliances.

"Well, Bertha, I guess you get a new kitchen. Any requests?" Tabatha asked.

Bertha's face brightened in a wide grin. "Anything but white."

"Or green," Derek muttered. "I hate green."

Tabatha smiled. "Maybe Italian country; decorated tiled backsplash, Italian floor tiles and marble countertops."

"And turn that servant's quarters into a butler's pantry," Bertha said getting into the game.

"Out of the twentieth century and into the twenty-first?" Tabatha smiled. "I think it's time to gut the place and start over. The ghosts of Grays past have had their say long enough."

"Now you're talking, baby girl. You know my son, Jacob, has his own construction company, right? I bet he'd be proud as a gater sunning on the levee to do the job for you. And he would do an honest job of it. He knows I'd tan his hide and use it for a rug if he didn't."

Tabatha nodded. "I'd like that, but, Bertha, *ask* if he has the time. Don't insist that he stop in the middle of another project."

Bertha waved her hand as if to dismiss her comment. "I'll just tell him the size of the job and see what he says."

"I know a good architect," Derek said with a grin. "He lives in Houston, but I bet he'd come if I gave him a yell."

"Your brother?" Tabatha asked. Derek nodded. "Ask him to come see what he has to work with and we'll talk money. I want it to be grand again, Derek. Something Paw-Paw would be proud of."

"I'm sure he'll do his best. Now, let's go get some rest. We can come back later."

Tabatha turned away. "No. I'm going upstairs. I want to see what Mom was talking about. She said I'd find everything I was looking for."

Bertha took Tabatha's hand in hers. "What *are* you looking for, baby girl?"

"Answers."

~

The stairs groaned with Tabatha and Derek's combined weight. A mixture of water and the remains of kerosene seeped over the tops of Tabatha's shoes, the caustic mixture burning her skin. Her eyes began to water and breathing became labored as she neared the second floor landing.

Derek glanced around the darkened hallway. "We need to get some air circulating and get these fumes out of here before we asphyxiate." He leaned over the railing, careful not to push against it, and yelled, "Bertha, open all the windows down there."

Tabatha went into the unoccupied bedroom first and flung the windows open, and drew in a deep breath of the fresh night air. She exited into the hallway as Derek entered Rhonda and Bobbie's bedrooms.

Tabatha stood at the entryway to Carla's suite but paused with her hand on the doorknob. Carla's voice echoed through her head, *Stay out of my room, Tabatha. This is the only place I have to myself. You don't belong in here. Get out! Stay out!*

Tabatha swallowed hard and turned the knob. She was greeted with a scented cloud of her mother's cologne mixed with the acrid odor from the fire. Her father's eyes stared down at her from the portrait above the mantel. She pulled her gaze from his and scanned the room. The area rug was saturated and squished under her footsteps. A broken cup and saucer cluttered the floor in front of the easy chair, and a basket of crocheting sat to the side, a colorful stack of granny squares waiting assembly. On the nightstand stood the framed cross-stitched family tree seven-year-old Tabatha had made as a birthday gift for her mother.

The doors leading to the other two rooms of the suite were closed. Tabatha made her way to the one on her left and turned the knob, pausing for a moment before entering. After several deep breaths, she opened the door.

Where the bedroom had been neat and orderly, this room was in disarray, but free of water and smoke damage. Paintings filled every inch of one wall; an Albrecht Dürer print Paw-Paw had given Tabatha centered the cluster of ornately framed art.

More paintings and etchings leaned against a sidewall below a large tapestry of an English foxhunt. At one time it had hung in the dining room over the eighteenth century dry sink. A set of antique Louis XV-style seating furniture sat to one side, her father's ivory chess set perched on an ornate walnut game table in front of the couch.

Three Persian rugs--rolled and tied--reclined in the center of the floor space. Everything looked well cared for. No dust had gathered. No cobwebs laced the corners. She returned to her mother's bedroom, but the memories followed her.

The door to the third room was locked. Tabatha ran her fingertips over the doorframe, checked the dresser drawers and nightstand, then checked the mantel. Nearly hidden from sight behind a stack of books she found what she was looking for--the key. With trepidation, she unlocked the door and entered.

She gasped at the sight before her. Her father's library had been kept as it had been on the day he'd died. Ceiling to floor books, interrupted only by an impressive, marbled fireplace topped with an ornately carved walnut mantel. An old grandfather clock filled the room with soft ticking, its time correct. In the far left corner sat a leather oxblood-hued, Early American style sofa and chair. She lifted the desk's roll top to look at the contents contained within its perfectly polished cherry wood patina. The desk appeared ready for Dunnock's return. She lifted the tops to three inkwells; each were filled with fresh ink, three pens lined up evenly in front of them, and unopened letters lay waiting for reply. Running her fingers over the intricately carved lid of her father's humidor, she remembered the time she'd snuck into his library and smoked one of his cigars. Her stomach lurched at the memory. She raised the lid to find it, too, had been filled with fresh cigars.

The large side drawer was jammed to capacity with manila envelopes. She removed one, noticing the typed address label: Mrs. Dunnock Gray. Return label: Dan Langton. She knew what she'd find before she slid the contents out. Every bank draft Dan had dutifully sent to her mother was inside, never cashed.

She sighed and slowly shook her head. "Oh, Mother."

"Tabatha?"

She jumped at the sound of Derek's voice shattering the silence of her reverie. "You can come in. It's okay." She leaned into his embrace when he came up behind her. "Welcome to Dunnock Gray's sanctuary."

Forty-six

Derek came up behind Tabatha. "What did you find?"

"Momma's bank drafts. I'm pretty sure they're all here. She didn't cash even one of them."

"Why? What could she possibly gain by keeping them?"

"Security, if Nyssa took everything and evicted her. Nyssa told her I was going to leave her in charge of the money. She had Mom convinced I was cutting her out of my will. If she saved all the checks, she'd have money to survive."

"Didn't you tell me she was missing some?" He withdrew an envelope in the back of the bottom drawer. "This one's postmarked fourteen months ago." He glanced inside before replacing it.

"That's about when she said they stopped." She reached over to lift the phone receiver but paused. It was the same phone she'd seen her father using so many times; an old black, 1950's rotary desk phone, the oversized numbers still sharp as they'd been in her childhood.

"Remind me to call my lawyer later."

He nodded. "You seen enough? I'm dead on my feet. I need some sleep and you look like you're about to drop."

"Yeah." She took one last look around before leaving the room, Derek close behind.

Bertha met them at the base of the stairs. "I'm going to run home and fix Oscar breakfast and take a little nap. You children gonna to be okay? You need a place to stay?"

Tabatha walked toward the door. "We'll stay at Derek's until I can find a place. Get some rest, then call Jacob and see when he can get started on the house." She paused on the porch and drew a fresh breath. "We'll need a place to store the things worth saving and a crew to load it up. Derek, call your brother and see when he can fly down here. Let's not waste time. Let's do this."

Her eyes roamed the property. She saw Nyssa pacing back and forth in front of her cottage, pausing every few steps to look over at Tabatha before pacing again. "I bet Nyssa's waiting for us to leave so she can get into the garage." Tabatha placed her fists on her hips.

Derek's eyes narrowed. "Tabatha, what are you thinking? I'm too tired to pick a fight with that crazy woman. She pisses me off right now and I'm liable to just shoot her and get it over with."

"Aren't you the least bit curious about what's in the garage? What's she hiding in there?"

Bertha clicked her tongue. "Baby girl, there ain't nothin' in there but old garden tools, though I have no idea what she wants with 'em. She's got a bunch of Mexicans that come do the yard work. She just stands around in her fancy duds and bosses 'em around."

"Wait. You're saying she doesn't do the grounds work herself?"

Bertha made a rude noise and rolled her eyes. "That woman never did much work. 'Fraid she'd break one of those fake fingernails of hers. When your grandpa was alive, he used to work in the yard and Nyssa would be by his side, actin' like she was workin', but it was your grandpa that did all the real work."

Tabatha glanced back as Nyssa stomped her foot then ran into her cottage. Tabatha kissed Bertha on the cheek. "Go home, Bertha. Take care of Oscar." Tabatha hooked her arm into the crook of Derek's. "Come on. Let's go check out the garage while Nyssa's in the cottage."

Derek glanced at Bertha and grimaced. "I guess I'd better go with her so she doesn't get in any trouble."

Bertha laughed. "Good luck, baby boy."

New padlocks, one about a third of the way down, another about a foot from the base of the door, made entering nearly impossible. Derek examined the latch. "It might destroy the door, but I've got a tire iron in the trunk."

Tabatha nodded. "Go for it. Nyssa doesn't like it, she can take it up with me."

He popped the back of the SUV open and returned with a small crowbar-like tool. He wedged it behind one latch then the next, ripping the screws out of the wood. Once they were gone, Derek tried the doorknob. "Locked."

Tabatha shrugged. "Pop it, too."

With a mighty push the lock ripped from the frame and the door cracked in half. They were in.

Tabatha found the light switch and flooded the space with light. She ran her gaze over the clutter filling the room. Several hoes and shovels leaned against a wall lined with snips, rakes, a sickle and a water hose.

Derek shrugged, a roll of muscle and sinew. He rubbed his eyes and yawned.

"You're exhausted. Let's go. We can come back later."

"What's this?" Derek asked as he squatted beside an old deep freeze sitting against the back wall. "Why's this freezer fastened to the wall?" He leaned closer. "With hinges?"

They rushed to clear two riding mowers out of the way and tugged on the freezer. It swung to the side revealing a dark maw big enough for them to pass through. A blast of cold air rushed past Derek and Tabatha, assaulting them with the retched stench of rotting meat, the coppery scent of blood and the lingering hint of death.

Derek gripped her upper arms. "Stay here. I'm going in."

The passage swallowed him whole as he walked into the darkness vanishing from sight for what felt like an eternity.

"Derek?"

A light came on. She saw him drop his hand away from the pull cord. The bulb hanging from the ceiling swung back and forth sending the shadows into a macabre dance. She stepped into the room. The combination of stench and the wavering shadows made her stomach roll in distress. The roof and back wall were a tangled mass of tree roots, the soil that once fed them, no longer visible. Several tap roots stretched from ceiling to floor like stately columns. Metal shelves jutted out from the wall, filled with jars and bottles; some filled, some empty.

Derek walked to the closest end of the long corridor to find a desk surrounded with old books. "The titles of these things would give a practicing warlock nightmares."

"Paw-Paw's," Tabatha said from behind him. "Mom wouldn't put up with them being in the house. He said he got rid of them. Guess he didn't."

She turned away and strolled toward the other end. "What is this? Looks like marbles in dirty dishwater." She picked up the small canning jar and carried it to the light. She rolled it in her hands and looked closely. She gasped and dropped the jar.

Derek snapped his hand out in time to stop the jar from smashing on the rock-hard soil floor. "Whatever it is, it can't hurt. . . ." His eyes grew large and his breathing quickened. "For the love of God. It's eyeballs." He set the jar on the table by the door and wiped his hands on his jeans.

Retching, Tabatha ran to the doorway. She wiped her mouth with the back of her hand and let her gaze wander the room once more. The other end still stood in darkness. She forced herself to take a step forward, then another. When she could no longer see, she waved her hand in front of her, searching for another light cord. Within seconds she felt the slight brush of its frayed end on her fingertips. She closed her eyes and pulled the cord. Taking several deep breaths she braced herself for what she might see next, but she wasn't prepared for what she found.

She opened her eyes and fell to her knees. "No. Oh, God, no."

Derek raced toward her. "Tabatha!" He came to a staggering halt.

Stretched out on a steel gurney lay Missy, naked, feeding lines in both arms. Gathered around her were tubes and empty containers, dirty scalpels and retractors.

"When Elizabeth said the killer was doing it right in her own back yard, I didn't know she meant it literally," Derek muttered.

Tabatha knew she had to pull herself together. With great effort she pushed herself to her feet, came to Missy's side and placed her fingers on the pulse point in the child's neck. "Please tell me I'm not too late, Missy. Please." She inspected the bags for labels and disconnected all but one. "Pulse is weak. She's malnourished, pale, but alive. Call for an ambulance, Derek. Tell them to hurry." She searched frantically through the cabinets, coming up with a tattered blanket and tucked it around the naked child.

Derek retrieved his cell and tried to connect. "Can't get service in here. I'm going outside." He turned taking a few steps and tried again. "Oh, hell."

Tabatha looked up from Missy to find Nyssa standing in the doorway wearing a long, flowing Irish-lace wedding gown. Its veil trailed from her hair to the floor, soiling the scalloped edge. In one hand she held a bouquet of dead roses and baby's breath surrounded by yellowed and frayed lace, in the other hand a gun.

Tabatha's heart thundered against her ribs. "Nyssa, how could you do something like this? This poor child, all the others, why? Why would you hurt these innocent children? What kind of monster are you?"

Nyssa's eyes darted back and forth from Derek to Tabatha. "The cheated kind. They're all *you*, you know. Every single one of them. You were the nearest I had to a child, so I couldn't very well kill you for real, now could I?"

"But why?"

"Because you refused to give me control of Gray Manor. You turned out to be just like all the rest."

"But you've always been taken care of. You always would have been. You have no right to more that that."

"Right?" Nyssa turned the gun and her attention away from Derek and toward Tabatha. "I have all the right. He loved me, you selfish bitch. Your father did everything he could to turn Raoul against me. Then he married that gold digger mother of yours. Raoul was going to marry me. He changed the will. I would control the money. He knew Carla would squander it. But that lawyer, he didn't file the will. He was probably screwing your mother. They probably cooked it up together. He--all of you--cheated me out of what's mine. Gray Manor is mine!"

In her peripheral vision Tabatha saw Derek's right hand edge toward his gun, and she tried to keep Nyssa's attention centered on her. "Why are you dressed in Grand-mama's wedding dress?"

"It's mine!" She swung the gun toward Derek. "I'm no fool, cop. Drop the damned weapon and get rid of the phone, too."

The sight of Nyssa's gun trained on Derek made Tabatha's heart skip a beat. She watched as he laid his pistol and cell phone on the table by the door.

Nyssa waved her gun. "Go stand beside your whore."

He edged to Tabatha's side and took her hand in his. "You'll not get away with this. You think someone else won't figure out what you've got in this garage? That it's you killing the kids?"

"You didn't figure it out, cop. Stumbled onto it." Nyssa laughed. The sound was so cold it added to the chill of the chamber. "Why, this isn't even my garage. It's hers." She gestured at Tabatha with a flip of her weapon. "I found out what she was doing. Tried to help that poor baby, but Tabatha attacked me. I had no choice but to kill her. And the child, well, I was too late to help her."

"What excuse will you use for killing me?" Derek asked.

"Oh." she shrugged. "They won't find you for a very long time. I'll just shove you in Raoul's place. He won't need it anymore."

Tabatha drew a sharp intake of breath and jerked her attention to the jugs on the shelves. "What have you done?"

The old woman brushed the veil away from her face. "I've dreamed of this since Raoul left me. I made sure you had the magic. Remember your puppy?" When Tabatha didn't answer she muttered a profanity. "You are so dumb, girl. You found him on your steps one morning. Dead. Someone had strangled it."

"Nyssa, what . . . you killed Mac?"

"I taught you how to bring him back to life. I had to do it. You understand, don't you? I had to know you could raise Raoul."

Tabatha slowly nodded. "I remember. You made me tell it to go back to sleep." Tears stung her eyes with the memory of having to take life from the poor animal again. "Then you told me I could raise my Daddy and Paw-Paw and talk to them any time I wanted. You just wanted me to raise Paw-Paw."

"But you never did. You went to the graveyard and talked to the crypt. I know. I followed you. Bertha always came to get you before you got the nerve to try it." She slapped at the veil once again as a breeze fluttered it back over her face. "I should have killed her before you got back. She's nothing but trouble, that old hag."

Her eyes went from Tabatha to Derek. "Load those bottles into your car. If you try anything I'll kill Tabatha."

"What's in them?" he asked.

Nyssa smiled. "It's the children's blood, my dear. The purest blood, that of an innocent. You can raise the long dead with such power. Now get moving."

Tabatha's heart twisted painfully. "Why did you save their eyes?"

Nyssa brought her hand to her cheek. "Oh, yes. I almost forgot. The eyes." She lifted the jar and unscrewed the top. She formed a strain with her fingers over the opening and drained the liquid. The strong smell of vinegar filled the small enclosure. The old woman yanked a filthy towel from a hook on the wall and dabbed gently at the orbs. With a nod, she smiled and held her prize in front of her. Like oversized pearls, six sets of eyeballs were strung together on a silver thread forming a choker necklace. Nyssa fastened it around her neck. "Eyes to watch for evil. To protect me from any who would mean me harm. No one can stop me."

Derek moved Tabatha behind him. "Stop you from what? What are you planning to do?"

"Tabatha is going to raise Raoul, of course. Today's our wedding day."

Forty-seven

Tabatha released a long-held breath as Derek returned from loading the jugs into the back of his Blazer. He leaned against the desk and reached for her.

She came to Derek's side and ran her hand over the back of his sweat-dampened shirt. "We'll figure something out. There's no way in hell I'm raising Paw-Paw." Her voice was a soft whisper in the small enclosure.

He leaned closer, the heat of his breath brushing against her shoulder. "We need to stall as long as possible. I managed to connect before I laid the phone down. Someone had to hear what's going on."

They turned their gaze toward Nyssa standing at Missy's side, uncoiling a drainage tube. "It's almost over. You can't hurt me anymore," she hissed to the unconscious child.

Tabatha swallowed past the dryness in her throat. "Leave Missy alone, Nyssa. You don't need any more blood. And did you ever think that all this blood has been sitting too long? Or that it's tainted with all the drugs you fed the children?"

"It's been frozen. It's good. But if it doesn't work, we'll just use a sacrifice." She gazed into Tabatha's eyes, a manic smile parting her lips. With a chuckle she glanced toward Derek. "Can't use Tabatha. No. Not Raoul's little baby. He'd rise with full fury if I committed such a sin against his very own blood." She moved away from Missy's side, coming closer to Derek and Tabatha. "Didn't know that, did you? That boy couldn't do anything right. Shooting blanks is what they call it today."

Tears stung Tabatha's eyes. Her blood turned to lava, thick with rage. "No. I don't believe you. My mother wouldn't do such a thing. She didn't even want me."

"Of course she didn't, dear. You were a reminder of what she did to keep Dunnock. He wanted a baby. She wanted to make him happy."

Derek gently touched her arm. "It doesn't add up, Tabatha. It doesn't make sense. She's just trying to hurt you."

Nyssa's laughter cut through Tabatha's brain like shards of glass. "You are a liar. Paw-Paw loved me and would have told me the truth. I'm Dunnock's daughter; the first daughter in hundreds of years to the Gray legacy. You are nothing but the gardener."

Movement at the back of the chamber caught her attention. At first she thought it was nothing but shadows fluttering over Missy's prone body, but then the shadows began to take form. Her breath caught in the back of her throat.

Swallowing hard, she jutted her chin forward. "Nyssa, you are nothing to me. I do not know you. You will not hurt my loved ones nor get what's mine. I want you off my property. You lose."

Derek gripped her arm tightly. "Tab, don't push it."

She leaned close and whispered, "Look behind her, Derek. Can you see them?"

He shifted his gaze behind Nyssa, his eyes widening with a mixture of fear and disbelief. "Mother of God."

The nearly transparent, ghostly forms of six little girls formed a semi-circle around Missy, as if to protect her.

Nyssa slowly turned to look behind her. She jerked her head back and forth. "No. Go away." She swung the gun toward them. "Why won't you die? Don't touch me."

Tabatha ran across the room and shoved the gurney out of harm's way before Nyssa began to fire upon the wraiths.

Derek leaped toward the corner table to retrieve his gun. "It's over, Nyssa. Drop it."

The children glided toward Nyssa, reaching out their hands, their mouths open in silent screams. Nyssa covered her ears as if her eardrums were splitting. The oldest child came closer, grasping at the necklace.

A whisper of pleading brushed Tabatha's ears. "Give them back. We want them back."

Nyssa chanted frantically between sobs.

Mason appeared in the doorway and shouted, "Drop the gun! Drop it now, Miss Boussard, or I'll shoot."

Relief flooded Nyssa's expression. "Thank God." She raised the gun and moved as if to hand it to Mason. He fired.

The bullet struck just above her heart, throwing her to the ground. She screamed, brought the gun up once again, and pulled the trigger. Mason readied to fire again, but Tabatha threw herself in front of Nyssa.

"No. The gun is empty. She can't hurt you. Don't kill her, please." She dropped to her knees beside the woman she'd loved and trusted. "Why? I would have done anything for you. Given you anything you wanted. Why?"

"You took him from me." Nyssa closed her eyes and released a heavy sigh.

Tabatha looked around at the children. "It's over. You're free. Go now."

Eyes wide with fear, Mason stumbled backward, grasping for anything to keep his footing. "What is that? This can't be." He turned accusing eyes to Tabatha. "What the hell are you? How can you do this?"

She accepted Derek's help to stand. "I didn't do this. I don't know how the children got here. Maybe they just needed to make sure someone knew what happened to them. Wanted Nyssa stopped."

The children smiled. A whisper of childish laughter flitted through the air, then they faded away.

Tabatha leaned down, jerked the necklace from around Nyssa's throat, and handed it to Mason. "Here. These are the little girls' eyes. I trust you can have them tested and buried with the right girl?"

He glanced at the necklace. His complexion lost all its color before he looked away. "Bainbridge, put them in something. God, man, this is beyond sick."

Stepping around Tabatha, Mason kept as much space as possible between them. He stooped down and placed his fingertips on Nyssa's throat. "She's still alive. I've already called for an ambulance on the way over here. I figured Bainbridge would find a way to get himself shot up again." He glanced over at Missy. "Dead?"

Derek said, "Weak, but alive."

Sirens grew closer, the lights of the ambulance streaking across the wall in a red flair of release.

A sob sounded before Tabatha could halt its escape. "It's over. Everyone is safe. Missy is alive."

Nyssa gasped and jerked to a seated position. Her lips moved in a steady rant of chants. Curses upon each of them, she swore. The EMTs lifted her onto a gurney and waited as Mason handcuffed her to the rails. Suddenly quiet, Nyssa lifted her head from the pillow and stared at Mason, eye to eye. His expression hardened and held a silent threat. He brought his face close to hers and began reading her rights. She bucked against the restraints, screeching, then fell back, her eyes boring into Mason's. "You will obey me. The monsters must die." She snapped her eyes toward Tabatha. "You think you've won. It won't end with me. We will be victorious."

Tabatha came to Nyssa's side and stared down at her. "You wanted it all, now you've lost everything. Goodbye, Nyssa."

Nyssa continued to rant as she was rolled away and put into the back of the first ambulance.

The next EMTs checked Missy before lifting her onto a gurney. One of them acknowledged Derek with a nod. "I think she'll be okay. Is this one of the missing kids I've been hearing about on the news?"

"Her name is Missy Lynn Blythe. I'll get in touch with her mother. She'll meet you at the hospital."

Mason shivered. "Let's get the hell out of here. This place gives me the damned creeps. Ghosts, curses, and it reeks of death."

Tabatha agreed. "Like the deaths of six little girls."

Once outside Mason unleashed his rage. "How could such a thing be happening in your own garage and you not know about it?"

"Look, Lieutenant--" Derek started.

"Did I ask you, Detective? I'm talking to Ms. Gray. I want to hear her answer the question."

Anger swirled in her brain. "I always parked my car outside. The garage was Nyssa's domain, has been since I was a small girl. My grandfather built it for her when she first came to work for us. Used it for her gardening tools and lawnmowers. I had no reason to rummage through there."

"Then why did you go in this time?"

"To piss her off!" she shouted into his face. "She told me to stay the hell out of *her* garage. I couldn't let her talk to me that way."

"I ought to take you in for questioning. This is--"

"You ain't taking her anywhere, Mason."

They all turned to discover themselves staring down the barrel of Phelps' gun. One eye covered with a patch, his face was bloated and discolored, his wounds beginning to fester. He leaned on his good leg; the other was still encased by a cast. "Come on, darlin', it's time to go. The plane is waiting."

"Mr. Phelps, stay out of this," Mason shouted. "Let it go. Get out of here."

Phelps reached out, grasping Tabatha by the arm and yanked her to his side. "You're a healer, too, ain't ya kid? I saw how you took your mother's pain away in the ambulance. You can make me better. I'm sick, baby."

Tabatha felt a moment of pity for the man. "I can't help you. You have to go back to the hospital."

"They're after me. They'll kill me."

"Why would anyone want to hurt you?" Derek asked. "Look at you. You should listen to Tabatha. You look like recycled shit, man."

Derek stepped closer.

"Stay back or I'll kill her," Phelps said, shifting the gun to Tabatha's head. "It's me or no one. Is that what you want, Bainbridge?"

A screech of rage came from above them and a black panther pounced from the limbs of the old oak. Phelps fell to the ground screaming and begging for help. He managed to shove the cat away and aim his gun but suddenly, his clothing burst into flames. He screamed and rolled about, slapping at the flames until they were out.

Tabatha searched the yard and finally found Rhonda leaning against the house. Her face was battered and bruised. She pointed to Phelps and said, "He caught me in the front yard. Hit me and left. Must've thought I was out for a while." She smiled weakly. "Fooled him."

Phelps whimpered and turned his tortured face to Tabatha. "Help me, darlin'. You can stop the pain."

She took a step toward Phelps, but Derek pulled Tabatha away. "Stay here until we get him handcuffed."

She rolled her eyes. "Lord, I'm tired of being told to stay like a dog."

Rhonda came to her side. "I did it, Tabatha. I was scared, but I did it."

Tabatha gathered her into her arms. "Yes, you did. You saved our lives, girlfriend. You're a hero."

Rhonda beamed. "Well, that's a bit much, but okay, I'll take it."

The panther curled at their feet and purred. Tabatha reached down and ran her fingers over the fur.

Derek ran over to check on Rhonda. "You okay, kid?"

She nodded. "Better than okay. Tabatha thinks I'm her hero."

"Won't get an argument from any of us. You two saved us all." He glanced down at the panther. "How about you, pussy cat? You okay?"

Bobbie rubbed her face up his leg and bared her teeth in a catty smile. In a cat's hiss she said, "You betcha, big boy. I'm always fine. Wanna see?"

Derek rolled his eyes. "Don't even think about it. I'm a one-woman man."

Forty-eight

Tabatha stepped under the crime scene tape surrounding the garage. Her inner voice screamed that she had no reason to return to its dark confines, but her dream the night before had been filled with her grandfather's urgings that she go back.

The dream was uncomplicated and easy to decipher. Raoul sat at his desk writing in his journal. He turned, his eyes meeting Tabatha's before he held out the journals. "You must find them. Your powers are strong, but your knowledge is weak. These hold the body of truth and the key to your survival."

Tabatha had awakened with a start from her dream, to find herself wrapped securely in Derek's arms. Her chest ached with each intake of breath, and her heart drummed against her ribs as if trying to escape. She crept out of Derek's embrace and left him to his own sleep phantoms.

And now she stood, running a reluctant gaze over her grandfather's hidden chamber. Dreams were just that--dreams, illusions of the subconscious. But this garage and its secrets were her reality.

Swallowing hard, she tried to force down the fear that nearly choked her. With little effort, she shoved the freezer from the yawning entry to her personal hell on earth. The odor of death gushed out with a foul breath, surrounding her with misery.

Tabatha's senses separated the smells. Gardening chemicals blended with blood, rotting flesh and vomit from the officers who had been ordered to gather evidence from the crime scene. Her own stomach lurched. She swallowed away the bile burning her throat, forced herself to enter and turn on the light.

"Concentrate on the desk and not the scene as a whole," she told herself as she opened the top drawer. It held pens, paper and an old pack of Clove gum, but no journals. Tabatha slammed it shut and fought the sobs building in her chest. The large bottom drawer opened with ease. Inside, tiny pairs of jeans, t-shirts and underwear were folded neatly away. "Where are they, Paw-Paw? Just tell me."

She flung the next drawer open with so much force its contents flew onto the floor. Paperclips, staples and typewriter ribbons scattered everywhere. The bottom half of a cardboard box containing barrettes and ribbons lay on its side. Tabatha ran her fingertips over each of the items, her heart aching for the dead children who'd once worn them. She placed them next to the clothing, vowing to return them to the girls' parents.

She grasped another handle and tugged but was refused entry. She screamed in frustration and kicked at the offending compartment. Her emotions rippled from her throat with a whimper and tears wet her cheeks. A scream tore from her lungs as arms surrounded her waist and pulled her backward.

"Tabatha, it's all right." Derek's voice flowed over her skin. "Calm down. I'm here. Nothing is going to hurt you."

"I can't get it open. I have to find them." She stepped out of his embrace and kicked the desk again with a scream of frustration. "I have to have the journals. Paw-Paw won't let me sleep until I do." A wail not unlike that of a wounded animal tore from her chest. "What does he want from me? Why can't he just leave me alone?"

"I don't know, honey." He held her close again, his heat seeping into her every pore. "Everything will be all right. I promise."

She sagged against him, drew a breath, then another. "Gads. I lost it for a minute there." She wiped her tears on his shoulder. "I'm okay now. You can let me go."

"Maybe I don't want to let you go. Ever."

Tabatha buried her face into his chest. "I didn't mean forever. Just until we find those damned notebooks." She stepped out of his comforting caress and released a breath. "Can you get this drawer open?"

He reached into the inside pocket of his jacket and pulled out a small zippered pouch holding an array of tools. He leaned down; peering at the lock, he chose two knife-like blades and with a flick of his wrist, released the latch. He opened the drawer. The journals lay side by side along with a book titled, *The Sorceress of Babylon.*

Tabatha gathered them into a pile. "Maybe now I can learn who or what I am."

"You're Tabatha Gray, the woman I love. That's all I need to know." He kissed her and pulled her so close she couldn't draw a full breath.

"Derek?"

"What, honey?"

"You're suffocating me."

He loosened his grip. "Sorry." He smiled. "Let's get out of here. This place stinks."

She agreed. "As soon as I can get the rest of Paw-Paw's books out of here, I'm going to have it bulldozed. I can't stand the sight of it." She picked the journals up and cradled them in the crook of her arm.

He took her hand and led her out of the garage and toward the front porch. Rhonda and Bobbie drove up in Tabatha's Grand Am and strolled toward them.

"Where've you two been?" Derek asked.

Bobbie flipped her hand in a dismissive gesture. "Women stuff. We went shopping for some clothes."

Derek snorted. "Yeah. Like you're so fond of wearing clothes."

She rushed to Tabatha's side. "Girlfriend, you look like hell. You been crying? What's wrong?" She gathered Tabatha into her arms.

"I'm just angry, tired, frustrated. Shall I go on?"

Bobbie shook her head. "I was so scared yesterday. I thought Phelps was going to kill you. I've got used to having you around. So don't go leaving me, you hear?"

The tears Tabatha saw in Bobbie's eyes were her undoing. She sobbed without shame or reservation. A moment later Rhonda was attached to her other side and the three of them held each other and wept.

Bertha's car pulled up behind Tabatha's. "Well, look at you, will ya? Sitting there like you've got nothing to do." Bertha rushed forward giving each of the girls a bear hug. "Now, the time for tears is over. You babies are fine." She grasped Derek by his shirt and drew him into her arms. "Son, you look like death on a sizzle plate."

Rhonda was the first to straighten away. "So. What's next?"

Tabatha wiped the tears from her cheeks. "Trying to figure out where we're going to stay? Any ideas?"

Rhonda nodded. "We can use my place. It's got three bedrooms."

"What about Momma? She won't stay there." Tabatha shook her head. "No. I don't think that'll work."

"My place isn't large enough for five people. Maybe two." Derek glanced at Tabatha. "But I think Tabatha and I need a place that's ours. No memories. No ghosts."

"You finally woke up and smelled the pancakes, big boy?" Bobbie stretched out her long legs and leaned her elbows on the porch.

Bertha clicked her tongue. "Baby girl, you got the perfect place for your momma to stay right over there." She pointed toward Nyssa's cottage.

"No," they shouted in chorus.

Tabatha rose. "Momma would never stay there. Hell, I wouldn't want to live in that house. I may just burn the damned place down and roast marshmallows over the flames."

"Just say the word," Rhonda said with a chuckle.

Bertha's eyes widened. "What? Oh mercy. It's such a nice house."

An idea came to Tabatha. "You and Oscar want it? He'll want to be involved with the rebuilding and you know it. You could live here and save a lot of travel time for both of you."

Bertha glanced at the cottage again. "You sure you don't mind? It would be better for Oscar. He's not as young as he used to be. That commute could be rough on him." Her face switched from one emotion to another as she thought. "Can we go look inside? See what the old biddy did to the place?"

Shivers run up Tabatha's spine. With an effort she smiled. "I think that's a good idea. See what needs to get tossed and cleaned up. No telling what she has lying around."

They tromped across the yard stopping at the front door of Nyssa's cottage. No one wanted to open it. Finally Derek reached out and turned the knob. The door swung freely, unlocked.

"Ready, girls?"

Tabatha wasn't but walked across the threshold, stopping three feet from the entry. "Well, now I know where everything went." Her grandfather's clock, armoire, end tables and coffee table decorated Nyssa's living room. An oriental rug from Raoul's study covered her floor. Settees and an armchair that had once decorated his library were now reupholstered in garish rose-print brocade and seemed out of place in the small surroundings.

Bertha cleared her throat. "We can put this stuff in storage until you get the new place built."

Tabatha shook her head. "No. There's no need moving your furniture unless you want to stay here for good. You'd have to just move it back again."

Bertha strode purposefully toward the other rooms. "How many bedrooms, baby girl?"

"Two. One to the left of the bathroom, the other is on the right."

Bertha opened the door to bedroom on the left, made the sign of the cross and gasped. "Jesus, Mary and Joseph."

They walked over to the doorway to see what had shocked Bertha so badly. The wall facing the doorway was covered with blood-red velvet. In the center of the wall hung a ceiling to floor crucifix, identical to the one on the Guardian's induction folder. The remaining walls were covered with glistening gold metallic paint. Twelve chairs surrounded a red silk upholstered throne. A tapestry covered the floor, the 12 zodiac signs circling the chairs.

"Well," Bertha said, "I see there's some redecorating needs to be done."

"The lord and her twelve disciples." Tabatha took one last look and turned away. "I've seen enough." Closing the door behind them, Tabatha felt a rush of sorrow grip her to her core. The woman she'd considered her best friend was a thief and murderer. The Nyssa she thought she'd known didn't exist. The warmth of Derek's hand on the small of her back comforted Tabatha. She leaned closer to absorb his love. "It's over. She'll never hurt anyone again."

"Honey, I doubt she'll see the outside world again. From the reports I've seen, she's a babbling idiot. Sits in a corner of her cell, telling the orderlies to let her go free and God will reward them. Mason came in this morning and told me Phelps died last night."

"Serves them well, if you ask me," Bertha said, handing Tabatha a large manila envelope. "Miss Carla's missing checks. Found them on the dresser in the bedroom."

Tabatha nodded. "I figured we'd find them here. Let's go. I've seen enough."

"And one more thing." Derek reached into his jacket packet and took out a stack of folded papers. "I got the toxicology results back on the soup. And from Carla's blood tests."

"And?" Tabatha asked, shutting the door to the cottage behind them.

"The soup had a large amount of a glycoside called convallatoxin. Same thing was found in your mother's system. Do you know what lily of the valley is?"

"Perennial plant with little white flowers and red berries," Bertha answered. "Lots of them under them trees around here."

"It's why Carla's so sick. The doctors said she's lucky to be alive. She'll be in the hospital for a week, maybe longer," Derek said.

"She was poisoning Momma?"

"It looks that way, but they've caught it in time. She'll be weak for a while, but she'll live." He held out a small plastic evidence envelope. "Mason thought this might help you accept the truth. Nyssa was wearing it."

Tabatha flipped the top flap open and emptied the contents into her palm. A gold chain dangled Jesus nailed to a stake. She let it slide back into the envelope and handed it back to Derek. "Give it back to him. I don't need it."

"They scraped the bottom of the freezer and found what proved to be human skin. So that's where she was keeping them until she delivered the body to the cemetery."

"Yuck," Rhonda said. "What ever happened with the glass from the warehouse?"

"Vanished. No one knows where it went. Shouldn't surprise me. Phelps had some pull everywhere, it seemed." Derek wrapped his arm around Tabatha's waist. "Let's go get something to eat and decide where to live."

She nodded. "It may be hard to find a place with at least four bedrooms, to rent quickly."

"Why four?" Bertha asked.

"Momma, Rhonda, Bobbie and me."

Tabatha and Derek settled on the porch steps. Derek cleared his throat. "Well, Carla could use my place. It'll be empty."

"Where would you stay?" she asked, trying to keep the hope out of her voice.

He reached into his pocket, pulled out a small, purple velvet box, and placed it in her hand. "With you, if you'll have me."

Her eyes burned with unshed tears, and her throat constricted, making her next words hard to speak. "What about Elizabeth?"

He brushed his lips across Tabatha's. "Elizabeth is my past, you are my future. Will you marry me, Tabatha Gray?"

She looked at the box in her hand and slowly opened it. A one-carat marquise diamond sparkled in the sunlight. "It's beautiful, Derek."

"For heaven's sake, baby girl," Bertha yelled. "Answer the man. You gonna marry him or what?"

Tabatha laughed, enjoying the surge of happiness filling her senses. "Yes. I'm gonna marry him."

"When?" he asked.

Tabatha glanced over her shoulder at Gray Manor. "When we can have the wedding here. It will be a new beginning for the house and us. We'll make it a double ceremony."

"Double ceremony?" Derek asked.

"A wedding," Tabatha said, "and the christening of our home. It will become Bainbridge Manor on our wedding day."

"Has a nice ring to it." He kissed her softly on the lips.

"Oh, hell." Bobbie moaned. They turned their gaze to follow hers.

Rhonda gasped. "My goodness. Who is that?"

Bertha clicked her tongue. "Trouble, I bet."

The man walking toward them could only be described as a mass of human form in continuous motion. Barefoot, bare-chested, clad in tight jeans, his muscles rippled with every stride. His complexion glowed with the same cinnamon hue as Bobbie's, his long black hair hung past his shoulders and a raven's feather dangled from his right earlobe. His hands hung at his sides in tight fists.

His lips parted and his voice seemed to sap the oxygen from the air. "Madam Luckman." He bowed. "Paco and his mate, Nahimana, were found this morning floating face down in Lake Pontchartrain. A bit far from home, don't you think?" His eyebrows rose sharply as he stared at her accusingly. "There are some who question your leadership to let this go on this long."

Bobbie jumped to her feet. "I've not been sitting idle doing nothing! We've killed their assassin. Their lord is behind bars."

"We?" He eyed the group before him. "You team up with mere humans to fight your battles?"

"Mere humans?" She turned and winked at Rhonda. "Show my friend how mere you are, Rhonda."

Rhonda stepped forward. "You really don't want to see me get upset. I have--um--hot attributes."

Tabatha stood and placed herself between her friends and the strange man. "Bobbie is my sister. We are her family."

He stepped forward, invading Tabatha's space. Her magic rushed forward and he staggered back, pulling in a gasp of air.

"Do not underestimate us," she warned.

Derek flashed his badge. "If you want to know a real battle, just threaten these women again."

The man inhaled a deep, greedy breath. "What the hell are you? Who are you?" he asked Tabatha.

"Multiple choice; either your worst enemy or your best friend. Who? I'm Tabatha Gray. And you are?"

The man pounded his chest with his fist. "I am Kangee."

Bobbie massaged her temples. "His animal is the eagle."

The group on the porch nodded their understanding.

Kangee darted his eyes away from Tabatha to Bobbie. "They know about us?"

Bobbie shrugged.

His eyes filled with rage before he lowered his head in a near bow and turned to leave.

"I'll be right back," Derek said and escorted Kangee to his car.

"Okay, Bobbie, what's the story with this Kangee? Who are the people he said they found in the lake?" Tabatha asked.

Bobbie crumbled into herself and dropped to the steps as if all her strength drained with the breath she'd released in a rush. "When we were children, Kangee and I were best friends. Both our fathers were dead. We used to tell my mother we would marry one day and build her a grand home and take care of her forever. Then she died when I was twelve. The community took me in, but I lived a while with one family then another until I felt like a refugee in my own village. I ran off to New York when I was seventeen. I didn't really think anyone would miss me. My brother inherited the leadership position when my father died. They didn't need me." She watched Kangee drive away. "He came to New York to find me, so in a way, it's my fault he's dead."

"Don't be silly," Bertha said.

Bobbie faced Tabatha. "I have to go back. They need me and I have an obligation to fulfill. I'm the last of my bloodline, the only leader they have."

Tabatha pulled her cell phone out of her jacket pocket and dialed. "Room 316 please." She waited in silence. "Hi. Feeling better today?"

"I'm fine. You okay?" Carla said, sounding stronger than she had the day before.

"Momma, I have to wrap up a few loose ends. I'll see you in a couple of days. Derek is going to let you live at his place until the house is finished. He'll be looking in on you until I get back. Is that okay with you?"

"Don't worry about me, Tabby. I'll be in good hands." She paused. "Um. Tabby. Will he be living with me?"

"No. We'll be staying at Rhonda's." She heard Carla release a sigh. "Okay. Rest. I'll see you soon. Bye, Momma." She handed the phone to Rhonda. "Can you get in touch with your mom?"

Rhonda drew a slip of paper out of her jeans pocket and accepted the phone from Tabatha.

Bobbie looked from one to the other. "What are you two thinking?"

Rhonda held up her hand. "Hi, Daddy. Is Mom around?" There was a moment of silence as she waited. "Hi, Mom. Look, I've got some business to attend to. You'll be back from Disney World on Thursday, right?" She nodded as if her mom could see her reaction to her answer. "Well, if I'm not back by then, can you watch Shane a while longer?" She smiled. "Great. And Mom, don't let him out of your sight. I'll explain when I get back. Love you. Bye." She flipped the phone shut and handed it back to Tabatha before they faced their friend.

"We're coming with you, Bobbie," Tabatha said. The decision was an easy one. Trying to figure out how to tell Derek what they were going to do was another matter altogether.

"No." Bobbie looked away as if her thoughts were anywhere but with them at the moment.

Rhonda stomped her foot on the ground. "We're a family. If you're in trouble, we're in trouble. We're in this together. I won't take no as an answer."

"Well, aren't you the bossy one all of a sudden?" Bobbie chuckled. "You don't know what you're saying. My world is much different than this one."

"We'll survive," Tabatha said.

Worry and relief warred in Rhonda's eyes. "Okay, what's the plan?"

Derek strolled across the yard and drew Tabatha into his arms. "You going to be okay? I need to go to the stationhouse for a while. I've got paperwork piled to the rafters. Where are we going to meet up?"

"Rhonda, why don't you give him your house key so he can have some copies made?" Tabatha suggested.

"Good idea." Derek took the key from Rhonda and slipped it into his shirt pocket. "You girls be careful."

Tabatha nearly sagged with relief. With all the love in her soul, she kissed him. "We'll be fine. See ya later."

Derek winked and waggled his eyebrows. "Hmm, sounds promising." He kissed her one last time, got into his car and drove away.

"Anyone have a pen and some paper?"

Bertha handed both to Tabatha from her purse. "What you up to?"

Tabatha began to write.

Derek, by the time you read this I'll be gone.

It's just for a few days.
Bobbie needs us. Don't worry about me.
I'll be fine. I love you.

She signed her name and handed the note to Bertha. "Give this to him. I'm not telling you where we're going, that way you can't tell him or have to lie for me. And don't you worry about us, either. We're big girls; we can take care of ourselves."

Bertha waved her hand in dismissal. "Oh, the Tree Lady will watch over you."

Bobbie spun around and stared at her. "What did you say?"

Bertha laughed. "I'll watch over Derek. He's gonna be plenty mad when he realizes you're at it again." She climbed into her car and waved goodbye. "See you girls later."

"What was that all about?" Rhonda asked.

"The Tree Lady." Bobbie ran her hands over her face. "She's one of my people. How does Bertha know about her?"

"Sometimes I think Bertha knows everyone and everything." Tabatha sat on the steps again and ran the situation over in her mind. "All right. Here's the plan. We go with Bobbie and see if what happened there was connected to our problems here." She stretched out her arm, hand palm down. "Derek's Devils. Together forever."

Rhonda placed her hand over Tabatha's. "Friends."

Bobbie placed her hand on top. "Family."

Tabatha searched her friends' faces and saw in them the same fatigue she felt down to her toes. "No rest for the wicked, or for those who fight against them."